Ba'el's beautiful face was streaked with Klingon and Romulan blood both. He suspected that the majority of the latter belonged to her father, Tokath, the leader of the colony, whose body lay over hers yet had somehow survived.

"Toq?" she said weakly. "You came back."

"Yes. What happened?"

"L'Kor."

Toq frowned. "What do you mean?"

"They came for . . . for L'Kor. Said they'd . . . they'd spare us if we . . . we gave them . . . him. Father re-refused. So they took . . . took him any . . ." She lapsed into unconsciousness.

Getting back to his feet, Toq said, "We must bring them to the *Gorlak* medical bay!"

"Must we?" Kuut asked. "All I see here is a righteous act. Klingons and Romulans living together—the only thing the attackers got wrong was to leave these two breathing." Unholstering his disruptor, he bared his teeth at Toq. "I will gladly rectify that error—and the error of leaving *you* alive."

He pointed the disruptor right at Toq's face.

**Other *Star Trek*® stories featuring
the Klingon Empire by Keith R.A. DeCandido**

Dedicated to the fond memory of
Rabbi David M. Honigsberg, 1958–2007.
I hope they have good Scotch in Sto-Vo-Kor.

HISTORIAN'S NOTE

This novel takes place in early November 2376 on the human calendar and at the beginning of the Year of Kahless 1002 on the Klingon calendar; shortly after the events of *I.K.S. Gorkon* Book 3: *Enemy Territory*, approximately a year after "What You Leave Behind," the final episode of *Star Trek: Deep Space Nine*, about three years prior to the feature film *Star Trek Nemesis*, and simultaneous with the *Worlds of Star Trek: Deep Space Nine* novel *Andor: Paradigm*.

And if a kingdom be divided against itself, that kingdom cannot stand. And if a house be divided against itself, that house cannot stand. And if Satan rise up against himself, and be divided, he cannot stand, but hath an end.

—the Gospel According to St. Mark 3:24–26

Only a fool fights in a burning house.

—Klingon proverb

ONE

I.K.S. *Gorkon*
Interstellar space

The *bat'leth* sliced through the air, heading straight for Captain Klag's neck.

Without even thinking, Klag turned his left wrist, flipping his own *bat'leth* upward, cradling the blade's curved handle in the crook of his left arm. The center of the other blade collided with the end of Klag's with a metallic clang that echoed off the walls.

Then Klag brought his own blade down, taking his adversary's *bat'leth* with it, and slammed his foe's jaw with his right palm heel. Pain glowed in Klag's right hand from the impact of bare hand on bone, but it sent his opponent reeling. His heart pounding faster against his ribs, Klag whipped his *bat'leth* up and over his head, intending to strike his foe's forehead crest.

The other *bat'leth* came up, blocking the strike, then

pressed forward, sending Klag stumbling back a few steps. In fact, it should have sent him only one step back, but Klag took a few extra to get his bearings. Klag knew his foe well and therefore was acutely aware how difficult victory would be.

The two warriors circled each other, staring face-to-face only a body's length apart. Klag held his *bat'leth* at an angle, his left hand gripping it tightly at chest level; his right hand, still sore from the blow to his foe's hard jaw, cupping the curved blade around his hip. His opponent swirled his blade around in a crisscross pattern. It was a common maneuver, one ostensibly intended to protect against any frontal attack; in practice Klag always thought it was at best merely a clever distraction, and he never bothered with it.

Again, his foe swung at his left side. Again, Klag blocked the strike with ease, but this time he was unable to entangle the other blade, and his foe tried to swing the downward part up toward Klag's chest. Klag was able to deflect with the upper part. That locked their blades, giving his foe an opportunity to kick up toward Klag's groin.

Klag instinctively blocked the kick with his left hand, which worked as far as it went, but when he tightened his grip on the weapon with his right hand, that hand twinged. Wincing, Klag almost dropped the *bat'leth* as his fingers loosened of their own accord, but he forced himself to hang on.

That gave his foe an opportunity to try another kick, this to Klag's right side, which Klag was unable to block.

But he didn't need to. Stumbling to the left with the blow from his foe's steel boot, and ignoring the pain that shot through his ribs from the impact, Klag let loose with a short punch to his foe's exposed right side, then swung up with the *bat'leth*, striking his foe's shoulder.

Klag cursed himself. Klingon armor was strong in general, and on the shoulders it was particularly thick, to protect the neck. He might as well have struck the air for all the good a shoulder strike would do.

A fist came at Klag's face, and he ducked his head so his forehead crest would take the brunt of the blow. Their blades were still entangled, so Klag brought his knee up into his foe's groin. That area was well armored as well, of course, but Klag's main interest was in putting some distance between them, and most warriors would back off instinctively after receiving such a blow, regardless of its actual damage.

Again, the pair faced off. This time, Klag's foe didn't bother with the crisscross motion, simply keeping his *bat'leth* ready in front of him.

Then he came at Klag from the right, swinging the *bat'leth* in a very tight arc, leaving him very little time to parry.

In one fluid motion, he swung the *bat'leth* up to block the strike and bring his foe's *bat'leth* down.

His foe smiled. "Well done, Captain!"

Klag returned the smile.

Then he punched his foe in the face.

As he fell to the floor, Klag threw his head back and laughed. "Do not assume the battle is over just because the mission is accomplished, Kohn."

Bekk Kohn laughed with his captain. "You are correct, of course, sir."

Kohn's swing to Klag's right had been the moment of truth for the captain. During the Dominion War, Klag lost his right arm at Marcan V while serving as first officer aboard the *I.K.S. Pagh*, which was destroyed on that planet. The only survivor of the *Pagh*'s crew, Klag slew one Vorta and half a dozen Jem'Hadar literally single-handedly. He was rewarded with a promotion and the captaincy of the *I.K.S. Gorkon*, one of the Chancellor-class vessels that were the cutting edge of the Klingon Defense Force.

At the advice of his ship's doctor, B'Oraq, Klag had a new right arm grafted on. B'Oraq, who studied to be a physician in the Federation and was on a one-woman crusade to improve the state of Klingon medicine, had wanted him to get a prosthetic, but Klag would not attach a machine to his body and call it his arm. Instead, he instructed her to transplant the limb of his father, M'Raq, who died like an old woman in his bed. Klag hoped to restore his father's honor by wearing his good right arm into battle.

But first he had to be accomplished with it. This had been a great stride in that direction.

More laughter came from the two figures standing against the wall of the workout chamber. Klag turned and saw B'Oraq along with the leader of Kohn's squad, Morr.

"Your opinion, Doctor?" Klag asked.

B'Oraq tugged on the auburn braid—bound at its base with a clasp in the shape of the emblem of her

House—that sat on her right shoulder. "Your reaction time has improved tremendously, Captain, and you've adjusted to the differing lengths of the arms. A few more months and you might approach your old levels of *bat'leth* fighting."

That was not what Klag wanted to hear. He felt as good as ever and resented the implication that he wasn't as good as he was before Marcan V. But he repressed that reaction quickly. In the months he had commanded this vessel, he had learned the hard way to respect B'Oraq's opinions, mostly by virtue of her never being wrong.

It had been the doctor's suggestion that Klag spar with Kohn rather than Morr. The leader of First Squad, the elite of the *Gorkon*'s massive complement of troops, Morr also served as Klag's bodyguard and was one of the most accomplished *bat'leth* fighters on the ship. Klag and Morr had also been sparring regularly since B'Oraq performed the graft of M'Raq's arm onto Klag, and B'Oraq was concerned that they were getting too used to each other. Morr concurred, so he assigned Kohn to this duty, with explicit instructions to continue fighting for a significant time before attacking Klag's right to see how he reacted.

Klag was about to tell Morr and Kohn to report back to their duty stations—Klag himself intended to return to his cabin, so he would not require Morr's services—when he felt the organs in his body shift upward ever so slightly, and his boots were no longer planted firmly on the deck.

With a snarl, he touched the control on his arm to contact his chief engineer. "Klag to Kurak."

"*I know, we've lost gravity. We're working on it. I did warn you this would happen.*"

"Yes, Commander, you did. What I wish to know now is how soon it will be fixed."

"*Two seconds. I suggest you brace yourself.*"

By the time Kurak finished that sentence, gravity had reasserted itself. Klag bent his knees as he came back to the deck, as did Kohn and Morr. B'Oraq was less agile and fell on her face, barely bracing herself with her hands.

Struggling to her feet, B'Oraq brushed herself off and said, "Well, that was embarrassing."

Klag grinned. "I suggest you report to yourself, Doctor. And Kurak? How much more of this must we endure?"

"*I told you before, Captain, the damage to the* Gorkon *is far too extensive for field repairs to be anything but temporary. Until we arrive at Praxis, these malfunctions will continue.*"

"Very well, Commander. Out." Klag snarled again. The *Gorkon* had been at the forefront of a very brief campaign against the Elabrej Hegemony, an upstart power that had attacked one of the *Gorkon*'s brother ships, the *I.K.S. Kravokh*, with no provocation and taken its captain and surviving crew prisoner and not permitted them to die. The Klingons' retaliation was swift and devastating, and now there was no Elabrej Hegemony but simply a broken world on which the empire might or might not plant its flag.

That decision was for General Goluk to make. He had remained behind to deal with that, while the surviving Chancellor-class vessels were to report back to the homeworld, with the exception of the *Kesh*, which remained with Goluk at Elabrej.

The *Gorkon* would have had to have done so in any case, for the ship suffered considerable damage at the Elabrej's hands, necessitating a crash landing on one of their moons. Kurak estimated that it would take at least two weeks in a shipyard for the mighty vessel to be fully repaired, and Kurak was not known for being inaccurate in such judgments.

After dismissing Morr and Kohn, Klag left the workout room, heading to his own cabin. B'Oraq followed, saying, "During your leave, I want you to continue the drills—with Morr, with Kohn, or with *someone*. And keep doing the exercises I prescribed."

Klag shot her a look as they walked down the *Gorkon*'s corridors. "I assumed, Doctor, that you would be present for my exercises even during my leave."

Tugging on her braid again, B'Oraq smiled. "I was under the impression that leave meant I was at liberty." The smile dropped. "Besides, I won't have the time. My presence has been requested by the Klingon Physicians Enclave to speak at their conference."

Frowning, Klag said, "I'm unfamiliar with that organization."

"That is not surprising," B'Oraq said with some small degree of bitterness. "Few know of the KPE outside the medical profession, and few in it care enough one way or the other. In fact, this is their first conference, and they're having it—and inviting me—only due to pressure from the High Council."

"Then I suppose congratulations are in order," Klag said neutrally.

B'Oraq, typically, saw right through it. "You don't approve."

"A conference sounds very . . . Vulcan. Sitting around and *discussing*." Klag's face scrunched up in disgust.

"Perhaps, but it's also the best way for us to learn more. Klingon doctors are not much for sharing, but with luck this conference will start to change that."

They reached Klag's cabin, and the captain fixed his doctor with a dubious expression. "That seems unlikely."

"Of course it's unlikely. The KPE is the most hidebound organization in the empire, and that's against some fairly stiff competition. Still, the longest journey begins with a single step, or so one of my instructors at Starfleet Medical insisted."

"That certainly sounds like a Federation sentiment," Klag said dismissively. Klag liked and respected many citizens of the Federation, in particular Picard and Riker of the *Enterprise*, with whom he had shared many battles, but in general he found their way of life to be repugnant.

The door to his cabin rumbled open. "I wish you success at your conference, B'Oraq. Where is it taking place?"

"At the Lukara Edifice in Novat."

Klag did not know the place, but he had also never been to the city of Novat. "When do you depart?"

"I'm due to present a monograph two days after we arrive on Qo'noS." She smiled and tugged her braid. "In fact, it's about you. Or, more accurately, your right arm. I'm off to complete the paper now—assuming Kurak's latest gravity disaster hasn't resulted in more patients. I no longer have a nurse to fob them off on." That last was added bitterly. B'Oraq's nurse, Gaj, had been put to death after she was exposed as being part of a mutiny against Klag.

"I hope you will not need me to provide a demonstration?" Klag asked.

B'Oraq shook her head. "It would probably help them pay attention, but no, that sort of thing isn't done. Klingon doctors pride themselves on getting their patients back out into the world as fast as possible. The idea of a patient hanging around to be examined is anathema."

"Even were it not, I would be unavailable. All the Chancellor-class captains have been ordered to report to General Kriz at Command."

Frowning, B'Oraq said, "*All* of them?"

"Well, except for Captain Kvaad, since the *Kesh* remained at Elabrej, but otherwise, yes—it will be to go over the entire Kavrot mission, not simply the war with the Elabrej."

"Even Dorrek?"

The mention of his estranged younger brother brought Klag up short. "I . . . I do not know."

"If all the Chancellor-class captains are to be present, it only makes sense that the captain of the *K'mpec* would attend as well."

"Yes," Klag said quietly. He had been hoping that he would not have to see Dorrek again so soon after Klag discommended him from their House. "He probably will be. Kriz has never been one to pay attention to family concerns." There would be a notation in Dorrek's file that he had been removed from the House of M'Raq by Klag, so when Kriz made the record of the gathering, he would see it, but that didn't mean he would necessarily pay attention to it.

Klag shook his head. "It matters not. We are both captains in the Defense Force, and we must report to our commander. We will do so." He looked down at B'Oraq. "*Qapla'*, Doctor."

"Captain—" B'Oraq put out an arm, then cut herself off.

"Yes?" Klag prompted when her pause threatened to go on forever.

"I . . . I wish to once again express my gratitude. My attempts to improve the state of our medicine—"

Unable to help himself, Klag smiled. "Your crusade, you mean."

"Call it what you will," B'Oraq said tartly, "I have made great strides over the past few months, and a great deal of it is due to your acceding to the transplant. Having the Hero of Marcan and Elabrej and the Conqueror of the San-Tarah undergo one of my 'barbaric' Federation-inspired procedures has done much to legitimize my work in the eyes of our people."

Klag beamed with pride that "Hero of Elabrej" was now being said of him. Already several songs had been composed about the battle, and Klag was pleased that his role was prominent in all of them. He was also grateful that the songwriters had not minimized Wirrk's contribution. The *Kravokh*'s captain died gloriously, restoring his ship's honor and dealing the decisive blow to the Elabrej, and that deserved to be memorialized.

To B'Oraq, however, he only said, "As I've told you in the past, I have done only what is necessary to make myself a better warrior and a more worthy captain of this vessel."

Smirking, B'Oraq said, "I'll take that as a 'you're welcome.'"

Klag sighed. B'Oraq's eight years living in the Federation had poisoned her speech to an appalling degree.

Then B'Oraq leaned forward and kissed Klag hungrily on the mouth, biting down hard on his lip.

At first Klag did not return the gesture, for once, very unsure of himself.

While there were no specific regulations against captains having sexual relations with subordinates—mostly because the regulations were written before women served on Defense Force vessels and had never been rewritten to accommodate the change, not even during Azetbur's reign—Klag had always been of the feeling that it was unwise to bed one's officers, as it might give way to making decisions on the wrong basis. A captain needed to think with his head and with his heart, not with his loins. It was for that reason that Klag had limited his sexual encounters to the *bekks*—troops he would never directly interact with on duty were the only people he slept with while off it.

But he was unlikely to treat B'Oraq any differently. For one thing, he already considered her indispensible. He was unlikely to change this opinion, regardless of the quality of the sex they were about to have. And B'Oraq

11

was too much the crusader to let *anything* interfere with her work as a physician.

So Klag grabbed B'Oraq's shoulder-length hair at the back and yanked hard on it, then dragged her into his cabin, the door rumbling shut behind her.

B'Oraq wore a lighter armor that had greater ease of movement, so she was out of her uniform far faster than Klag was able to extricate himself from his. She spent the time it took him to unfasten the parts of his armor biting on the bits of flesh he had exposed, sending quivers of magnificent pain through Klag. At first, she nibbled, then worked her way up to furious bites, practically chewing on his flesh. Once his pants were gone, he grabbed her, digging his finger into her spinal ridge at her hip bone and dragging that finger up to her neck. She shivered at his touch.

Then he threw her onto his bunk, flesh and bone colliding enticingly with metal. Klag had never truly noticed how magnificent B'Oraq was as a woman. In fact, he had never truly thought of her as a woman before— she was simply the doctor, the one who harassed him about replacing his right arm and the one who later did everything she could to make his new arm function to the best of its ability.

Now, though, she was an attractive woman who was as hungry for him as he was now coming to realize he was for her.

She reached over at the stand next to his bed, grabbing the candleholder that his mother had given him when he got his commission. Rearing back, she threw it at him. He let the wrought iron strike him on his crest, reveling in the pain, snarling with ecstasy as he leapt on top of her. Klag had never been one for poetry, so he decided to forgo that part of the ritual, finding himself far too impatient to bother with such nonsense. It was amazing—up until the moment she kissed him, he never considered B'Oraq as a potential bedmate, but from the moment she bit his lip, his thoughts were suddenly consumed with her. The meeting with Kriz, the *Gorkon's* considerable damage, the prospect of seeing his estranged brother—none of it mattered. All he cared about was his own body intertwined with that of the daughter of Grala.

Klag was honestly not sure how much later it was when he heard Commander Toq's words over the speaker: "*Bridge to Klag.*"

Disentangling himself from B'Oraq—no easy feat, for they had wound up on the floor under his desk—Klag clambered to his feet and activated the intercom. "Klag."

The *Gorkon* first officer said, "*Sir, we have entered the home system, on approach to Praxis Station. Leskit estimates our docking time in seventeen minutes.*"

Checking the timepiece that had been next to the candleholder, Klag saw that he was supposed to have reported to the bridge twenty minutes earlier. Toq, to his credit, had not interrupted his captain until it was absolutely necessary. Klag needed to be on the bridge when the ship arrived at the homeworld, however, and Toq had given him sufficient warning to get dressed and be there.

"I will be on the bridge shortly, Toq. Out."

B'Oraq had also gotten to her feet. "I truly hope that no one needed my services."

"One did," Klag said with a smile.

They both laughed, and B'Oraq walked up to him, tracing a line on the faint scar where M'Raq's arm met with Klag's shoulder. "You know, I could make that scar fainter."

Klag shook his head. They'd had this conversation back when she did the procedure. "I do not ever wish to forget that this is my father's right arm. I did this as much for him—and for my House—as I did for myself."

"As you wish." She turned away, searching for her clothes in the mess they'd made on the floor. "I can safely say that this has been good medicine for *me*. I feel much better about speaking before the KPE." She turned and stared at him ferally. "I have a firsthand notion of how strong your right arm is."

Throwing his head back, Klag laughed heartily.

When he was done, he noticed a concerned look on B'Oraq's face. "Captain," she said hesitantly, "you don't . . . you don't expect us to take the oath now, do you?"

In all honesty, Klag hadn't given it a thought. Ancient tradition dictated that Klingons who had sexual relations then had to mate. It wasn't observed in the breach very often, in Klag's experience. "No," he said emphatically. "In truth, I have never understood that particular practice."

B'Oraq shrugged into her tunic. "It actually has its roots from Emperor Kligrok's time. He felt that there was too many extramarital affairs among the nobility, and too many younger nobles who spent too much time fornicating and not enough strengthening their Houses. Many Houses were feuding, also, and most of those feuds went back to bad ends to sexual relations between the Houses in question. So Kligrok decreed that all who had sexual relations were automatically mated."

As Klag fastened his armor, he shook his head with mild amusement. He hadn't known any of this, mostly by virtue of not caring all that much. Most of the stories he knew about Emperor Kligrok were about his conquests and his fealty to the teachings of Kahless.

"At first there was great resistance," B'Oraq continued, "but by the time of Emperor Kahrl, the oath had been codified." She finished putting on her armor and then stared at Klag. "In any case, Captain, while there are many ways in which uniting our Houses might be advantageous, I doubt it would be possible."

Although Klag agreed, he found himself slightly resentful of her complete rejection of the notion. "Why?"

She smiled. "My uncle. He is the head of our House, and he *hates* the Defense Force. He was disgusted when I joined, and approved only because he felt that my reforms had the best chance of succeeding across the empire if I made them to the Defense Force first. The people of the empire often take their cues from the military, after all. But if I brought you home and said we were to be mated, I would be discommendated instantly."

"Yes," Klag said, "but if we mated, you would be of the House of M'Raq, and it would not matter."

"Perhaps, but a feud between our Houses would get in the way of both of us actually accomplishing anything."

She rested her hands on his shoulders and stared up at him, giving Klag pause to notice how lovely her eyes were. Then she said, "But I would hope that you would not be averse to this happening again."

"Not in the least," Klag said without hesitation. The problem with taking low-ranking *bekks* into his bed was that he was never sure if they were genuinely interested in bedding him or simply following orders—and he'd never get a straight answer on the question from them. With B'Oraq, though, he knew the desire was genuine, and that made it far sweeter.

"Good." She moved to the door. "Now I *really* do need to finish my speech, and you need to get to the bridge."

"Indeed." Now both dressed, they departed his cabin together.

It was the *Gorkon's* first trip back to Qo'noS in many months. Klag decided that it was good to be home.

You sit in the captain's chair on the Hegh'ta. *The ship is badly damaged, being hemmed in by two vessels loyal to the House of Duras. Several warriors are lying dead at your feet.*

"Maintain course!" you cry out. "Status of warp engines!"

From behind you at the operations console, one of your warriors says, "Warp engines at sixty percent."

Then you ask, "Status of shields?"

A console explodes, sparks flying through the bridge. Once there was a warrior stationed there, but she is dead, and so no one else was affected.

Your gunner, who is familiar to you, says, "Aft shields buckling."

Though you order auxiliary power to shields, another shot takes down the aft shields completely.

Showing appalling judgment, the gunner leaves his post and approaches you. "We cannot win," he says, the coward. "We must withdraw!"

"Keep your place," you tell him, your voice a snarl.

He gives you an angry look, but he does so.

"New course," you tell the pilot. "Three-zero-seven mark two-seven-five."

You take the Hegh'ta into the corona of a star. The two enemy vessels follow, as you expect. Then, once you've entered the photosphere, you order the ship into warp, an action that kicks up several solar flares, which incinerate the dishonorable petaQpu' of House Duras.

It is a glorious sight. Duras disgraced your family. While you have no love for Gowron, you remember the words of Kahless: "The enemy of my enemy is my ally." So you fight for Gowron against those who took away your family name, those who dishonored you and kept you from taking your rightful place as—

Rodek, son of Noggra woke up screaming—not in pain or fear, but in frustration. Again, he'd had a dream that felt as real as any memory, yet he'd dreamed of events that Rodek knew could not possibly have happened to him. He'd not served in the Defense Force until the commencement of the Dominion War in the Year of Kahless 999, yet there he was fighting the forces of Duras during the civil war that raged in 993. It—like all the other dreams—made no sense.

He had told no one of the dreams, thinking them to merely be side effects of his injuries. On San-Tarah, he'd nearly had his head blown off and was only still drawing breath thanks to the good graces of Doctor B'Oraq, who healed him. Then at Elabrej, he took a disruptor hit to the face.

Since then, the dreams had not stopped. He had performed his duties as second officer and primary gunner for the *Gorkon* during the trip back to Qo'noS from Elabrej, but it had been a struggle. Toq and Leskit had both noticed that he seemed odd, but Rodek had brushed them off, assuming they would get better the farther he got from his injuries.

They did not; they grew worse.

Turning to look at the chronometer in his cabin, Rodek saw that it was not long before he had to report for what would be his final bridge shift for some time. As was customary, he would be required to present Toq with the record of battle, which meant he would need to look it over one final time to make sure it was both up to date and accurate. It was all well and good for warriors to exaggerate their feats over bloodwine, but formal records needed to be free of such indulgences.

Clambering off his *QongDaq*, Rodek stretched, feeling the vertebrae in his back snap. Perhaps he should seek medical attention.

Immediately, he dismissed the notion. It was weakness, and he was a Klingon warrior, not some mewlish human who ran to a physician at the first sign of injury.

He would be home soon. He would see his father, Noggra. And things would improve.

* * *

Wol stared dolefully at the food on her tray.

When she had first reported to the *Gorkon*, she had heard stories of how much better the ship's replicated food was. The Chancellor-class vessels had food replicators obtained through trade with the Federation in order to maximize space. By requiring less storage space for food, the *Gorkon* and its brother ships were able to take on more crew. A ship this size in the old days would have been able to carry only a bit more than a thousand instead of the twenty-seven hundred the *Gorkon* had at capacity. But the presence of the replicators meant a much smaller store of real food and therefore room for more crew.

The ship had a complement of fifteen hundred troops, which were divided into twenty companies, each of which contained fifteen five-soldier squads. Since the beginning of the mission to explore the Kavrot sector, and through the *Gorkon*'s campaigns at San-Tarah and Elabrej, Wol had served as leader of the fifteenth, in charge of one of the squads in First Company under the command of *QaS DevwI'* Vok.

Wol joined the surviving members of her squad—the oversized Goran, the white-haired G'joth, and the newest recruit Kagak—at their usual table, Goran taking up the space of two people with his girth. For them, she assumed it to be their last meal aboard ship for some time.

But Wol had nowhere to go. Now that they were on approach to the homeworld, she had to face that possibility for the first time. It was not a happy one. She would ask Vok if she could remain on ship during the repair cycle, though she doubted that would be possible. Even the most tolerant engineers, she knew, hated having soldiers underfoot when they were fixing things, and Kurak was far from the most tolerant engineer.

As she sat down between G'joth and Goran, Kagak said, "Your hair grows back well, Leader."

Unconsciously, Wol's right hand went to the top of her head, where her dark red tresses were at almost shoulder length. Her head had been shorn when she had been captured and experimented on by the Elabrej. She had escaped and helped Commander Toq take down the Elabrej's government headquarters, thus regaining her honor, but her hair had to regrow on its own.

"Thank you, *Bekk*," Wol said. "In truth, it grows more slowly than I would prefer." She had cut her hair down almost to the scalp once before, and it had grown back more quickly then. However, she preferred not to think about that part of her life, even though her squad was aware of it.

Nor did she particularly wish to dwell on her imprisonment at the hands of the Elabrej, so she changed the subject. "I assume you all have plans for your leave."

G'joth chewed on his *racht*. "I'm returning home to Krennla. It's been far too long. My sister Lakras has joined an opera company."

Wol turned in surprise at G'joth as she scooped up the meat from her skull stew. "The way you always talk about Lakras, I assumed her to be an infant."

"Merely describing how she *acts*. And it *has* been several turns since last I was home. Duty has never permitted it at any time since we were last at war with the Federation."

Kagak's eyes grew wide. "That's a long time to be away from home."

At that, G'joth simply shrugged. "My duties have kept me busy."

"I could never stay away from home for five years." Kagak laughed as he stuffed some *bregit* lung into his mouth. "My grandmother would have me executed."

"Where are you from, Kagak?" Goran asked.

"Pheben III. One of the *loSpev* farms."

G'joth sputtered his *racht*. "You come from farming stock? I'm impressed—I didn't think you had that much honor in you." Then he laughed heartily.

They all did likewise. Though most farmers were not of noble blood, they nevertheless served a critical function in feeding the empire.

"You must be the shame of the family," Wol said, "joining the Defense Force."

"It would be more accurate to say that I *stopped* being the shame of the family when I joined. I am far more skilled with a disruptor and a *bat'leth* than ever I was with a thresher or an animal feeder." Kagak swallowed the rest of his *bregit* lung and washed it down with some *warnog*. "What of you, Leader?"

Wol sighed. She had been hoping no one would ask, but she knew that was a forlorn hope. "I have made no plans."

"Neither have I," Goran said. Wol noted that Goran sounded sad.

"Don't you have family, big man?" Kagak asked.

Goran shook his head. "My family died long ago. I have only me now."

"That is not true," Kagak said. "You have the fifteenth. And since I am now part of the fifteenth, that means you also have somewhere to go."

Picking at her skull stew, Wol said, "What do you mean, Kagak?"

"I mean, you both should come with me to Pheben III! Mine is a large family, and Grandmother always makes enough food to feed entire armies—especially at *yobta' yupma'*."

Frowning, Wol said, "I'm not familiar with *yobta' yupma'*."

"It's a holiday celebrated at the harvest, usually involving a very big feast," G'joth said. "My mother was born on a farm, and we still have a feast. In fact, she's already crest-deep in the preparations for it."

Kagak nodded. "It's my favorite time of year, and I haven't been home for it for many turns. Grandmother would gladly welcome two more mouths at the table— even one as big as yours, Goran."

Goran chuckled, which caused the table to shake. "I do not wish to impose on your family's hospitality."

"Nor I," Wol said. She wasn't even entirely sure she *liked* Kagak. True, he had warned them of a possible mutiny among his former crewmates on the *Kreltek*, which had come to pass, and he had fought well on Elabrej, but he had yet to prove his worth as a member of the fifteenth.

"I insist. Grandmother is the finest cook in the empire, and she always wants me to bring people home to visit, *especially* at *yobta' yupma'*. She loves showing off the farm for strangers."

Goran stared down at his tray. "I have not had a home-cooked meal in a very long time. And when I did, it wasn't very good. My mother was a terrible chef."

They all chortled at the big man's bluntness. Wol swallowed some of her replicated, bland skull stew and thought that perhaps Goran had a point.

"And you'll love my family. They're the finest people the empire has to offer, you'll see."

That clinched it. The last thing in the galaxy Wol wanted to encounter was a happy family. She'd been part of a happy family, once. The House of Varnak had been a most noble House, one of the finest on Qo'noS, until the House head's impulsive daughter Eral bore a son by a commoner, rather than the man she was to mate with. Eral's son was taken from her, her lover killed, and Eral herself exiled, left a Houseless common woman. Left without alternatives, she changed her name to Wol and joined the Defense Force.

Ironically, she was the only member of House Varnak to survive. Her family supported the usurper Morjod, who attempted to remove Chancellor Martok from power, and when that coup failed, Varnak was dissolved, most of its members put to death.

Wol did not think she could bear being amid Kagak's family.

"I am grateful for the offer, Kagak—and Goran, you should definitely accept—but I must decline." Wol added before Kagak could object further, "We will speak no more of it, *Bekk*!"

Kagak practically shrank into the bench. "Yes, Leader."

"How are we to get there?" Goran asked.

"There's a cargo ship, the *Mahochu*, that makes regular runs between Pheben and Qo'noS. The cargo master's a friend of the family."

"Where will you fit?" G'joth asked with a chuckle.

"Anywhere we want—the ship's always empty when it goes *to* Pheben. It goes to each planet, picks up its goods, and then returns to Qo'noS to pass on the items to their distributors."

Wol swallowed the last of her stew. "That won't get you back to Qo'noS—and I doubt that the captain will divert the *Gorkon* to Pheben to pick the pair of you up."

Kagak laughed, spitting out some of his *warnog*. "I will find a way to return. I always have in the past."

"Enjoy yourself," G'joth said. "I'm sure your feast will be far better than mine." He laughed in Goran's direction. "My mother prepares Klingon food with the same skill as yours did, big man."

Goran frowned. "I thought your mother was a chef."

"She is—in an Andorian restaurant. For so long has she prepared those blue-skins' food, she's forgotten how to make proper meals."

"Then why not come with us?" Kagak asked. Wol found herself both amused and annoyed by his insistence.

"Because there is more to my return to Krennla than my mother's inability to keep from bringing her work home," G'joth said angrily. "I have not seen my family in far too long." The anger dissipated, G'joth's easy smile returning. Wol had not seen that smile as much since G'joth's best friend Davok died at San-Tarah, and she was always grateful for its return. "The same also for Klaad and Krom. We grew up together on the streets of the Kenta District, but I haven't seen them since I enlisted."

Wol shivered involuntarily. She had grown up on the estates of House Varnak, which weren't far from Krennla. At first, she had known of that city only as the thing she looked down on from the aircar in disdain when she came into town with the family—when she even bothered to give them a thought in the first place—grateful that she had been born to a noble House and wasn't forced to live in such squalor.

Then, after she was exiled, she *was* forced to live in that squalor. A woman without a House, she had few options, and the ones that presented themselves in Krennla were repugnant at best. She had joined the Defense Force out of desperation.

And G'joth is nostalgic *for this?* She shuddered at the very thought. But she did not wish to insult her subordinate, so she said nothing.

To her relief, G'joth himself changed the subject. "Do we have any idea who our fifth will be?" The fifteenth had been one soldier short since Trant's death on Elabrej.

Wol shook her head. "Unlikely. I will ask Vok when next I speak to him, but such decisions are generally made after the repair cycle is through."

"I look forward to it," Kagak said.

"Why?" Goran asked.

Grinning, Kagak said, "Because then I won't be the *chu'wI'* anymore."

Everyone else at the table laughed at that, including Goran, causing the table to shake again. Wol couldn't bring herself to, though. As Kagak had said, he was the newest member of the squad. Something about him annoyed her, still. Unlike Goran and G'joth, not to mention their dead comrades Krevor and Davok, Kagak wasn't, she felt, entirely part of the fifteenth yet. While she wasn't sure if he was the traitor that both Maris and Trant had proved to be before their unmourned deaths, she was equally unsure if he yet deserved to be a part of their squad.

She certainly had no intention of going to celebrate this ridiculous *yobta' yupma'* with him.

"Excellent," Toq said to the white-haired image of Captain Quvmoh on the screen before him. "I will see you tomorrow."

"Do not be late, Toq. The Gorlak will leave orbit of Qo'noS at high sun. I will not wait for you."

"I will arrive on time. I thank you, Captain."

"Thank your father," Quvmoh grumbled. *"He's the one I owe half a dozen favors to."*

Toq grinned. Lorgh was not Toq's biological father, but he had taken Toq in after he was rescued from Carraya, and made Toq part of his House. Most people thought that, when Toq called Lorgh "Father," he meant it literally, and it was too much trouble to explain the truth to people.

Besides, few people knew the *real* truth—even Lorgh himself.

Still, having a high-ranking member of Imperial Intelligence for a House head, regardless of whether or not they shared blood, was handy for getting rides. And in this case, it was to visit Lorgh himself. The old man was currently stationed at a base near the Romulan border and couldn't get away, but thanks to the *Gorkon*'s repair cycle, he didn't need to. Toq could come to him.

After switching off the screen, Toq walked away from the communications console, leaving it to Ensign Kline, and moved to the front of the bridge. "Leskit, what is our time of arrival at Praxis?"

Turning from the helm control, the white-haired pilot drawled, "Two minutes. Unless Klarr is on duty, in which case it will be more like seven." Leskit shook his head. "I came up through the ranks with that *petaQ*. He's half blind, half stupid, and half drunk."

Toq sat in the first officer's seat to the right of the command chair. "How has he retained his position?"

"He hasn't. He used to be a pilot. Now they let him dock ships at Praxis because the *real* pilots usually do all the work. Still, I expect he will find a way to make my life more difficult." Leskit said that last with an exaggerated sigh.

Toq shook his head and chuckled at the old razor-beast. Then the rear door rumbled aside to reveal Klag.

"Captain!" Toq rose to his feet. "We will dock at Praxis Station shortly."

"Excellent." Klag strode forward, his bodyguard, Morr, taking up his position at the rear of the bridge. As he passed the operations console, which was right behind the captain's chair, Klag said, "Ensign Kallo, open intership."

The young ensign nodded. "Done, sir."

"Attention crew of the *I.K.S. Gorkon*. We have, at last, come home. Our journey to the Kavrot sector has been a success. We placed the Klingon flag on San-Tarah and we were victorious against the foul Elabrej. We have served the cause of honor, we have served the empire, and we have been victorious. I am proud to call you my crew. *Qapla'*!"

The entire bridge cried out, "*Qapla'*!" in response.

Toq turned toward Rodek, standing at the weapons console, and held out his hand. "Lieutenant Rodek, the record of battle."

Rodek reached under the console and removed an ornate padd. He touched a control, then held it out to Toq. "I, Rodek, son of Noggra, gunner for the ship *Gorkon*, conclude the record of battle for this ship on the twelfth day in the year of Kahless, 1002."

Taking the padd, Toq walked two steps down to where Klag stood. "I present the record of battle, Captain Klag. It is filled with exploits of glory and honor, and you will find it worthy of your leadership."

Klag took the padd and smiled.

A *bekk* at the back of the bridge cheered. Kline started singing the Warrior's Anthem. Several others shouted "*Qapla'*!"

Somehow, Leskit made himself heard over the din. "We have docked at Praxis Station, Captain. It seems they had someone sober on duty."

Toq laughed. "Not your friend, then."

"Hardly," Leskit said dryly. Then he looked back at Klag. "We are home, Captain."

"Home," Klag said quietly. "Yes. You have done very well, my warriors. Very well indeed. Now let us leave the ship to Kurak and her minions, so we may once again return to the fields of battle and bring glory to the empire!"

Toq joined in the cheers that provoked.

But his duty was now finished. Once Kurak was done, he would once again speak for this fine crew to the captain. For now, though, he was going to be with the only family he'd known since Carraya.

TWO

The Commercial Quarter
First City, Qo'noS

"I find myself reminded why I hate the First City so much," Leskit muttered as he and Kurak walked through the cobblestone streets of the Commercial Quarter. Most of the First City's businesses were concentrated here: shops, restaurants, trading posts, and so on. Some were concentrated in single structures, others stood on their own in boxy buildings that acted as satellites to the larger buildings.

The street on which the two officers walked was crowded with pedestrians, primarily Klingon civilians, along with the occasional offworlder. Indeed, by wearing their Defense Force armor, Leskit and Kurak stood out, and most of the others on the street gave them a wide berth out of respect. Their insignia indicated that they were officers, and that meant they were of the upper classes of empire society.

In truth, Leskit would have been happy to have worn civilian clothing, but, as per regulations, he had none aboard ship, and he hadn't yet had the chance to go home to Kopf's Cliff to retrieve any. As for Kurak, the *Gorkon*'s chief engineer and Leskit's sometime *par'Mach'kai*, he had picked her up at Command Headquarters, where she'd been requisitioning matériel and personnel for the repair work, and so was also in uniform.

Kurak stared up at him, and Leskit could feel her penetrating brown eyes boring a hole in his crest. "Why do you hate the First City?" she asked, sounding more than a little surprised.

"Oh, the place was very impressive—hundreds of years ago. But now? Time has marched on."

Now Kurak's face modulated into one of confusion. "What do you mean? This is where all the finest buildings are."

Leskit snorted at that. "Finest? Hardly. Perhaps when this style was in vogue during Emperor Sompek's reign, but now?"

Shaking her head, Kurak said, "Leskit, *what* are you talking about? And where are we going? We've been walking for hours."

Chuckling, the Cardassian neckbones he wore jangling on his chest, Leskit said, "It's only been a few minutes, and we'll be there shortly."

"We couldn't simply transport?"

"We're not on Defense Force business, and I didn't feel like waiting in a public transporter queue. Besides, it's a nice night for a walk." That much was true. Lightning crackled through the cloudy sky. Leskit couldn't have asked for a finer night to take Kurak to his favorite restaurant.

"If you say so," Kurak said sourly. "And that still doesn't explain your disdain for Emperor Sompek."

"Oh, I have nothing against Emperor Sompek—I simply wish the architects seventy-five years ago felt the same."

"Sompek's reign was a lot more than seventy-five years ago."

With a chuckle, Leskit said, "Yes, I'm aware of that."

"Leskit, if you do not start making sense, I'm going back to the *Gorkon*. I shouldn't even be indulging in this, there is still a great deal of work to be done. Praxis Station has not nearly enough engineers to do the job. Most of the Chancellor-class ships are in for repair *and* they're shorthanded because of *yobta' yupma'*."

"Do people still celebrate that?" Leskit asked with surprise.

"Oh, yes. When I worked with Makros, the place ground to a halt when *yobta' yupma'* came around. That's another reason why I find the Defense Force to be populated with indolent fools—they don't even appreciate the important holidays."

That prompted a laugh from Leskit. "Your definition of 'important' differs from mine, Kurak."

"Be that as it may, the few engineers that *are* available are incompetents and fools."

"As I recall, that has been your description of every engineer who is not yourself."

"That is *not* true." Now Kurak almost sounded petulant. "Vall was competent. A filthy, sniveling worm, but he was quite the engineer."

"Indeed. Though I'm shocked to hear *you* admit that."

"I am capable of admitting when I am wrong, Leskit. You of all people should be aware of that."

They turned a corner onto another, narrower cobblestone road, one with fewer pedestrians—just a few older Klingon civilians ahead of them and two Ferengi walking rapidly in the other direction—and the structures now were all the smaller, one-story rectangular buildings that never made it to the First City's skyline. "True. After all, some of the first words you said to me were that you were not interested in me or in any other male on the ship." He chuckled. "I must admit a part of me thought that meant you were interested only in other females. Though you disabused me of that notion when you explained your disdain for the Defense Force in general."

"A disdain I still hold firmly in my heart," she said with a wicked smile. "Present company not at all excepted. I've simply learned to tolerate your idiocy."

Leskit bowed his head. "Very generous of you, Commander."

"Thank you, Lieutenant." Kurak still wore the smile. Leskit had found her to be an ill-tempered shrew of a woman who hated the Defense Force and everything it stood for. One of the finest civilian warp-field specialists in the empire, she had helped design the previous chancellor's flagship, the *Negh'Var*. However, when the Dominion War broke out, her family pressured her into joining the military, her skill and reputation earning her the rank of commander.

After the Founders of the Dominion surrendered to the allies of the Alpha Quadrant, she found herself forced to remain commissioned. The House of Palkar must always serve the empire, as she had apparently been told since birth, and all the other able-bodied adults of her House who served had died in battle against the Jem'Hadar, the Cardassians, and the Breen. Until her nephew, Gevnar, was old enough to begin officer training—which he would not be for another year—Kurak had to remain in the Defense Force. If she did not, the House *ghIntaq*, Moloj, who had been running the House of Palkar since Kurak's parents' deaths, had promised to discommendate her. Kurak's father had made that threat at the war's commencement, and Kurak was of the opinion that Moloj would follow through on it.

At first, Kurak had promised herself not to form any attachments or do anything more than was absolutely necessary to do her duty, but Leskit was proud to have forced her to rethink the first, and serving on the *Gorkon*—and almost being killed in a mutiny—had changed her mind on the latter.

"So," she said, "why is Emperor Sompek to blame for the architecture of seventy-five years ago?"

"The entire city was built up during Sompek's reign. Prior to that, it wasn't even called the First City, it was simply the Great Hall, located on the highest point on the continent, and had been the fortress from which various Klingons had defended their land for centuries. After Kahless united us, it became the seat of power, but it was not until Sompek that it became a *city*. It was transformed into a thriving metropolis, with the Great Hall at its center, and each quarter radiating out from it."

"I know all this, Leskit. Klingons learn this before they can walk." Kurak sounded impatient, and when she got impatient, she tended to hit things, and Leskit wasn't in the mood for foreplay right now.

Quickly, he said, "What you may not realize is that, at first, all the architecture followed the pyramidlike style of the Great Hall."

"As it does now," Kurak said.

"Yes, but at the time, it was done because Sompek ordered it so. Some had triangular roofs, others had spires, but they all looked more or less alike. The main reason, of course, was defense. Air travel was still relatively new, then, and that construction style allowed weapons to be emplaced within the spires. Only the larger structures, the ones that could be seen from the sky, were built like that. Less care was given to smaller buildings—as you can see." He indicated the places on this street, all of which were jammed together and favored function over aesthetics. "But then, they were not required to defend the city against an aerial attack. Over time, as technology improved and the fleet that could protect the First City grew, there was a touch more variety—as indeed there was all over the planet. In my own home city—"

"Where is that?"

Leskit blinked. "You don't know?"

She smiled. "It never came up. And where *is* this place you're bringing me?"

"Soon." Leskit tried to sound reassuring, but he could tell it wasn't working. Luckily, the restaurant was only another eighth of a *qell'qam* away. "I grew up in Kopf's Cliff, and my mate and child still live there."

"I've never been there. The Palkar estate is just outside the First City, along the Qam-Chee River, and I've only lived there on Qo'noS." She smiled. "I also left the homeworld as fast as I could once I reached the Age of Ascension."

"No surprise there." Leskit knew that Kurak had been working with the legendary engineer Makros at the Science Institute on Mempa V before she was conscripted by her father. "The Cliff is a wondrous city. The center of town has almost entirely cylindrical buildings. That style was actually pilfered from the Phebens after we conquered them. In fact, most of the Cliff is built in the style of species we've conquered." He smiled. "The architects of our city have always been experimental, and the city administrators have always approved, as it made the city unique."

"I suppose 'unique' is one word for it," Kurak muttered. "How do you know all this?"

"My mother. She was an administrator for an architect. She loved the art, though she had no talent for it herself. So instead she went to work for one, so she could indulge her passion by proxy. Supper-table conversations were almost always about this building or that building, and my sister and I—"

"You have a *sister?*"

"Am I not permitted siblings?" Leskit asked with a huge smile.

"Leskit, we've been sleeping with each other for months now. We've had plenty of conversations, and typically *you've* done most of the talking. Indeed, you've done most of the talking for the entire crew. How is it that in all the inane conversations you've subjected me to, you've never discussed your family?"

Shrugging, Leskit said, "Simply your good fortune."

"I'm surprised your mother worked at all. Was she not the Lady of the House?"

Chuckling, Leskit said, "Our House is not quite on the same level as that of Palkar, I'm afraid. Being Lady of the House of Graf is not a luxury we could afford, particularly once my father died. In any event, Mother loved to discourse about this, and she railed against the First City every third night. You see, after Praxis blew up—"

"What? Oh." Kurak shook her head. "Of course, the moon."

Leskit grinned. The orbital station where the *Gorkon* was being repaired had been named Praxis Station after the moon of Qo'noS that had blown up eighty-three years previous. That was where Kurak was going to be spending most of her time for the next several weeks, so Leskit wasn't surprised at her initial confusion.

"The damage done to the First City from Praxis's fall-out was considerable," Leskit said. "Many buildings had to be condemned and the Great Hall had to be rebuilt. That was a time of great change in the empire—an alliance with the Federation, a woman in the chancellor's chair—and so, probably in reaction to that, Chancellor Azetbur decreed that all new construction follow that of the Great Hall, to make the First City look as it did in Sompek's time. Many of the buildings still have weapons emplacements, too—disruptor cannons rather than the projectiles of old—though I can't imagine why they'd be used now, when the First City has far more useful defensive measures."

Kurak stared up at him as they walked. "You told me all this to distract me from the fact that we're lost, haven't you?"

"Not at all." He stopped walking, having sighted their goal several paces back. "Here we are."

Looking around, Kurak said, "Where?"

Leskit chortled to himself. He had been expecting this reaction, since there was only one eatery in sight.

"We are at our destination."

She looked up at that one eatery, which had the words VULCAN CUISINE in austere Klingon script over the door. "Is it behind the Vulcan restaurant?"

"It *is* the Vulcan restaurant."

Kurak stared up at Leskit, and took a step back, as if suddenly afraid to be close enough to touch him. She gripped her right wrist with her left arm, a sure sign that she was extremely angry. "*What?*"

Holding up a finger, Leskit said, "Before you pass judgment—"

"You expect me to eat *Vulcan* food?"

"Have you ever *had* Vulcan food?"

Eyes ablaze, Kurak said, "No. Nor have I ever dove

naked into a vat of hungry *taknar*. Neither is an experience I am eager to undertake."

Pausing long enough to enjoy the mental image Kurak just gave him, Leskit said, "I thought much the same thing when my sister dragged me here years ago, shortly after it opened. Then I tasted the food. Nothing to make you swear off meat, but quite edifying."

"Please tell me you're joking."

Putting his hand over his heart, Leskit said, "Have you ever known me to jest?"

Kurak just stared at him.

"All right, have you ever known me to jest about food? I was the one who thanked whatever deceased deity was responsible for bringing Vall on board as your assistant, since he fine-tuned the replicators to make *edible* food, remember?"

"Leskit—"

"Very well," he said quickly, holding out his hands. "I shall make a wager with you. You will try the food here. If it is not to your liking, then you may make any request of me, and I will fulfill it, or die trying."

Regarding him with obvious suspicion, Kurak said, "*Any* request?"

"Anything."

"No conditions?"

"None."

Finally, Kurak let go of her wrist. Leskit viewed that as a good sign. "I look forward to your doing my bidding, Lieutenant."

Grinning, Leskit indicated the door. "Never assume, Commander."

The front door slid aside quietly at their approach. That set the tone for the inside. No matter how many times Leskit returned to Vulcan Cuisine—the owners, T'Lisik and Syruk, had never seen the need to use more distinctive nomenclature, since that name alone made it unique on Qo'noS—he never quite got used to how *quiet* it was inside.

Kurak's eyes went wide, and Leskit suspected she had the same sense of foreboding that he had felt when K'dot, his sister, had taken him here for the first time right before he went off on his first assignment for the Defense Force. "You're going into space," K'dot had said. "You'll be encountering many different species. You should know how they eat."

Leskit had never quite followed that logic, but he had been surprised by how well prepared the Vulcan food was. Unlike humans, who cooked all the flavor out of their food, Vulcans generally cooked it only enough to remove potential viruses and germs. They also had an appreciation for spice that had surprised Leskit. K'dot, who was an anthropologist, had said that it was a hold-over from the Vulcans' days as desert nomads, where spices were necessary to preserve food.

The front door opened to a small receiving area where spare couches and sand paintings were all that lay against the walls. An open entryway to the restaurant proper was flanked by a podium, behind which stood a Vulcan woman with long, dark hair, wearing a loose red robe etched with the lettering of her people. This was T'Lisik, one of the two proprietors, and the one who seated the customers.

"This," Kurak whispered, "is an obscenity."

"There's no need to whisper," Leskit said, though he still spoke in a subdued tone. "Greetings, T'Lisik."

Bowing her head, T'Lisik spoke the Klingon language flawlessly. "It has been some time since your last visit to our establishment, Lieutenant." She then turned to Kurak. "Commander, welcome. On behalf of he who is my husband and myself, we hope you find the meal satisfactory."

"I would not count on that," Kurak said darkly.

T'Lisik bowed her head again and then led them into the main part of the restaurant. Wood was at a premium on Vulcan, and to maintain authenticity, the tables were made of stone, even though Qo'noS suffered from no such shortage. The decorations were spare and modest. About two-thirds of the tables were filled. The patrons appeared to be a quarter Klingons, three-quarters outsiders, the bulk of the latter being Vulcanoids of some form. Leskit knew that many Romulans lived on Qo'noS, though few in the First City, and many of them patronized this place. Syruk had told him once that if it weren't for the Romulans, the restaurant would not be able to stay in business.

As she sat opposite Leskit, Kurak stared at him. "And you come here on *purpose*?"

"Why shouldn't I? I'm as Klingon as the next person, Kurak. I can debauch with the best of them. But sometimes, it is good to be calm and relaxed and enjoy food of a different type in quiet and solitude."

"I dislike quiet and solitude," she said as she peered at the display on the table that provided the menu options. "They are usually a prelude to disaster."

Leskit chuckled. "Would you like me to order for you?"

"I'm not a *child*, Leskit. I'm capable of choosing my own meal."

"I do not doubt it, but I know the cuisine somewhat better than you, and—"

Now Kurak grinned. "You assume much, Leskit. I never said I've never eaten Vulcan food."

That brought the pilot up short. "Oh?"

"Father entertained some Vulcan diplomats when I was a girl. Moloj went to great lengths to obtain proper Vulcan food, since he knew they had that ridiculous taboo against meat." She shook her head. "I remember that old *toDSaH* whining like a Ferengi when he couldn't get the right leaves for the salad—especially when the houseboy who usually did the shopping threw up his hands and said, 'We cannot have this in our house! This isn't food, it's what food eats!'"

Both of them shared a laugh at that. Kurak perused the menu for a bit more, then ordered a *vranto* salad, *t'mirak* rice, and *ulan* soup. Leskit was silently impressed that Kurak knew the order of dishes—soup always came last.

For his part, he knew better than to have anything but Syruk's *plomeek* to finish; he began with *lirs*, a grain dish.

The first course came in fairly short order, along with utensils. Kurak frowned in annoyance, but Leskit smiled. He recalled the first time K'dot brought him here, and Leskit had asked why weapons were provided with the food. In later years, Syruk had admitted that when the restaurant first opened, they hadn't bothered providing utensils because they assumed the Klingon patrons wouldn't use them anyhow, but enough complaints from the assorted Vulcanoids led to them providing such for all.

Lirs was a specialty of the house. Leskit had been told by experts that Syruk's *lirs* was far superior to what one got on Vulcan; for his part, he'd never had Vulcan food anywhere else and so could not judge. Kurak ate her food silently and without complaint—though without compliment, either.

That ended when the soups arrived. Kurak stared at it, leaned in and smelled it, then finally picked up the spoon.

Leskit had already taken two sips of his *plomeek*, and it was as magnificent as ever. Vulcan soups were usually palate cleansers, washing down the meal, and also providing a distinctive, if not overwhelming, flavor.

The *ulan* did likewise but had more flavor than the *plomeek*. Apparently, that flavor was to Kurak's liking, as she wore an expression of pleasure. Leskit recognized it mainly by virtue of being the only person in the empire who'd ever seen such an expression on her face.

"It would seem," Kurak said with a smile, "that you win the bet, Leskit. Once again, you have proved me wrong about something. This is rapidly becoming a habit."

"One I'm more than happy to maintain."

"Do you mean that?" Kurak asked.

Leskit frowned. "What do you mean?"

"I mean, Leskit, that we have been sleeping together,

43

eating together, *being* together for months now. You've seen me through some of the worst times of my life. We have been acting as mates do."

Not sure he liked where this was going, Leskit said, "My dear Kurak—you forget that I am already mated."

"Divorce is a simple enough procedure," Kurak said with a shrug.

"True, but I would not leave my son Houseless."

"What do you mean?"

Pausing to finish his own soup, Leskit then set the bowl aside. "I said earlier that my House was as nothing to that of the mighty Palkar."

Kurak snorted at that.

"However, it is a great and noble House compared to Karreka's. Before we were mated, she belonged to the House of Krolt."

"I do not know that House."

Smiling wryly, Leskit said, "No reason you should. It was never much of a House even before it was dissolved."

Now Kurak nodded in understanding. "If you divorce her, she will be left destitute."

"As will my son."

"You could petition the High Council for custody. You are a member of the crew that just won the war against the Elabrej. I can't imagine you would be refused."

Leskit shook his head. He'd thought this all through months ago. "And then what? Karreka *should* have custody. I have no skills in child rearing. Nor do I have any desire to see her left Houseless and childless."

That seemed to render Kurak mute. She silently slurped the rest of her *ulan*. Leskit did not like the implications of the silence.

Finally, when she had finished the soup, she looked up at him. "Then where does that leave us?"

"In a Vulcan restaurant enjoying each other's company. What more is required?"

"Perhaps nothing." She got to her feet. "I must return to Praxis Station. There is much to be done."

Also rising, Leskit said, "Kurak—"

She held up her hands. "You are correct, of course, Leskit. It would be dishonorable of you to abandon your mate and child to such a fate simply to please me. It was wrong of me to even ask it of you." Then she smiled, which came to Leskit as something of a relief. "We will dine again tomorrow night."

"Yes," Leskit said. "This time, you may pick the eatery."

"Then we shall return here."

With that, Kurak left the restaurant. Leskit thought with amusement that this obviously meant that he was paying for the meal.

He wished Kurak hadn't brought up the subject of mating. All things being equal, Leskit would gladly mate with Kurak—particularly this new improved version that wasn't drunk all the time and smiled a lot and ate Vulcan food. But things were not equal. For starters, their relationship primarily worked because they served on the same vessel. But what would happen if one of them were transferred? It had already happened once— after the mission to taD, Leskit had been rotated back to the *Rotarran*, not returning to the *Gorkon* until their Kavrot sector exploration months later.

Plus, a year from now she would be resigning her commission. Her nephew would reach the Age of Ascension and she would go back to being a civilian engineer, far away from the fools and incompetents of the Defense Force.

And finally, there was Karreka and young Ch'kan. It was neither of their faults that their mate and father was a reprobate who was unfit for either job. He could not abandon them so callously. As Kurak had said, it would be the height of dishonor, and Leskit's honor was weak enough without doing that to erode it.

He ordered a bread dish called *saffir* for dessert. *Perhaps tomorrow night, I will try the* ulan.

THREE

Klag refused to look at his brother.

Eight of the twelve captains who had been assigned to vessels of the Chancellor class were present in General Kriz's office. Of the remaining four, three of them—the commanders of the *Gowron*, *Kravokh*, and *Azetbur*—had died in battle. The fourth was Captain Kvaad of the *Kesh*, who had remained behind with General Goluk at Elabrej.

Dorrek, son of M'Raq, former member of M'Raq's House and current captain of the *K'mpec*, stood on the far side of the large office from Klag, which certainly made it easier for Klag to avoid eye contact.

Kriz had been asking the captains in turn for their reports on the conquests they'd made in the Kavrot sector. To Klag's relief, the general did not ask him first, nor did he ask Dorrek. Instead, Captain Vikagh told of the *Ditagh*'s accomplishments, finding three uninhabited but quite habitable worlds.

When he finished, Kriz nodded at Vikagh, then turned to Captain Gatrell of the *Sturka*. Kriz was a tall, wiry Klingon with a pockmarked crest and small eyes. Gatrell, who stood to Klag's left, was much shorter, with broad shoulders, a boxy build, and a very simple crest. He'd been shifting his weight from foot to foot throughout Vikagh's entire report, showing a lack of discipline that Klag found surprising in the captain of one of the fleet's finest.

Then again, they gave Dorrek a command, he thought uncharitably, then added with wry amusement, *not to mention giving one to me, so perhaps the standards are not as high as one might hope.*

After staring down at a padd for a second, Kriz looked back up at Gatrell. "Captain, you reported finding several inhabitable worlds in the system designated Kavrot *javmaH jav*. Your report to General Goluk indicated that its conquest was imminent, so much so that you were unable to participate in the battle against the Elabrej."

Angrily, Gatrell said, "We were too distant to join in that war! Even had we broken off our attempted conquest, we would not have arrived until long after the battle had ceased!"

"Yes," Kriz said in a low, menacing tone, "your 'attempted' conquest. That same report said that you would plant the flag in that system within the week. Yet when the summons to return to Qo'noS was given, you returned to the homeworld with no conquests in your record of battle. What happened?"

Again, Gatrell started shifting uncomfortably. "Our scans were . . . misleading. My second officer insisted that the world had no technology, but he misunderstood the readings. The natives of the planet had biological tools, spaceships—and weapons. They were quite effective. We were unable to defend ourselves against their living spaceships with their bioelectric weapons. I put the second officer to death and returned to Qo'noS as ordered."

"That is your story, Captain?"

Now Gatrell stepped forward, standing against the edge of Kriz's desk. "It is the *truth*! I will not stand here and have my honor impugned!"

Still using the low, menacing tone, Kriz said, "You will modify the tone you take with a superior officer, *Captain*, or you will have far more to worry about than what you laughingly refer to as your honor."

Gatrell's hand went to his *d'k tahg* as he said, "How *dare* you! I—"

Interrupting, and sounding wholly unimpressed with Gatrell's bluster, Kriz held up a padd. "This is a report made by First Officer K'Draq—one she made directly to Command. In it, she says that both she and Second Officer Grokla expressed concern that the natives of that system had *some* sort of organic technology, but that you disregarded that concern and then blamed Grokla for your own failure. She also reports—and this is verified by your gunner *and* your pilot—that she challenged you and you not only refused the challenge but had your bodyguard restrict K'Draq's movements, as well as those of anyone else in the bridge crew in order to prevent any others from challenging you."

"That is a lie! The record of battle will bear out that K'Draq is a mutinous shrew, who—"

"Enough!" Kriz said, holding up a hand. "Even if this report were false, your failure to conquer that system is alone enough to condemn you. Hand me your *d'k tahg*."

Klag watched Gatrell's face contort into a rictus of rage. "Never!" Gatrell cried, though he did unsheathe the weapon, unfurling the side blades with a double click. "I will kill any who dare to—"

Kriz pulled out a disruptor pistol seemingly from nowhere and fired it upon Gatrell.

Before his body even fell to the floor, Kriz touched a control on his desk. "This is General Kriz, son of K'Mat. K'Draq, daughter of Sangra, is promoted to captain and given command of the *I.K.S. Sturka*." Looking up at the guards who stood at the door, Kriz said, "Get rid of that."

As the guards moved to follow that order, Vikagh stepped forward.

"What are you doing?" Kriz asked.

Vikagh looked at the general as if he were mad. Before he could respond, Klag found himself speaking and also stepping forward. "A warrior has fallen. The Black Fleet must be informed of his impending arrival."

Letting out an annoyed growl, Kriz said, "If you feel you must."

After nodding up at Klag, Vikagh knelt down and

pried open Gatrell's eyes. He and Klag then threw their heads back and screamed to the ceiling.

Several of the other captains joined in the scream. Klag couldn't help but notice that Dorrek was not one of them. Perhaps Dorrek agreed with the general that Gatrell did not deserve the consideration. Or perhaps he simply didn't wish to do something Klag endorsed.

It did not matter to Klag either way. It simply confirmed Klag's opinion of his younger brother.

"If you're *quite* finished," Kriz said when they were done, "as it happens, Klag, you are the one I will hear from next."

Standing at attention, Klag said, "Sir!"

"A concern has been expressed," Kriz said slowly, "regarding the treatment of Imperial Intelligence agents on your vessel." Quickly, the general added, "Let me assure you, Captain, that this concern has not been expressed by me, but rather by the head of I.I."

Stiffly, Klag said, "And what precisely *is* that concern, General?"

"You have an agent named B'Etloj on board your vessel, whom you rescued from the Elabrej homeworld. You refused to speak to her."

"B'Etloj was the only member of the *Kravokh* crew who did *not* remain behind on Elabrej to regain their honor after being taken prisoner. Regardless, she had served her function in providing us with intelligence on the Elabrej in the first place."

"Which she provided to an I.I. agent on your ship."

"*Bekk* Trant, yes." Klag was wondering what the point was of this line of questioning.

The general looked down at his padd. "This *Bekk* Trant was killed on Elabrej?"

"Yes."

"I.I. reports that you have not returned his body to them, as per regulations."

Klag couldn't believe what he was hearing. To the general's credit, Kriz sounded like he couldn't believe what he was saying, either. But he was evidently under orders. "Those regulations," the captain said, "state that the body is to be returned to I.I. *if at all possible.* It was not. The warriors who were with Trant when he was killed were soon thereafter taken prisoner and experimented on like they were animals. I do not know what became of Trant's body, nor does anyone else, save possibly the Elabrej."

Kriz thumbed his padd. "B'Etloj also claims that you disobeyed Trant's instruction to yield command of the *Gorkon* to him when he learned of the Elabrej's destruction of the *Kravokh.*"

At that, Klag bristled. "Trant had no authority to take command of my ship, General—and Chancellor Martok himself approved of my decision. Trant attempted to usurp control of the *Gorkon* from me. I believe the usual punishment for mutiny is death." Klag smiled. "In which case, the Elabrej were kind enough to carry out the sentence."

Nodding, Kriz set aside the padd. "Very well. Captain, you also are to be commended. Your actions at San-Tarah were correct. General Talak has paid for his dishonor with his life, as it should be. According to Governor Huss, the Children of San-Tarah are being integrated into the empire." He smiled. "Klingons have already begun petitioning to join them on their Great Hunt."

Klag was glad to hear that. He had put everything on the line at San-Tarah and turned what could have been an embarrassing, honorless defeat into the greatest of victories. "I may be joining those petitioners, General."

"If your duties permit," Kriz said acidly. "And that leads me to Captain Dorrek. Step forward."

Dorrek did so. "The *K'mpec*'s repairs are complete, General. What is our next mission to be?"

Gazing pitilessly upon Klag's brother, the general said, "This meeting is not about the future, Captain, but rather an examination of the past. In your case, it's regarding whether or not you are fit to take the *K'mpec* on its next mission."

The look on Dorrek's face, Klag thought, was quite similar to that of Gatrell shortly before Kriz shot him.

Kriz continued: "Those serving under General Talak in his fleet may be forgiven for taking up arms against their fellow Klingons at San-Tarah. The general did not reveal the truth, merely informing his subordinates that Klag had disobeyed his orders. That it was a point of honor was of no interest to him, nor did he share that rather important fact with his warriors.

"He did, however, share that with *you*. Also you do not have the mitigating factor of being part of his fleet and therefore being under Talak's direct command. Your actions were as dishonorable as those of Talak, and you are not worthy to command one of the finest ships in the Defense Force." Again, Kriz touched a control on his desk. "This is General Kriz, son of K'Mat. Mikar, son of Kri'stol, is promoted to captain and given command of the *I.K.S. K'mpec.*"

Klag continued to stare straight ahead, but out of the corner of his eye he could see the smoldering expression on his brother's face.

But it was not directed at General Kriz—rather, he stared murderously at Klag.

The meeting continued through several more captains, and eventually they were all dismissed—save for Klag, whom Kriz told to remain behind.

Once the other captains had departed the room, Kriz said, "Let me assure you, Captain, that I would have been quite content to let those ridiculous questions from I.I. go unasked. However, the choice was *not* mine." He snarled. "I have little use for those shadowy *yIntaghpu'.*"

"Nor I, General, but they *do* have their uses. We won the campaign at Elabrej at least in part because of their intelligence."

"And if all they did was gather intelligence, the galaxy would be a better place." Kriz snarled, which was an impressive gesture from his already unpleasantly featured face. "It is when they insert themselves into politics that I wish to have them all disemboweled with a rusty *d'k tahg.*"

Klag hesitated. Since he had the general's ear, he thought he would take a risk. "Sir, what is to become of Captain Dorrek?"

Kriz regarded him with confusion. "Why do you care? From what I understand, Dorrek is your enemy. Or do you wish to know how far he is to fall?"

To Klag's shock and dismay, that was *not* the reason. "No, sir, I . . . I wonder if he might be afforded the same clemency you gave to his fleet. Dorrek *was* following the orders of a general."

Shaking his head, Kriz said, "Dorrek was your brother once, yes? Until you discommendated him from your House over this *very* conflict?"

"Yes." Klag hated how weak his voice sounded when he said that.

"Make up your mind, Captain. Either he is cast out of the House of M'Raq, in which case his welfare is of no matter to you, or he is your brother and you are concerned for his well-being, in which case you let him back into your damned House. Dismissed."

That is that, Klag thought sourly as he turned on his heel and left the general's company. *I was a fool to plead Dorrek's case.*

Klag knew in his mind that removing Dorrek from the family was the right thing to do. In addition to all the other offenses Kriz had listed, Dorrek committed one other crime: he disobeyed the wishes of the head of his House. Klag specifically told him to fight by his brother's side at San-Tarah, and Dorrek refused. Doing so cost Dorrek a House, and now had cost him his command.

And it cost me a brother.

In his heart, though, Klag questioned his harshness. Klag and Dorrek had been as close as twins when they were youths and remained so into adulthood.

Right up until M'Raq escaped his Romulan imprisonment and went home to the House M'Raq estates to die in his sleep. Dorrek and their mother, Tarilla, both felt that M'Raq had earned that right after all he went through, but Klag thought otherwise. A warrior died in battle, and Klag had always believed his father to be a warrior. Even now, Klag wore his father's right arm to regain the honor that M'Raq had let atrophy in the decade that he waited for death.

Klag walked through the corridors of Command Headquarters, nodding to those he knew and admiring the new statuary that adorned the halls since last he was here. He suspected the hand of General Goluk, who had replaced Talak as chief of staff. The artwork that now graced the dark passageways was more austere, reflecting the new person in command.

Headquarters were located in a large plaza overlooking the Qam-Chee River, about half a *qell'qam* from the Great Hall. The main entrance was huge double doors made of wood, reinforced with duranium that had been cut and shaped into the form of two Klingons facing each other with *bat'leth*s. During the day, the doors were left open, and Klag felt the wind brush against his beard as he approached. It was gloriously cloudy today, with electrical storms visible over the Qam-Chee. The plaza was large and crowded with armored warriors going about their business as well as civilian support staff who were performing errands for their superiors. The plaza ended with an overlook of the Qam-Chee, and even from here, Klag could see the mighty river's whitecaps.

In the plaza's center was the *qaDrav*, a raised rectangular platform surrounded on three sides by a low iron fence. Stairs led up to the fourth side. There was a time when all challenges were played out in the *qa-Drav*. These days, challenges tended to be made and met wherever the two disputing parties happened to be standing, but things, Klag knew, had been more ritualized in the old days.

As soon as Klag set foot on the ancient stonework of the plaza, a fist collided with his jaw, sending him sprawling to the ground. Instinctively, he unsheathed his *d'k tahg* and looked up.

He saw his brother standing over him.

Angrily, Klag got to his feet and sheathed his weapon. Around them, many warriors (though none of the civilians) stopped what they were doing to see what would happen next.

"Is it not enough that you cast me out of our House for no good reason, Klag? Is it not enough that you slew a great man to further your own misguided attempts at glory? Now you cost me my command!"

Protocol demanded that Klag ignore Dorrek's words and turn his back on him—unless they had Defense Force business to discuss, they had nothing to say to each other—but Klag found himself responding. "You disobeyed the orders of the head of the House, choosing instead to take arms against him. And Talak accepted my challenge on San-Tarah willingly. As for your command, I knew nothing of that until you did. You may take it up with General Kriz—*if* you have the courage."

"You *dare!*"

"I dare nothing, *Captain*. I but speak the truth to one who does not deserve it."

57

Then, finally, Klag crossed his arms at the wrists in front of his face, clenched his fists, and turned his back on Dorrek.

As he walked away from his brother, he heard the shouts: "This is not over, 'brother.' There will be a reckoning!"

Klag ignored his former sibling. He had made his report, done his duty. Now it was time to go home.

FOUR

G'joth crawled around his bunk one final time, making sure he hadn't forgotten anything.

It was fairly unlikely. He had very few possessions of his own. Defense Force soldiers learned early on to travel light. *Bekks* and leaders had only one thing to call their own: a two-meter bunk. Soldiers could have anything they wanted at their posts, as long as it would fit in that two meters. On the *Gorkon*, those bunks were set into the bulkheads on deck eighteen, and G'joth's was one of five stacked on one section of that bulkhead reserved for Fifteenth Squad.

The words of the *QaS DevwI'* who trained him came back to G'joth: "Inside those two meters, you are allowed to be yourself. Once you set foot outside those two meters, you become a tool of the Defense Force.

Nothing outside those two meters belongs to you—not even your honor. *Never* forget that."

Over his years of service, G'joth had found those words to be less than the truism the *QaS DevwI'* claimed. For one thing, even the lowliest soldiers had their own honor.

The bunk was clear, save for G'joth's satchel. With a glance inside, he made sure everything was present: the padd on which he did all his writing, the data spike on which he backed up those files, the spikes that had the late, unlamented *Bekk* Tarmeth's recordings of *Battle-cruiser Vengeance* that G'joth had claimed after that mutineer was put to death, his *bat'leth*, and a small box.

Reaching into the satchel, he pulled out the box and opened it. A lock of dark hair sat curled inside it.

G'joth never used to be sentimental. He had lost many comrades over his decade in the service. Yet when Davok and Krevor had died, he'd felt it keenly.

Though he was a tiresome little *petaQ* with whom he spent most of his waking hours arguing (and many of his sleeping ones, if it came to that), Davok had still been G'joth's best friend. They'd served together for all ten years that they'd both been in the Defense Force, and nothing had been able to fill the gap left by his death.

As for Krevor, they had shared a bunk on more than one occasion, and it had been quite glorious.

They both died well at San-Tarah. He'd had remembrances of both of them, but only Krevor's beautiful hair—a gift from her shortly after she'd cut it—remained. G'joth also had Davok's prized *qutluch*, but he'd later given it to Captain Wirrk on Elabrej. Davok probably would've hated G'joth's giving it to an officer, but it seemed like the right thing to do at the time.

In retrospect, G'joth wished he'd kept it. *But no—I hate those damned things. The weight's all wrong. Better for it to have gone to someone who had use of it.* The weapon of a paid assassin, a *qutluch* was a very specialized weapon, heavier and more difficult to use properly than the more common *d'k tahg*. Davok claimed to have taken it off an assassin who tried to kill him years ago. G'joth had no idea if that was true or not, but he certainly had no trouble believing that Davok could have annoyed someone enough to drive him to hiring an assassin.

Closing the satchel, he climbed out of the bunk and onto the ladder that would take him to the deck.

Only Wol was standing there, and the other bunks were all empty. "Where are Kagak and the big man?" G'joth asked.

"The commode," Wol said.

Checking his timepiece, G'joth said, "They'd best hurry. They'll be calling us to the transporter soon, and if they miss it—"

"They know, G'joth," Wol said testily. "They'll get bumped to the end of the line, and they won't leave until all the troops have beamed off, and then they'll probably miss their cargo flight to Pheben and they'll miss Kagak's precious *yobta' yupma'* meal."

G'joth stared at Wol. "You seem irked, Leader."

That broke her, and she burst out in a laugh. "Indeed. I find myself with nowhere to go."

"I do not understand."

Wol stared at him. "It was a simple enough statement, G'joth, that even you should have been able to parse it."

Smiling, G'joth said, "No, I mean I do not understand how that can be. You declined Kagak's offer—I assumed it was because you had a better one."

"No."

G'joth read a significant amount of regret in Wol's tone. "Then why *did* you decline the offer?"

"That is not your concern, *Bekk*." The testy tone returned.

However, G'joth was having none of it. "Come off it, Leader. We've been through too much, you and I. If being with Kagak and Goran offends you—and I can't blame you if that's the case—then come with me. My mother is not quite as gregarious as Kagak describes his own grandmother to be, but I'm sure she wouldn't object to one more place at the table."

"No," Wol said forcefully. "I would sooner slice out my own heart then set foot in that *targ*pit of a city you call home, G'joth."

With a chuckle, G'joth said, "I can assure you, Leader, that were my family not present, I would feel the same. Sadly, my parents and sister did not show the same wisdom as I, and remained in Krennla." Then G'joth frowned. "What was the occasion that brought you to live in Krennla the first time?"

"What makes you think I lived there?" Wol asked defensively.

"Yours is a contempt that can come only from residency. Trust me, Leader, I know it well."

Wol's defenses dropped. "It was . . . it was after I was

discommendated from the House of Varnak and before I thought to enlist in the Defense Force. It is a time in my life I am *not* eager to be reminded of." She ran her hand through what there was of her hair. "That is also why I do not wish to go to Pheben and Kagak's festival. I have lived at the heights of Klingon aristocracy and the depths of the Klingon common life. I want no more of either."

G'joth found the flaw in her logic. "Leader, do you *really* think that Krennla and a farm on Pheben are the same?" He laughed. "You know, when you first told us that you were once a highborn *petaQ*, I doubted it, but now I see that it is very much so. I suppose from the lofty heights of the warrior class, all those beneath are the same. Leader, the depths that you experienced in Krennla were likely the nadir of life in the empire—I know, because I grew up there, and I at least had a family. You didn't even have that much, and I know what can happen to women on their own in Krennla, even ones as capable as you."

In a surprisingly small voice, Wol said, "I was not so capable then."

At that, G'joth simply nodded in acknowledgment. "But do not assume that it will be the same on Kagak's farm."

"There is more than that," Wol said. "I do not think I could bear to be in the company of a happy family."

"Why? You have no trouble being in the company of the fifteenth."

"It's not the same."

"Of course it isn't. The fifteenth isn't the same as the

House of Varnak, which isn't the same as my family, which isn't the same as Kagak's family. They're all different. And I can assure you that nothing on Pheben will remind you of Krennla." He smiled. "It couldn't be that bad."

Wol had been staring straight ahead at the bunk in front of her.

"Leader?"

Shaking her head, Wol looked up at G'joth. "If you're wrong, G'joth, I will personally slit your throat."

Smiling, G'joth said, "If I *am* wrong, Leader, I will hand you my *d'k tahg* to perform the act."

"First Company, report to transporter rooms. First Company, report to transporter rooms."

Just as that notice came over the speakers, Goran and Kagak walked around the corner corridor to rejoin them at their bunks. "We are ready to go," Goran said.

Wol looked at Kagak. "*Bekk*, can your friend accommodate one more in his cargo ship?"

In all the weeks that Kagak had been with the fifteenth, G'joth had never seen quite so gleeful a look on the young soldier's face. "Of course, Leader!"

"Good." She looked at G'joth. "Perhaps a homemade meal is just what I need."

G'joth laughed heartily, and all four of them proceeded down the corridor.

FIVE

The Lukara Edifice
Novat, Qo'noS

It was the second day of the KPE conference, and B'Oraq was already convinced that this was to be a disaster.

The first day had only one activity: the opening ceremonies, which consisted of a lot of bloodwine, a lot of head butting, and almost no discussion of medicine beyond complaints of headaches. The Lukara Edifice—named after Kahless's mate and the woman who was responsible for keeping the Great One's message alive after his ascension to *Sto-Vo-Kor*—had one giant hall on the ground floor and several dozen smaller rooms on the three upper levels. The Edifice had served as a substitute Great Hall when the one in the First City was under construction or renovations in the past—after the Praxis explosion, as well as during Morjod's coup attempt shortly after the Dominion War—and also housed functions that required large gatherings. The Age of Ascension ceremonies of many a highborn Klingon had been held here—including B'Oraq's.

The previous day's drunken revelry was held in the ground-floor hall. The various other events of the conference were to be held in the smaller rooms, which had been set up with a stage facing dozens of stools. Two talks and one demonstration were to be given today. Two more were scheduled for tomorrow, the second of which was to be B'Oraq's description of the transplant procedure she did on Klag.

Whatever hopes B'Oraq had that this might be a true medical conference were all but dashed when she saw that she was one of only three people attending the first talk, and that number included the speaker. Worse, the talk was supposed to be on emergency surgical procedures but was instead a discussion of different knife techniques.

The second talk was slightly better attended: a workshop on medical interrogation methods. B'Oraq had actually found that talk to be useful, but the point of this had been, she thought, to move Klingon medicine forward, and this talk did nothing to accomplish that goal.

As for the demonstration, it was in triage techniques, and B'Oraq found herself correcting the speaker—a doctor serving on the *I.K.S. Klivin*. She wasn't even the only one. A man and a woman—the former a civilian, the latter in a Defense Force uniform—also pointed out better and more efficient methods of field diagnoses.

Another person in the audience asked, "What if a woman is about to give birth?"

The doctor frowned. "I do not understand."

"What is the procedure?"

Laughing now, the doctor said, "Summon a midwife, of course. The task of birthing new warriors falls to them—it is hardly a medical matter."

B'Oraq shook her head. That was a fight she'd given up long ago, but only because there was no circumstance under which she would trust the average Klingon doctor over the average Klingon midwife to aid in the birth of a child. In many ways, midwives were better physicians than the doctors.

Eventually, the doctor threw up his hands and said, "Pfagh! If you know so much, then you hardly require *my* presence on this stage!"

He stomped out. By this point, most of the audience had done likewise.

B'Oraq walked over to the two doctors and said, "Thank you for your *qI'bI'tlhIng*." At the physicians' confused look, B'Oraq laughed. "It is a human term; it refers to people who comment on what others are doing."

They both nodded, then glanced at each other with apprehension.

"I am B'Oraq, daughter of—"

"We know who you are," the man said. "I am Kandless, this is Valatra. We must depart."

They turned to go, but B'Oraq called out after them. "Will you be attending my talk tomorrow at low sun?"

Kandless turned around and said, "Of course."

Valatra also turned, smiled quickly, and added, "We

would not miss it for all the bloodwine in the empire, Doctor."

Then they both left as if they were being pursued by a wild *klongat*.

Departing the room at a more leisurely pace, she exited to find a familiar face standing under a poorly sculpted statue of some generic warrior or other. He was a short, squat man with a dull crest, small, beady eyes, an unkempt beard, and puffed-out cheeks. This was Kowag, the doctor in charge of the Great Hall.

"Ah, the butcher herself. I had been hoping we would meet before your presentation. It gives me the opportunity to spit on your boots."

"Go right ahead," B'Oraq said with an insincere smile. "I do hope that you plan to attend the presentation, as you are quoted quite extensively in it."

"Am I?"

"Oh, yes."

Kowag walked toward B'Oraq and stared up at her. B'Oraq took a certain pleasure in the fact that she herself stood half a head taller than this incompetent *toD-SaH*. "You are a fool to think this is anything other than a sham to make Chancellor One-Eye happy. We will have this charade, and then life will go on as before. You have done *nothing*."

"No, Kowag, *you* have done nothing. It has been the hallmark of your career as a physician."

Now Kowag did spit on her boots. "You violate every tenet of Klingon life, butcher. I will live to see you put to death for your barbarity."

Tugging on her braid, B'Oraq said, "As I recall, Kowag,

the last prediction you made was in that monograph you published saying that Klag's transplant would fail within the next four months following the monograph's release— that release was *five* months ago, and I last saw Klag doing *bat'leth* drills with his right hand." In truth, she last saw Klag naked in his bunk, but she saw no need to share that with Kowag. Instead, she leaned in and smiled down at him, trying to ignore the cheap *warnog* on his breath. "I'm sure this prediction will come just as true."

Then she turned her back on him and walked away.

She went down the grand staircase at the rear of the Edifice to the ground-floor hall. Several Klingons were milling about, drinking and talking and laughing. She saw Kandless and Valatra at one table, and decided to take a chance.

First she went to the bar and asked for a mug of *chech'tluth*. The bartender, a bored-looking *jeghpu'wI'*, dolefully filled a mug with the steaming beverage and handed it to B'Oraq. After she paid for it, she turned to move toward the two physicians.

Upon sighting her, they both got to their feet, draining their mugs.

"May I join you?" B'Oraq asked.

"Doctor," Valatra said, "we're sorry but we cannot stay. I must report back to headquarters."

"And I have just received an emergency call," Kandless added.

B'Oraq debated pointing out that she had heard no such call, and the room was empty enough that any communication device would have been heard. *But perhaps his is silent.*

"We will see you tomorrow, Doctor," Valatra said as they retreated. "*Qapla'*."

"*Qapla'*," B'Oraq said with little enthusiasm.

"Get used to it, butcher."

B'Oraq turned around to see two more Defense Force–armored men—though in both cases, it was the lighter armor of the medical division. The one who had spoken was Tiklor, who served at the base on Mempa V, last she'd heard. She didn't know the other one. While she'd seen both of them drinking heavily the previous night, neither of them had shown up for any of the three presentations. "What did you say, Tiklor?"

"I said, get used to it. No one wants you here. No one wishes to be seen with the likes of you. No one cares what you have to say. And none will drink with you, for you *are* the enemy. You are contaminating a once-noble profession with barbarism."

Gulping down some of her drink, B'Oraq said, "I would say the same of you, Tiklor. I still remember how you nearly killed Captain Grannk with your bungled incisions. You were lucky not to be put to death."

Slamming down his mug, Tiklor stood up. "I saved his life!"

"It should never have been in danger in the first place! You could train a *trigak* to perform that operation, it's so simple, yet you botched it. Had I the position I have now, I could have had you put to death for that."

Tiklor unsheathed his *d'k tahg*. "How dare you! I will not stand here and be insulted."

"A bit late for that, don't you think?"

"Perhaps." Tiklor unfurled the side blades of the weapon. "But the insult will *not* go unanswered."

There it is, then. B'Oraq sighed. She had been hoping to get through this conference without a duel.

Making a show of finishing her drink first, she unsheathed her own *d'k tahg*.

Suddenly, the hall seemed more crowded. *It's as if they smelled the blood before it was spilled,* B'Oraq thought uncharitably. Given the disdain most were showing for this whole endeavor, most probably viewed this as the most exciting thing that was likely to happen during the conference's duration.

Tiklor started circling B'Oraq. She stayed in place, pivoting only so she could continue to face him. The other physician had a large grin on his long face. "I will be hailed as one of the great heroes of the empire today, butcher. They will build statues to me as the one who rid the empire of a tiresome—"

Suddenly, B'Oraq lunged with her own *d'k tahg*, striking right under one of the seams in the armor, which was also between the fifth and sixth transverse ribs. Mentally, she made a note to have that weakness in the armor covered up.

The blade sliced right into Tiklor's third aorta.

To his credit, he managed to swing his own blade at B'Oraq's side, which was left open by her lunge. She felt the metal slice into her flesh, but not even cutting all the way through. Fire burned in her belly at the intoxicating smell of both Tiklor's and her own blood. She figured she could afford to lose *some* blood, so she didn't bother trying to hold the wound shut. It would be several minutes before blood loss would be a concern.

However, that turned out not to be an issue. As B'Oraq had thought, she had penetrated his heart, and Tiklor fell to the ground, dead.

The battle lust had barely had time to build before it subsided with her opponent's death, and B'Oraq looked around the hall.

Silence.

Normally, in such a duel, there would be cheers as people goaded on one or the other or both to victory. But she ended the fight too fast, and the resounding silence that greeted her victory showed that nobody here was goading her on to anything save the Black Fleet.

Shaking her head, B'Oraq knelt in front of Tiklor and moved to pry his dead eyes open so she could perform the death ritual. But then Tiklor's drinking companion rose to his feet and roared, "Away from him!"

She looked up. Tiklor's friend had a snarl on his face and spittle mixed with *warnog* flew from his mouth.

"You will not defile Tiklor's body!"

In a tight voice, B'Oraq said, "I had no intention of doing so. He died honorably, and I was going to—"

"No!" The man batted his arm at B'Oraq's. "Such as you are not worthy to herald his arrival in *Sto-Vo-Kor!*"

The notion was ridiculous. Klingon tradition was that, if one died honorably in a duel—as Tiklor had done—the victor had the honor of performing the ritual: prying the deceased's eyes open and screaming to the other warriors in *Sto-Vo-Kor* that another warrior was about to cross the River of Blood to join them in the Black Fleet.

Grumbles from around the hall indicated that most of those present were in agreement with Tiklor's friend. Or, at the very least, were unwilling to say that they weren't.

Snarling, B'Oraq got to her feet. Pain sliced through her left side. She had forgotten about her injury. Though she was in a hall full of alleged physicians, she could not bring herself to ask any of them for aid in binding the wound.

In fact, she couldn't even bear to walk past them. Activating her communicator, she said, "B'Oraq to Praxis Station—one to beam to the *Gorkon*."

As the transporter whisked her away, she heard Tiklor's friend lead the others in the scream to the heavens.

SIX

Office of Doctor Qa'Hos
Kri'stak City, Qo'noS

The dreams continued to plague Rodek.

He finally admitted to himself that he needed medical advice, but B'Oraq was now unavailable. Since he was on leave anyhow, he went home to his father Noggra's estate in Kri'stak City. They almost missed each other, as Noggra was traveling to Mempa XII on a case. Noggra was a top advocate, and one of his clients was having some difficulties in the Mempa sector. When Rodek told his father of the dreams, Noggra immediately made an appointment with Qa'Hos, an old friend of Noggra's family, for the following morning, right after Noggra was to depart.

Rodek arrived at Qa'Hos's office on time for the appointment. His office was located on a back street of Kri'stak, inside a large green building with dozens of pri-

vate offices. The door to the office labeled QA'HOS, PHYSI-
CIAN rumbled aside at Rodek's approach, but no one was
inside. There was a desk with a computer station, various medical implements on the walls—at least, Rodek
assumed them to be medical implements. Several of
them resembled items that he'd seen in medical bays on
the *Lallek* and the *Gorkon*, at least.

He went to the computer station to find it inactive
and with no data. Now the open door made sense—
Qa'Hos probably kept all of his data on a spike, so the
only items would-be thieves could obtain were the
pieces of equipment.

After a few moments, Rodek was ready to leave and
question his father's friendship with this fool, but then
a tall Klingon with short, white hair entered. "Who are
you?" he asked testily upon entering.

"I am Rodek, son of Noggra. I—"

"Oh, yes, yes, yes, of course. Well, come in, come
in."

"I am already in."

"Right, yes, of course." Qa'Hos stepped around the
desk, took a seat, and removed a data spike from his
pocket. "You're Noggra's boy, eh? Mm. Surprised I never
saw you before. Well, not *that* surprised, Noggra's like
most advocates."

Rodek frowned. "And how is that?"

Qa'Hos grinned, showing very few teeth. "A damned
secretive old *toDSaH*. So, what's the issue?"

Slowly, Rodek explained what had happened on San-
Tarah and at Elabrej. "Since then, I have been having
odd dreams."

"What kind of dreams would those be?"

For a moment, Rodek hesitated. Then he castigated himself. *You came to him because of the dreams, fool. Tell him!*

"I keep remembering myself in places where I have never been. In the captain's chair on a *Vakk*-class vessel. On a Federation starship. In a cargo bay wearing a Bajoran Militia uniform. In the council chambers in the Great Hall."

"How do you know that that is what those places are?" Qa'Hos asked. "I mean, all right, everyone knows what the council chambers look like, but have you ever even *seen* a Federation starship or a Bajoran Militia uniform? I didn't even know the Bajorans *had* a militia. I mean, I suppose they must have, but I hadn't given it any thought."

Shaking his head, Rodek said, "I do not know. I have only been to the Bajoran sector once, and that was when I had my accident."

"What accident?"

Rodek looked up. "Of course, you could not know. I have no recollection of my life prior to four years ago, when I was in a shuttle accident near Bajor. I was hit with a plasma discharge that damaged my hippocampus. According to the Starfleet doctor who treated me, I suffered irreparable brain damage."

Qa'Hos frowned. "Hmm. All right, then, let me look you over." He reached into a pocket and took out a scanner that looked similar to the one B'Oraq used. "If I recall correctly from what Noggra said when he made the appointment, you're in the Defense Force."

"Yes," Rodek said, trying to sit still for the scan, though he knew it probably wasn't necessary. "I am a lieutenant aboard the *Gorkon*."

"Not surprised you didn't go to your regular doctor, then. Defense Force physicians're all insane."

"In fact, I would have gone to our doctor, but she was busy."

"Wait, you said the *Gorkon*? Oh, by Kahless's left toe, you don't serve with that animal B'Oraq, do you?"

"Yes," Rodek said, unappreciative of the doctor's tone toward his crewmate. "She has saved my life on more than one occasion."

Qa'Hos shrugged. "The moon shines on a *targ*'s ass every once in a while, I suppose. She learned medicine in the *Federation*, of all places. As if outsiders can tell you anything about how to treat Klingons. I suppose she couldn't look at you 'cause of that absurd conference of hers?"

Rodek knew only that B'Oraq was to speak at the Klingon Physicians Enclave's first medical conference, but from what Toq had told him before the young first officer went off on his trip, it was the High Council who had called it, not B'Oraq. Indeed, B'Oraq had been far too busy as the *Gorkon*'s physician to have organized it.

However, he said nothing. He only wished to find out what was wrong with him.

The old doctor looked at the results of his scan. "Now that's damned odd."

"What is?"

"Well, for starters, your crest. It isn't the one you were born with."

Rodek frowned. "That *is* odd." He knew that some people had their crests surgically altered for a variety of reasons—most often, to disassociate themselves from family, or in some cases for simple vanity—but Rodek could not imagine a circumstance under which he would do so.

"Recent, too—within the last ten years, definitely. And here's another thing—you've got brain damage, that's for sure, but it's all recent."

"What do you mean?"

Qa'Hos looked up and stared at Rodek with his rheumy eyes. "Somebody lied to you, Rodek, son of Noggra. You said it was a Starfleet doctor that treated you back on Bajor?"

"Yes."

"That explains it." He wagged a finger at Rodek. "You see, *that's* why your friend B'Oraq's a fool. Federation doesn't know anything about *real* medicine. That Starfleet animal didn't know what he was talking about."

In a low, threatening tone, Rodek said, "I do not know what *you* are talking about, Doctor. Explain yourself."

"What I mean is this." Qa'Hos sounded wholly unintimidated, to Rodek's annoyance. "You didn't suffer any brain damage ever, in your entire life, until that alien weapon blew up in your face on—what was it? Santerio?"

"San-Tarah."

"Right, there. That's it. There's no evidence in your hippocampus of the damage that would arise from a plasma discharge."

"That is impossible." Rodek could not believe what he was hearing. The surgical alteration of his crest was bizarre enough, but there could have been a good reason for it in his life before. And, as Qa'Hos had indicated, Noggra had always been quite secretive.

But this—this was new.

Someone had lied to him.

Possibly several someones. *Why didn't Noggra tell me of the alteration of my crest? And was he part of the Starfleet doctor's lie?*

If a lie it was. Perhaps he was simply incompetent.

No. Despite this old *petaQ*'s words, Rodek knew that Starfleet doctors were not ones for misdiagnoses on this level. And Bashir, the doctor on the Bajoran space station, was one who had treated Chancellor Martok himself. For that matter, Worf, the current Federation ambassador to the empire, was born a Klingon and had served on that station during his years in Starfleet. No, Bashir knew how to treat Klingons.

So what is going on?

Getting to his feet, Rodek said, "I thank you, Doctor. You have—enlightened me. You may bill the House of Noggra for your services today."

"Hold on." Qa'Hos reached into another pocket and pulled out a box and opened it to reveal several compartments, then opened a drawer in the desk and took out an empty bottle. "I know you Defense Force types don't like to take drugs, but in this case, it might not be a bad idea." He removed seven pills from one compartment and put them in the bottle. "Take one of these before you go to sleep, and you shouldn't dream no matter what."

Rodek eyed the bottle with suspicion. However, he was on leave, so he did not need to worry about the drugs affecting his performance.

"Very well." He took the bottle from the doctor.

He then departed, planning to return to the estate and find a ship that would take him to Deep Space 9.

It is time I had words with Doctor Bashir.

SEVEN

I.K.S. Gorlak
Interstellar space

"**I** regret that we were unable to see each other before I departed Qo'noS," Toq said to the face of the man who saved him.

Ambassador Worf stared back at him through the viewscreen in Toq's cabin on the *Gorlak*. "*As do I. Unfortunately, I was unable to excuse myself from this particular obligation.*"

"What was that?"

Worf hesitated, and Toq saw a look of distaste cross the ambassador's face. "*A Benzite theater company has started performing* The Battle of Gal-Mok. *They requested permission to perform it at Ty'Gokor, and I was obliged to attend the opening night.*"

Grinning, Toq asked, "How bad was it?"

"My aide stated that Kovikh was turning over in his grave."

"I do not know what that means." Toq knew that Worf's aide was a human, and this was no doubt one of their peculiar turns of phrase.

"It is a human saying that means, were Kovikh alive today, he would be displeased with the performance. As it is, only the desire to maintain good relations with the Federation kept Governor J'Bris from ordering the entire company put to death."

Toq laughed heartily. "That must have been a challenge for you, since I am sure your desire was the same."

Worf inclined his head briefly, then said, "You are visiting Lorgh?"

"Yes. He is stationed at the border and could not get away."

"Tell him that we must hunt when he returns to Qo'noS."

"Hah! If I am still at liberty, I will join you!"

"Good. It has been too long since we hunted together, Toq."

"Indeed. And I am far more proficient than I was then."

"So I have been led to understand."

Toq grinned. Worf had been the one to teach Toq to hunt, but it had been Lorgh—an old family friend of Worf's—who refined Toq's skills to the point where he had achieved high standing in the sport. Only the onset of the Dominion War and Toq's joining the Defense Force derailed him from what might have been an impressive career as a hunter.

At the time, Worf was teaching Toq only what he should have already known. While the official story—which Worf had even told to Lorgh—was that Toq was one of several children who were the only survivors of a ship that crashed on Carraya long ago, the truth was far worse.

Thirty years ago, Romulans attacked the Khitomer outpost, aided by a Klingon traitor named Ja'rod. A few Klingons survived the attack and were taken back to Romulan space and not permitted to die. After three months, the Romulans attempted to negotiate their return, but the High Council refused to believe that they were alive. A Romulan centurion named Tokath volunteered to be their jailer, and they were sent to the fourth planet in the Carraya system. Klingon and Romulan lived in peace, away from the rest of the galaxy.

That was the world Toq had been born into. He had thought it to be a haven, a refuge from "the wars," a vague conflict that his elders often mentioned but never described.

And then Worf came.

He was seeking his father, who might have survived the massacre, though that information turned out to be false. Tokath could not risk Worf exposing his haven to the galaxy at large, so he kept Worf prisoner.

But Worf saw that the Klingon children who grew up on this world had not been taught Klingon ways. Worf showed them *mok'bara* and taught Toq how to hunt.

It had been the most amazing experience of Toq's life. The scent of the animal, the thrill of the kill—it was as if he'd been granted sight after not even realizing he was blind.

The man on the viewscreen had saved him, taught him what it meant to be a Klingon, and Toq was forever in his debt.

"It would be an honor to hunt with you once again, Worf. In fact, even if Lorgh does not come back to Qo'noS, I would ask that we do hunt upon my return to the homeworld."

"*Of course.*" Worf almost smiled, which was as close as he ever came to one. The one thing Worf did not have was Klingon passion, the result of living most of his life among humans. While Worf taught him what it meant to be Klingon, it was Lorgh who taught him how to live like one. "*Perhaps,*" the ambassador said, "*the chancellor will also join us.*"

Toq's eyes grew wide. "You hunt with Martok?"

"*Often. He once said a condition of my accepting the diplomatic post was that there would be a Federation ambassador that he could hunt* targ *with.*"

At that, Toq's face fell. "The chancellor hunts *targ?*"

"*Yes.*" Worf frowned. "*He finds it . . . relaxing.*"

Somehow, Toq stopped himself from saying he found it the same, by virtue of the boredom of hunting *targ* putting him to sleep. *It would not be politic to speak ill of the chancellor's choices, especially since he and Worf shared a House.*

"I would find such a hunt diverting," he said neutrally.

"*I am a diplomat, Toq, but that does not require you to lie to me. You find such a hunt beneath your notice.*"

"Yes." Toq cursed Worf for his perspicacity. But then, Worf had always known how to read him. Though the ambassador had never said as much, Toq always suspected that Worf insisted on being allowed to hunt on Carraya only because he knew that Toq would take to it.

"*I believe that, should you join the hunt, the chancellor might be amenable to altering the target.*"

"Good," Toq said with perhaps a bit too much enthusiasm.

Worf suddenly looked away. After a moment, he nodded and said, "*Of course.*" He looked back at the screen. "*I must depart.*"

Toq bowed to the screen. "*Qapla'*, Ambassador. I will give Lorgh your message."

"*Qapla', Toq. Klag made the best choice when he made you his first. May you serve with honor and die well.*"

After closing the connection, Toq checked the computer to see what the ETA was, only to be told that it was unknown due to course correction.

Frowning, Toq activated his communicator. "Toq to bridge. Why have we changed course?"

"*We have received a distress call,*" Quvmoh said. "*Your arrival will be delayed.*"

"Who sent the distress call?"

"*It is from a system outside the empire's boundaries called Carraya. However, a Klingon sent it. The base has been alerted of our delay.*"

Toq felt as if the deck had shifted under him. "Did you say Carraya?"

"*Yes. Why?*"

"I will be on the bridge shortly." Toq cut off the communication before Quvmoh could reply.

He immediately ran out to the corridor and climbed the ladder to the bridge. Larger vessels like the *Gorkon* had turbolifts, but the majority of Defense Force ships were not so equipped.

As soon as the door to the bridge rumbled aside, two *bekks* stood in his way. "You may not enter the bridge," one of them said. "Captain's orders."

Ignoring them, Toq said, "Captain, I have information about the Carraya system."

Silence followed that pronouncement for several seconds. Toq held his breath. He knew it was a breach of protocol—indeed, if a guest on the *Gorkon* had behaved as Toq was, neither Klag nor Toq as his first officer would tolerate it.

But this was where Toq was born and raised. He had promised on his word of honor to maintain the secret of the Romulan-Klingon camp located on the fourth planet, and so had Tokath, L'Kor, and all the others.

If that word had been broken, Toq needed to know the reason why.

Finally, Quvmoh spoke. "Let him through."

The two *bekks* parted like a doorway, and Toq burst onto the bridge, which was tiny and cramped. He squeezed past the gunnery console and under the angled ceiling supports and stood next to Quvmoh, who stared straight ahead at the viewscreen from his seat in the captain's chair. "Speak."

"Who is the Klingon who sent the distress call?"

Still without looking at Toq, Quvmoh said, "You claimed to have information."

"Much of the information is classified, and how much I may tell you depends upon who sent the signal." Strictly speaking, what he said was true, though it was not classified by Command or the High Council but merely by tacit agreement of a collection of Klingons and Romulans.

"The Klingon who sent the signal did not identify herself—she said only that the fourth planet was under attack by an unknown assailant and that they had many dead."

Herself—possibly Gi'ral, Toq thought. "There was . . . an experiment being undertaken on Carraya," he said slowly.

Finally, Quvmoh looked at Toq. "What manner of 'experiment'?"

"A secret one," Toq said tartly. "That secret has now been exposed, and once the survivors are rescued, we must determine how that happened."

"Oh, 'we' must, must 'we'? May I remind you, *Commander,* that you are a guest on *my* ship, and *I* will determine what the *Gorlak* must or must not do."

"You are right, of course," Toq said, feeling ashamed. His instinct was to apologize, but that was due to how he was raised on Carraya. It had taken him years to beat the habit out of himself once he joined Klingon society, for warriors who apologized did not last long as warriors.

"Yes, *of course,* I am right. Now you will tell me about this planet."

Toq considered his words. "The planet has no physical defenses worth mentioning. So the attacking vessel could literally be anything that is armed, and it would stand a fair chance of success."

It was Quvmoh's first officer who then spoke. "What kind of Klingon experiment has no defenses?"

"I said no *physical* defenses." Toq cast a sidelong glance at the first officer, keeping his eyes mainly on Quvmoh. "Secrecy was its best security. You cannot attack what you do not know."

"Secrets." Quvmoh leaned forward and spit on the deck. "Warriors do not keep secrets."

"The people on that planet are not warriors." That was almost the truth. L'Kor, Gi'ral, and many of the other older Klingons were indeed warriors once, though that time was three decades in the past.

Before Quvmoh could respond to that, the pilot said, "Entering Carraya system now."

"Slow to sublight and engage cloak," the first officer said. "Scan for ships."

The operations officer said, "Nothing on sensors. However, there are indications of recent warp activity."

"Scan the fourth planet."

Toq stared at the viewscreen, which showed the entirety of the Carraya system, and he felt . . . nothing. He had thought that coming back to the place where he spent his early years would fill him with a nostalgic joy. But the Toq who grew up on Carraya was long dead—he died the day Worf brought him out to hunt. He belonged in the empire now, not on a planet that hid from it.

However, while he had no desire to return to that home, he still had affection for its inhabitants. Ba'el had been like a sister to him (at least, sometimes; sometimes he spied on her when she bathed, since she wasn't *actually* his sister . . .), his parents, Pitzh and Q'Idar, had been good people, and L'Kor had been the leader of the Klingons on Carraya for all Toq's life, and done so well.

If they were hurt, he *would* avenge them, no matter what Quvmoh decided to do.

After a moment, the operations officer said, "Most of the planet is devoid of artificial construction or industrialization. There is a collection of material both organic and inorganic concentrated in one area of the largest continent."

Toq didn't like the sound of that.

"Any life signs?" the first officer asked.

"Two." The operations officer then looked up in shock. "One is indeterminate—but the other is Romulan!"

"Then this was a Romulan attack," the first officer said.

Pointedly, Toq said nothing. The indeterminate reading was likely one of the half-breeds, like Ba'el.

Quvmoh, however, glared at Toq. "You do not look surprised."

Since the captain did not phrase it as a question, Toq said nothing.

"Pilot, defensive orbit. Prepare to drop cloak for transport." To his first officer, Quvmoh said, "Commander Kuut, you will take a squad down." He looked at Toq. "You will go down as well, as an observer. You will provide whatever aid Commander Kuut requires." Back to Kuut: "If he does not, kill him."

I have made an enemy today, Toq thought sourly. Quvmoh hadn't been thrilled with having Toq on board in the first place, no doubt in part because it was at the insistence of I.I. The captain's disdainful comment about secrets had not been lost on Toq: Quvmoh obviously had very little use for those who kept them, and that number included I.I.

Toq followed Kuut to the transporter room in silence. Four *bekks* and a leader awaited them.

As they stepped onto the platform, Kuut turned to Toq. "Why would a Romulan be on that world, if he is not one of the attackers?"

At first, Toq was tempted to remain silent, but Kuut struck him as the type who followed orders to the letter, and he would have all five troops open fire on him if he did not answer. "He was defending his home."

Kuut stared at Toq. "What?"

"We will know for sure when we beam down, Commander. I suggest we do so."

After giving Toq an aggrieved snarl, Kuut turned to the transporter operator. "Beam us to the life signs."

The operator nodded and worked the controls. Toq felt a red glow overtake him as the transporter room faded to indistinction, then coalesced into an almost-familiar sight.

And then it hit him. Seeing Carraya had instilled surprisingly few feelings in Toq, but as soon as the scent of the trees and of the animals and birds and of the stream that Ba'el always bathed in came to him, he almost grew weak in the knees.

Then his nose detected the acrid stench of smoke and spilled blood—both the iron tinge of the Klingons' blood and the copper tinge of the Romulans'—and burned flesh, and the feeling grew worse.

His home had been destroyed.

Rubble was piled where buildings used to be. The house he grew up in was a smoking ruin. The garden where he used to throw his *ghIntaq* spear was pulverized.

And there were bodies *everywhere*. Toq recognized each one of them. Virlak, the Romulan guard who always scored the *ghIntaq*-throwing contests. Maj, who made the best cakes. Klon, who had thought Toq a fool for leaving Carraya. Hanril, the Romulan cook, who had refused to prepare the results of Toq's first hunt. Jurok, who always told the best stories, at least until Worf came.

Then there was Q'Idar, his mother.

Upon seeing her, Toq finally did fall to his knees. "No! This wasn't supposed to happen! They were supposed to be safe!"

Leaning over, he pried open his mother's eyes, then screamed to the heavens. His mother was no kind of warrior—she didn't even like to argue. But Toq didn't care. She gave him birth, raised him, fed him, clothed him. He didn't even really *believe* in the Black Fleet, but damn it all, Toq would announce her arrival there, just in case he was wrong. She deserved that much and more.

So he screamed.

None of the *Gorlak* crew joined in the scream, however. Instead, when Toq was finished, Kuut asked, "Who is that woman?"

Toq rose to his feet. "She is—she *was* my mother."

Then he heard a groan. Running toward its source, Toq saw a hand moving from under a pile of rubble. Grabbing one piece of stone, he threw it aside.

From behind him, one of the *bekk*s said, "The life signs are under there."

"Help the commander with his digging," Kuut said.

With the aid of the troops, Toq was able to clear the rubble. What he saw probably shocked the Klingons present.

A Romulan male had shielded a Klingon female from the bulk of the impact.

Toq of course knew them both.

"This woman may appear Klingon," one of the *bekk*s said, "but she is not."

"A disguise?" Kuut asked.

"No," Toq said. The truth would come out soon enough, once someone got a look at her ears. "A halfbreed." He turned to Kuut. "I told you that a Romulan would die here to protect his home? This Romulan was protecting his daughter."

"This Romulan is still alive," the leader said.

A look of disgust on his face, Kuut asked, "Is *this* your 'experiment'?"

"In a manner of speaking." Toq turned his back on Kuut before he could ask another question and knelt down beside Ba'el. "Ba'el, it's Toq. We've come to save you."

Ba'el's beautiful face was streaked with Klingon and Romulan blood both. He suspected that the majority of the latter belonged to her father, Tokath, the leader of the colony, whose body lay over hers yet had somehow survived.

"Toq?" she said weakly. "You came back."

"Yes. What happened?"

"L'Kor."

Toq frowned. "What do you mean?"

"They came for . . . for L'Kor. Said they'd . . . they'd spare us if we . . . we gave them . . . him. Father re-refused. So they took . . . took him any—" She lapsed into unconsciousness.

Getting back to his feet, Toq said, "We must bring them to the *Gorlak* medical bay!"

"Must we?" Kuut asked. "All I see here is a righteous act. Klingons and Romulans living together—the only thing the attackers got wrong was to leave these two breathing." Unholstering his disruptor, he bared his teeth at Toq. "I will gladly rectify that error—and the error of leaving *you* alive."

He pointed the disruptor right at Toq's face.

EIGHT

Kenta District
Krennla, Qo'noS

When the public transporter deposited him at the Kenta District Station, which was nearest to the street where he'd grown up, G'joth wasn't sure what surprised him more: how much had changed, or how little had.

On the one hand, most of the short, boxy buildings were the same as they'd always been. On the other, several he knew should be there, weren't. An eatery he'd patronized in his youth was gone, replaced by a jewel merchant, and that was just one example.

There also seemed to be fewer people on the streets. He wondered if that was good or bad.

Most Klingon cities were built around a system of roads that could accommodate pedestrians and people astride a mount—usually, a *klongat* or a *khrun*. After the Hur'q invasion, Klingon technological development went into overdrive. Where most worlds—as G'joth had learned in his decade in the Defense Force—developed powered ground travel, then air travel, then space travel, Qo'noS bypassed the first step and did the next two simultaneously, all in an effort to prevent another invasion like that of the Hur'q.

Years ago, when G'joth had first started thinking about writing an opera, he had considered undertaking a heroic epic that portrayed the Hur'q as the heroes of the empire. After all, if they hadn't invaded, Klingons would probably have stayed on Qo'noS, their lives occupied by tribal feuds that were far more vicious than the House disputes you saw these days. Thanks to the anger at the Hur'q plundering of the world—including taking the Sword of Kahless from its rightful place—the Klingon Empire spanned the heavens and was one of the great powers of the quadrant. It was G'joth's considered opinion that the empire owed everything to the Hur'q, though he knew that to be a minority opinion. However, he'd never completed the opera, and when he'd returned to opera composing in recent months, he'd tried for more mundane subjects.

When he turned a corner onto the road that had his parents' dwelling, he saw three youths throwing tiny *ghIntaqs* into the air. Looking up, G'joth saw that they were aiming at a group of small *lotlhmoq* chicks that circled overhead. G'joth figured the birds had just come from the nearby river to feed and now were the victims of these children's games.

Not that they were in much danger, truly—the children had awful aim. Of course, when G'joth had been the youth practicing with his spear, his aim had been wretched, too. He generally preferred a *bat'leth* to a *ghIntaq* anyhow.

Even as G'joth approached the children from one direction, a man in leather armor approached from the other. Armed with a curved *tik'leth* decorated with ornate characters that was more for show than anything, and a bright green painstik that wasn't, this was a member of the Imperial Guard, who were charged with maintaining law on Qo'noS. This was the third guardsman G'joth had seen since transporting in, which was the other change from ten years ago. He used to see only one, maybe two, on a normal day; almost never three in two minutes.

"Disperse!" the guardsman yelled.

One of the youths said, "We're just practicing our aim!"

"There's a range for that in the park," the guardsman said. "Disperse!"

That was something else new. There never used to be a spear-tossing range in the park.

"We can't afford the entrance fees!" another boy said.

The guardsman now brandished his painstik. "That is not my problem. You tossing your *ghIntaqs* into the air where they might cause harm—*that* is my problem. And it will be your problem if you do not *disperse!*" Then he looked up and saw G'joth. "Sir!" he barked, straightening, holding his painstik straight upward as if it were a salute. "Excuse me, I did not see you here."

"Settle down, Guardsman," G'joth said. "And don't

call me 'sir.' I work for a living. I'm *Bekk* G'joth. What is the difficulty?"

The children were now all staring in awe at G'joth. *Well, in truth, they're staring in awe at my uniform, as is the guardsman. Obviously they don't know what it means, if they can't even tell that I'm not an officer.*

"No difficulty, honored *Bekk*," the guardsman said. "I was merely telling these youths to disperse."

"So I noticed. Why? They're not doing anything I didn't do growing up on these streets."

"There wasn't a spear-tossing range when you were growing up, honored *Bekk*. It was specifically constructed three turns ago in order to keep the residents of these streets safe."

"But they charge an admission fee?"

Now the guardsman smiled. "Ranges do not pay for themselves, honored *Bekk*."

"I suppose not." He looked down at the children. "Where do you live?"

Each of the youths pointed in a different direction.

Looking back up at the guardsman, G'joth said, "Why not simply tell them to stop throwing the spears?"

"Because the only way to guarantee that they will follow that instruction once I leave this street is to confiscate their spears." He smiled again. "They are very poor spears, and I have no desire to have them clutter up the weapons locker at headquarters."

Suddenly, one of the children asked, "Are you the same *Bekk* G'joth who serves on the *Gorkon*?"

"Yes, I am."

"My father says your captain is a great man—and that you don't deserve to be on the same ship as him."

Chuckling, G'joth said, "Your father is correct. He wouldn't happen to be Klaad, would he?"

The youth nodded. "I am Kimm, son of Klaad."

G'joth had noticed earlier that the boy had the same crest as his old friend. And, looking at the second youth, he realized it was another familiar forehead. "Your father must be Krom."

"Yes, sir," the boy said with a nod. "I am Gurlk, son of Krom."

"You don't have to call me 'sir,' either. I knew both your fathers when we were all younger than you." He turned back to the guardsman. "I will take charge of these three."

Bowing his head, the guardsman said, "As you command, honored *Bekk*. The *Gorkon* is a great ship, and we are honored by your presence in our meager city." With that, the guardsman took his leave.

"You shouldn't have done that," the third boy said. "After you're gone, he'll come back and take our *ghIntaqs* and beat us—or maybe use the painstik."

"I won't be leaving for some time," G'joth said. "Besides, he cannot do violence to you unless you disobey him, which you have not done. His job is to protect you, unless you are a criminal." He stared down at the boy. "Are you a criminal?"

"*He* thinks so."

"Perhaps." G'joth looked down the street after him, then turned to look at all three. "Either way, you are three and he is one. If he treats you unjustly, you may challenge him."

"No we can't!" Gurlk looked at him as if he were mad. *In fact, Davok used to look at me like that all the time*, G'joth thought sadly.

"Of course you can. Warriors may challenge any who dishonor them."

"We're not warriors, we're just children."

Reaching down and grabbing the *ghIntaq* out of Gurlk's hands, G'joth said, "If you can hold this, you are already a warrior."

The third boy said, "If we were warriors, we could hit the birds!"

G'joth laughed. "An excellent point! One thing I was told when I was a youth was to hold up one's other arm." He did so with his left, then held the *ghIntaq* above his right shoulder with his right hand. "Use it as a scope to find your target." Then he handed Gurlk back his spear. "But not now. I took responsibility for you, and that means you must no longer throw your spears, or I will be dishonored."

Kimm said, "My father says you don't have any honor."

That brought G'joth up short. "He said that? In so many words?"

"No." Kimm hesitated, looking as if he were trying to dredge up the exact phrasing. "He said, 'G'joth wouldn't know honor if it bit him on the ankle.'"

Again, G'joth laughed. "*That* is definitely my old friend Klaad. I must go now."

The third boy said, "But you just arrived!"

"Yes, and my parents are waiting for me. I must not keep them waiting. But if you are here at this time tomorrow, I will come back and tell you stories of the *Gorkon*."

"Will you tell us about Captain Klag?" Gurlk asked eagerly.

"Actually, I was going to tell you of the exploits of the finest squad on the ship: the fifteenth!"

"Who cares about the troops?" Kimm asked.

The third one added, "They never do anything."

By Kahless's hand, what are Krom and Klaad teaching these infants? Despairing for the youth of the empire, G'joth said, "You will hear my tales tomorrow, and then you will find out who is the subject. And Kimm, Gurlk? Tell your fathers I will visit them while I am home."

They all nodded. Then they looked at each other, stood up straight, and put their right fists over their hearts. *"Qapla'!"*

Smiling, G'joth returned the gesture and the exclamation.

He continued on his way to the small four-story building that housed twelve small flats. The façade was tarnished and pockmarked and filthy, the front door broken and left open. As he climbed the warped, creaky wooden stairs to his parents' flat on the third floor, he thought about Wol, and how she had to go from the estates of House Varnak to living in the two meters of a Defense Force soldier. *It was probably very difficult for her.*

For G'joth, however, his two meters were only a little bit smaller than what he was used to.

He approached the doorway to his parents' flat. The

door had a tarnished handle on it, and G'joth shook his head with annoyance that the owners still hadn't put in an automatic door.

They had, however, put in intercoms. He touched the control, which made a buzzing noise. Then he said, "It is G'joth."

Moments later, the handle moved downward, then up again, then down again. After another second, the door flew inward to reveal the short, stout form of G'joth's mother, Tektra.

"G'joth! You're home!" She wrapped her stubby arms around G'joth's armor in a happy embrace. "It's so good to see you alive and well!" Breaking the embrace, she stepped back to look at him. "We've heard so much about your ship—it's all anyone's talking about. First fighting on behalf of the Order of the *Bat'leth*, then the war with the Elabrej. I'm glad you came home alive, so we can find out the truth." She looked around. "Where's your friend Davok? Oh, no, I forgot, he always goes back to that House his father worked for for two days, then comes here when he can't stand it anymore. A pity, he'll miss the *yobta' yupma'* feast."

"Mother, Davok is dead. He died at San-Tarah."

"Oh." Mother's face fell. "That's too bad. I always liked him. He was an irritating little *petaQ*, but he always made me laugh."

"Me as well," G'joth said sadly. He knew Mother would understand. Warriors just went on about how Davok died well, and that was all fine, and G'joth was sure that Davok was in *Sto-Vo-Kor* complaining about everything *there*, but G'joth still missed him.

"So come in, come in. Your father and sister are both working. I have the night off from the restaurant, since I knew you were coming home. I have to be there tomorrow, though; *yobta' yupma'* is always a busy time. We'll just eat early."

G'joth followed his mother into the kitchen, which also served as dining area and sitting room. He remembered Davok complaining the first time he came with G'joth to this place, whining about how this room served functions that would be served by six rooms at the House Kazag estate. It and the two bedrooms made up the entirety of the flat. G'joth would share with Lakras, a state of affairs that G'joth knew would make Lakras whine like the little girl he still thought of her as.

Speaking of whom, G'joth asked as he sat at the table, "How is Lakras's opera career going?"

Mother walked over to the cabinet and pulled out a bottle of cheap *warnog*. It was what Mother always took out when she had guests, though G'joth had never understood how he qualified as such. "She is eager to see you again. And she wishes to bring you to the theater tomorrow."

G'joth frowned. "Why?"

Mother just smiled as she poured the *warnog* into two mugs. "I'll let her tell you."

At that, G'joth sighed. He wasn't sure what frightened him more, Lakras plotting something, or Mother being in on it. "I will not be able to go until low sun. I made a promise to three young boys."

"Oh?" Mother sat down next to him and handed over one of the *warnog* mugs.

"Klaad and Krom's boys were playing with another boy."

"Yorikk. Those three are always getting into trouble." Mother shook her head. "It's a wonder they haven't been bound by law yet."

"Mother, they weren't doing anything I didn't do at their age."

"Nonsense. You were a good boy. These children today, they're a disgrace. They could learn a lot from you and their parents, if they just paid attention."

G'joth didn't bother to argue, as he'd never won an argument with Mother in his life, and he doubted he would start now.

"A shame about Davok," she said, sipping her *warnog*. "What happened?"

For anyone else, G'joth would have embellished, but this was Mother. "It was during the contests on San-Tarah. We were assigned to protect a prize that the San-Tarah would attempt to capture. All five of us were wounded—except for Goran, of course, but no one can harm the big man—and one of the aliens cut off Davok's head."

She shook her head. "That's awful. After all you've been through, to die like that. At least he died on duty. Not like that friend of yours, what was his name?"

"I do not know who you—"

"Korlak!" Mother said, eyes widening. "The one who died in the shuttle accident while on his way to a *bat'leth* tournament."

Shaking his head, G'joth said, "Of course." He'd forgotten about Korlak. They'd served on the *Kalvis* together and survived many campaigns. In fact, he, G'joth, and Davok had been the only survivors in their company in a battle against the Kinshaya. Then he died because someone hadn't performed maintenance on the shuttle he was using to get to the tournament.

"I also wish to see Klaad and Krom while I am home," G'joth said after a moment.

"I'm sure they'll be glad to see you."

Somehow G'joth doubted that, especially given what Klaad had said to his son, but G'joth didn't care.

As he sipped his *warnog*, he thought, *It's good to be home*.

NINE

Yopak Port
Pheben III

Wol stared angrily at her subordinate and wondered how difficult it would be to find a ship that would take her back to Qo'noS.

They had arrived at Pheben III on time, a two-day journey on the *Mahochu* that went without incident. Wol actually had an entire space to herself: a sectioned-off part of the cargo hold that smelled of rotted fruit and dried-out *loSpev*. The odor notwithstanding, it was still several times larger than her two meters on the *Gorkon*, and she was grateful for that, though she had trouble sleeping on the straw pallet, missing her metal bunk. Several of the crew played *grinnak*, and Wol had enjoyed taking their money, which was going toward a new cleaning kit for her blades.

Then they waited.

The waiting area at Yopak Port was a small room just off the processing station, which was, in turn, next to the public transporter, as well as a corridor that led to the housing area for the planet-based vehicles. Once the *Mahochu* achieved orbit, the three of them beamed down to Yopak Port, which was the only place on Pheben III that was authorized to receive public transporter beams. As Klingons and as soldiers, the three of them went through processing without a second glance, and then they waited, where Kagak had said his brother Fuhrman would meet them.

Kagak had been surprised that Fuhrman had not been waiting for them and said so about a dozen times during the two hours they waited.

Just when Wol was about to stab Kagak through the neck and then go to the controller's desk and find a ship that would take her and Goran back home, a man who was as wide as Goran but shorter than Wol came stomping in, his stubby arms spread wide.

"Brother!" he cried.

Kagak's own face lit up. "Brother!"

They embraced—or, rather, Fuhrman engulfed Kagak and Kagak attempted to breathe. "I did not intend to be late, but the vehicle malfunctioned!" He laughed, a sound that echoed off the metal walls of the waiting area and vibrated in Wol's crest. "I beat it until it ran again!" He released Kagak and stared at Goran and Wol. "You must be my brother's shipmates! Welcome to Pheben! Prepare yourselves, for you are about to have the finest *yobta' yupma'* feast in the history of the galaxy!"

Fuhrman still held his arms wide, and Wol feared he

would try to embrace them, but he refrained. *Though it might be amusing to see what an embrace between this one and Goran would look like.*

"Leader Wol, *Bekk* Goran, this is my brother Fuhrman."

"I gathered," Wol said. "Thank you for finally arriving. I was beginning to think that Kagak had planned an elaborate deception."

That prompted another crest-vibrating guffaw from Fuhrman. "You give my brother far too much credit for imagination! Why do you think he joined the Defense Force?"

Goran frowned. "He told us it was because he was a terrible farmer."

"That is the *other* reason!" Fuhrman slapped Kagak on the back. To his credit, the *bekk* only stumbled a little bit. "The vehicle is waiting for us outside—come!"

With a due sense of anticipation and dread as to what manner of aircar the "vehicle" in question was, Wol followed Fuhrman out the door.

It rumbled aside to reveal hot temperatures, the yellow sun baking the open air. Yopak Port seemed to be located in the middle of nowhere, as there was nothing around them but flat land. Not even any trees.

She also saw several ground cars sitting at various spots around the port, which surprised her. Wol had seen wheeled vehicles in the past, of course, and she figured these were used by the port.

Then Fuhrman led them to one of those vehicles. It was a large boxlike shape with six wheels, three on either side, each wheel as high as Wol's chest. The front of the vehicle had a large transparency, and the back appeared to be cargo space of some sort, as the top was hinged and looked as if it could be easily opened.

Wol stopped walking. "No."

Everyone stopped and turned to look at her. "What is it, Leader?" Kagak asked.

"We are not riding in *that*."

Again, Fuhrman laughed, but in the open air the effect was lessened. "Of course we are! How else would we get to the farm?"

"Aircar?" Wol ventured her question quietly.

Another laugh, but this time Fuhrman was joined by his brother. When he caught his breath, Kagak said, "Leader, aircars are a luxury we cannot afford. Some of the planetary officials travel in that manner, though they prefer the transporters, but we lowly farmers get by on the land."

"Besides," Fuhrman added, "those *khest'n* things never work right. No, if you wish to be transported *properly*, you use a Vikak." He walked up to the vehicle and waved his hand over a plate.

The Vikak made a noise, then a gurgling sound.

Snarling, Fuhrman waved his hand over the plate a second time.

This time, the rear of the Vikak unfolded to reveal an open space filled with tools and bags of things that Wol did not recognize. All the way in front were two benches behind one stool. In front of the stool were three long levers that went from the floor of the Vikak to about chest level. Presumably, they were used for steering.

It was quickly determined that the wooden benches

could not support Goran's girth, so he sat on the floor in the cargo area with their luggage, while Wol and Kagak took the bench behind the stool.

Transported properly, indeed. I should've stayed on Qo'noS.

Fuhrman settled his wide frame onto the small stool and ran his hand over another plate, which resulted in the whirring sound of an engine of some kind.

Then the engine went dead.

Kagak shook his head. "When was the last time you changed the battery, Brother?"

"It isn't the battery," Fuhrman said, waving his hand over the plate again. "The battery's fine."

"You did not answer my question."

"A month ago. The battery is *fine.*" The engine started, then gurgled and stopped again. *"Qu'vatlh!"*

Fuhrman kicked the area near his feet on the other side of the levers.

The Vikak started up again and stayed running.

Wol looked at Kagak. "He beat it until it ran again?"

"That is the way of things with my brother," Kagak said.

The ride to the family farm took several hours. It wasn't so bad for the first half hour or so, since the Vikak was driving over flat ground of either stone or dirt, but the farther they got from the port, the worse it got. Several times, Wol was thrown from the bench as Fuhrman drove over a rock or a divot. Her buttocks ached from the constant jerking motions the Vikak made. She was able to distract herself by thinking of all the ways she was going to kill G'joth for talking her into this.

From the rear, Goran asked at one point, "Is it always this bumpy?"

"No," Furhman bellowed from up front as he used the levers to make a right turn down an incline, "it used to be worse, back when we had the Sporak! Those things have *no* suspension! The Vikak is much better!"

Wol had always had a fairly vivid imagination, but she found, as the Vikak rumbled over a boulder with a bone-bruising impact, that she could not imagine a ride worse than this.

She had tried to distract herself with the scenery of a new world, but that proved useless after a while, because it was all the same: flat ground filled with crops, occasionally broken by a long, one-story structure. From this distance, it was hard to tell the crops apart, especially given that Wol had no idea what any of them were. Farming was always something that other people did; Wol was perfectly happy to simply reap the rewards of it, as it were.

Of course, she could have asked Kagak, but he was third on Wol's list of people she wanted to disembowel, right after G'joth and Fuhrman.

There were people visible, including several on wheeled vehicles she did not recognize. Wol was starting to think that farmers were all mad, if they preferred this type of transportation to a sensible aircar—or just walking. Not that there weren't people on their feet: she saw many Klingons, and quite a considerable number of *jeghpu'wI'*, mostly multitentacled Phebens, who operated equipment that Wol also didn't recognize.

The Vikak came to an abrupt halt, the engine ceasing its noise, and Wol feared that it had broken down again and they'd be stuck for hours, but then Fuhrman said, "We have arrived!"

Wol blinked. "We have?" Then she admonished herself. If all the farms looked alike, how was she to know that the one they were driving past was the right one?

Fuhrman had brought the Vikak to a halt right in front of a long path that led to a one-story structure. The north end (assuming the Vikak's perambulations hadn't completely destroyed Wol's sense of direction) of the building had many small windows, with the center and south end having fewer and bigger windows, so she assumed that to be storage, with Kagak's family living in the north end.

Without asking, Furhman opened the rear and removed the luggage, carrying it all himself. Wol considered objecting, but after being bounced all the way here, she was willing to let someone else carry her duffel, and Fuhrman was wide enough to be able to carry all three. Besides, they were Klingon soldiers—they didn't carry much.

Removed from the stench of the Vikak, Wol took a deep breath, taking in the new scents of this farm. In some ways, it reminded her of the hunting preserves on House Varnak's estate, but there were a lot more scents here. More animals, for one thing, beyond the avian and reptilian ones you expected in a hunting ground, and plants she didn't recognize, plus the expected tinge of fertilizer. While Wol knew little about farming, even she knew of that ingredient.

The large wooden front door of the house, which

was on the north side at the end of the path, was engraved with the words GOOD HARVEST in an ornate, old-fashioned script.

"I like your door," Goran said.

Kagak said, "My great-grandmother had that put in after the previous door was destroyed by a tornado."

That brought Wol up short. "Tornado?"

"This was in the days before weather control," Kagak said quickly. "That doesn't happen anymore."

Wol exhaled. "Good." This trip was going to be nightmarish enough without weather difficulties added to it.

Kagak then ran ahead to open the door for the laden Fuhrman.

As soon as the large piece of engraved wood swung open with a creak, Wol found herself awash in familiar scents. *Alien this world may be, but anywhere in the empire, a kitchen in use smells like a kitchen in use.* Spices, sauces, and raw meat all wafted across Wol's nostrils, reminding her of the hours before the evening meals growing up.

Before she had a chance to dwell on that, Fuhrman bellowed, "We have returned!"

Kagak held the door open for Wol and Goran—the latter had to duck his head to get through the doorway, but the big man was used to that.

The foyer they entered was dark and cluttered with an amazing amount of *things*: padds, figurines, rolled-up scrolls, codex books (Wol hadn't seen any of those in *years*), assorted weapons in various states of disrepair, containers of varying sorts ranging from jars to boxes, data spikes, and other things Wol couldn't identify, all of which was strewn about against the walls and on the floor and on shelves. There were two open doorways on the far side of the foyer, the right one leading to a hallway, the left one leading to a kitchen, where Wol could see an older woman wearing a cooking drape, slicing something on a countertop. Next to her was a younger woman, also wearing a drape and also chopping something.

The older woman said, "Be right out!" She chopped a few more things, then said to the younger woman, "Cut them smaller than that, B'Ellor." B'Ellor—who, if Wol remembered right, was Kagak's other sibling—nodded, and started chopping in a smaller arc. "Much better."

Then the woman came out from around the counter and entered the foyer. Wol could see that her hands were covered with what smelled like animal blood.

Breaking into a smile, she said, "Kagak! Welcome home!"

"Thank you, Grandmother. These are my crewmates: Leader Wol, the commander of our squad, and *Bekk* Goran. This is my grandmother, Tabona, daughter of Jirak."

Tabona opened her arms wide. "My house is yours, Leader, *Bekk*."

Bowing her head, Wol said, "We are honored, Tabona."

Then Tabona laughed. "Enough of that ritualized nonsense." She looked at Fuhrman. "Where are my gizzards?"

Fuhrman, who was still carrying all three duffels,

bowed his head into his all-but-nonexistent neck. "I was unable to procure them."

"You were gone half the *khest'n* day, you stupid *yIntagh*. Why couldn't you get me my gizzards?" For good measure, she smacked Fuhrman on the back of the head.

"The Vikak broke down again, and by the time I was able to make it run, Kinvoh's was closed."

Staring angrily at him now, Tabona said, "When was the last time you changed the battery?"

"It is *not* the battery!" Unlike the last time Fuhrman made this declaration, he sounded a bit whinier. "I changed it a month ago."

Shaking her head, Tabona said, "I should never have let you talk me into getting that *khest'n* Vikak. The Sporak was just *fine*." She looked at Wol. "I suppose he spent the whole time from the port extolling the Vikak's virtues?"

Wol smiled. "Not the *whole* time, no."

"And now I can't make the gizzards, which ruins the *entire* meal."

From the kitchen, B'Ellor called out, "We still have those *klongats* in stasis! We can use their gizzards!"

Turning around, Tabona said, "Did I teach you *nothing*, B'Ellor? You do *not* serve *klongat* gizzards with *zilm'kach*." Again shaking her head, she said to Wol, "You try to teach them the way of things, but they simply will not listen."

"I like *klongat* gizzards," Goran said. "I eat them with *zilm'kach* all the time."

Tabona glowered up at Goran. "Are you telling me how to prepare food in my own home?"

"No, ma'am. I was merely saying that I would not object if you served that."

Wol held in a laugh. Goran was simply being Goran.

"Good to know," Tabona said dryly. Then to Fuhrman: "Boy, why are you standing there? Go put down those bags in the guest rooms."

Wol blinked. "Rooms?" She had expected to be placed with Goran in the storage area or with the animals.

"Of course 'rooms,' girl, what do you think this is? You're a guest in my house, and I won't have you sleeping in the straw when I've got plenty of perfectly good *QongDaqpu'*." To Fuhrman: "Boy, will you *move*?"

Nodding quickly, Fuhrman moved to the right-hand door down the hallway, which presumably led to the guest rooms.

Kagak asked, "Where is everyone else?"

"Did they take out your brains on that ship of yours? It's low sun the day before *yobta' yupma'*, where do you *think* they are? There's *loSpev* to be brought in, you *know* that." To Wol, she asked, "He always this dumb, or just lately?"

"He only recently joined my squad," Wol said truthfully, "so I am unaware of precisely when the removal of his brain occurred."

At that, Tabona laughed. "Oh, I *like* this one. Kagak, take them to their rooms so they can change. I need to get back into the kitchen before B'Ellor completely fouls it up. Besides, I gotta figure out what to make now, since I don't have my *khest'n* gizzards. I swear, that boy's brains leaked right outta his damn ears. Damn Vikak probably didn't even break down, he was just joyridin' on the thing."

She turned around and walked back into the kitchen, still muttering to herself.

Wol turned to Kagak. "Change?"

Kagak smiled. "Grandmother will not serve you food if you sit at the supper table in uniform, Leader."

"Oh." Wol let out a snarl. "I do not have any civilian clothing."

Goran asked, "Why not? I have some for when I am off duty."

I have not been off duty since I joined the Defense Force. Wol managed not to say that out loud. "The need has never arisen."

Kagak turned toward the kitchen. "Grandmother! Leader Wol has no other clothing!"

"What?" Tabona came back out, her bloodstained carving knife still in hand, and holding it in such a way that Wol half expected the old woman to come at her with it. "You just wear that *khest'n* armor?"

"I have no need for other clothing," Wol said, choosing her words carefully, as she had no desire to share her life story with this woman, who probably didn't care about it in any case. "Whenever I am away from my post, the uniform affords me respect." *Respect I would not have otherwise as a Houseless outcast.*

Tabona stared at her for a moment, then said, "B'Ellor, get out here."

B'Ellor came running out, also still carrying a bloody knife. "Yes, Grandmother?"

"Take Wol here to your room and get her some

clothes. You two are almost the same height." She smiled. "I wouldn't want you to starve to death while you were here."

Wol bowed, Tabona's implication confirming Kagak's earlier statement that she would not be allowed at the supper table in uniform. She was not pleased about it, but she had accepted this mad old woman's hospitality.

After nodding to Tabona, B'Ellor walked to the corridor. Wol followed her.

B'Ellor's room had four beds. *No wonder they have space for guests*, Wol thought. The young woman moved to a pile of clothing in one corner—not to be confused with the other piles in the room, which were even worse than the ones in the foyer, which at least were pushed against the walls to allow space to move. You could barely see the floor in this room.

"Here." B'Ellor held out a brown one-piece outfit with a flared bottom, with the middle cut out. It looked like a low-class version of the dresses she wore when she was Eral, daughter of B'Etakk—which, she supposed, it was.

Wol began removing her armor, snarling as she did so.

"What is wrong?" B'Ellor asked.

"I do not wish to remove my armor. I will abide by your grandmother's rules of hospitality, of course," she added quickly, not wishing to insult her host.

"Why?"

Wol hesitated, using the removal of her boots to cover it. Finally, she said, "When I wear this armor, I am Leader Wol, commander of the fifteenth. I am a soldier, a warrior, worthy of respect."

"Aren't you still Leader Wol without the armor?"

"No one sees that," Wol said as she removed her leg-wear. She held up the outfit B'Ellor had handed her as if it were a diseased animal. Then she held it up over her head and shrugged into it. As her head poked out through the neck, she went on: "Without the two medallions on my biceps, I simply become Wol, a woman without a House."

"So?" B'Ellor sounded genuinely confused. "Nobody here has a House, either. We don't need all that silly stuff. Besides, Grandmother welcomed you—that means you're part of the family as long as you stay here. So you don't need the uniform, because you have us."

Wol straightened the dress out, adjusting the cutout around her breasts. "It is not that simple."

"Of course it is," B'Ellor said. "You are Kagak's squad leader. That makes you as welcome here as he is."

"Because your grandmother says so?"

"Yes. It's her house." She smiled shyly. "Is that any different from you having respect based on what you're wearing?"

Wol found she didn't have an answer for that.

TEN

The Lukara Edifice
Novat, Qo'noS

The third day of the KPE conference had actually gone worse than the first two.

The first of two talks scheduled for that day was at high sun, and it was intended to discuss the mapping of the brain that was done for criminal prisoners and apply it to healing head injuries. B'Oraq entered the room to find only three people in the audience and nobody on the stage. Two of those present were Kandless and Valatra; she did not recognize the third.

B'Oraq took a seat and overheard Valatra telling Kandless about an operation she had performed at B'Alda'ar Base after the Kreel attacked it. The procedure she described was one B'Oraq had learned at Starfleet Medical to treat belly wounds, and she wondered where Valatra had discovered it.

119

Unfortunately, the speaker never bothered to show up, which might have created more of a fuss if there weren't only four people in the audience. After it was clear that there would be no talk, B'Oraq walked over to the physician she did not know, who quickly ran out of the room at her approach.

When she turned toward Kandless and Valatra, they too were departing. She considered calling after them but decided that it was a wasted effort. It was obvious from the overheard conversation—not to mention their questions yesterday—that they were far more dedicated than the average Klingon doctor, but it was also obvious that they didn't want to get anywhere near her. She supposed she couldn't blame them. For all that she had become one of Klag's closest advisers, and for all that Chancellor Martok was on her side, she had made herself an outcast in the Klingon medical community. Associating with her would be professional suicide for Valatra and Kandless, and suicide was dishonorable.

She beamed back to the *Gorkon* and went to her cabin, stepping over and around dozens of engineers on the way. As she turned one corner, she saw Kurak yelling at one of them. "What *petaQ* told you to use *that* to repair the junction? By Kahless's hand, I am surrounded by imbeciles!"

The tone surprised B'Oraq. Since Elabrej, Kurak's perpetual bad mood had been ameliorated, presumably by her liaisons with Lieutenant Leskit combined with her cessation of excessive alcohol consumption. B'Oraq had never known a Klingon who drank enough to endanger her life until Kurak.

"If this junction is not repaired, and *properly*, by the end of the shift, I will put you to death myself!"

B'Oraq noticed that Kurak was gripping her right wrist with her left hand, something else she hadn't done since Elabrej.

Kurak seemed to notice that B'Oraq was looking at her, as she whirled on the doctor and said, "What do *you* want?"

"Merely concerned about your health, Commander. I—"

"My health is *fine*, Doctor. If it changes, I will let you know."

With that, she turned on her heel. The engineer she had upbraided was digging through a toolbox, apparently seeking out the correct tool for the job.

Tugging on her braid, B'Oraq turned and continued on to her cabin.

As soon as the door rumbled shut behind her, she sat at her desk and opened a communication to the House of M'Raq estate.

The face of an older man appeared on the screen. *"What?"*

"I would speak with Captain Klag."

"Very well." The man, whom B'Oraq presumed to be the House *ghIntaq*, reached for a control, and then his image was replaced with the empire's trefoil.

Moments later, Klag's more pleasant features appeared. *"B'Oraq. How goes the conference?"*

"There are many things I would be happy to speak to you about, Captain, but the conference is *not* one of them."

Klag smiled. "*It goes that poorly?*"

"Yes." She shook her head. "In truth, I expected little else, but that makes it no less frustrating. I contacted you to see how your drills were progressing, so I can provide as recent an update as possible for my talk this afternoon."

"*I have not been able to schedule one. The servant with whom I intended to spar is not here. My mother, despite knowing that I was coming home, has taken a trip to Qimpo, and she took most of the staff with her, leaving only Dokil— that was the sour-faced toDSaH who answered your call.*"

"Is he your *ghIntaq?*"

"*Hardly.*" Klag chuckled. "*He is in charge of the cleaning staff. No, my darling mother took the ghIntaq with her, along with everyone else. I have been forced to transport to the First City in order to eat, as the larder barely has enough for the cleaning staff.*"

"She did not even leave enough food for you?"

Klag shook his head. "*It is possible that Mother simply forgot. She is not as young as she used to be.*" Then he let out a breath. "*It is equally possible that she has taken Dorrek's side.*"

"Aren't you House head now? By denying you food—"

"*I will not upbraid my own mother.*"

B'Oraq refrained from pointing out that he did far worse to his father when he was alive. *Perhaps he sees now that that was a mistake.*

His face softened as he continued. "*Besides—Dorrek did not pay attention to my being the House head, so why should she? It is of no consequence.*"

"When will she return?"

"*She provided no timetable for such. I suspect it will relate to when the* Gorkon *is spaceworthy again. In the meanwhile, I have been summoned to the Great Hall in a week's time, a summons that includes all the shipmasters who fought at Elabrej.*"

"All of them? Even General Goluk?"

Klag nodded. "*And the vessels with him. That is the reason for the delay, as it will take that long for his fleet and the* Kesh *to return. They would be returning in any case—apparently, the Elabrej were not deemed worthy of conquest. They will be left to their own devices and to reflect on the folly of firing unprovoked on an alien ship.*"

B'Oraq thought that to be an abrogation of responsibility. True, the Elabrej fired on the *Kravokh* first, but should an entire nation suffer because of the actions of one foolish ship captain?

Then she shrugged the thought off. *You are thinking like a Federation politician, not a Klingon doctor.* The Elabrej had many opportunities to surrender with honor, and they chose to fight instead. Worse, they experimented on their prisoners instead of letting them die. B'Oraq recalled with disgust the report Leader Wol had written about her treatment at the hands of Elabrej "scientists" before she was able to escape.

"Perhaps you will be rewarded for a well-fought campaign."

"*I have my doubts.*" Klag then told her of the questions I.I. had required General Kriz to ask Klag during his report. "*I suspect that I.I. is displeased with how their agents were treated and is causing problems for the High Council.*"

"If you say so." B'Oraq had enough trouble dealing

with the politics of her profession. If she tried to follow the greater politics of the empire with any but a cursory interest, she'd go mad.

"That is simply a guess, but it fits the evidence. After all, the abused always kick downward. I.I. kicks the High Council, the High Council kicks General Goluk and the ship captains."

"And you kick Toq?" B'Oraq asked with a smile.

Klag returned the smile. *"Either him or the cleaning staff."*

B'Oraq laughed, then looked at the screen. She had not intended to make this request of Klag, but since the estate was all but empty . . . "Captain, I was wondering if you wouldn't object to company tonight after the conference."

Laughing, Klag said, *"Your uncle will not object?"*

"My uncle will never know."

"I will send the estate's coordinates to the Gorkon," he said, his smile widening.

"Then I will see you tonight."

After receiving those coordinates—which were, B'Oraq noted, to a transporter station just outside the estate, as one did not beam directly into a home, especially that of a noble House—B'Oraq went over her talk one final time, reciting it as much from memory as she could. Consulting notes might be construed as a sign of weakness, after all. True, most physicians would not care one way or the other, but B'Oraq's talk would be under the finest of sensors, and her every movement would be dissected like a lab animal. It would be best if she did not provide her detractors with additional reasons to dismiss her.

An alarm sang out when it was fifteen minutes before low sun, which gave B'Oraq just enough time to go to one of the *Gorkon*'s transporter rooms and beam down to the Lukara Edifice.

When she arrived at the room where her talk was to be given, she nearly fell over from shock to see that most of the stools were occupied. Tugging nervously on her braid, she walked to the front of the room, an action that served to quiet all those in the audience, aside from the occasional whisper.

She walked up onto the stage, at which point the silence was almost deafening. B'Oraq wouldn't have believed it possible for so many Klingons to be so quiet. What's more, most of them gazed upon her with hostility. The only exceptions were Kandless and Valatra, who were in the front row, and perhaps one or two others. Valatra, she noticed, was in her full Defense Force armor, not the more casual medical uniform, a token of respect that B'Oraq appreciated.

Right in the center of the front row, and with the nastiest expression on his visage, was Doctor Kowag. *Wonderful.*

Setting the padd with her notes down on the podium, B'Oraq took a moment to compose herself, realizing that Kowag's presence did a lot more to explain the crowds. These people—like the ones who gathered around her duel with Tiklor yesterday—didn't want to hear about Klag's transplant procedure.

They were here to see a fight. And Kowag had made it clear that he was going to give her one.

So be it. The moment she decided to apply to study at the Starfleet Medical Academy—a process that itself was a mighty battle against the bureaucracies of two large interstellar nations—she had commenced a war. That war had seen dozens of battles, some of which she lost and left her bloody, but none of which led to her defeat. What's more, she'd won more than she'd lost, and the very existence of this conference, regardless of what happened during it, counted as one of her finest victories.

"Honored physicians," she began, as all the talks had begun, "I salute you. I will be telling you this day about a procedure that I performed half a turn ago: the grafting of an arm onto a living warrior who had lost the limb during the Dominion War."

She touched a control on her padd, which lit up the screen behind her with an image of Klag from after Marcan V, but before the procedure, when he had no right arm.

"Klag, son of M'Raq, was the sole survivor of the crash landing of the *I.K.S. Pagh* during the Battle of Marcan. However, the crash took his right arm. Klag continued to fight against the Jem'Hadar until he was rescued by the *I.K.S. Ro'Kronos*. The wound was sealed, and Klag continued to serve the empire."

Now she changed the image, this time to one of Klag's holodeck sessions. Klag had often re-created the Battle of Marcan on the *Gorkon's* holodeck, but that was not what B'Oraq showed now. Instead, she showed the time that Klag changed the parameters of the program so that it was *not* a re-creation of a battle Klag had long since memorized but instead a random encounter with half a dozen Jem'Hadar. The audience members watched as Klag fared very poorly, able to use only one arm and a *mek'leth*.

"When Klag first faced six Jem'Hadar and one Vorta—"

One audience member interrupted. "I heard it was a dozen Jem'Hadar and three Vorta!"

B'Oraq sighed. The story of Marcan V had been told many times, and each telling exaggerated it more. B'Oraq herself had heard Klag go as high as twenty Jem'Hadar. However, while such exaggerations were acceptable for stories told around a bloodwine barrel, for a talk such as this, precision was important.

Well, maybe not that important. "Perhaps it was," she said. "But the numbers matter less than Klag himself. His ship had been destroyed, his crewmates lost. On Marcan V, he had adrenaline, fueled by anger at the loss of his ship, aiding him. In that state, he may well have slaughtered dozens of Jem'Hadar. In the *Gorkon* holodeck, however, he had no such aid, and he paid for it. Indeed, the circumstances under which he would be a whole warrior again were unlikely ever to return."

Again she changed the image, this to Klag as a youth, holding a *bat'leth*. "When Klag was a child, he participated in the Young Warrior *Bat'leth* Tournament five times and never finished lower than second. As he grew older, that skill improved tremendously. But the *bat'leth* is a two-handed weapon. When Klag realized that he would not be a whole warrior without a good right arm, I was able to provide him with options."

At this stage, B'Oraq had planned to list those options, but she decided that this room would be no more receptive to artificial prosthetics than Klag was, so she skipped over that. "The option that he chose was a transplant."

Now she provided a moving image, one of a Klingon with no right arm, one of an arm, both fairly generic. The arm then moved toward the empty shoulder.

"The procedure involves the attachment of a limb that the patient was not born with. Now there are risks—"

Kowag suddenly spoke. "Did you warn your captain of these risks?"

"Of course." *And of course you're going to heckle me with inane questions, you brainless* targ. "I also told him of other procedures that carried less risk, but this was the method Captain Klag preferred for personal reasons."

"And what would those reasons be?" Kowag asked.

Glowering at Kowag, B'Oraq said, "They would be *personal* ones. If you wish the answer, I suggest you ask Captain Klag." That was a conversation B'Oraq would have paid to see, especially given the turn her and Klag's relationship had taken of late. "In any event, the first thing that had to be done was to remove the limb from the donor, Klag's recently dead father, M'Raq."

"What would have happened if the arm was not compatible?"

B'Oraq sighed. "That had already been determined, as you would have learned had you shown some patience, Doctor. Klag and his father have the same blood type. The greatest risk with this procedure is the possibility of the nerve endings not lining up. However, I was able to adapt a procedure by a Vulcan physician, Doctor Survan, originally intended for use on burn victims, to redirect the pathways of the central nervous system to return feeling to limbs that had been burned. I performed this CNS therapy on M'Raq's limb so that the nerves of the arm would line up with the nerves of Captain Klag's shoulder."

Another audience member spoke up. "And what of the arm's spirit?"

That brought B'Oraq up short. "What?"

"What of the arm's spirit?"

B'Oraq looked around and saw that the questioner was an older woman in the back row. "If the arm had any spirit—and a cleric would be better qualified to speak to this than I—then that spirit was Klag's own father and should be able to coexist with his son's." This was not the place to bring up Klag's paternal feud. "And if M'Raq's spirit had moved on to the afterlife, then it was free for Klag's spirit to infuse it."

The woman was standing now. Her hair flew wildly about her head, and for a moment B'Oraq thought that perhaps she was a madwoman who wandered in off the streets. Normally, she would expect security to be too tight to allow that, but somehow she suspected that nobody cared enough to secure this conference all that well. "But there is a third possibility: that the arm has *no* spirit whatsoever, in which case, your captain carries a dead weight on his body."

"Again, that is a question best left to a cleric. My concern is the physical well-being of my patient—"

Kowag got to his feet. "Physical well-being begins with the spirit, does it not? Did you consider these implications when you performed your barbarity on an honored captain of the Defense Force?"

"No, I did not—Klag had made those considerations for himself." Once again, she restrained herself from discussing Klag's tempestuous relationship with his father, not to mention his rather absurd insistence that it be the arm of a warrior attached to his right shoulder. "Once again, I suggest you pose such questions to him. My concern is with the physical procedure—"

"And I wonder, Doctor, what you would have done had your procedure failed."

"But it did *not* fail," B'Oraq said tightly.

"Fortunately for you, yes. You had to suppress his immune system in order to allow his body to accept this foreign limb, which made him susceptible to any number of diseases and ailments that a Klingon would normally fight off with ease. Even with that, he could still have rejected the arm. In fact, Doctor, what you did was increase the risk that he would die—not in battle but on your operating table. A Klingon warrior fights so he may die honorably, in battle against his foe. How, I ask you, is it serving your patient to increase the risk that he die in his bed, writhing in agony from a limb that has betrayed him, or an immune system that has done the same?"

"That has not happened—"

"Yet! There is still that risk, is there not?"

B'Oraq paused a moment to gather herself. She had expected hostility, of course, but not of this nature. Kowag was showing a knowledge of medicine that B'Oraq hadn't credited the incompetent old *toDSaH* with having.

Tugging on her braid, she said, "Klag thought it more important to be a whole warrior. To be the *bat'leth* champion he once was. Without his right arm, he was less than he was. He was willing to accept the risk. I am his physician, but he is also my captain. He ordered me to do the procedure."

"Which he would not have known about had you not revealed it to him!" Kowag bared his teeth at her. "You manipulated him into accepting your vile experiments as medicine, just as you manipulated the High Council into convening this farce. You are a sorceress, and a fraud, and you are not fit to belong among the ranks of Klingon physicians."

With that, Kowag crossed his wrists in front of his face, clenched his fists, and turned his back on B'Oraq.

The two men who had been sitting on either side of Kowag stood up and did likewise.

In turn, virtually everyone in the room also stood up and turned their backs on her, some crossing their wrists, others not bothering.

To her relief, Valatra and Kandless were not among those who turned their back on her. To her surprise, the old woman who questioned her spirituality also hadn't stood up but faced her as if waiting for her to continue her talk.

She's going to have a long wait. B'Oraq stepped off the

stage and walked slowly toward the exit at the rear. Besides Kandless, Valatra, and the old woman, there was a fourth person who hadn't turned his back on her, but as she walked closer to him, she saw that he had fallen asleep.

To the two doctors and the old woman, she said, "Thank you for attending."

Then she walked out of her own talk.

As she went downstairs to the large hall on the ground floor, B'Oraq found that she had no disappointment in her heart. To be disappointed, one had to have expectations, and she had none for this conference. The KPE was not going to change its ways because the High Council forced them to talk to each other. This was just one very small step on one very long road. B'Oraq had already accomplished more than she'd ever hoped to. She'd take her victories where she could.

Today simply would not be one of them.

She walked onto the promenade outside the Lukara Edifice's front doors, feeling the cool breeze blowing through her auburn hair. Looking up, she saw the statue of Lukara. Unlike most public statuary, Lukara was not depicted holding a weapon. Instead, she had her hands out as if in exhortation. When B'Oraq had her Age of Ascension ceremony here, she heard one of her cousins disdainfully saying that Lukara was so portrayed because she was "just a woman." When B'Oraq angrily pointed out that women could do anything men could do—something her own parents had instilled in her from birth—her cousin said, "I agree with you, B'Oraq, but my point is that Lukara was *just* a woman. We do not remember her for her great deeds but because she was Kahless's woman. What else did she do?"

Had her cousin bothered to read the plaque on the statue, he would have had an answer. As it happened, B'Oraq hadn't yet read the plaque, so she had no answer either. It wasn't until years later that she read that Lukara had been the one to spread Kahless's word after he was gone, and she had founded the Order of the *Bat'leth* as a means of ensuring that Kahless's words would still be heard. But the average Klingon knew her only as Kahless's woman and nothing else.

B'Oraq had never given much thought to her own legacy—she was far more concerned with the here and now to worry herself about the future—but times like this, she wondered if she would even *have* a legacy. Would anyone think to build a statue for her, or would her deeds be stricken from history by the Kowags of the empire?

Or would she be remembered as Lukara was? After all, Kahless might well have been forgotten had Lukara not lived on to spread his teachings, but by doing so, she ensured that she herself was all but forgotten. Decades from now, B'Oraq could imagine her medical techniques being standard in the empire but her own work as forgotten as Lukara's.

Look at me, she thought, shaking her head. *How arrogant am I, to put myself on the same level as Kahless's mate?*

She lifted her wrist, about to contact the *Gorkon* for a site-to-site transport to Klag's estate, when she heard a whining sound.

Looking up, she saw an aircar plummeting toward the ground at a great rate. There was no visible damage to the aircar; it was simply diving straight toward one of the large office buildings down the street from the Edifice. The whining quickly became a scream as the aircar streaked right at the structure.

Then it crashed in a deafening conflagration that sent B'Oraq sprawling to the stone ground at the base of the Lukara statue.

ELEVEN

The remains of Tokath's camp
Carraya IV

Even as Kuut pointed the disruptor right at his face, Toq heard the voice of Captain Quvmoh over everyone's wrist communicators, even his own.

"Quvmoh to Kuut. Prepare the survivors for transport."

"Captain—"

However, Quvmoh wasn't finished. *"Imperial Intelligence has taken over this mission, Commander. They have a ship in orbit, and they have ordered that Commander Toq and the two survivors be beamed directly to them."*

Toq could almost feel the anger in Quvmoh's voice and could not bring himself to cast blame on the captain. He recalled the anger with which Klag had greeted Trant's attempt to take over the *Gorkon* on the Elabrej mission. Most Defense Force captains preferred it when I.I. remained out of sight, in the shadows where they could gather their intelligence, not out in the open where they interfered with duty.

"Captain," Kuut said, "you do not know what is happening here."

"But apparently, I.I. does. Is there any reason why you cannot carry out their orders?"

Toq's heart raced faster. Kuut could easily tell Quvmoh that he had to kill Toq, and then shoot him after the communiqué ended in order to fulfill that lie. Deciding to help aiding in his decision *not* to do that, Toq said, "I.I. no doubt has sensors trained on this location. They know that I am still alive, as are Tokath and Ba'el."

"You know the survivors?" Quvmoh said.

"Yes, sir, I do. There is more going on here than Commander Kuut knows or understands. He believes that I should be put to death. However, if he carries out his intention to do so, I believe that I.I. would be displeased."

"I tend to agree with my first officer," Quvmoh said, and Kuut's face lit up, *"but you are also correct, Commander. Kuut, lower your weapon."*

Toq could see the war playing out on Kuut's face. He obviously very much wanted to kill Toq. What he saw on this world was an abomination to him, and he needed to strike out at someone.

There had been many elements of Klingon life that Toq had had trouble adjusting to, but the one that gave him the most difficulty was the instinctive hatred that Klingons had for Romulans—and, as he'd seen during the Dominion War, that Romulans had for Klingons.

Some of the finest people Toq had known in his youth were Romulans, and he had never been able to subscribe to that hatred.

Toq could see into Kuut's heart, and this was a man who might well disobey his superior's orders if it meant doing what he felt was right, and he obviously felt that killing Toq was the right thing to do.

But then he lowered his disruptor. "As you command, sir."

Another voice spoke, one quite familiar to Toq. *"You made the right choice, Commander."*

"Who is this?" Kuut asked belligerently.

"Mind your tone, Kuut. I am Lorgh of Imperial Intelligence. You will beam back to the Gorlak. Captain Quvmoh has been instructed to remove all record of this rescue mission from the Gorlak's logs. If you or any of your warriors speak of this planet to anyone, it will be considered treason."

Now there was no conflict on Kuut's face or on those of the soldiers: Toq saw fear. It was one thing to have I.I. spoken of, but when an agent threatened you with treason, you listened. I.I. did not make idle threats, and anyone foolish enough to think otherwise rarely lived to regret that decision.

Treason carried even more weight than simply being put to death, as such a sentence condemned not only the accused but also the accused's family for ten generations.

Then Toq felt the glow of the transporter, and moments later he found himself in a medical bay that was as sophisticated as the one on the *Gorkon*. Toq had been led to believe that only the Chancellor-class vessels were so equipped.

Two Klingons placed first Ba'el, then Tokath onto biobeds. Even as the scanning equipment provided readouts on a large screen, each Klingon examined each patient.

While the doctors—at least, Toq assumed them to be physicians—did their work, the door rumbled open to reveal the craggy features of Lorgh. "So," he said, staring at Tokath and Ba'el, "it seems that someone learned of the centurion's secret."

"You knew all along?" Toq asked.

"Yes. Does this surprise you?"

Instinctively, Toq thought it should have, but thinking about it, he found that he could muster no shock. "No. It explains why you were willing to take me in."

"I was willing to take you in, Toq, because Worf asked me."

Toq knew that Lorgh was an old friend of Worf's, having been a friend of the ambassador's grandfather, who was a general in the Defense Force Political Corps. Lorgh also took in Worf's brother after the Khitomer massacre.

"We will speak more of this later." Lorgh turned to the doctors. "Will they live?"

The doctor examining Tokath said, "Yes. Their injuries are substantial but treatable."

"Wake him."

Nodding, the doctor grabbed a needle and applied it to Tokath's neck.

The Romulan's eyes opened a moment later. His

voice, normally deep and resonant, sounded weak. "Where—?"

"You are in the custody of Klingon Imperial Intelligence, Centurion Tokath."

That prompted a ragged smile. "I have not . . . not been a centurion for some time." His bleary eyes focused on Toq. "Is . . . is that you, Toq?"

Toq approached the biobed. "Yes, Tokath, it is I."

"You became a soldier. How . . . how disappointing."

Lorgh said, "Do not be so quick to judge the boy, Tokath. Had he not been on the ship that responded to your distress call, we would not be having this conversation, because the captain of the *Gorlak* would have finished the job your attackers began."

Tokath let out a ragged breath. "Your people are always so . . . so quick to judge."

"Not all of us. Believe me, I would have been more than happy to let you live in peace." Lorgh snarled that last word. "Until you would be of use to me, in any event."

"How . . . how long has Imperial Intelligence known?"

"Long enough. And we would have used you, should we have required a club to use against the Romulans— always assuming *they* continued to tolerate you."

"The camp was privately funded," Tokath said. "Our patron would not have abandoned us."

"Your optimism is touching, but all it requires is one regime change to alter that, and given the rate at which Neral is acquiring enemies, I suspect that he will not be in the praetor's chair for much longer than two turns."

Lorgh smiled. "But this matters little, since your camp is no more. What I require now is that you tell me who attacked you, and why."

"It was a Klingon vessel," Tokath said after a moment, "but *not* from the Defense Force. They fired on the periphery of the compound by way of getting our attention. Then they contacted us, saying they wanted L'Kor."

Lorgh nodded. "One of the Khitomer survivors."

"He was more than that," Toq said. "He was the leader of the Klingons in the camp."

Tokath nodded. "L'Kor has been my friend and comrade for three decades. I would not surrender him, and even if I would, none of the Klingons would allow it."

"You said 'they' contacted you," Lorgh said. "Who, precisely?"

"A Klingon. A civilian. He did not provide a name, and I did not recognize the type of ship he flew."

Lorgh nodded. "And your planet's sensors were all eliminated in the assault."

"Yes."

"L'Kor was taken?"

Tokath nodded. Toq noticed that his eyes were getting even more rheumy. "They transported to the surface and disposed of my guards quickly. And then they killed everyone else—except for L'Kor, who was the only one they took. They no doubt believed Ba'el and me to be dead after the building fell on us. In fact, I am surprised that we *did* survive."

"A crossbeam fell just over you," Toq said. "I noticed when I removed the rubble from your person."

"I am grateful for that, Toq. And grateful for your appearance."

Toq bowed his head.

"Can you think of anything else that might aid our investigation?" Lorgh asked.

Tokath raised an eyebrow. "Oh, this is an investigation, is it?"

"Yes. Klingon lives were taken. That requires a response."

"Romulan lives were taken also."

Lorgh smiled again. "There are those who would say that *that* requires only a celebration." The smile fell. "*All* of those who died this day will be avenged, Centurion."

Tokath, though, was obviously falling asleep. "I . . . I appreciate . . . appreciate that."

Lorgh turned his back on the Romulan, letting him rest. He looked at Ba'el, who also slept. "She is his daughter?"

Toq nodded. "Gi'ral is—was her mother."

"I assume her ability to recognize Klingon civilian ships is even less than that of her father."

"Yes."

Lorgh folded his arms, looking thoughtful for a moment. Then he scratched his crest and turned to Toq. "Come with me."

Toq followed his foster father out of the medical bay. As they walked down the cramped corridor, Lorgh said, "We have recovered the bodies. There are several older Klingons who are matches for the Klingons who were assigned to the control room at Khitomer. They were missing after the Romulan attack, but that was true of many who died that day. There are only two missing from the dead on Carraya: L'Kor and Gi'ral."

Toq blinked. "Tokath said that only L'Kor was taken."

"I doubt he would lie about that, especially since it was his mate. However, vaporization is always a possibility, though it was not true of any of the others. Still, there isn't time to do a more intensive scan." Lorgh arrived at another door that rumbled aside only after he peered into an optical scanner. Inside was a desk that was piled high with padds, around which Lorgh walked. He sat and then looked up at Toq.

"There is another reason why I kept Carraya a secret—even from my fellow agents."

That brought Toq up short. "I.I. does not know?"

Lorgh let out a low growl. "It is possible that other agents know of it but are keeping it secret for their own reasons."

"And what are yours?" The question was presumptuous, Toq knew, but his own honor—not to mention his life—was at stake here.

"If the truth about Carraya were to be revealed, so too would Worf's role in keeping that a secret. The empire cannot afford to have him disgraced, especially now that he is of the House of Martok."

Toq suspected that there was more to the answer than that, but he had already pushed his luck with Lorgh. "Then what is the next step in this investigation?"

Lorgh riffled through the padds on the desk, then

found the one he was looking for and handed it to Toq. "When he was assigned to Khitomer, L'Kor had an unresolved feud with a warrior named Gannik. It related to a financial transaction."

Toq looked down at the padd's display and saw that, at L'Kor's advice, Gannik had invested in the Turok shipbuilding company instead of the Sokor company. He looked up in confusion at Lorgh. "I have not heard of either of these. I assume Turok went under, since that was the source of the feud, but Sokor?"

"That was during Chancellor Kravokh's reign," Lorgh said. "It was several decades after Praxis exploded, and the empire was, for the first time in fifty turns, entering a time of prosperity. There was a shipbuilding boom, and dozens of businesses started up attempting to cash in on it. Most of them failed, including both Sokor and Turok. Gannik lost a considerable amount when Turok went under, and blamed L'Kor."

Again reading the padd, Toq shook his head. "The fact that L'Kor lost just as much did not matter?"

"I have never known a highborn Klingon to use such insignificant criteria as facts to get in the way of a good fight, have you?"

"No." Toq set the padd down. He'd read about Chancellor Kravokh's golden age. *That must have been a glorious time to live in the empire*. Looking at Lorgh he said, "You believe that Gannik is responsible for the attack on Carraya?"

"That is not possible." He handed Toq another padd.

Looking at it, Toq saw that Gannik had died of an

infection two months ago. According to the report, his oldest son Gorrik was now the head of the House. "Gorrik, then. It would not be unusual for the new House head to settle the debts of the old one." Toq frowned. "But how did he know L'Kor was even alive?"

"Someone told him." Yet another padd was handed to Toq, this a report on communications coming in and out of the Great Hall. One was highlighted as coming from within the hall and being sent to the House Gannik estates. It had no identifier, which bespoke great resources on the part of the sender.

"You do not know who sent this?" Toq asked.

"No, but right after this message was sent, Gorrik hired a ship. Its flight plan was never filed, but its course away from Qo'noS could easily have taken it to Carraya. When he awakens, I will show Tokath images of Gorrik's ship to see if it matches what he recalls. But that will simply confirm what we already know: Gorrik took L'Kor—and possibly Gi'ral. Now we must find out where."

"Gorrik's ship may have left a warp trail."

Lorgh shook his head. "I have already scanned for one."

Toq thought a moment. "What type of ship did Gorrik procure?"

"One of those Ferengi Star-Hopper models that they designed for Klingon use."

Brightening, Toq said, "A Mark 7?"

Consulting another padd, Lorgh said, "Yes."

"Good. We had to trace Kinshaya pirates who had stolen a Mark 7 several months ago. I was able to trace their movements by retuning the sensors. It must be done while the ship has a clear path ahead, as it requires taking navigation sensors off-line."

"Then when we have finished here, you will accompany me to the bridge, where we will perform this retuning. And once the ship is found, you will have a mission."

That surprised Toq. Technically, he was on leave. He would, of course, do whatever Lorgh asked, but he was worried that whatever he did now for I.I. would affect his job as first officer of the *Gorkon*.

On the other hand, if it had to do with finding Gorrik, Toq had already sworn to avenge the deaths of his comrades.

"There is a shuttle on this vessel, which you will use to go after Gorrik. If Tokath or Ba'el wish to join you, they may. I have people watching the House Gannik estate in case he returns to Qo'noS, but I suspect he will go somewhere more secret until he concludes the feud with L'Kor. That gives us time, but not a great deal."

"I will, of course, do this for you, Father, gladly—but why not use your own people?"

Shaking his head, Lorgh said, "I cannot use any I.I. personnel because then I must report the truth about Carraya. The people who serve on this ship are loyal to me and will keep it secret. If I divert any other agents to this, I will be required to write an official report, which will bring about the very disgrace to Worf, and therefore to Martok, that I would rather prevent. There are several councillors who would prefer to see Martok fall, and I suspect that one of them provided the information to

Gorrik that led to this. That traitor must not be allowed to achieve that particular victory."

Toq shook his head. "I thought Martok appointed all of the current council. How can he have enemies on it?"

"There are always enemies in politics, boy," Lorgh said with a growl. "Do not forget that." He got to his feet. "Your primary mission is to ensure the secrecy of the camp on Carraya IV. Do you understand me, Toq?"

All too well, he thought angrily. Lorgh had made it clear that vengeance against Gorrik was secondary to preserving secrets. While Toq did not share Captain Quvmoh's disdain for keeping them, Toq still was a good enough Klingon that he preferred never to lie.

Yet he'd spent his entire life since leaving Carraya lying, and on Carraya he'd lived a lie. *So for whose benefit, precisely, is this insistence on being truthful?*

Besides, the best way to get Gorrik to stay quiet would be to kill him.

"I understand," he said.

Lorgh had come around to the other side of the desk and now put a gauntleted hand on Toq's shoulder. "Good. We will repair to the bridge."

As he followed Lorgh out of his office, Toq swore that he would fulfill *all* his missions this day.

TWELVE

Rodek really detested aliens.

It didn't bother him so very much on the *Gorkon*, as the only aliens were the various *jeghpu'wI'* who performed menial tasks. They were beneath his notice and therefore easy to ignore. His position as ship's gunner had kept him on the bridge for most of the *Gorkon*'s mission to date, so his encounters with aliens were limited to blowing them out of the stars.

What he hated most about aliens was the *smell*. All of them, the *jeghpu'wI'*, the Children of San-Tarah, the humans they'd worked with against Malkus, the Elabrej resistance fighters they'd encountered, they all smelled like *taknar* droppings.

Walking around this Federation space station again made Rodek want to plug up his nose forever—that or

147

vomit all over the deck. He'd not seen so many aliens in one place since he last set foot here, and the stench of all of them—Bajorans, humans, Cardassians, Ferengi, Bolians, Vulcans and Romulans, Andorians, Yridians, even his fellow Klingons—was overwhelming.

This station used to be Bajoran, but they had joined the Federation recently, so now it was entirely run by Starfleet. Rodek looked for someone in one of their drab gray-and-black uniforms. As soon as he saw one—a Bajoran woman, whose collar was gold—he grabbed her arm.

"Infirmary!" he bellowed.

The woman's initial reaction was anger, but when she got a look at Rodek's face, she relented, no doubt recognizing how much Rodek needed to get out of this damned Promenade. Turning, she pointed at an open doorway farther down the Promenade. "That way."

Nodding his head, Rodek quickly moved toward the doorway in question, pushing aside several foul-smelling Bolians and another Starfleet officer.

When he entered, he saw a woman sitting at a desk, studying a Cardassian shatterframe display. Rodek was confused about that at first, then recalled that this station was originally a Cardassian mining outpost before the Bajorans took their world back.

"I am looking for Doctor Bashir," he said upon entering.

The woman turned around. "He's seeing a patient right now. Can I help you with something, Lieutenant?"

Rodek managed to get his breathing under control. The stenches had lessened with his ingress to the infirmary, in part due to the many medicines that were stored here, plus the place was kept particularly clean due to the human need to scrub the life out of everything. Rodek had never understood why a species with such poor olfactory senses had such a need for cleanliness.

"No," he said after a moment. "I must see Doctor Bashir. I will wait for him."

Pointing to a bench against one wall, the woman said, "You can have a seat over there, Lieutenant—?"

Ignoring the prompt to give his name—he did not wish Bashir to know he was coming—he took the proffered seat.

The trip to the station had been relatively easy to arrange. The *I.K.S. Yorkang* was travelling from Qo'noS to DS9 with the intent of going through the Bajoran wormhole to the Gamma Quadrant. The captain was an old friend of Noggra's and was happy to provide passage for Rodek.

In the days spent on the *Yorkang*, the dreams grew even more vivid. Qa'Hos's drugs had done him no good whatsoever.

"Lieutenant?"

He looked up to see a frail human with wide eyes and a sickeningly sweet voice. It was Bashir.

"I am Lieutenant Rodek, son of Noggra. I will speak to you."

"Of course, Lieutenant. It's good to see you again."

"Is it?"

The human seemed taken aback by the harshness of Rodek's words. "Well, it's been a few years, but I still recall the shuttle accident you and your father were in. Are you suffering any ill effects?"

"Yes, Doctor, you might say that I am suffering 'ill effects.'" Rodek got to his feet and approached Bashir, deliberately towering over the human. "I have twice in recent times suffered head injuries. Since then, I have had strange dreams and fragments of memories that are not my own."

"Are you sure—I mean," Bashir added quickly, "are you sure that they're not your own?"

"I am the son of an advocate from a minor House, Doctor. Until the Dominion War, I had never served in the Defense Force, and to this day I have never set foot in the Great Hall. Yet my memories are of *captaining* a Defense Force vessel and of serving on the High Council! These are not my memories, Doctor—or, at least, not the memories I should have."

"I'm afraid I can't say anything without examining you first, Lieutenant. If you'd like, I'll do so now."

"Yes, Doctor, I would 'like.' And while you perform this examination, you may also explain why my crest has been altered."

"Excuse me?"

Rodek pointed to the top of his head. "According to Qa'Hos, the doctor I saw on the homeworld—the same doctor who told me that there was no evidence of plasma damage to my hippocampus—my crest has been surgically altered. Why would I have done this?"

"The reasons are legion, Lieutenant," Bashir said tightly, "as you well know, and I don't appreciate your tone. I'm perfectly happy to examine you, but you seem to be accusing me of something."

"I am doing no such thing, Doctor—yet. Perform

your tests. We will see what they tell you—and what you tell me."

Julian Bashir had never expected *this* to bite him on the ass.

He went through the motions, of course. He examined the man who called himself Rodek—but whom Bashir had first met as Kurn, son of Mogh, younger brother to Worf—quite thoroughly. The lieutenant had indeed suffered brain damage, some from physical trauma, more from disruptor fire, but whoever treated him did excellent work in repairing the damage—which alone was a surprise on a Klingon Defense Force vessel. Klingon doctors' ideas of healing an injury was to cut off the offending limb—or to prescribe bloodwine for the pain.

Checking Rodek's service record, he saw that he served on the *I.K.S. Gorkon*, which meant his physician was B'Oraq. That explained a great deal. Some of Bashir's time at Starfleet Medical Academy overlapped with B'Oraq's, and he remembered her as a revolutionary. In truth, Bashir was amazed she'd survived this long in the Defense Force. She'd wanted to change the state of Klingon medicine, and it was Bashir's considered opinion, after treating Klingons on and off for years, that that was a lost cause.

On the other hand, he wouldn't have expected a Klingon doctor, this Qa'Hos person, to notice the lack of plasma traces on the hippocampus. Bashir concocted some nonsense about how the traces fade with time, and while they don't often do so in so short a time as four years, it wasn't outside the realm of possibility.

Rodek greeted that news with a snarl.

Finally, when he was done, he said, "All right, Lieutenant, we're done. I'm afraid I have other business to take care of before I can process these tests. Will you be remaining on the station?"

"I have not taken quarters. I will be in the Klingon restaurant for the next several hours. You may find me there."

With that, Rodek turned and left the infirmary. Only then did Bashir allow himself to breathe regularly again.

Seeing Rodek in a Klingon Defense Force uniform had been frightening enough. The last time he saw the man in question, he'd been a civilian, the amnesiac child of an advocate named Noggra—or, at least, that was the fiction Worf had devised, with Noggra's help. In the normal course of events, he would never have returned to DS9.

But he said he enlisted after the Dominion War started. Bashir sighed. That war changed so much . . .

Shaking it off, he then said, "Computer, locate Lieutenant Dax."

"Lieutenant Dax is aboard Runabout Rio Grande, *en route to Deep Space 9 from Bajor."*

"Right, the meeting with the ministers." Dax had accompanied Captain Kira and Commander Vaughn for a meeting with the Chamber of Ministers and Councillor Krim on Bajor. He tapped his combadge. "Bashir to Dax."

"Go ahead, Julian."

"When you return to the station and have a moment, could you come to the infirmary, please? It's nothing urgent," he added quickly, so neither Kira nor Vaughn assumed a medical emergency. "It has to do with a patient."

"Sure. I'll be there in two hours?"

"Fine."

Two hours later, Ezri Dax came into the infirmary. She had ended her relationship with Bashir on Trill, and given the recentness of that breakup, he might not have come to her for advice. But she was the only person on the station to whom he could talk right now.

"What can I do for you, Julian?" she asked, all business.

"I just received a visit from a Lieutenant Rodek, son of Noggra."

Dax frowned. "I know that name."

"You should. As I recall, you were the one who suggested it to Worf."

She snapped her fingers. "Right! Curzon knew a Klingon named Rodek—he was an aide of Kang's back in the day. Really good *grinnak* player." She regarded Bashir curiously. "It can't have been him, he died fifty years ago. No, wait, you said Worf. That was the name we gave Kurn!"

"Yes, and he's back, with some rather interesting complaints."

After Bashir shared with her what "Rodek" had said to him, as well as the results of his examination, Dax said, "I can't believe you actually did that."

"You can't believe *I* did that? Worf found him drunk with a disruptor at his head. He'd already tried to commit suicide on any number of other occasions prior to

153

that, including when he served as one of Odo's deputies. He tried to have Worf commit *Mauk-to'Vor* on him, but Captain Sisko wouldn't permit it. The procedure—which, by the way, you endorsed at the time—was the only alternative to killing him."

"You may as well have killed him," Dax said angrily, "and I didn't endorse a damn thing—Jadzia did."

Bashir shook his head. "It's amazing, isn't it? Whenever a previous host does something wonderful or funny or thrilling, or you want to go on about how you've been around for three centuries, then it's something 'I' did. But if it's anything you don't approve of, *then* all of a sudden, that was a different host and you're not responsible."

Through clenched teeth, Dax said, "This isn't about me."

"Yes, Ezri, it is, because you—or one of your previous hosts, however you wish to rationalize it—came to me with Worf four years ago and said that Worf's brother Kurn needed to have his crest altered, his genetic profile changed, and his memory erased. Simple enough procedure—now, though, it's unraveling."

"How?" she yelled. "You said it was impossible to reverse!"

Holding up a finger, Bashir said, "No I said it was *almost* impossible to reverse!" Realizing that they were both shouting, he forced himself to breathe out slowly. More calmly, he continued. "Humanoid brains remember everything they're exposed to. After that, it's a question of access. What I did to Kurn was remove his ability to access his memories."

"What changed?"

Shrugging and moving to sit at a console—he suddenly found himself to be exhausted—Bashir said, "Head trauma. He lived through an explosion that almost killed him and took a disruptor hit to the face."

Dax moved over to sit next to him. Her own anger seemed to have burned to ashes as his had. "Wouldn't that make it worse?"

"The damage? Almost certainly. But the ship Rodek serves on is blessed with one of the few Klingon doctors who actually deserve a medical degree. When she repaired the damage to his brain, she unknowingly reconstructed several of the neural pathways to the hippocampus that my procedure cut off. He's started remembering aspects of his life as Kurn, like being a captain in the Klingon Defense Force, like serving on the High Council—even being one of Odo's deputies."

Now sounding concerned, Dax leaned forward. "Julian, I think you need to tell him the truth. And maybe give him the rest of his memory back."

Bashir closed his eyes and let out a long breath. "You're probably right."

"I *am* right. Look, let's say I agree with what Jadzia did four years ago—in fact, in some ways I do, since at least this didn't kill him. But what made sense then doesn't now. Kurn was dishonored because Worf opposed Gowron's invasion of Cardassia, so Gowron eliminated the House of Mogh. But now Gowron's dead, and Worf is part of Martok's House. The dishonor you operated on Kurn to eliminate doesn't exist anymore. I can't think of any good reason why we can't have Kurn back. Can you?"

At first, Bashir said nothing, simply stared at the bench where "Rodek" had sat while waiting to see him. "You know," he finally said, "at the time, I had my doubts. But you—Jadzia—and Worf both made such a compelling case that I went ahead with it, especially once I met Noggra. He seemed willing to do whatever was necessary to make Rodek a real part of Klingon society. And look at him." He turned around and called up Rodek's service record. "He's second officer on one of the finest ships in the Klingon fleet. He has commendations, medals, citations—he's had a good life." Turning to look at Dax, he said, "I'm not disagreeing with you, Ezri. In fact, I think I asked you in here because I knew you'd say what you just said. But it's not as simple as that. Four years ago, yes, Rodek was a tabula rasa that Noggra and Worf added lies to—but now? Rodek's a *person*. It's not as cut-and-dried as that."

Dax nodded and put a hand on his shoulder. "Maybe not, but I think he deserves to know the truth. What's more, precisely *because* he's a Klingon warrior in his own right now, he *needs* to know the truth, for the sake of his own honor."

Bashir chuckled. "That's the difficulty with honor. It's not a measurable quality."

With a small smile, Dax said, "It can be."

He got to his feet. "The lieutenant said he was going to Kaga's. We'll find him there."

After departing the infirmary, Rodek moved as quickly as possible through the Promenade toward the restaurant. The last time the *Gorkon* had come to DS9, Rodek had stayed on board, but Toq had taken advantage of the Promenade and sung the praises of both the Ferengi bar's dabo tables and the Klingon restaurant. Rodek had no use for dabo, and even less for Ferengi, but he had an urge for *krada* legs.

For some reason, after seeing the doctor, the stench of the station didn't bother him. Perhaps it was the doctor's own diagnoses casting doubt on that of Qa'Hos. Or perhaps it was the feeling that he would get answers soon enough. If the ones provided by the human did not please him, Rodek would kill the doctor and seek satisfaction elsewhere.

The restaurant was run by a chef, a short, rotund individual who introduced himself as Kaga. When Rodek expressed his desire for *krada* legs, Kaga laughed and said, "Of course, Lieutenant. The *krada* came in this very morning. However, the *taknar* came in this afternoon."

After smelling what he imagined to be *taknar* droppings all day, Rodek couldn't bear the notion of eating any. "Just the *krada* legs."

Kaga bowed and walked off to fulfill the order.

Rodek liked it here. The walls were decorated with weaponry and Klingon statues and tapestries, the chairs were proper stools, and the smells were almost like he was back on the *Gorkon*. True, there were many aliens fouling the place with their presence, but the whiff of *grapok* sauce and animal meat both living and dead overcame that.

Soon, Kaga walked back and dropped a table filled with *krada* legs and a pool of *grapok* sauce. Then he held up his *may'ron* and started playing it while singing the final song from the opera *Kahless and Lukara.*

Rodek appreciated the touch. On the *Gorkon,* it was traditional for there to be a song before the evening meal. That tradition did not exist on the *Yorkang,* and Rodek found he'd missed it. Somehow, song made the food taste sweeter.

Kaga finished the aria just as Rodek swallowed the last of the legs. As he was considering whether to order some skull stew, a familiar-looking Klingon sat opposite him.

"I would speak with you," the Klingon said, staring at Rodek with small, beady eyes.

"*Would* you?" Rodek said angrily, not pleased at the interruption. He wondered if the right of challenge existed on this station, or at least in this restaurant. *Probably not—it is not a diplomatic space, merely an eatery.*

"Yes, Lieutenant, I would. I have information that will be of value to you. I am Dorrek, son of M'Raq, and I know who you *really* are."

THIRTEEN

Kenta District
Krennla, Qo'noS

When Lakras told G'joth that the name of the opera she was performing in was *The Battle at San-Tarah*, he nearly choked on his *zilm'kach*.

He might have done so in any event, as Mother had prepared it with her usual lack of skill. G'joth had never really acquired a taste for Andorian food, but he found himself longing for Mother to prepare *that*, simply because she was good at it. Not that it would have done any good, as Mother said doing so at home was "too much like work."

Once he managed to swallow the *zilm'kach*, G'joth said, "Say that again."

Lakras sat across from him at the small kitchen table, both sitting between Mother and Father, practically bouncing up and down on her stool, holding a piece of *bok-rat* liver without actually eating it. "It's called *The Battle of San-Tarah*. It's a brand-new opera by Reshtarc that was first performed on Ty'Gokor last month. This will be its debut on Qo'noS, and I'm in the chorus!"

On the one hand, G'joth had been hoping that Lakras would have had an actual part. On the other, she was a commoner—rarely did they get the named parts. On the third hand—if one was a Pheben, anyhow—at least she got to sing. Many commoners were just given roles that were little more than bodies, playing the cannon fodder or soldiers or relatives or what have you. The chorus, though, stood at the back and narrated the action through song. While individual singers rarely were noticed, at least the chorus as a whole played an important role.

This, however, was the first time G'joth could think of where an opera was about a specific event that he participated directly in. Though he suspected it wasn't a major work. True, the opera house in Krennla—located in the Baldi'maj District, the closest Krennla had to a respectable neighborhood—was well regarded, major operas generally had their Qo'noS debut in Novat or the First City.

"That is . . . amazing." He looked at Mother. "This is what you would not tell me?"

Leaning over, Mother said, "She would have been very cross if I had told you. She wanted that privilege for herself."

"Isn't it *wonderful*?" Lakras was practically squeaking. "What's more, the leading man is *Kenni*."

Lakras spoke as if that name should mean something.

Then, suddenly, it hit him, from the last time he saw an opera on Ty'Gokor. Kenni had a powerful voice and performed decently with a *bat'leth* (for a stage performer, anyhow—stage fighting always left G'joth cold, as it bore no resemblance to actual combat). He had played Jokis in *Goqlath Castle*, an opera about the Kol'Vat Campaign allegedly written by Chancellor Sturka himself, though G'joth always assumed that to be propaganda and that he'd hired someone to do it for him. Still, it was a fine opera, and Kenni had performed the role of Jokis well.

However, Kenni also looked nothing like Klag. "He is playing Captain Klag?"

"*No*, you silly *petaQ*, he's playing General Talak."

"Talak is the villain of the piece," Father said in the long-suffering voice he often used in conversations with his daughter. "Which means Kenni *can't* be the leading man."

"Well, he's the leading man to *me*. Besides, he's the big draw. Nobody's even *heard* of Klivv. *He's* the one playing your captain. In any case, that's not the really good news. The *really* good news is that, when I told the director that you were coming home, he said that you *had* to come to the theater and be a technical adviser."

Again, G'joth almost choked on his *zilm'kach* and finally just threw it down, determined to cease all attempts to eat until Lakras was done talking. "Adviser on *what*, exactly?"

Father stared at G'joth from under his pronounced eyebrow ridge. "What do you mean 'on what'? Son, you were *there*. You know more than some idiot opera composer about what happened in that battle."

"Reshtarc is *not* an idiot!" Lakras almost pouted when she said that, and G'joth had to restrain himself from throwing his *zilm'kach* at her. "He's a great composer! And Konn is a great director."

While G'joth had heard of Reshtarc, he knew nothing of this Konn person. Of course, what he knew of Reshtarc was that he was exactly the type of ignorant *yIntagh* whose operas led G'joth to want to compose his own just so *somebody* would get it right. Still, at least this Konn person seemed to understand that problem, if he wanted G'joth to consult. "What else has this Konn done?"

"This is his first time directing an opera," Lakras said, "but he's Reshtarc's third-born son, so he knows the composer's intentions."

G'joth wasn't sure how he saw that as a good thing but refrained from comment. "When must I arrive at the theater?"

Lakras stared at him as if he were mad. "First thing in the morning, obviously."

"I had hoped that on leave, at least I would be spared having to rise with the sun."

"You work in *space*. There *is* no first sun in space," Father muttered into his *chech'tluth*.

"Besides, we need your help right away," Lakras said. "We're about to rehearse the scene where Captain Klag faces the San-Tarah in the square for the fate of the planet."

"Ah, so you've already done the other contests?"

"What contests?" Lakras asked as she finally swallowed her liver.

Getting a queasy feeling in both stomachs, G'joth said, "The other contests prior to the swordfight—which, by the way, was in a circle, not a square."

For the first time since she served the meal, Mother spoke: "You see, G'joth, this is why your presence is required. You can correct things like that."

Lakras winced as she chewed off more liver. "I do not believe that will be possible. You see, there's an entire song leading up to the battle, and if you change *square* to *circle* it will ruin the meter."

"This," G'joth said with a long-suffering sigh, "is why I grow weary of operas—and why I tried to write my own."

That got Mother's attention. "You wrote an *opera*? Why did you not tell us?"

"Because I never finished it. Operas are . . . difficult." He smiled snidely at Lakras. "For starters, you have to alter facts in order to make the meter work."

Primly, Lakras said, "It's an important part of the creative process. And anyway, Konn *wants* you there so you can tell him things like this."

"Very well." G'joth finally decided it was safe to chew his *zilm'kach*. While doing so, he added, "But I will need to depart at high sun for a time, in order to fulfill a promise I made to three children."

G'joth accompanied Lakras the following morning in the opera house's aircar, which came and picked up several members of the company, bringing them to the opera house in Baldi'maj District. The theater itself was an artificial re-creation of a natural amphitheater. From above, G'joth could see the circular stage, surrounded by ever-rising circles of benches. The benches were made of stone in what G'joth assumed was an attempt to duplicate the feel of the amphitheater on Ty'Gokor. After the top row was a sheer drop down a wall that was all that could be seen of the theater from ground level. As the aircar moved to land behind the opera house, G'joth could see poorly rendered images of opera performers carved into the wall's surface.

The people in the aircar all spoke of either their singing, about which G'joth knew nothing, or about people whom G'joth had never met. He noticed that several of them were passing around mugs of bloodwine. Even G'joth thought it was a bit early for that, but Lakras told him archly that bloodwine helped coat the throat to improve singing ability. For his part, G'joth stuck with a *raktajino*, which was the one Klingon food Mother knew how to prepare properly, mostly for Father. There were times growing up that G'joth was convinced that the empire would be a better place if Father just had a permanent intravenous feed of *raktajino* all day long.

The aircar landed behind the theater, right near a small door inset into a corner of the theater. Presumably this area—which was surrounded by fences on three sides and the curved wall of the theater on the fourth, leaving it accessible only by air or transporter—was set off to keep the performers away from the audiences. Kenni, G'joth knew, had a huge following and likely had many devotees who would kill for a chance to meet him.

There was another aircar in the landing area, this

one much more lavishly appointed than the one G'joth was in. A figure stepped out dressed in a white cloak made from al'Hmatti fur. His hair had been carefully styled to look like it was wild, and his crest looked carefully sanded.

Lakras smiled. "Kenni," she whispered and ran toward him.

He smiled back at her, and he clasped her hand in his, squeezing so that her fingernails drew blood. She sniffed him, and he her.

The rest of the cast ignored the public display of affection. For his part, G'joth wondered what, exactly, he would extract from Lakras to keep this information from Mother and Father. There was simply no way she could have forgotten to mention that she and Kenni were lovers, though it did explain her insistence on his being the leading man.

To one of the other chorus members, G'joth asked, "How long has *that* been going on?"

She shrugged. "Since he discarded his last toy. He'll discard her soon enough."

The others all went inside. G'joth remained, not wishing to enter without Lakras to introduce him.

"Ah," Kenni said after he and Lakras were done, "you must be the famed G'joth." The Klingon spoke with a deep, resounding voice that no doubt served him well on the stage. He also projected his voice so that G'joth was sure it could be heard back in Kenta District.

Dryly, G'joth said, "I was unaware I had any fame to precede me."

"My dear Lakras speaks quite highly of her brave older

brother, who fights for honor on the great ship *Gorkon*. When I first accepted this role, I had simply assumed it to be another opera. But now, thanks to Lakras, I have learned just what a privilege it is to be permitted to help tell the story of your ship's grand exploits for the empire."

Unable to resist, G'joth added, "By playing the villain who forced Klingon to fight against Klingon?"

"Ah, but without great villains, whom would the great heroes fight to prove their heroism? Besides, General Talak believed he was in the right, and in the end, he dies with honor. What more can anyone ask?"

One could ask that Talak not have been an honorless fool. But G'joth did not say that. Besides, even if Talak hadn't forced Klag to disobey orders or go back on his word to the Children of San-Tarah, Davok and Krevor would still be dead.

Indicating the door, Kenni said, "Come, let us enter, so you may see what we have made of your battle."

G'joth followed his sister and the singer through the small door that the others had already entered. Looking at Kenni, the only thing he could think was, *He doesn't look a damn thing like Talak.*

The door led down a flight of stairs to a large room with a low roof. People had split off into groups of three and four and five, chatting at a low volume.

There were two exceptions to that. In one corner sat an older man with bone-white hair sitting alone at a battered and tarnished *tIngDagh* with strings of at least four different colors. G'joth seriously hoped that the stringed instrument was merely used for practice and that the actual performances were accompanied by a proper *tIngDagh* that didn't look like it had been through the Dominion War.

The other exception was a short-haired Klingon wearing a garish green one-piece outfit. He was engaged in an animated conversation with a man wearing a cloak that looked remarkably similar to that of Kenni, though it was made from *klongat* fur rather than al'Hmatti, and was a ruddy color.

The one in the green suit said, "Remember, Klag has watched as his beloved first officer died, so he is distracted. That is why the alien creature is able to defeat him."

G'joth could not help but burst out laughing. "That is *not* how it happened."

Turning around, the man—whom G'joth assumed to be Konn—said, "Who are you?"

Ignoring the question, G'joth said, "First of all, Captain Klag lost the duel because he fought with a *bat'leth* when both arms didn't yet work properly. Second, Commander Kornan wasn't killed until *after* the captain's duel with Me-Larr."

"Who is Commander Kornan?" Kenni asked.

Konn said, "Ah, you must be Lakras's brother G'joth. I'm told you served as an officer on the *Gorkon*."

Sparing a glare at his sister, G'joth said, "No, I serve as one of the soldiers."

"Oh." That seemed to deflate Konn. "It matters not. You were there *at* San-Tarah! Your input will be of great value to our endeavor!"

"I can begin by telling you that the San-Tarah have their duels in a circle, not a square."

Konn sighed. "Yes, I tried to tell Father that that was a mistake, but he did insist that it needed to be changed for the song's meter. The circle would look better, as well, matching the contours of the stage itself. Alas, we cannot rewrite the songs, so we must work with what we have."

Before G'joth could respond to that, Konn clapped his hands once, loud enough that G'joth's ears almost popped. Everyone grew silent.

"Now then," he bellowed to all in the room, "the chorus will remain here and practice the overture with Kruq." Kruq, obviously, was the one at the *tlngDagh*. "Once Klivv arrives, we'll rehearse both duels, first with Gowrik here, then with Kenni. G'joth, you will join us. Any insight you can provide into adding verisimilitude to the duels would be welcome. Let us commence!"

The members of the chorus all gathered near Kruq, who was now tuning the *tlngDagh*. Konn moved toward a staircase in the back, Gowrik and Kenni following. A woman moved to pick up a box off the floor, and she followed. After a moment, G'joth ran to catch up to them, asking Kenni, "Why did you ask who Kornan is?"

"There's no character by that name in the opera."

"What? He was the first officer!"

"The only first officer in this story is Captain Klag's lover, Commander Tereth."

G'joth could not help but burst out laughing at that as he followed the others up the stairs. "Commander Tereth died at Narendra III before we ever set off for the Kavrot sector! And I can assure you that, of all the lovers she had on the ship, Captain Klag was *not* among them. She preferred her own sex for a bed partner."

From the top of the stairs, Konn said, "There must be a love story. There is no opera without it."

"But there wasn't one!" G'joth said.

"Then we create one for the story!" Konn laughed. "Come now, G'joth, you know how opera must be. The audiences will not accept it if there is no love story. When Father's first production of this played at Ty'Gokor, the greatest cheers came after the final love song after General Talak's assassin kills Commander Tereth."

G'joth snarled. "Tereth was killed at Narendra III when—"

"Yes, yes, yes, I'm sure she died with honor, but that does not fit the needs of the story. And that is of no concern, for the opera has already been written, and I would not dare to change Father's words. No, what I require from you, G'joth, is your memory of the fight between Captain Klag and Me-Larr of the San-Tarah."

As he said that, they all reached the top of the stairs in succession, which emptied onto the stage itself. Surrounded by rows and rows of rising seats, and the almost deafening silence of the empty amphitheater, G'joth suddenly felt very small.

The woman put down the box and removed several items, the first of which was a headpiece, which she handed to Gowrik. He placed it on top of his head and suddenly, with that and the *klongat* cloak, he almost looked like one of the Children of San-Tarah. *In truth, he looks like he killed one and is wearing his fur as a trophy, but it will do for the purposes of theater.* Were this being recorded instead of staged, the aliens would be re-created more precisely, but symbolism was always enough for the opera. From his studies of the history of opera, undertaken after he first attempted to write one, he knew that this was a recent development, that operas used to go to great lengths to re-create the original events with holographic trickery and complex costuming, but the trend over the past seventy-five years or so was to return to the older ways of performing opera, the way it was supposedly done in Kahless's time.

The other three items in the box were *bat'leths*. She handed one each to Gowrik and Kenni. The third, presumably, was for Klivv. As soon as they took them, G'joth realized that they were not real *bat'leths*. The one manner in which modern theater tended away from the time of Kahless was in the use of weaponry. In the old days, performers used real weapons. When performances became ever more enhanced with false images and illusions, the weapons followed suit. But when theater became more stripped down, the weaponry remained false. It had always struck G'joth as hypocritical—and dishonorable.

But that was the least of the problems. He said, "The Children of San-Tarah did not use Klingon weapons."

"I am aware," Konn said. "However, we already have the *bat'leths*. To create new weapons would force us to go over budget, and Father would *kill* me."

G'joth sighed. "I cannot provide you with advice as to the accuracy of the fight if you are not using the same weapons. For that matter, for the captain's duel against Talak, he used a *mek'leth*."

The woman, whom G'joth assumed to be the prop master, spoke for the first time. "Can't use a *mek'leth*."

"Why not?"

She indicated the upper rows with her head. "Can't see them from the high seats."

Snarling, G'joth said, "Very well."

Then he heard panting and running feet, both noises growing louder. A short, squat man came onto the stage. He had broad shoulders and small, beady eyes.

Angrily, Konn said, "You are late, Klivv. If you are late again, I will kill you and replace you with a performer who is punctual."

Klivv spoke in a high, whiny voice. "The aircar was late."

G'joth was aghast. This little *petaQ* looked more like the captain's traitorous brother Captain Dorrek than like Klag, and sounded more like a Ferengi than a Klingon.

The prop master held out his *bat'leth*, which he took. "Which are we doing first?" Klivv asked.

"The duel with Me-Larr. This is *Bekk* G'joth. He serves on the *Gorkon* and will provide technical advice."

Klivv's beady eyes grew wide. "Really? Oh, that is *excellent*! I will speak with you when rehearsal has ended, honored *Bekk*. There is much I may learn from you about the great Captain Klag."

"Of course," G'joth said, though he wondered what excuses this little *toDSaH* would contrive to avoid being accurate. *Then again, perhaps he is not as maddening as his director.*

"Take your stations," Konn said. He and Kenni, as well as the prop master, moved to the edge of the stage. G'joth joined them a moment later. Klivv and Gowrik, meanwhile, went to center stage, each holding his *bat'leth*.

"Computer," Konn said, "begin playback of soundtrack for Act 2, scene 9 of *The Battle at San-Tarah*."

Some rather bombastic music began playing, and G'joth remembered the other thing he disliked about Reshtarc's operas: the noise. The best operas, to G'joth's mind, kept the music simple to allow the singers free rein. After all, the music was there only to support the singers. Reshtarc, though, subscribed to the theory that the music was the important part, with the words being only the *grapok* sauce to garnish the meat of the instrumentation.

As soon as the music started, Gowrik and Klivv got into character. Gowrik hunched downward, almost pulling his body into the cloak, which, G'joth realized, was meant to emphasize his cloak and mask to the audience. As for Klivv, he danced back and forth lightly on his feet. It looked quite elegant and graceful, and it made G'joth's crest ache.

"No," he said, "this is wrong!"

"Computer, cease playback," Konn said. The music stopped, which G'joth saw as a kindness. "What is wrong, G'joth?"

"Klivv. Those movements are wrong."

Frowning, Klivv asked, "Does Klag not move like that?"

"*Nobody* moves like that when wielding a *bat'leth*. It

is a two-handed weapon, and a heavy one. Proper use of it requires that one's footing be solid." He walked over to Klivv and took the prop *bat'leth* from his hands. Sure enough, it was lighter than G'joth's *d'k tahg*, much less a real *bat'leth*. "You must stand with your feet slightly inverted, your hip thrust slightly outward, and dropping your stance so that your center of gravity is lowered. That provides you with stability. Otherwise, at the first clash of blade on blade, you will fall down." He shook his head. "This is the first thing you are taught when you learn the *bat'leth*. *Children* know this."

"Perhaps," Konn said, "but that is not what will play to the high seats. We will continue."

Angrily, G'joth handed the *bat'leth* back to Klivv. To his credit, Klivv inverted his feet slightly after taking the weapon back.

Then Konn said, "Klivv, cease that idiotic stance. Do it the way it was choreographed. Computer, restart playback."

G'joth started thinking up ways of killing his sister.

FOURTEEN

The Lukara Edifice
Novat, Qo'noS

B'Oraq clambered to her feet, the smell of burning plastiform and acrid smoke climbing into her nostrils. The aircar, she remembered from seeing its descent toward Novat, was an old Yivoq—those things had thruster packs that burned quickly and catastrophically with any kind of impact.

She ran toward the pyramid structure of the office building that the car had crashed into. Most everyone else was either running away from it or standing and staring.

There was a guardsman talking on a wrist comm, and when he saw B'Oraq, he whipped out his painstik and said, "Stay back! The guard will be by to put this out."

Although she was in civilian garb—a brown tunic and loose black pants—B'Oraq had thought to wear her rank insignia on the sleeve of her tunic, and she turned her right arm toward the guardsman. "I am Lieutenant B'Oraq of the Klingon Defense Force, and you *will* let me pass!"

The guardsman hesitated. Had she been in uniform, there would have been no question. Even a lowly *bekk* in the Defense Force outranked anyone in the Imperial Guard.

"Who is your supervisor," B'Oraq then said, "so I may tell him that his subordinate is a foolish little *chuSwI'* who—"

The guardsman lowered the painstik and stood aside.

"Tell the fire crews to wait for my signal before emplacing the force fields." The Imperial Guard's mandate included not only maintaining Klingon law on the homeworld but also disaster control. In case of a fire, they had ships that would project a force field around the fire until it was smothered. Technically, they were under no obligation to wait until people were evacuated, but that, B'Oraq knew, was due to a tendency to think that anyone caught in a fire was automatically dead. B'Oraq knew better, and she was not going to let any more people die than she absolutely had to. It was for that reason that she swore an oath to personally maim that guardsman with his own painstik if his delay caused her to lose anyone.

B'Oraq ran toward the conflagration. She heard a scream to her right and ran toward it. Klingons tended not to scream when in pain, so this had to be a critical case. In no time, she traced the scream to a man lying on the pavement, a twisted, charred chunk of metal impaling his left leg near the groin. Blood soaked the pant leg. She watched for a quick moment, trying to judge if the blood flow was pulsatile or not, but she couldn't be certain. *Could be the artery or the vein. Of course, I don't have my hand scanner with me.* She knelt down next to him and said, "I'm a doctor. Hold still."

"I was trying to run away from that *khest'n* lunatic, and this thing hit me. Get it out!"

She took the man's wrist in her left hand and found his radial pulse. It was tachycardic, to her lack of surprise. Then she lightly touched the protruding end of the shrapnel and felt the metal throb. Closing her eyes, she focused on the thrum of the metal that transmitted to one hand and compared it to the flow of his blood from the radial pulse going to her other hand. She was hoping for a disconnect between the two, because the venous return should lag by a mere fraction of a second.

But they matched perfectly, which meant it hit an artery.

Quickly, she made a visual inspection of the man and patted down his back—to his obvious annoyance. Miraculously, there were no other visible wounds. With the amount of debris that had been flying around, he was lucky to be hit only once.

"Stop touching me and get this thing out of me—if you truly *are* a doctor," the man said with a snarl.

"If I remove it, you'll bleed to death in a matter of minutes. Not that *that* isn't tempting. However . . ." She unholstered her disruptor, smiling at how appalled her teachers at Starfleet Medical would have been if they knew she was armed while giving a talk at a medical conference. *But given the reception I was expecting . . .*

She used the disruptor to slice off the ends of the shrapnel, which reduced the danger of something or someone hitting the protruding ends and making things worse until she could get him to a proper medical facility. In aid of that, she activated her wrist comm with the intention of having this man beamed up to the *Gorkon*—she did not trust any planet-based medical facility, especially since most of the planet's physicians were a quarter *qell'qam* away at the conference and not at their posts. Of course, they could be there in an instant, but then there was the issue of their catastrophic lack of competence.

Unfortunately, she couldn't send him to the *Gorkon* right now, because the only trained medical person currently assigned to the ship was B'Oraq herself, since Gaj had been put to death.

"I'll get you to a medical facility soon. Wait here," she said.

"I am not likely to go anywhere," the Klingon said through clenched teeth.

Smiling the most encouraging smile she could manage—which probably confused the man, but human medical training had corrupted her in several ways—she got up and ran to see who else needed her help. The smoke was thick, and she ran in a low crouch. *No point in both polluting and flash-frying my lungs while trying to save lives.* The heat, which had started out intense, was starting to build, baking her face and hands.

"B'Oraq to *Gorkon*."

"*K'Nir.*"

Grateful that the second-shift commander had answered rather than, say, Kurak, B'Oraq said, "Lieutenant, is there power to the medical bay?"

"*No.*"

"Please make it so—there was an aircar crash in Novat and I'm about to send several patients to the ship."

"*Doctor, that's not authorized by—*"

"It's authorized by *me*, Lieutenant. If you want, I'll contact Captain Klag at home and disturb his leave to authorize this, but how do you think he'll react—"

"*I'm diverting power to the medical bay now, Doctor.*" A pause. "*And when Commander Kurak lodges her inevitable complaint, I'll direct her to you. Out.*"

I suppose I deserved that, B'Oraq thought as she ran toward a woman lying facedown on the pavement. *And I wish that just once I could get something accomplished without having to resort to intimidation.*

As she got closer, she smelled the stench of burning hair and saw that the woman's shirt had been burned off. Those same burns probably took her hair, which was singed at the ends and quite short.

A single glance at the woman's back and spinal ridge confirmed her worst fears. The skin of the affected region was white, nearly translucent, with wormy ropes of purplish-pink blood vessels visible beneath. But she knew that the blood inside those veins and arterioles could no longer flow. These were third-degree burns, and the blood in those vessels had been boiled and then had coagulated. As expected, an area of second-degree burns—skin reddened, blistered, cracked—rimmed the perimeter.

She checked the woman's breathing and then her radial pulse—with all those burns, B'Oraq didn't risk contaminating the woman's damaged flesh any further by touching her neck to try for a carotid pulse—and it was thready and rapid but strong enough. The woman was unconscious, which B'Oraq saw as a blessing, given how painful the burns probably were.

Then she heard a wonderfully familiar voice. "What may we do to help, Doctor?"

Getting up and turning around, she saw Kandless and Valatra, the latter still in her full Defense Force uniform, which had no doubt got them past the guardsman. "I need you two to beam to the *Gorkon* with this woman and that man over there." She pointed to the man with the shrapnel. "You'll find state-of-the-art equipment there. If you need anything, talk to Lieutenant K'Nir on the bridge. I'll keep doing triage down here and will send up patients as I find them."

"Of course," Valatra said.

Kandless hesitated. "I'm not authorized to perform medicine on a Defense Force ship—"

"I'll authorize it, Kandless, and I'll take responsibility," B'Oraq said. Then she hesitated. "But it's probably best if Valatra takes charge while on board. Valatra, go stand with the other patient. Signal the *Gorkon* when I nod to you."

"As you command, Doctor," Valatra said with a quick salute, then ran over to the man with the shrapnel.

B'Oraq reactivated her wrist comm. "B'Oraq to

Gorkon. K'Nir, there are two people with me—beam them, but not me, directly to the medical bay. You will then be contacted by a Defense Force doctor named Valatra—beam her and the person next to her to the medical bay. I will be sending more patients as well. Treat any request from Valatra as if it were from me."

She nodded to Valatra, who activated her own comm. Shortly thereafter, all four disappeared in a red glow.

Running closer to the flames, now crouched even lower, B'Oraq found more bodies, but these were beyond her help. Some were being consumed by the fire, some had shrapnel that penetrated the heart or head or spine.

Then she found someone who still had a weak, hitching pulse and shallow respirations. She had him beamed to the *Gorkon* with instructions to take him ahead of everyone else.

Finally, she got to the crash site itself. Flames danced all around her, heat conducting through the metal of her armor and boots to make it feel as though her flesh was being boiled. *I can't stay here much longer. And if these flames start to spread, I wouldn't put it past the guard to go ahead and activate the force field without my signal.*

Looking up, she saw that an Imperial Guard ship was approaching this position. *I'd better hurry.*

There was only one place left to look: the aircar itself. Climbing over debris, she pushed her way into it, jumping over burning consoles, coughing half a dozen times as she inhaled smoke. She cursed herself for not holding her breath, as she knew full well what kind of damage that smoke and heat would do to her throat and lungs, but done was done. She had to find the pilot—if he was alive, he needed to answer for his crime. If he was dead, then he already had.

She found him draped over the flight console. He had no pulse and wasn't breathing. She pried open his eyelids, and both pupils were dilated.

That gave her pause. Pupillary dilatation normally did not occur for approximately seven hours postmortem. *If his pupils are blown now, it could be herniation of the brain stem through the foramen magnum. An intracranial bleed?*

She swept her eyes over the surrounding area: the console, the viewscreen (currently showing the static of a destroyed image translator), the chair. Of course, there was no restraining harness—that was a battle even she gave up fighting. She saw no sign of an impact on any of the bulkheads or equipment.

Lightly brushing aside the pilot's shock of black hair, she saw a stellate bursting of the skin along his crest. A moment later, she was able to pick out a minute stain of blood amid the static on the viewscreen. The wound itself showed only oozing, nothing that suggested a massive bleed. But head wounds bled insanely. *Which means his heart had stopped pumping prior to his impact with the viewscreen.* The impact itself was certainly enough to kill him all by itself. And then there were the blown pupils . . .

So perhaps an intracranial bleed, something that would create enough pressure that the only direction the brain could go is down. A herniation of the brain stem through the foramen magnum, and death would've been nearly instantaneous—no chance for him even to react.

To make matters worse, this wasn't just some Klingon flying an aircar into a building. He wore Defense Force armor and had the rank insignia of a captain. Under other circumstances, she might be willing to let the flames consume his unworthy corpse, but all was not as it appeared here. She needed to perform a proper autopsy, one that she knew would not happen unless she took it upon herself.

A whooshing sound, and then B'Oraq found herself thrown backward for the second time in ten minutes. The hatch to the aft compartment had collapsed, and the fires from the thrusters that had built up back there exploded into the fore compartment.

Ignoring the pain in her head, the nausea that started to well up her throat, and the way the aircar was suddenly jumping all around, B'Oraq signaled the *Gorkon* to have her and the body next to her beamed up.

As soon as the transporter beam caught her, she felt relief at being out of the heat of the fire. Materializing in the comparative cool of the medical bay was a relief. But why did the nausea remain? And her head was pounding . . .

"B'Oraq to . . . to K'Nir."

"*Doctor?*"

"Signal the . . . the Imperial Guard ship hovering

over Novat . . . tell them they're . . . they're authorized to . . . to put the fire out."

"Yes, Doctor. And Commander Kurak wishes to speak to you."

Two Valatras walked up to her and said, "B'Oraq?"

"I'm fine, Valatra, I—"

Then the world went black.

FIFTEEN

Imperial Intelligence shuttlecraft D'jaq
Interstellar space

Both Tokath and Ba'el asked to be allowed to accompany Toq to find Gorrik. Carraya was their home, and it was gone now. Tokath had said, "I have nowhere else to go," and Ba'el had said she would stay with her father. Toq had objected to Ba'el coming but did so only to Tokath, not wishing to offend his childhood friend.

"Where would you have her go, Toq?" Tokath had asked him. "If she travels to either of our empires, she will be an outcast. There is only one place where she would be welcome, and that place was destroyed."

"She could go to the Federation. Ambassador Worf—"

That had brought Tokath up short. "*Ambassador* Worf?"

"Yes. He is now the Federation ambassador to the empire, and he could easily facilitate her entry into—"

In a cold and quiet voice that Toq knew meant the old Romulan was greatly displeased, Tokath had then said, "She will *not* live in the Federation, and she will not do anything facilitated by that *veruul*."

Toq should have realized that Tokath would hold a bit of a grudge, since Worf's presence had badly disrupted life on Carraya.

His retuning of the sensors having been a success, Toq had gone with Tokath and Ba'el into one of Lorgh's shuttles, the *D'jaq*, and set a course along the warp trail of Gorrik's ship.

There was only one star system on the projected course: the Kovris system, which was even farther outside Klingon space than Carraya was. At the *D'jaq*'s maximum speed, it would take two days to reach it.

Ba'el was sleeping in the aft compartment when Toq finally asked Tokath the question he'd been wondering about for several years now. "Why did you keep the camp a secret?"

"You know the reasons, Toq. The disgrace—"

"No, I mean after the Dominion War began—after the Romulans joined the alliance against the Dominion. Why keep it a secret then? Why hide from the war that—"

"Hiding from the war was the camp's reason for existing, Toq."

Toq let out a breath through his teeth. "But there *was* no war! Yes, there were tensions between our peoples—there always have been, and I suspect there always will be. But the Dominion threatened the entire quadrant. Once there truly *was* a war—"

"That was not our concern," Tokath said calmly. "The only effect the war had on us was that the supply ships came less often. But we made do, as we always did."

Putting the *D'jaq* on autopilot, he turned to face Tokath, who sat in the copilot's seat. There were four seats in this front compartment, with four bunks in the rear, and very little space to move around. "What would you have done if the war found you? The front lines of the battle were in the Bajoran sector, which is only a few light-years from here."

"No one knew of this place, save for—"

"A few Romulans. And if the Dominion conquered Romulus? Your people entered the war because of intelligence that the Vorta were targeting your homeworld. One civilian ship was able to destroy everything you built in less than an hour. What do you think would have happened if it was a Jem'Hadar strike ship?"

Slowly, his deep voice like ice, Tokath said, "But it was not, Toq. Even as conflict raged all across the stars, we remained safe." Tokath looked away from Toq, staring out of the viewscreen. "When we find this Gorrik, I will learn who it is who betrayed us before I kill him."

"That is my desire as well," Toq said, also facing forward again, disengaging the autopilot. "First blood should go to you, as leader of the camp."

Tokath gave a half smile at that. "How very Klingon of you."

"I *am* a Klingon, Tokath."

"More's the pity."

Putting the autopilot back on, Toq whirled on the man who once ruled his existence. "I am *proud* of what

I have accomplished! I am a warrior in the Defense Force, first officer of one of the finest ships in the fleet. I am also a champion hunter. I became alive in the empire, Tokath, in a way I *never* could have living on your prison camp."

Continuing to look straight ahead, Tokath said, "Yet you kept our secret. Why?"

Toq could not believe he could even ask the question. "I gave you my word, as did Worf and all those who went with him. Did you think so little of us that you expected us to go back on it? We left Carraya because we wanted to be *more* Klingon, not less."

"It has been my experience that Klingon honor is observed more in theory than it is when faced with the realities of life."

Readjusting the *D'jaq*'s course slightly, Toq said, "I have observed that as well—occasionally. But you *knew* us, Tokath."

Now, Tokath looked at him again. "Yes, I did know you once, Toq. And I saw the person I once knew transform before my very eyes into a stranger. You lived among us for all your young life up to that point, yet a few days with that Worf creature, and you betrayed us."

Aghast, Toq said, "I *never* betrayed you! Worf simply opened my eyes to—"

"To what? Hunting like a cave dweller? Embracing violence like some kind of animal? Nonsense stories about an impossible honor told around primitive campfires?" Tokath shook his head. "When I offered to house the Khitomer survivors, I did it because I could offer them a better life than the one they left behind."

Toq stared for several seconds at Tokath. "I never realized."

"Realized what?" Tokath asked, eyebrow raised.

"You really hate us."

"Of course not, Toq, I—"

Throwing up his arms, Toq asked, "What else am I to make of the contempt with which you dismiss the very heart of what makes us—of what makes *me* a Klingon?" He shook his head. "All my life, I respected you. Do you know that I was just yesterday thinking about how living with you made me appreciate Romulans far more than my fellow Klingons, who view you with nothing but contempt?"

"And can you express this appreciation openly? Or do you risk being stabbed in a back alley duel?" Tokath's contempt dripped from his every word.

"Sometimes," Toq said, remembering more than one mess hall conversation with Leskit and Rodek on that very subject. "And I have that appreciation because of *you*. I see Romulans as *people*, not as enemies to be despised." Turning away from Tokath, he said, "I had hoped that respect was returned. I see now that I was a fool to think that—and I must wonder if that respect is truly deserved."

"I did what no one else has done, Toq. Nowhere else in history have Romulans and Klingons lived in peace as they did on Carraya."

"Yes, they have, Tokath. The Klingons and Romulans are allies now and have been since the war."

"An alliance of necessity—oh, yes, Toq, I am familiar with what happened. But there was no respect between our two peoples, only uniting against a common foe. The war has been over less than a year. I can assure you that within another year, our people will be at each other's throats once again."

Toq stared at Tokath, and he realized that, just as Worf opened his eyes that day on the hunt and allowed him to see for the first time, he was now truly seeing Tokath for what he was. "Our people did *not* live side by side. Our parents were your prisoners. And we were not allowed to be Klingons. We were no different from the Romulans in the camp. When Worf gave his word to you, you scoffed, as if honor meant nothing to you—and now I realize that it does. We were *not* living in harmony, Tokath, we were assimilated!"

Tokath rose quickly to his feet. "I will not be judged by you, Toq—you who abandoned your home, and for what? Honor? Glory? Of what use are such commodities?"

"If you have to ask that question, then you do not understand us."

"I am not a Klingon, Toq. I am under no obligation to understand you—nor do I particularly want to."

"Why not?" Toq also got up, wishing to look Tokath in the face. "You accepted the responsibility of caring for the Khitomer survivors. It seems to me that you *should* have at least attempted to learn of our ways." He smiled. "Unless, of course, you were only a jailer, and we were only your prisoners. In which case, can you blame me for wanting to escape, once I saw your cage for what it was?"

Tokath apparently had nothing to say to that, for he got up without a word and moved to the aft section.

Left alone, Toq sat back down and pulled out the padd Lorgh had given him, which had the complete dossier on the House of Gannik.

As he read on, Toq grew confused. Then he grew angry—even more than he had been when speaking to Tokath.

The aft door rumbled aside, and Ba'el came out. "Hello, Toq." She sat in the copilot's seat that her father had vacated.

"You do not wish to remain with your father?"

Ba'el stared at the viewscreen. "I love the way the stars streak by like that."

"They are not truly moving," Toq said. "It is merely the distortion of warp space."

"I understand the theory, Toq," Ba'el said with an annoyed glance. Then she looked back at the stars. "I've been doing a lot of studying the past few years. But sometimes it's nice just to *look* and enjoy what you see instead of trying to look below the surface."

"You have become philosophical."

"I've had a lot of time to myself—it makes it easy to think."

Toq stared at her. "What do you mean?"

Ba'el took a deep breath. Toq hadn't really been paying attention before, as he was focused on larger concerns, but Ba'el's eyes, which used to be bright and cheerful, were now sad and lonely.

After several moments, she finally answered his question. "After you left, Father and I stopped speaking. He said that if it weren't for me, Worf wouldn't have been able to do what he did. And I don't think he forgave me joining you and the others in the group to be sacrificed with Worf." She gave a small smile, but it was a sad one. "Or what I asked him afterward."

Gently, Toq said, "What did you ask him?"

Still staring at the stars, Ba'el said, "I asked him, 'Would you have given the order if I hadn't stood with them?'" Now she looked at Toq, and her eyes were sadder than ever. "To this day, he hasn't answered. We've hardly spoken since."

And yet, he threw himself over you, intending to sacrifice his own life in the hope of saving yours. Toq wondered if Ba'el realized that but thought it best not to bring it up. It wasn't as if he had any great desire to effect a reconciliation between these two, given his recent conversation with Tokath.

Ba'el stared ahead again. "Mother left him after that. Oh, she stayed in the camp, obviously—until one day she took that rusty *d'k tahg* out of its trunk and plunged it into her chest."

Toq's eyes widened, and he felt a rumbling in his stomachs. "Gi'ral killed herself?"

Ba'el snorted. "Her last words were that her place in *Gre'thor* had been guaranteed from the day she was captured. Assuming you believe that. I certainly don't. After you left, those of us who stayed behind asked L'Kor to tell us more of the stories Worf told us, and I learned all about the afterlife and honor and Kahless. And they're good stories—L'Kor didn't tell them as well as Worf did, but I enjoyed them." She looked away. "I can't *believe* them, though. Not the way Worf did."

Toq leaned toward her. "Do you wish to know the truth? I do not believe them, either."

Ba'el stared at him. "And here I thought you'd completely transformed yourself."

"Not completely. Oh, when I am among my fellow warriors, then I speak as if I believe in *Sto-Vo-Kor* and *Gre'thor*, and when my comrades die in battle, I pry their eyes open and scream a warning to the Black Fleet that another warrior is crossing the River of Blood." He let out a sigh. "But I do not truly believe it. When you die, you die."

"Like everyone on Carraya," Ba'el said in a whisper that Toq imagined was a haunted one.

"I know," Toq said in almost as quiet a voice. "I still have trouble believing it is true."

"I watched them die, Toq. All of them." She turned her sad eyes to look at him. "I've never seen anyone die before. It's so different than what I was expecting." Again, she looked out at the stars. "The only home I've ever known is gone, Toq. I suppose this is how Worf felt."

Frowning, Toq asked, "What do you mean?"

"After Khitomer. That was another story L'Kor finally told us: about thousands of Klingons who died at the Khitomer outpost thanks to a Romulan attack. An attack that my father was a part of. Even if we were speaking then, we would not have been after that. I cannot look at my father without seeing a murderer. All those people—including Worf's parents." She stared at Toq. "You know, he never told me?"

"Who?"

"Worf. Never once did he tell me that his parents were killed at Khitomer." She shook her head. "So much made sense after that. Once L'Kor told me that, I realized that Worf would never have been able to live with us. Even if Father wasn't the one directly responsible, he was part of what took his parents away from him." Ba'el stared at Toq. "You said 'fellow warriors,' Toq, and you're wearing a soldier's uniform. What are you now that you no longer try to spy on me when I bathe?"

Toq looked away. "You knew I did that?"

"I could hardly not. You were never very subtle, Toq."

"Perhaps not. At first, I was taken in by a family friend of Worf's—Lorgh, the man who commanded the ship that rescued you and Tokath. I harnessed my hunting skills for many turns and soon attained championship standing."

"Worf chose his hunting partner well," Ba'el said.

Toq went on, telling her of his enlistment in the Defense Force during the Dominion War and his assignment to the *Gorkon* after the war's end. "A blind old razorbeast named Kegren served as second officer—until I challenged him. After I slew his honorless self, Captain Klag made me his replacement."

"You *killed* him?" Ba'el shook her head. "And this is how you advance in rank?"

"One of the ways, and only when the warrior in question is unworthy. I became first officer after the previous one, Kornan, died nobly in battle. I am honored to carry on for him and to speak for the crew."

"It sounds so . . . so *brutal*. You advance through the death of others."

Toq shrugged. "We are warriors. Battle is our life."

"Farming used to be your life."

Smiling, Toq said, "After that, it was hunting. If I have learned anything, Ba'el, it is that life is never constant."

"What about Worf?" she asked.

Toq quickly filled Ba'el in on Worf's life since Carraya. She looked disheartened when Toq said that he had married, yet sad when he told her that his mate died a year later. However, she was not at all surprised at his new career as a diplomat.

"It's a good use of his skills," Ba'el said. "I didn't see it then, but looking back on it now? He manipulated everyone in that camp in order to get his way. So he represents the Klingon Empire?"

"No. He serves as the Federation ambassador *to* the empire."

"The which ambassador?"

Blinking, Toq said, "The Federation. That is where Worf has lived most of his life. He was six when he was at Khitomer, and he was rescued by a Starfleet vessel and brought to live in—"

Now Ba'el's eyes were a mass of confusion. "Toq, what are you *talking* about?"

"Ba'el," Toq said slowly, "there are others in the galaxy besides Klingons and Romulans. The United Federation of Planets is a nation of many species, and there is also the Cardassian Union, the Breen Confederacy, the Tholian Assembly, the Ferengi Alliance, the—"

Holding up her hands, Ba'el almost screamed. "Stop! Toq, this is madness!"

"No, it is not. I have met these people—in some cases fought against them, in others fought by their side. There was a great war, where an empire from halfway across the galaxy—"

"Stop!" Ba'el got to her feet, her hands still raised as if defending herself from an attack. "Why did no one tell me of this?"

"I was surprised, too." Toq also rose and reached around her upraised arms to put his hands on her shoulders. "But that is the way of the universe. And you must adapt to it."

Ba'el closed her eyes. "I do not believe it. Yet *another* lie." She stared back at the aft door. "I should never have stayed. I should have left with Worf, but I wanted to remain with my family. Besides, was there truly a place for me out there where Klingons and Romulans hated each other?" She shook her head. "But now you tell me there is more to the galaxy. I had other choices besides my parents' two worlds, didn't I?" She scrubbed her face with her hands. "Worf offered to take me with him—had I known he meant to this Federation, I might have said yes. And it's not like my family was worth staying for," she added bitterly.

An alarm beeped. Toq looked down at the console. "We are approaching the Kovris system." He sat down at the pilot's seat. "Activating cloak."

Ba'el joined him.

After a moment, Toq asked, "Why did you come with me?"

"I owe it to L'Kor. After Father and I stopped talking, L'Kor became my father in all but name. I want to get him back. And all those people who died deserve to be avenged." She ran her hands through her long auburn hair. "I may not be much of a Klingon, but I won't just sit around and let the person who destroyed my home and killed my friends get away with it." She looked at Toq. "After that, Toq, could you do me a favor?"

"Of course."

"Take me to see Worf. He's somewhere nearby, right?"

"He is based in the Federation embassy on Qo'noS. If we survive, I will bring you to him."

Ba'el nodded. "Thank you." She sighed. "If we live. I never used to think like that. And I *still* can't believe that everyone's dead."

Tokath came fore. "I assume by our coming out of warp and cloaking that we have arrived at our destination?"

"Our assumed one, yes," Toq said. "I'm scanning now for Gorrik's ship." After a moment, he smiled. "There it is—a Mark 7 Ferengi Star-Hopper, one running with a Klingon civilian ID. It is in orbit around the fifth planet." He frowned. "There are no life signs on board. Scanning the surface."

"Why would he abandon his ship?" Ba'el asked.

Though he had no answer for Ba'el's question, Toq had found what he was looking for. "The fifth planet is breathable but has no sentient life—except for two Klingon life signs." He looked at the other two. "It makes sense. Gorrik may wish to keep this entire thing secret, and one person can operate the Star-Hopper if he is a talented enough pilot. According to the dossier Lorgh provided me, Gorrik has the skill."

"That works to our advantage," Tokath said. "There are three of us—four, counting L'Kor—and only one of him. It will be a pleasure to kill him."

Toq turned to the console, setting a course for orbit around the fifth planet. "I believe, Tokath, that that is the one thing on which all three of us agree."

SIXTEEN

Tabona's farm
Pheben III

Wol had never seen so much food in one place in her life.

The House of Varnak had had its share of feasts over the years, and no one ever starved in a Defense Force mess hall, but they all paled in comparison to the huge piles of food that were placed all around the big wooden table in the middle of the clearing in front of the farmhouse.

"I can't remember the last time I ate outside," Wol said to Kagak.

The *bekk* said, "I can't remember the last time we ever ate inside on the farm, when it wasn't midwinter." He laughed. "And sometimes, even then, if Grandmother was feeling particularly vicious."

Tabona passed by, carrying another tray, this one piled high with *gagh*—in fact, they were the largest serpent worms Wol had ever seen. The old woman said, "Viciousness got nothin' to do with it, boy. I just don't think folks should eat indoors. Isn't natural."

"We have very little choice aboard ship," Wol said with a smile. "Where did you get those *gagh*?"

"What, these?" Tabona looked down at her tray. "They're all right, I guess. Hurgor brought them. Usually he brings bigger."

Wol's eyes widened as Tabona brought the tray to the already-overloaded table. She didn't think they bred *gagh* that large, much less larger.

She and Kagak were standing between the table and the house. The table sat right in front of the north end of the house, bordered on two sides by farm, and on the fourth by the pathway to the main road, where Wol saw the accursed Vikak still parked. Only the fact that it seemed to be the family's only distance vehicle kept Wol from firebombing the damn thing.

The wooden table was surrounded on each of its two long sides by a bench, with stools on the two ends. It looked like at least thirty Klingons could fit—more if they didn't mind bumping elbows.

She asked Kagak, "How big *is* your family? I didn't see that many bedrooms in the house."

"Two of the neighboring farms also dine here—particularly on a special occasion such as this."

Wol frowned. "What special occasion? I thought *yobta' yupma'* was tomorrow."

Tabona, having somehow contrived to find room for the *gagh* on the table, said, "It's for you, of course. Ain't every day my grandson returns to the nest, and ain't every day we have guests of your caliber. Now what're you standing here for? Sit! Eat!"

Wol let Kagak lead her to an appropriate spot. He sat at one corner, next to one end of the table. Wol sat next to him. She looked around and saw Goran talking to B'Ellor, Kagak's sister. Tabona approached them, waving her arms and pointing at the table.

Shortly thereafter, the two of them walked over, even as Klingons and Phebens started pouring in from all sides—some from the house, some from the farm, some from the path to the road. Everyone's clothes (well, the Klingons' clothes, as Phebens didn't dress themselves) were covered in a certain amount of grime and dirt, adding the peaty aroma that seemed to hang over this place.

People greeted each other with laughs and head butts, and welcomed Kagak with equal enthusiasm. Goran eventually managed to squeeze his way onto one of the benches next to Wol, and B'Ellor took a seat opposite the big man, leaving room for Fuhrman, who sat between her and the head of the table, which Wol presumed to be Tabona's place.

Now seated, Wol had a chance to examine the contents of the table more closely and saw plenty of familiar foods, but the proportion was different from what she was accustomed to. No doubt due to what they produced, there were a lot more vegetable- and grain-based plates. Where such would be only a side dish or garnish at House Varnak or on the *Gorkon*, they were in greater evidence here. She also saw a basket full of *jInjoq* bread—only this had the odd shapes and sizes that indicated that it was handmade. One of House Varnak's chefs had made *jInjoq* by hand; it had been a sad day for Wol when she died.

From the far end of the table, one of the Klingons said, "Hey, Fuhrman, ain't you gonna set traps for the *korvit*? Didn't see any when I walked over here."

Wincing, Fuhrman said, "*QI'yaH*, is that thing back *again?*"

The Klingon nodded. "Ate through half my *khest'n* fence and tore through my *hurkik*."

Another Klingon settled in next to B'Ellor. He had a scar on his cheek and a patch missing on the chin of his beard. "So, you work with Kagak, eh?"

"Yes. And you farm?"

He laughed. "I provide food for the empire, yes." He grabbed some food off a plate and started to move it toward his mouth.

"Kaseli! Stop that!"

Wol turned to see Tabona heading for the table, fury in her eyes.

Quickly, Kaseli threw the food back onto the table.

"You know better than to start eating before we've all sat down," she said as she walked around and hit him on the back of the head. Then she turned to Wol. "Feel free to ignore this *petaQ*, Wol. I wonder why I continue to let him sit at my table."

His mouth widening into a huge grin, one that

accentuated the bald spot in his beard, Kaseli said, "Because you cannot deny my charm?"

"Oh, watch me deny your charm, Kaseli." She rolled her eyes and went back toward the house.

Wol regarded her retreating form with apprehension. "She isn't getting *more* food, is she?"

"Probably," Kagak said. "This is less than we usually have."

Wol swallowed, then said, "It is nice to see that some things remain constant."

"What do you mean?" Kaseli asked.

"On the *Gorkon*," Wol said, "we also do not eat until the appropriate time."

Kagak added, "Though in our case, we wait for a song." He smiled. "When B'Elath sings—"

"We all suffer," Wol said with a laugh, "for B'Elath is a terrible singer. But the day after she sings, we are always victorious in battle."

"So," Kaseli said, "what is it, exactly, that you *do* on that ship? Do you fly it?"

"No, that's for the bridge officers."

"Engineers, then?"

Emphatically, Wol said, "No." She'd managed to avoid encountering Kurak during her tour, but she'd heard plenty of stories about that madwoman. "We are the ship's soldiers—the ground troops who fight our captain's battles."

Kaseli grunted. "Seems to me he should fight his own battles."

Wol bristled. "He does. But most battles require more than one participant."

"So let all the captains do it," Kaseli said with a laugh. "What else do you do?"

"We have many duties—they vary depending on the situation. We guard sensitive areas of the ship, we provide the ship's security, we—"

"So you fight? All day? That is all?"

"That is enough. We fight for the empire."

Kaseli frowned. "Seems risky to me. Doesn't that increase the likelihood that you'll die?"

"Of course." Wol couldn't believe she was even being asked this.

A few other Klingons had sat down around them. One said, "C'mon, Kaseli, that's what the Defense Force is *there* for. To die for us."

"I don't want anyone to die for me," Kaseli said.

Snorting, Wol said, "Trust me, Kaseli, when I die, it won't be for *you*. Besides, I believe your friend meant all the peoples of the empire when he said 'us.'"

The other Klingon asked, "Why do you do it, if it carries such great risk?"

"It is the wish of every Klingon to die in service of the empire."

That got a bark of laughter from Kaseli. "Every Klingon *warrior*, perhaps, but we are not all so fortunate as to be warriors. Besides, I have no wish to die in the service of the empire or anyone else. If I die, who will till the fields for my family?"

The one next to him said, "Any one of a dozen other members of your family, and they'd all do it better than you, you lazy *toDSaH*."

"Hah! I still do it better than you, Kosted."

A Pheben sat next to Kosted, which surprised Wol. Others did likewise. "The *jeghpu'wI'* sits at the table?"

"Of course he does," Tabona said, on her way back from the house. "Where else would he sit?"

The Pheben said, "Tabona honors us by allowing our lowly selves to sit with her."

"Oh, stop that," Tabona said as she placed yet another tray, this one containing a huge *rokeg* blood pie, on the table, squeezing it between the skull stew and the mutant *gagh*. "You work the fields, you eat the food." Then she stood at the stool at the head of the table and shouted, "Everyone sit down! It's time to eat!"

The few who were still standing took their seats on the benches. Only the stool at the other end was left empty. Wol was considering suggesting Goran be allowed to use it—he was straining the capacity of the bench as it was—but assumed that, with this many people, if a seat was left empty, it was done so for a reason.

Everyone quieted down, which was Wol's latest surprise. Even on the *Gorkon*, when the premeal song was sung, no one ever got completely quiet.

Tabona held up a mug that appeared to be empty. In fact, there were mugs throughout the table—much more battered than the ones Wol was used to on the *Gorkon*, though in better shape than the malformed things she was forced to drink from in Krennla—all empty.

"K'Zinn, daughter of Kasara, was my cousin. When we were younger, a tornado came, one that was far stronger than our *yIntagh* of a governor said it would be. The force field generator went out, and K'Zinn immediately, without thought to herself, ran out of the house to repair it. My cousin died that day, as the winds carried her off and straight into a tree. But before that, she fixed the generator. The force field activated, and the crops were saved. It was the day before *yobta' yupma'*, just as it is today, and if the force field hadn't protected the crops, our family would have had nothing—nothing for *yobta' yupma'*, nothing for the market, nothing for our market buyers. We would have had no food for the winter—no surplus crops to store, no crops to sell to pay for food. That would have been the end of us. We continue to live because she died. She cannot drink with us, nor eat with us, so the first drink is empty to honor her!"

Everyone raised their mugs and shouted, "K'Zinn!" Wol and Goran said nothing, of course, since they hadn't known what to shout until it was too late. She noticed that the Phebens also joined in the toast.

After that, they all dry-sipped their mugs and threw them aside.

"Now let us eat!" Tabona cried.

Wol held back as everyone else dove into the food, grabbing bits of everything and tossing it onto their plates. *Another way in which this is familiar*, she thought.

She leaned over to Kagak. "I have never heard of that manner of tribute before."

"Really?" Kagak asked through a mouth filled with some kind of vegetable Wol belatedly realized was a *gonklik*—she was used to them being sliced. "It is an old tradition—I thought everyone did it."

Wol shook her head. "In all my days, I never saw such a thing." She smiled. "However, I do like it."

Once the initial frenzy had died down, Wol grabbed some food at random, though she made sure to get some of the *gagh*. Her teeth bit into the wriggling creature's flesh, and the worm's blood was rich and thick, saltier than usual. "Tabona, you must tell me where you get this *gagh*."

From down the table, someone said, "Oh, no! You let the Defense Force know about this, and they'll buy them all up! We'll never see it again!"

"I have no intention of telling the Defense Force," Wol said, "merely my ship's quartermaster."

Several laughed at that.

B'Ellor said to Goran, "Have you always been a soldier?"

"No," Goran said, his mouth full of skull stew. "My parents were prison guards on Rura Penthe, and I did as they did. Then they were killed, and I left to join the Defense Force."

Her eyes growing wide, B'Ellor said, "You've *been* to Rura Penthe?"

"I was born there."

Kaseli said, "I've heard that all the prisoners there are killed by wild animals and eaten for food by the guards."

Goran straightened with outrage, making his already large form seem considerably larger. "That is not true!"

"I don't see why not," a Pheben said. "Why else have the prisoners?"

"They do the work," Goran said. "The prison has to be maintained."

"Why?" Kaseli asked. "They cannot leave the prison, and the prison is maintained only so it can house the prisoners."

Fuhrman gave one of his ground-shaking laughs, though it was muted in the greater ambient noise of Tabona's supper table. "Someone mark this day down! Kaseli has said something intelligent!"

"No, he hasn't," Wol said with a wicked grin as she swallowed more *gagh*.

"Really?" Kaseli chewed on a piece of *zilm'kach*. "I'd say my logic is quite sound."

"Were this a Vulcan supper table, that would matter—but no Vulcan would have the stomach for Klingon food." Wol chewed on another serpent worm for good measure. "And even if it were a Vulcan table, you would be cast away from it like a fool, because your logic is flawed. The prisoners on Rura Penthe are there to be punished for their crimes."

"Is death not the ultimate punishment?" Kosted asked.

Goran answered that. "Death is an *honor*. It should not to be wasted on the likes of prisoners."

"Death is death," said the Pheben who sat on the other side of B'Ellor from Goran. "Why does it matter?"

"*Because* death is death," Wol said. "It is the only surety of life—that it will end. So how you achieve it matters more than anything."

Kaseli laughed, spitting *grapok* sauce. "I suppose you

have to believe that in order to fight the idiotic battles of the Defense Force."

Goran slammed a fist on the table, shaking several pieces of food off their trays and plates. "We fight for the honor of the empire!"

"And to preserve it," Kagak said. "And you're all wasting your breath. Kaseli has made this argument before."

"Yes, right before you decided to throw your life away," Kaseli said.

Fuhrman said, "It is his life to throw, Kaseli! Besides which, you'll notice he is still here!"

"For now." He turned to Wol. "Tell me, how many of your soldiers died in order to defend some aliens you'd only just met? Yes, I know all about your ship. We could hardly not, what with them composing operas about it."

"Operas?" Wol frowned as she tore off a piece of the still-warm *jInjoq*.

Tabona said, "On Ty'Gokor a month or two ago, they debuted a new Reshtarc opera about your ship's battle at San-Tarah."

"It's now playing on Qo'noS," B'Ellor said, "at the opera house in Krennla."

Kagak turned to Wol. "Didn't G'joth say his sister performed at that opera house?"

Wol nodded absently as she chewed the soft, delicious *jInjoq* but was focused on Kaseli. "You feel that we fought for no reason?"

"The world was conquered anyhow. Why sacrifice so many warriors like that? Your captain should have just done what the general told him to do and taken the planet."

"He gave his word," Wol said.

"So?"

Wol laughed. "Strange sentiments from a man who shares a table with *jeghpu'wI'*."

Kaseli snarled. "That is different."

"How? Would you renege on a promise made to any of the Phebens sitting at this table?"

Tabona glared at Kaseli. "Not if he wants to ever sit at this table again."

"Elddeh, Kralc, and Atorec have earned the right to be treated as equals by laboring with us to provide the empire's food." Kaseli angrily grabbed some more of one of the salads and slammed it onto his plate.

"The San-Tarah earned the same respect from us," Wol said. "Without honor, we are nothing."

"Oh, I wouldn't go that far," Tabona said. "But without honor, we're not really Klingons, are we?"

Kaseli shook his head. "I still say it was ridiculous for so many to die that day. It was a waste."

"Was it?" Wol stuffed another handful of *gagh* into her mouth, then said, "I might say the same of Tabona's cousin."

Tabona threw her food onto her plate. "What?"

"She threw her life away to activate a generator. Why would she do that? It was a waste of a life."

"If she had not done that—" Tabona started, but Wol cut her off.

"Yes, yes, so you said, Tabona, but as Kaseli pointed out, it was a waste. True, this farm might not have survived, but there are other farms on this planet, and more still elsewhere in the empire. People would not starve. Why should a woman, who was obviously important to all of you, or you would not have waited to eat until proper tribute was paid to her memory, allow herself to be killed like that?"

"She sacrificed herself for—" Kaseli started.

"For this farm, yes. For something she believed in. If I dismiss that, Tabona looks on me with disfavor." Wol looked over at Tabona, who in fact was no longer regarding her that way, having figured out what she was talking about, which was more than could be said for Kaseli. Wol continued: "Yet you feel free to dismiss our sacrifices, when we fight for the very foundation of what makes our empire strong."

"So say you." Kaseli bared his teeth. "I say that the food we grow makes our empire strong!"

Several people cheered raggedly at that. Tabona was not one of them. She looked at Wol, then looked at Kagak. "I like these two *much* more than the last ones you brought home."

Wol inclined her head. "Thank you, Tabona."

Kosted asked, "How long will you be staying?"

"I do not know," Wol said honestly. Her first instinct upon arrival was to leave the morning after *yobta' yupma'*, but the more she sat at this table, and the more of this excellent food she ate, the less she wanted to leave. The *Gorkon* would be under repair for half a month, after all.

"You are welcome to stay as long as you like," Tabona said.

"If you remain for a few days, you can see the tournament!" Fuhrman bellowed.

Kagak practically bounced in his seat. "There's a tournament? Excellent! I was hoping to see one!"

"What manner of tournament?" Wol asked.

"Fistfighting," Kaseli said. "We've had one every season for almost twenty turns now. And I wouldn't get too excited. Lak's going to win anyhow."

B'Ellor said, "He can't possibly win all of them."

"He's won the last seven," Fuhrman said dolefully. "I faced him last time, and he nearly killed me!"

Wol chewed thoughtfully on a piece of blood pie that she'd liberated from the tray. "How does the tournament work?"

Tabona said, "It happens in the market circle. Whoever won the previous tournament fights until he is defeated. Any may challenge him, as long as he is a farmer on this world."

"No outsiders?"

"This is *our* tournament," Tabona said fiercely. She smiled. "Besides, the side bets are how many of us make our money."

"Or we would," Fuhrman grumbled, "if we won any of them. With Lak's victories, it becomes difficult to lay a wager!"

"True," Tabona said. "We could use some better clothes for this winter. We almost lost B'Ellor last winter when the worst of the frost came."

Goran turned to look down at Kagak's sister. "That is awful. You should wear furs."

"Furs are expensive, boy," Tabona said. "The animals

hereabouts have weak pelts, and importing real fur from offworld costs coin we don't have."

"Huh." Goran scratched his chin. "On Rura Penthe, we just hunted for fur. It cost us nothing."

"At last," Kaseli said, "a reason to move to Rura Penthe."

To B'Ellor, Goran said, "I still have one of my fur cloaks. If you want, I will give it to you, so you do not freeze again this winter."

"That won't be necessary," Tabona said quickly before B'Ellor could speak. "You should not give up your trophy."

"But I want to." Goran sounded confused. "I do not need it anymore. I serve on a ship where it does not get cold."

Chuckling, Kosted asked, "What if they send you to a cold planet to kill more people for the empire?"

"Our armor protects us," Kagak said. "Besides, the big man's cloak would be considered an improper addition to the uniform. I am stunned that you continue to carry it, Goran."

"I killed the *torgot* myself."

Kaseli sputtered his *zilm'kach*. "You killed a *torgot*?"

Goran nodded.

B'Ellor stared up at him. "That's incredible."

"It was not difficult. I am the biggest and the strongest."

Tabona said, "A pity he cannot fight Lak."

Angrily, Fuhrman said, "I will defeat him this time, Grandmother!"

"You said that last season, and the season before that, boy, and yet he still reigns."

The meal continued on for some time. At one point, Tabona told Fuhrman and Kagak to get the torches, which confused Wol; Pheben had only just started to set in the west. Soon, though, the sky was painted the color of blood, and darkness came alarmingly quickly. Every once in a while, Tabona rose and fetched something else from the house, to the point where Wol swore there was more food on the table at meal's end than there was at its commencement. She also brought out a fresh set of mugs and a barrel full of homemade *chech'tluth*, which was far stronger than almost anything Wol had ever consumed.

When she said as much, Kagak asked, "Leader, when did you ever have anything stronger than *this*?"

"It was in Krennla," she said.

"Oh." Kagak looked away and sipped some more.

Kaseli, though, asked, "Is that all? Will you not tell us the story of your drunken exploits on the homeworld?"

"No," Wol said, "I will not." That required her to remember the Kitchen, and that she would not do.

"Is this how you repay our hospitality, Wol?" Tabona asked. "By denying us a story?"

Wol smiled. "I will gladly tell you stories of my experiences in the Defense Force. I will tell you of how we took Mempa IX from the Jem'Hadar. I will tell you of my training at the hands of a brutal *QaS DevwI'* named Skragg. I will tell you of how we held the line on San-

Tarah. I will tell you of how I escaped an Elabrej scientist who tried to experiment on me. I will even tell you tales of a highborn fool of a woman who let herself be impregnated by a lowborn man who was not her mate. But I will not tell you of Krennla."

Laughing, Kaseli said, "I want to hear the one about the high-born fool of a woman."

"That's a redundancy," Kosted said. "All highborn are fools."

As laughter spread around the table, Wol reached and grabbed some of the delicious *gagh*, of which there seemed to be an infinite supply. She was starting to suspect that the worms on the bottom were breeding.

After swallowing two more, she said, "Very well. I heard this story for the first time when I was training as a soldier under Skragg. It was our last night before training ended, and those of us who survived would be moving on to our first assignments the next morning. We stayed up all night drinking and singing and telling stories. This was one of the stories told."

The truth, of course, was that Wol had told the story herself—though, technically, it was indeed the first time she'd heard it, as she had never told it to a soul prior to that. She told it that night only because she had had a great deal of very bad bloodwine.

Pausing only to lubricate herself with a quick sip of the homemade *chech'tluth*, Wol began her tale. "It is said that one should mate only with one to whom one is willing to devote one's life. In fact, Kahless himself said that mating without love is living a lie, and lying is the greatest dishonor."

From down the table, someone said, "But what if he was lying when he said that?"

Laughter echoed into the darkening sky. Wol said, "Perhaps. But whether or not Kahless was lying, his words are not always observed in the breach. After all, the House of Varnak was an old and noble House, and they could not let their daughter mate with just anyone. It did not matter to Koradan or B'Etakk whether or not their daughter Eral cared about Vranx. What did matter was that Vranx was of the House of Jorn, a very strong House indeed. The alliance of these two Houses would be good for everyone."

"Obviously not," Tabona said wryly, "or you would not be telling the story."

"Indeed," Wol said, "though my words *should* have been true. Vranx wanted the union, the head of the House of Jorn wanted the union, Koradan and B'Etakk wanted the union."

"But this Eral did not?" Fuhrman asked.

"No. She had given her heart to another. He was a servant in House Varnak, a man named Kylor. He was strong where Vranx was weak, solicitous where Vranx was uncaring, passionate where Vranx was timid."

"So why didn't she mate with Kylor?" someone asked.

"Oh, she would have if that were possible. But women from noble Houses do not mate with servants. And alliances between noble Houses are not sundered by women who do not understand their place." She smiled. "Of course, Eral was a fool. She could have simply had Kylor be her bedmate. Women had been doing this since long before Kahless's time. But they were discreet, for to do otherwise was to bring dishonor upon the House, and that could not be tolerated. However, their discretion was sufficiently great that the thought of following their example never even occurred to Eral."

"Are all highborn women that stupid?" Kaseli asked.

"No, but this story is not about them."

Several people chuckled at Wol's response.

She went on: "This bit of foolishness was compounded by another. Eral became with child by Kylor. Vranx was surprised when a DNA test showed that the child was not his—even though Eral had never been able to bear the notion of taking him to her bed." Wol sipped some more of her drink. She found it went down easier the third time, due in part to it numbing her entire throat. "The child was taken from her, Kylor was put to death—and Eral was cast out."

"They didn't kill her?" Kosted asked. "I thought that was the answer to everything for you warrior types."

"No," B'Ellor said, "she probably killed herself. In the stories, the lovers always give each other *Mauk-to'Vor.*"

"Sadly," Wol said, "Eral was not that bright. Besides, Kylor had already been put to death, so there was no one to do this for her. Instead, she was cast out, never to be heard from again."

"They should have let her stay," one of the Phebens said. "Didn't they lose the alliance with the House of Jorn?"

Surprised that a Pheben would catch that nuance, Wol said, "Yes, but that would have happened in any event. Vranx was dishonored by the behavior of a member of the House of Varnak. The alliance was dust." She smiled. "But the House paid the price for their betrayal of Eral, for they cast their lot in with Morjod when he attempted to remove Martok from the chancellor's chair. Like all those who supported the traitor, the members of the House were put to death, the House dissolved, its lands and assets seized by the High Council."

"Sounds like a happy ending to me," Kagak—who knew the whole story—said with a smile.

"So in the end, Eral was the only one who lived?" B'Ellor asked.

"Yes."

"It isn't very romantic," she said.

"Oh, if you wanted a romantic story," Wol said, "I would have told a different one." Recalling the one that had been told right before hers during that all-night celebration, she said, "Like the one about Maelgwyn and Gha'rek, who both loved B'Urad."

Wol continued telling that story. At one point, Tabona came out with what looked like *racht*—only it was dead. Worse, it looked as if it had been frozen and dipped in something.

"Candied *racht*," Kagak whispered to her when she cut off her storytelling to stare at the platter. "I've been *waiting* for this. It is the most wonderful thing you will ever eat in all your days, Leader."

The moment the platter touched the table, a dozen hands grabbed at the dead *racht*, a concept that made Wol feel a bit ill. But she would not insult Tabona's hospitality—and she could not deny the looks of pleasure from those around her who ate the candied *racht* with pleasure—and so she grabbed one and bit down on it.

Wol had never had anything this delicious in her life. The tough flesh of the *racht* mixed perfectly with the sweetness of the coating. She chewed through one serpent quickly and then grabbed a handful more before they were all gone.

Perhaps this will not be so bad after all, she thought.

SEVENTEEN

I.K.S. Gorkon
Praxis Station, in orbit of Qo'noS

Kurak stomped toward the medical bay. She had waited
a full day for this. Her initial attempts had been stymied
by B'Oraq being unconscious. However that *petaQ* Valatra had just informed her that B'Oraq was awake. She
also said that the doctor could not see her right now,
but Kurak was hardly about to listen to the words of a
physician whom she outranked and who wasn't even assigned to this ship.

The medical bay doors rumbled aside to reveal
B'Oraq sitting at her desk, talking with someone on a
comm screen. Valatra and that civilian she'd brought
with her were checking on the patients in the medical
bay, many of whom seemed healed enough to Kurak's
untrained eye.

"B'Oraq," she said, "I will speak to you."

Holding up a hand, B'Oraq said, "I will be with you in a moment. Cou—"

Kurak stepped forward, her arm gripping her wrist. "Now, Doctor, this can wait no longer."

The voice on the comm screen said, *"What is that noise I hear in the background?"*

Her eyes smoldering, B'Oraq said, "It is the *Gorkon's* chief engineer, Councillor Krozek. I am sure she has what she believes is important ship's business to discuss."

As she walked closer to the desk, Kurak saw the emblem that indicated that the communication was with the Great Hall, and based on B'Oraq's words, it was a member of the High Council to whom she was speaking. With the greatest reluctance, Kurak said, "I will wait."

At no point during this conversation did B'Oraq take her eyes off the viewscreen. "You were saying, Councillor?"

"I was saying, Doctor, that you may not speak to Kryan. The actions of Captain Stren speak for themselves."

"No, Councillor, they do not. I am not sure that—"

Krozek looked to Kurak as if he wished to be doing anything other than talking to this woman. *"Doctor, this is a waste of time. Kryan has been removed from the High Council pending his case being heard before the full council session that will commence in one week's time. His brother's actions have brought shame upon his House and upon the High Council."*

"Councillor, I do not believe that Captain Stren's actions were—"

"What you believe is of very little interest to me, Doctor.

220

If you wish to speak on Stren's or Kryan's behalf, you may do so in one week in open council. In the meantime, as part of that session, there will be a meqba'. *We require Captain Stren's body be sent to Doctor Kowag for examination."*

B'Oraq hesitated. "Stren is a patient in my medical bay, Councillor. Standard procedure dictates that I do a full examination and write a report before I release him."

"You are welcome to do so, but do it quickly and send the body to Kowag. That is all."

With that, the screen went dark. Kurak had to admit to taking considerable enjoyment from the look of frustration on B'Oraq's face.

"If you're done wasting the High Council's time," Kurak said with a wicked smile, "perhaps you can take a moment to explain to me why you have commandeered—"

Pointing to the biobeds in the medical bay, B'Oraq said, "Kurak, do you see all these Klingons?"

"Of course."

"Do you know why they're alive right now?"

Pointing at one of them, Kurak said, "That one isn't."

"He was dead before I got to him. But the rest of them are alive because I diverted power to the medical bay. The reason I did it was to save these people's lives, which, you might recall, is my job. The power requirements of the medical bay are less than five percent of what is required to run this entire vessel on its own, and the *Gorkon* is currently receiving a power feed from Praxis Station, is it not?"

"That is hardly the point. You did not receive authorization to—"

"On medical matters, the only authorization that can supersede mine is Captain Klag's. As it happens, I was about to contact him. Would you like to ask him if I did anything wrong?"

"Yes, actually," Kurak said. She was getting tired of this loathsome woman putting on airs as if she were in some way important to the functioning of this ship.

The remarkable thing was that she actually gave any thought *to* the functioning of the ship beyond engineering.

B'Oraq seemed taken aback by Kurak's response. No doubt, the *bolmaq*—as the late, unlamented Nurse Gaj had referred to B'Oraq—had expected her threat to be enough. But Kurak was made of sterner stuff, and if the doctor was going to hide behind the captain's shields, she was damn well going to make her activate them herself.

"Very well," the *bolmaq* said sourly. She turned back to her console and put through a communication to the House M'Raq estates.

Klag's face appeared on the viewer a moment later. *"Greetings, B'Oraq. How goes the rescue?"*

"Well enough, Captain. We were able to save all those that were not already dead. Doctor Valatra in particular is to be commended—she saved one person who was very close to death."

"Doctor," Kurak said, growing impatient with the doctor's bleating.

"Captain, Commander Kurak is with me, and she has a complaint."

"*That is hardly surprising,*" Klag said. "*After all, she is awake.*"

Kurak stepped forward, a growl building in her throat. "That is hardly fair, Captain."

"*It is my ship, Commander—I am under no obligation to be 'fair.' What is the nature of your complaint?*"

Opening her mouth to form a reply, Kurak realized she was going to sound foolish. The captain had begun the conversation asking B'Oraq about the rescue. Of course, it was all over the information net, so Klag could hardly not be aware of it. It had been a huge scandal, as the aircar's pilot, Captain Stren, was the brother of Councillor Kryan. Or, based on what she had overheard, *former* Councillor Kryan. Stren's cowardly, brutal, and wholly unprovoked attack on the city of Novat had resulted in disgrace for the entire House of Kryan. B'Oraq had even been mentioned in some of those reports, especially since one of the people whose lives she had saved was a member of the House of Kurita.

However, the casualness of Klag's tone indicated his likely response to Kurak's protest.

Still, she had come this far. "I do not appreciate medical personnel who are on leave commandeering ship's power without consulting with the chief engineer. We are in the midst of repairs, and it is possible—"

Holding up a hand, Klag said, "*Stop there, Commander. This was a medical emergency, and thus procedure becomes secondary to duty. B'Oraq made the proper decision.*"

That was that, then. Kurak's only option at this point was to challenge either B'Oraq or Klag, neither of which was particularly attractive. She probably could kill B'Oraq, but that would serve only to alienate Kurak farther from a captain she was only just starting to appreciate and under whom she had to serve for another year.

"Very well, Captain."

"Are the repairs proceeding apace?"

"Despite the imbecility of the Praxis Station personnel, who have managed the unbelievable task of being even more incompetent than my own engineers, we have maintained the repair schedule, yes. I believe we will be able to achieve our intended departure date."

"Good. I will inspect the repairs in three days before I go to the Great Hall."

Kurak frowned. "The Great Hall?"

Klag's upswept eyebrows knit into a furrow of annoyance. *"I have been summoned to a meeting with Chancellor Martok and several councillors. The state of the Gorkon's repairs may well be a subject of the meeting, so I wish to be as cognizant as possible of them."*

"I will be happy to assist you in whatever way necessary, Captain." Kurak surprised herself with the words.

Grinning, Klag said, *"That would be appreciated. That will be all, Commander."*

Recognizing the dismissal, Kurak gave the *bolmaq* one final glower before departing.

That was foolish, she thought as she walked down the corridor toward her cabin. *Klag was never going to favor any but the* bolmaq. *If they haven't actually bedded each other, it is only a matter of time before they do, and even if they do not, he will always favor her over me. Indeed, he is likely to favor* anyone *over me*. Kurak could not blame the captain. After all, Kurak had spent most of her tenure on the *Gorkon* trying to do as little work as possible. This was not someone for whom the captain would ever be an advocate. Trust had to be earned, and Kurak had a long way to go to start accumulating such coin.

So why did I revert to my old self and barrel into the medical bay to step on B'Oraq?

She knew the answer: Leskit.

He was right to stay mated to Karreka, Kurak *knew* that. It would be a stain on both their honor if Leskit divorced her.

Yet she could not help but feel that she was being denied true happiness, that what she had with Leskit was an illusion that could be shattered at a moment's notice. The only way she would believe that it wasn't would be for them to mate.

As soon as she walked into her cabin, she noticed the light on the workstation blinking, indicating that she had a message. She activated the station and sat at the desk.

The face of an old woman appeared on the screen. It took Kurak a moment to place it as belonging to Torj, one of the chambermaids at the House Palkar estate.

"Greetings, Kurak. I bring grave news. Moloj is dead."

Kurak hesitated, waiting for the grave news to actually be given. The House *ghIntaq* since before Kurak's father was born, that tiresome old *toDSaH* had been Kurak's nemesis since birth. She had been hoping for his death since her Age of Ascension, and Kurak's only regret at his dying was that it took this long to happen.

In addition to all the other indignities Moloj had visited upon her, he had forced Kurak to stay in the Defense Force until Gevnar came of age, or face discommendation.

That threat, however, died with him. Now the House was in control of—

Of no one. Even as Torj droned on with the irrelevant details of Moloj's joyous passage to *Gre'thor*—Kurak couldn't imagine that *petaQ* getting anywhere near *Sto-Vo-Kor*—Kurak frowned. That there were no able-bodied men of Palkar to serve in the Defense Force also meant that there were none such to take over the House.

Then, suddenly, the frown turned into a smile, as Kurak realized that she could solve all her problems in one *d'k tahg* thrust. She cut off Torj's ramblings and connected to the Great Hall. Krozek said that the next full session of the High Council was in one week, and Kurak needed to be on that session's agenda.

Once that was accomplished, she had to track down a woman in Kopf's Cliff named Karreka.

EIGHTEEN

Kaga's Restaurant
Federation Starbase Deep Space 9

Dorrek sat opposite the Klingon who believed himself to be Rodek, son of Noggra, and said, "You are a difficult man to find, Lieutenant. I had come to your father's home to speak with you but was told you had gone offworld. Luckily for both of us I was able to commandeer a ship to take me to this forsaken place." He glanced around. For years, this station had been a dreary Cardassian backwater. Now, thanks to the discovery of the Bajoran wormhole, it was a major Federation outpost—but still, it was dreary, and still quite far from civilized space.

Rodek bared his teeth. "Is your vessel still under repair from the damage it took thanks to your dishonor?"

Dorrek refused to take the bait. "The *K'mpec* is spaceworthy again; however, it now has a new captain. I have been removed from my post thanks to the actions of a coward."

"And which coward would that be, Captain?" Rodek all but snarled the rank.

The disdain Rodek expressed had not been entirely unexpected. After all, the *Gorkon* fought hard at San-Tarah against Dorrek, General Talak, and their forces, and Rodek was the ship's gunner. If he was not loyal to Klag, Klag would have replaced him rather than promote him as he did.

Still and all, he barged ahead. The plan required it.

"The coward would be my older brother, Lieutenant. Klag, most unworthy son of M'Raq. It is not enough that he soiled the honor of our family, and that of the House of K'Tal, but he did likewise for your family as well."

As expected, Rodek unsheathed his *d'k tahg*. "You dare to insult my captain?"

Holding up a hand, Dorrek said, "Let me speak, Lieutenant. If, after you have heard my tale, you still wish to challenge me for insulting your captain, then I will accept. But you do not know Klag as I do, and you do not know what he has done."

The restaurateur came by then. Dorrek waved him off, but Rodek said, "Bring me a skull stew."

After the chef bowed and went to fill the order, Rodek looked at Dorrek. "I never killed anyone at the supper table, Captain. You have until I finish my stew to convince me that I should not cut you down where you stand."

Dorrek inclined his head. *All I need is for you to sit and listen, and then, at last, vengeance shall be mine!*

He had spent a full day after General Kriz took his command from him going over the service records of the *Gorkon* crew, convinced that there was someone among his brother's subordinates who could be used against him. The best choice seemed to be Rodek, son of Noggra, especially when Dorrek did some investigating and learned that Rodek had not existed until four turns previous.

Now facing the object of his research, Dorrek said, "You were not born with the name Rodek, Lieutenant. Your name is Kurn, son of Mogh, brother of Worf."

"What?" Rodek's mouth widened with shock. "That cannot be!"

"I see the doubt in your eyes that belies your words, my friend. Your ship has transported Worf since his posting to the Federation embassy, has it not?"

"Yes," Rodek said in a low voice. "And he said to me that I reminded him of someone he once knew who was now dead."

"An entertaining fiction," Dorrek said wryly. "When you were an infant, your father, Mogh, as well as his mate, Kaasin, your older brother, Worf, and your family's *ghoj-moq*, all traveled to Khitomer. You were deemed too young to go and stayed with a family friend named Lorgh."

Dorrek could see that Rodek was doing the arithmetic in his head. "The massacre?"

Nodding, Dorrek said, "Yes. The Romulan attack on Khitomer claimed thousands of lives, including those of

Mogh and Kaasin. Your brother survived, rescued by a Starfleet vessel. One of their crew took him in and raised him in the Federation, eventually to become their ambassador to the empire. Lorgh took you as his own son, not telling you the truth until you reached the Age of Ascension. Eventually, you joined the Defense Force as an officer, rising to the rank of captain. But you did not share your true bloodline until your father was accused of betraying Khitomer to the Romulans."

The chef came by with the skull stew, but Rodek barely acknowledged it. It was as Dorrek hoped: the true story was prompting long-dead memories.

But then Dorrek's hopes were dimmed when Rodek said, "I recall none of this."

"Do you recall approaching your older brother, revealing the truth to him, and aiding him when he challenged the High Council's ruling against your father? Do you recall learning the truth—that Ja'rod of the House of Duras, whose son served on the High Council, was the true traitor at Khitomer. Do you—"

"All of this is in the public record, *Captain*," Rodek said, spitting the stew on which he chewed. "Chancellor Gowron restored the House of Mogh in exchange for the House's support in his civil war against Duras's sisters, who tried to put Duras's bastard in the chancellor's chair."

"And when they failed, Gowron ascended to that chair—and appointed *you* one of his councillors."

That seemed to bring the lieutenant up short. "I served on the council?" he asked in a much quieter voice than he'd been using.

"Yes. After commanding the *Hegh'ta* against House Duras's forces, Chancellor Gowron rewarded you with a seat."

Rodek got a faraway look in his eyes, and Dorrek knew that he had, at last, struck home. *Perhaps he has some memories of his time on the High Council.* The reasons why did not matter; Dorrek knew that he had him.

Which was fortunate, as the rest of his story would be pure falsehood.

"And then four years ago, your memories were taken from you by Klag."

That brought Rodek out of whatever fugue he'd been in. "Klag did this to me?"

"Yes. My brother has always been ambitious. Throughout our childhoods, he always needed to be best at everything." That much, at least, was true. "Being an officer was never good enough. Being a ship captain was never good enough. He was not to be satisfied until he ruled the empire. To that end, he had targeted several councillors in the hopes of making them allies. But you refused, so he had you brought here and blackmailed the human doctor into making you into Rodek. Apparently, the doctor had broken some Federation laws regarding genetic enhancement; Klag learned of this and threatened to expose him. He altered your crest and erased your memory."

"No wonder the human was so reluctant to assist me just now." Rodek looked at Dorrek. "He covered it well, but he was hiding *something* from me."

"Now you know what it is. Klag's plans were curtailed by the Dominion War, but after its end, he redoubled his efforts. The House of K'Tal has also stood against him, which is why Klag contrived to have both Captain Kargan and General Talak killed, and I was cast out of my own House. Klag was able to get you assigned to his command so he could keep an eye on you."

Rodek shook his head, his skull stew lying abandoned in front of him. "I was so blind—I saw none of this."

"You saw only what my brother wished you to see, my friend." Dorrek leaned in, speaking in an intense whisper. "There is more. This is by far the worst sin."

Pulling a padd out of a pouch in his armor, Dorrek keyed up the display to show the recording that he'd liberated from the House Noggra estate's security system. He'd called in his last remaining favors with a friend in I.I. to obtain this footage.

He knew what was on it before he'd ever gotten it, of course, by virtue of being in it, which was also why he had the need to edit it.

Rodek—or, rather, Kurn—stared at the padd with eager eyes. He saw Noggra returning home from a trip he'd been on. As he walked in the door, he was assaulted by a figure dressed in black who kept his face obscured behind what Rodek, as a lieutenant in the Defense Force, had to recognize as a holomask. That figure beat Noggra repeatedly, who fell to the floor. The mystery figure then unsheathed a *d'k tahg*, picked Noggra up (though the old man's face was obscured from the security sensor), and stabbed Noggra in his heart.

"*QI'yaH!*" Rodek cried and got to his feet, the padd clattering to the restaurant floor. The non-Klingons in the place looked up in surprise. "Who has done this?"

Leaning over, Dorrek retrieved the padd from the floor and handed it back to Rodek, after thumbing the display back a few seconds so he could see what he missed by tossing it aside.

Rodek snatched it from his hands and started the playback going again. Dorrek heard the words, filtered through the holomask, of the assassin: *"Die, traitor, in the name of the House of M'Raq!"*

Dorrek knew the words well, for he had spoken them himself. He had also spent quite some time interrogating Noggra from behind the holomask before killing him, but that footage was edited out before it was placed on this padd.

Again, Rodek tossed the padd aside. "Klag did this?"

"And more, though not to you. He *must* answer for these crimes, Rodek—or should I say Kurn?"

Shaking his head, the lieutenant clenched his fist. "I no longer know who I am—and for that, and his other crimes, Klag must *pay!*"

Dorrek stood and put a hand on his shoulder. "Then return to the homeworld with me, son of Mogh, that we both may have our revenge."

As the pair of them left the restaurant, Dorrek smiled when his face was out of the lieutenant's sight. *All is going according to plan. Soon Klag will be dead and I will be restored to my rightful place as the head of the House—as it should have been all along.*

Julian Bashir and Ezri Dax entered Kaga's Restaurant but saw no sign of Rodek.

"He said he'd be here," Bashir said. He sighted Kaga

placing three plates on the table of a Bajoran couple and made a beeline for the chef, Dax trailing behind his longer strides.

"Doctor!" Kaga said with a hearty smile. "Do you wish more *zilm'kach?*"

Rubbing his belly from the stomachache that even the thought of more *zilm'kach* gave him, he said, "Er, no, I'm sorry, we're not here to eat. We're looking for someone—a Defense Force lieutenant by the name of Rodek?"

"Yes, he was here, but he left half an hour ago. He had been joined by a captain named Dorrek—who did not eat anything, the *petaQ!*"

"His loss," Bashir said with a small smile. "Did they leave together?"

Kaga nodded. Bashir thanked him, and he and Dax went out onto the Promenade. Dax tapped her combadge. "Computer, locate Lieutenant Rodek and Captain Dorrek."

"Lieutenant Rodek is not on the station. Captain Dorrek is not on the station."

"When did they leave?"

"Unknown."

Bashir muttered a curse. Dax, however, was undaunted. "Computer, check outgoing vessels manifest for both those names."

"Captain Dorrek, son of M'Raq, and Lieutenant Rodek, son of Noggra, are listed as passengers on the Klingon transport vessel Ky'rok."

"Dax to ops."

"Nog here."

"Nog, has the *Ky'rok* left yet?"

"*Uh, hang on, let me check.*" After a pause that seemed interminable to Bashir, the young Ferengi ops officer said, "*I'm sorry, Ezri, it left ten minutes ago, bound for Qo'noS.*"

"Dammit," Bashir muttered.

"Thanks, Nog. Dax out." Looking up at Bashir, Dax asked, "Now what?"

Bashir sighed. "I don't know. I suppose we could contact the *Ky'rok*, but this isn't the sort of thing I want to broadcast over subspace. It would be best if we could bring him back here, but I don't see a Klingon transport turning around for us, do you?"

"No," Dax said emphatically. "But we don't need any of that. Remember, we've got an in at the Federation embassy." She smiled.

Moments later, they were back in the infirmary. Bashir was seated at his desk, Dax standing behind him instructing ops to put a call through to the Federation embassy on Qo'noS.

A human face of mixed ancestry appeared on Bashir's workstation screen a minute or two later. "*Greetings—I am Giancarlo Wu, the ambassador's aide. How may I assist you?*"

Bashir said, "You may put the ambassador on, Mister Wu. My name is Julian Bashir, and this is Ezri Dax. We're—"

"*The ambassador's former crewmates from Deep Space 9, of course. My apologies for not recognizing you straight away. The ambassador is in the midst of a call.*"

Dax said, "We can contact him later, if—"

Keith R.A. DeCandido

Wu gave a small smile. *"No need. I believe the ambassador would find a call from the pair of you a convenient excuse to end a rather onerous discussion. If you'll excuse me for one moment, I'll fetch him."*

"Thank you, Mister Wu," Bashir said.

"Very good, sir." With that, the screen went back to the Federation emblem.

Bashir fidgeted in his seat. Dax, standing behind him, said, "Stop fidgeting, Julian." Bashir sighed.

Worf's face replaced the emblem a moment later. Bashir had served with Worf for four years and had eventually learned to be able to tell the taciturn Klingon's emotions from his eyes. When they widened, he was angry or surprised. When they squinted slightly, he was amused. A deep squint meant caution or respect.

If the expression didn't change, but his features relaxed ever so slightly, then he was glad to see you. That was the expression he had now, though Bashir suspected it wouldn't last very long.

"Doctor. Ezri. It is good to hear from you."

"I doubt you'll say the same once we tell you why we called, Worf." Bashir took a deep breath and filled him in.

Worf squinted deeply as Bashir talked, and somehow he didn't think respect was involved.

Bashir ended by saying, "But by the time we reached Kaga's, he had already left with some captain or other. He's on a civilian transport back to Qo'noS even as we speak."

236

"Which captain was it?" Worf asked, which struck Bashir as an odd question.

"Dorrek," Dax said.

Now the eyes widened.

Dax asked, "Do you know him?"

"Yes." Worf's voice had deepened, which Bashir did not view as a good sign. *"Thank you for bringing this to my attention. I will deal with it."*

And with that, he signed off.

Bashir leaned back. "Good to hear from you, too."

Frowning, Dax said, "Computer, display Klingon Defense Force service record for Captain Dorrek, son of M'Raq."

A moment later, a Klingon military record appeared. Bashir's Klingon was a bit rusty, but he recognized his most recent posting as the *I.K.S. K'mpec.*

"There's a notation in his file that he was discommendated from the House of M'Raq by his older brother, Klag."

Bashir frowned. "I know that name." He rubbed his chin. "Of course, Klag's the captain of the *Gorkon*—that's Rodek's posting!"

"I don't like this," Dax said, arms folded. "Why would Rodek leave without even waiting to speak to you with the disgraced brother of his captain?"

"I couldn't even begin to guess," Bashir said with a smirk, "primarily because the nuances of Klingon feuds give me a headache."

"Me, too." Dax smirked back. She shook her head. "Well, forget it. It's Worf's problem now. Curzon said it best: the only people who can deal with Klingons are Klingons. We've put the ball in Worf's court—let him deal with it."

Nodding, Bashir said, "You're probably right. I just hope for his sake that it's relatively painless."

"That's one thing I can guarantee it won't be," Dax said gravely. "Klingon feuds usually result in much worse than a headache."

NINETEEN

Kenta District
Krennla, Qo'noS

The three boys weren't around when G'joth went to meet them. He had cut short his "consulting" on *The Battle at San-Tarah* in order to fulfill his promise to the boys from the previous day.

Not that he minded having an excuse to bolt from the opera house. In addition to every other indignity, Klivv did no justice to the role of the captain. The only point in his favor was that he had an amazing singing voice.

If only what he sang was worthy of his talent. Not that G'joth was in any position to judge, as he was so disgusted with the whole enterprise that by the time he started actually paying attention to the songs, he was incapable of judging them objectively.

When he came back to the street where he'd met

Kimm, Yorikk, and Gurlk, the boys were nowhere to be found.

The guardsman who'd threatened them, though, was walking casually down the street, brandishing his painstik.

Upon sighting G'joth, the guardsman stood at attention and saluted in the style of the Defense Force, lowering his painstik. "Honored *Bekk*. How may I serve you this day?"

G'joth somehow managed not to roll his eyes. He was the last person in the empire to rail about what constituted a true warrior, but even he would admit that this obsequiousness was unbecoming. "I was supposed to meet the three boys I saw you speak to yesterday, the ones using the chicks for *ghIntaq* practice."

"I did tell them to disperse," the guardsman said matter-of-factly. "They are not foolish enough to disobey me."

"I see."

Inclining his head, the guardsman said, "Is there anything else, honored *Bekk*?"

"No." G'joth snarled and walked away from the guardsman, who continued on his rounds.

For his part, G'joth went to where Mother had told him that Klaad now lived. He wanted to see his childhood friends, and by visiting Klaad he might see Kimm as well and find out what had happened.

Based on the guardsman's words, G'joth had his suspicions.

Klaad's residence was similar to G'joth's own, except the building's façade was much more crumbled. The front door did work, though it took several seconds to slide open at G'joth's approach; the inside smelled far worse. This building also didn't have an intercom, so when G'joth got up to the fifth floor, he had to pound on the door with his fist.

The door was opened with a creak of metal on dry hinges by an old man. G'joth was only a few turns younger than Klaad, but Klaad seemed decades older. G'joth had a warrior's build. Klaad, though, with his ample belly, rheumy eyes, thin hair, and stooped posture, had let age overtake him. Klaad worked at the same construction company as G'joth's father, Ch'lan, and therefore should have been in better condition.

"So," Klaad said, his voice like sandpaper over gravel, "you're here."

"Yes. It is good to see you, Klaad. It has been too long."

"That's hardly my fault." Klaad did not step aside. "What do you want?"

"I had hoped to meet with your son and his friends, as I promised them yesterday, but they were not there, so I thought—"

"What?" Klaad said belligerently. "What did you *think*, G'joth? Do you wish to see my son? Do you?"

Now Klaad stepped aside, allowing G'joth to enter a space that was even smaller than G'joth's own: one common room that included kitchen facilities and two doorways.

As G'joth entered, Klaad called out, "Kimm! Show yourself!"

One of the two doors opened, and G'joth saw a young

man that he was hard-pressed to recognize as the same youth who yesterday was throwing a *ghIntaq* nowhere near its intended target. Welts and bruises covered his beardless face, and one eye had swollen shut. Lacerations covered his arms, and he walked gingerly, as if ribs were broken.

"What happened?" G'joth angrily asked.

"*You* happened, G'joth. You made the guardsman look a fool in front of the children, and the children had to be reminded of his position."

Looking at Kimm, G'joth stared incredulously. "The guardsman did this?"

In a weak voice, Kimm said, "Right . . . right after you left. He . . . he found us and . . . and then he started using his . . . his painstik on Y-Yorikk. I t-tried to . . . to stop him, and he . . ."

Kimm trailed off, but G'joth got the idea. "I will kill him."

"Oh, really?" Klaad asked. "And then what happens, exactly? There are hundreds of guardsmen assigned to Krennla. They won't touch you, of course, you're part of the all-hallowed Defense Force—and they'll probably tell you that you did the right thing and praise you and maybe even give you a barrel of bloodwine for your troubles. But once you go back to that *khest'n* ship of yours? They'll be out in force, and the minute my boy or any of his friends shows his face, they'll beat it until it's bloody. So well done, G'joth."

Shaking his head and clenching his fist, G'joth said, "I did not intend—"

"No, of course you didn't. You didn't intend to betray all of us."

The lunch he'd hastily grabbed at the opera house started welling up G'joth's throat from one of his stomachs. "I betrayed *no one*, Klaad! You and Krom could have come with me! I *asked* you to come with me!"

Klaad was still holding the door open, presumably because he did not wish G'joth to stay for any length of time. "We have discussed this before, G'joth. Unlike you, we had families."

"And they would be treated better if you had come with me." He pointed at Kimm. "Certainly, *that* would never have happened!"

"A son should know his father," Klaad said.

G'joth shook his head. "So better that you grow flabby and old working with *my* father. Did they transfer you to a desk position, Klaad? Is that why you disgrace yourself?"

That prompted a bitter laugh from Klaad. "Your father and I do not work together, you stupid *petaQ*, because we do not work. The company went out of business half a turn ago."

"No." G'joth shook his head. "Father was at work yesterday. He is home today because of *yobta' yupma'*, but—"

"Your father lies, G'joth. I would think even you would be astute enough to see that. He preserves the illusion for the sake of you and your sister, but he does not work."

He knew Lakras wasn't being paid much at the opera

house, and G'joth sent only some of his earnings home, which meant that Mother's cooking at the Andorian place was now the household's only serious source of income.

Looking again at Kimm, he said, "Why do you not challenge the guardsmen? They would never have done this before."

"Ours was not the only company that has gone out of business in Krennla, G'joth. The city produces nothing of value to the empire. Even our cultural contributions are secondary. And so we wither on the vine and eventually will die." Klaad snarled. "In some ways, G'joth, you are right. Krom and I might have been better off going with you to fight the empire's battles. Instead, we chose to fight one here to simply survive."

"No." G'joth looked at the man he had once considered a friend with disgust. "You have not fought, Klaad, you have simply accepted. You were named for a great warrior, who served in the Defense Force a century ago, both before and after Praxis. I remember your father telling me when we were children that he hoped that you would follow the path of your namesake and bring honor to your family. I now see that it is good that you did not. Such as you would never survive in the Defense Force."

"Perhaps not. But at least I would have died with honor, as I'm sure you will, G'joth. Such is not my fate. So go and do that and leave this place. Krennla is a dying city, and you should not die with it."

G'joth stormed past Klaad toward the exit but

stopped on the threshold. He looked back at Kimm, who still stood, his body ravaged by the guardsman. Then he looked at Klaad and did something a warrior was never supposed to do—but was perhaps the duty of a friend. "I am sorry for my role in what happened to your son."

Klaad's face softened for the first time since G'joth arrived. "In truth, you are not to blame. It is not the first time that the guard have done this. If it had not been you, another excuse would have been contrived. The only profession that thrives in a place such as this are those who enforce the law, because lawlessness has increased."

"What those boys did was not lawless!"

"Of course not, but it did disrupt order. And the guard cannot abide that."

A growl building in his throat, G'joth left.

He walked the streets of Kenta District for almost an hour. As he did so, he observed that there were more guardsmen, but also more people, and those people looked worn-down, destitute.

Defeated.

G'joth wondered if it had always been this bad and he hadn't noticed, or if things had indeed grown worse as Klaad had said. He recalled Leader Wol's revulsion at the very idea of even setting foot in Krennla.

Eventually, his feet took him to a tavern called Kravokh's Beard. The place had been built during Chancellor Kravokh's reign by a shipbuilder whose fortunes prospered under that chancellor's rule, and it was filled with images of Kravokh from throughout his life. G'joth had always found the place to be irritating, but Father and his friends loved it.

Sure enough, there they all were, sitting quietly around the large table in the corner, just as they were ten years ago.

No, not just as they were, G'joth thought with displeasure. *Ten years ago, they would not have been sitting quietly. The drinks would be flowing freely, heads colliding, songs being sung.*

Now, though, they simply sat and sipped their drinks—cheap bloodwine, from the smell of it—and had low, muttered conversations.

Father looked up at G'joth's arrival. "Greetings, my son. Have you and Lakras finished your rehearsals?"

"Hers is still going on," G'joth said. "I, however, had to depart."

The man who used to be Father's supervisor, a fat old *toDSaH* named Korvaq, said, "Are both your children part of the opera now, Ch'lan?"

"Did you not hear?" That was Trolk, whom Father had always described as the worst worker on any construction site. "They are portraying one of G'joth's battles!"

"One of my ship's battles," G'joth said quickly. "The director wishes me, as someone who was there at San-Tarah, to be a consultant. However, in truth this means he wishes to *say* that he had someone who was at San-Tarah to be a consultant. The events are jumbled, the weaponry is wrong, Klivv bears about as much resemblance to Captain Klag as a dead *klongat*, and I have been reminded that stage combat bears little to no resemblance to real combat."

"You know," Korvaq said, "in the old days, actors *had* to know how to fight. There wasn't no such thing as 'stage combat'—if two people fought onstage, dammit, there'd be *blood*. Klingons nowadays, they're soft. It's a disgrace, really. S'what happens when commoners get in the chancellor's chair."

Trolk laughed heartily, spitting his drink on the table. "*You're* a commoner, you stupid *petaQ*."

"Exactly—could you imagine what a disaster it'd be if *I* led the High Council?"

"Couldn't make things any worse, I can tell you *that*," one of the others, whom G'joth did not recognize, muttered.

But G'joth was looking at his father, who refused to look up at his son. "Father," he finally said.

Now he looked up. Droplets from his beverage were dripping out of his stringy white beard. "Yes, son?"

"When, precisely, were you going to tell me?"

"I wasn't." He looked back down at his drink, which G'joth finally placed the smell of as being cheap *warnog*. "There was no need for you to know, and there is no need for Lakras to know. She has enough to worry her—and your mother makes enough that we get by."

"How did this happen?" G'joth asked.

Trolk spoke with a snarl. "No one's *building* anything in Krennla. And why should they? It's *Krennla*. We produce nothing of use for the empire, and the empire gives us nothing in return."

"We produce taxes for the High Council to waste

on new ships," Korvaq said, "like that luxury liner you serve on, G'joth."

G'joth growled, his fists clenched. "The *Gorkon* has a crew of twenty-seven hundred, Korvaq. My quarters are a space smaller than this table at which you sit. And we fight to keep the empire strong."

"Have you looked around, G'joth?" Father said. "The empire does not feel very strong from here."

G'joth looked down on his father. "You have lied to your own kin and brought disgrace to our family."

Korvaq stood up, his fists slamming on the table as he did so. "You will not speak to your father that way, whelp!"

"Or *what*, old man? Will you throw up on me to show how valiantly you defend your putrid state?"

"Krennla has brought disgrace, G'joth. We are simply trapped in its path."

"You are *Klingons*! When Klingons are trapped, they fight their way out, or die in the attempt."

Sitting back down, Korvaq said, "Then we will die. And few will care."

Before G'joth could respond to that, his father said, "Go, G'joth. If you will not drink with us, then leave this place. You are not welcome." And then Ch'lan turned his body in the chair so his back was turned.

His instinctive response to his father's insult was to insert his *d'k tahg* into Ch'lan's spine, but G'joth reined in that instinct. This was still his father, and he was not a warrior.

None of them were.

G'joth left Kravokh's Beard without another word.

He could have stayed and fought these drunken old fools, and probably killed all of them, but to what purpose? They were already dead; they simply hadn't stopped moving yet.

He went back to the opera house. Even simulated battle was preferable to this.

TWENTY

An unnamed cave
Kovris V

Red-hot talons of fire clawed into L'Kor's mind, and he screamed.

Memories . . .

. . . he is on the homeworld, speaking to his friend Gannik about an investment opportunity that will improve the fortunes of both their Houses . . .

"Trust me, my friend, the Turok people are among the empire's finest. Your House's debts will be a thing of the past within the first few months."

. . . he is on a transport ship that takes him and hundreds of others to the Khitomer outpost, as replacements for the station's crew . . .

"So, Gi'ral, I hear Moraq's a good commander."

"I could not say, L'Kor. We will learn when we arrive."

. . . months after he arrives on Khitomer, he learns that Turok has gone out of business . . .

"What do you mean, he never hired anyone? What was our money used for?"

"I do not know, L'Kor, but Turok was found dead in his office following the announcement, a qutluch lodged in his heart. I would say he has paid the price for his betrayal."

"Whereas we shall pay the price for years to come."

. . . Gannik contacts him, furious . . .

"You assured me—"

"I suffered as much as you, Gannik."

"But you do not have my debts! When next we meet, I will kill you for this!"

"You are welcome to make the attempt, Gannik, and I will kill you when you do. But we have no quarrel. We are both victims of Turok's betrayal."

"I am scheduled to deliver goods to Khitomer in two months' time."

. . . only one month later, a warrior named Mogh is assigned to Khitomer to supervise upgrades to the outpost's defenses . . .

"I wish to run a simulation on the new shields. I assume we have enough information on Romulan weaponry to do so?"

"Do you think such an attack likely?"

"I think such an attack is possible. After all, one praetor has been overthrown—who is to say another might not be? Politics are unpredictable."

"That is certainly the case. But I cannot imagine why Romulans would attack this base. There is much about them that is honorable."

. . . and then the very Romulan attack Mogh predicted occurs . . .

"The shields have gone down!"

"Get them back up!"

"I am attempting to do so, but—"

"What is that?"

"Gas!"

. . . being taken prisoner by the Romulans and not allowed to die, but nor do they give up any intelligence . . .

"My name is Tokath. The Klingon Empire has refused to acknowledge that you still live. Your commanders, your loved ones—they all think you dead. Therefore I offer you the opportunity to live out your lives in secret on a planet outside both our empires. You will be cared for, you will be fed and housed. What say you?"

. . . growing accustomed to life on Carraya, even taking a mate and having children, and giving his word to Tokath that he would remain, until the day a warrior named Worf arrived . . .

"I am Worf, son of Mogh."

"Why have you come here?"

"I have come to find my father. Is he alive? Is he here?"

"Your father fell at Khitomer."

. . . Tokath confronting him after Worf, Toq, and the other children departed . . .

"Why did you do it, L'Kor? Why did you stand with Worf? You gave your word that you would not betray me."

"I gave my word that I would remain your prisoner, Tokath. I never promised you that I would stop being a Klingon."

. . . Gi'ral leaving Tokath and later taking her own life; Tokath growing more distant; L'Kor caring for Ba'el . . .

"There is an unauthorized ship in orbit! We must—"

"This is madness!"

A low hum that L'Kor had not even noticed suddenly stopped, filling the cave with a loud silence. Through bleary eyes, L'Kor saw the tall, gangly form of Gorrik, Gannik's firstborn son.

For days, they had done this dance. Somehow, Gorrik had gotten his hands on a mind-sifter, an old Defense Force tool that was banned by the Khitomer Accords. With a certain irony, L'Kor thought, *My life seems to consist of betrayals related to that planet.*

But whatever memory Gorrik was attempting to pry out of L'Kor's mind, he had yet to find it. Nor had he articulated what, precisely, it was he searched for.

"You have stymied me at every turn, L'Kor, just as you stymied my father by dying on Khitomer."

"But . . . but I did *not* die."

The youth rolled his eyes. "Obviously."

"Then how did you know that I lived?"

Gorrik started to pace back and forth in the cave. L'Kor wondered where they were, exactly. The House of Gannik had lands aplenty—or at least they had three decades ago. The Turok investments had hurt Gannik sufficiently that, for all L'Kor knew, the House had no lands left.

Gorrik wore a one-piece brown suit that accentuated his slim form. Were L'Kor not strapped to the mind-sifter, he was quite sure he could break the boy in two, even at his advanced age. True, he was not in prime condition anymore—years of inaction on Carraya could sap any warrior's strength, especially one who was, for all intents and purposes, dead—but this whelp had killed everyone L'Kor loved and those he had sworn to protect. *The latest failure in a series of them*, he thought bitterly.

"There were always rumors," Gorrik was saying, "that there were some who survived Khitomer. Father had always followed those rumors—I had assumed it was because he wished to learn if you were still alive, so he could at last avenge the wrong you perpetrated upon him. But it was more than that. He told me before he died that *all* those who survived Khitomer, if any there truly were, had to be found—but he did not tell me why!" Gorrik's childish screams echoed weakly off the cave walls.

Then he turned to face L'Kor. "There is a higher setting on the mind-sifter that might still be used. I have refrained from doing so, because that will leave you a mindless vegetable, and I want you to be aware of your suffering." He moved closer, resting his hands on the sides of the chair to which L'Kor was strapped, his *raktajino*-laden breath burning L'Kor's nostrils. "But I need to know Father's secret."

L'Kor did not bother to point out that he had no secret to give Gorrik. The only dealings he ever had with Gannik were completely public, ending with the Turok investment. A cursory check of the information net would reveal anything that Gorrik needed to know.

Again, L'Kor struggled against his bonds. He knew it to be futile—the restraints were made of rodinium.

Were L'Kor at the peak of physical condition, he could not shatter these bonds.

But he struggled anyhow. He had been a Klingon once, and if he was to die this day, he preferred to be one when he did so. The past thirty years of his life guaranteed he would ride the Barge of the Dead to *Gre'thor*, but at least his final act would be that of a warrior.

He wasn't sure how he could do that, exactly, but he hoped that the desire counted for something.

As Gorrik walked to the controls, he said, "Feel free to scream all you like, L'Kor. We are alone on this world. If, by some miracle, anyone heard your distress call and managed to trace us here, there is a shield around this location that will prevent any from finding us, even if they do see my ship in orbit. And then—"

An alarm cut off Gorrik's rant. It echoed in L'Kor's skull, convincing the old Klingon that the sound could be heard *from* Gorrik's orbiting vessel. The youth pulled a padd out of a pocket and touched some controls.

"Someone has penetrated the shield! But that's impossible!"

"Hardly," said a very familiar voice from the cave entrance.

L'Kor looked over and saw Tokath—alive! *But Gorrik said that everyone else was killed.*

Tokath fired his disruptor even as Gorrik touched a control on his padd. While the green beam sliced into Gorrik's arm, causing him to drop the padd and wince with pain, a beam fired from the cave ceiling and struck Tokath in the shoulder.

Gorrik crabwalked behind the mind-sifter's console,

which was well for him, as Tokath, though he lay grimacing on the cave floor, sweat beading on his high forehead, still held his disruptor. He fired it at the console.

While it did not have Tokath's intended effect of striking Gorrik, it did damage the device's controls enough that L'Kor's bonds retracted into the chair, freeing him.

He attempted to leap to his feet, but two days of sitting and having his mind scanned had left his body weak and impotent. Instead of leaping, he fell clumsily to the ground, no better than an old woman.

Another beam struck Tokath from the ceiling.

Pull yourself together, you old fool, L'Kor admonished himself. He gathered every muscle up and forced himself to his feet, using the mind-sifter's chair to support his body.

"Father!" Another familiar voice screamed from the cave entrance. It sounded like Ba'el. L'Kor wondered who else survived. *Perhaps they all did, and Gorrik lied.* But no, L'Kor recalled several dying in front of him.

It does not matter. This must end, now.

"I do not know who you people are," Gorrik said from behind the console, "but you will not keep me from my destiny!"

Yet another familiar voice: "Ba'el, get down!" Those words were immediately followed by an armored body knocking Ba'el to the floor. Gorrik's damned weapon just missed both of them, firing harmlessly into the cave wall.

L'Kor forced himself to put one foot in front of the

other, abandoning the chair's support but quickly grabbing the mangled console. Gorrik still hid behind it like
a *chuSwI'* in the dirt.

Sparing a glance, L'Kor saw that it was indeed Toq—
and in the armor of a Defense Force commander, no
less—who had brought Ba'el down, saving her life. He
had a beard now, did Toq, and had apparently risen
quickly through the ranks. *I am proud of you, Toq, as if
you were my own son.*

Toq spoke from the ground, his own disruptor now
unholstered, his body protecting that of Ba'el. "Show
yourself, Gorrik!"

"How do you know who I am?"

"I know everything about you, son of Gannik. I know
your father died with an unresolved feud. I know you
killed virtually everyone on Carraya IV with information given you by a member of the High Council. And I
know that today is the day you die."

The High Council? That information shook L'Kor.
How could anyone on the council know of Carraya?
L'Kor knew things must have changed in the years since
Khitomer, and knew that the empire had allied with the
Romulans in order to fight the Dominion—but if the
council knew of Carraya, why would they let it stand?

Unless, of course, the council didn't know—simply
one councillor, who wished to keep it secret.

But why?

L'Kor's vision swam, and he realized that he would
die never knowing the answer to any of these questions.
His limbs again grew weak, and an odd acidic taste filled
his mouth.

I am dying. But I will take that honorless coward with me.

Using his weakened arms, L'Kor pushed himself off the console, and he stumbled behind it, literally falling on top of a surprised Gorrik. Pinning the youth with his knees, L'Kor lifted his arms and let them fall on Gorrik's face.

Over and over again, he pummeled Gorrik, even though after a few times, gravity proved more powerful in bringing his fists down than any effort he expended. L'Kor felt the life drain out of him, began to lose feeling in his legs, but still he beat and beat and beat on Gorrik's face.

In his mind, he saw the faces of Pitzh and Q'Idar and Virlak and Maj and Klon and Hanril and Jurok and Tokath and all the others who had died because of Gorrik's insanity. His fists became slick with the *petaQ's* blood as L'Kor continued to pound his face into bloody mulch.

"L'Kor, that is enough!"

With a supreme effort of will, L'Kor stopped and looked up to see Toq, his face now partially obscured by a strong man's beard. "Toq?"

"He is dead, L'Kor. Vengeance has been satisfied."

"No," L'Kor said, weakly, "it can never be completely satisfied. But it is enough."

Then L'Kor let go.

Toq knelt next to the bodies of Gorrik and L'Kor.

Of the former, he cared not a whit, but L'Kor had been as much of a father to him as Pitzh, and he died taking vengeance on his enemies, avenging those who died needlessly. He died as a Klingon.

As with his mother, Toq didn't care whether or not there really was a Black Fleet, whether or not *Sto-Vo-Kor* really existed. He still pried L'Kor's eyes open, growled low in his throat, then threw his head back and screamed to the heavens, his voice echoing off the stalactites.

When he was finished, Ba'el said, "Is that the death scream you were telling me about?"

Rising to his feet, Toq nodded.

"But you don't really believe it?" she asked.

"No." He turned to look at Ba'el. "But I could be wrong."

She looked down at Tokath. "What about my father?"

"He is a Romulan. Romulans do not go to *Sto-Vo-Kor*." Toq smiled sadly. "And he would not wish to go even if he had earned the right to do so." He walked over to Ba'el. "We will take his body with us. I will arrange to have it delivered to Romulus. Their military will take care of him."

"But he wasn't in their military anymore."

"It does not matter. Romulans honor those who serve."

In a small voice, Ba'el said, "I didn't know that." She looked at Toq with sad eyes. "I never knew anything about either heritage, did I? And I never—" Her voice broke. "I never got to tell him I loved him."

"You must have told him," Toq said.

She shook her head, her curly auburn tresses bouncing. "Not recently."

Toq put a hand on her shoulder. "He knew, Ba'el. He

leaped on top of you to save your life, fully expecting to die in the attempt. That was not the action of a man who did not know the love of a daughter." He removed the hand and activated his communicator, standing close to Tokath's body. "Computer—two people and one corpse to beam up."

They materialized on the *D'jaq* transporter platform a moment later. He and Ba'el stepped off and Toq walked to the console embedded in the shuttle wall. "I will put his body in stasis."

"What about L'Kor and the other one—Gorrik?"

"L'Kor's body is but a shell and can be disposed of. As for Gorrik—he is dead, and if there truly is an afterlife, then Fek'lhr is escorting him to the Barge of the Dead even as we speak."

"Good," Ba'el said quietly.

Once he finished taking care of Tokath's body, Toq moved to the pilot seat and set a course for Qo'noS. Before going to warp, he armed the shuttle's torpedo bay and fired upon Gorrik's ship. It was consumed by fire that was in turn consumed by the vacuum of space, leaving only debris and dust.

It gave him some small satisfaction.

But it was not enough. The fire in his heart had not yet abated, and would not, until he returned to Qo'noS for the conversation he knew he must have with Lorgh.

TWENTY-ONE

The Great Hall
First City, Qo'noS

When Klag entered the meeting room in the Great Hall, the faces of the previous six chancellors looked down on him.

In the original Great Hall, this was the emperor's study. As one came in, one passed through a gauntlet of statuary, three on each side, representing the six prior emperors. When the Great Hall was rebuilt after Morjod's abortive coup d'état, Martok had a new version of the study constructed, now called the chancellor's study. Battles were to be planned here and the fate of the empire decided. Continuing the old tradition, Martok lined both sides of the entrance with statues of the half dozen who'd preceded him in the chancellor's chair. In order to save time, Martok had a different sculptor do each one.

The first to stare down at Klag on the right was K'mpec. He had led the empire longer than anyone in history, even the great Emperor Sompek, and he had taken the empire to new heights of prosperity, taking advantage of the alliance with the Federation and his ability to bring consensus to good effect. His sculptor placed him on the chancellor's chair—the only one of the six chancellors depicted sitting down—his arms on the armrests, looking both relaxed yet ready to leap forward without hesitation.

Across K'mpec, to Klag's left, was his successor, and Martok's predecessor, Gowron. The sculptor had put him standing ramrod straight, his arms folded. Gowron had been a political agitator for many turns, feeling that K'mpec's compromises had made the empire weak. Upon K'mpec's death, Gowron had gained enough followers that he was considered a viable candidate to replace him. The statue represented Gowron as he was before he led the empire: a defiant agitator, who refused to accept things as they were.

As he proceeded inside, he was then looked down upon by Kravokh and Ditagh. While his allowing the Romulans to attack first Narendra III and then the Khitomer outpost resulted in K'mpec challenging and defeating him, Kravokh was still primarily remembered as the chancellor who brought the empire out of the dark times following Praxis and made the Klingon Empire a force to be reckoned with in the quadrant again. Mindful of that, this sculptor had Kravokh standing straight, a *bat'leth* raised over his head.

Facing Kravokh was Ditagh. Klag felt pity for whoever got that commission, for Ditagh was not a chancellor one cared to recall for very long. The sculptor portrayed him holding a disruptor pistol at an unseen foe, perhaps symbolizing Ditagh's military career, which was more impressive than his political one.

The last two were Azetbur and Kaarg, and one could not imagine two more distinct personalities. The only woman to serve on the High Council in *any* capacity, the daughter of the great Gorkon, Azetbur had served a tumultuous reign, having to deal with the catastrophic aftermath of the Praxis disaster, her father's assassination, and the early days of the Federation alliance. She was considered the greatest and the weakest Klingon leader, sometimes at the same time. Her sculptor portrayed her with open hands, perhaps representing the role of peacemaker that Praxis forced her into. Klag couldn't help but notice that she was portrayed as shorter than any of her male counterparts, yet her eyes were fiercer even than wide-eyed Gowron's.

Finally there was Kaarg, a reactionary who had dismantled many of the reforms Azetbur had put forward, including that of her very service: he decreed that no women could serve on the High Council forevermore. Kaarg was portrayed holding a *d'k tahg*, looking ready to insert it between the ribs of his foe.

As Klag moved past the gauntlet of chancellors to take his seat on the far end of the table, four others entered. Two of them, dressed in formal cassocks, took their seats at the opposite end of the table from where Klag had gone to sit. Klag recognized them from the information net as two councillors, though he could not recall their names. The other two wore Defense Force armor and took up positions behind them—obviously, they were the councillors' bodyguards. Only members of the High Council were permitted to have bodyguards in this structure.

Two familiar captains entered the room a few moments later, and they moved to sit near Klag as soon as they all recognized each other. Rising to his feet, Klag head-butted each in turn, warmly greeting them.

"It is good to see you, son of M'Raq," Captain Vikagh of the *Ditagh* said with a hearty laugh. The old captain still carried the burned flesh from an old battle with a cabal of slave traders, his white beard having grown around it.

Captain Puklik of the *Kaarg* added, "Though not here. Why do we waste our time filling the air with words?"

One of the councillors said, "That will be made clear to you soon enough, Captains. Be seated until the others arrive."

"Who else is to be part of this insanity?" Vikagh asked. "Martok, I assume, since it was his seal on the summons I received."

"That will *also* be made clear to you," the councillor said archly.

Unsheathing his *d'k tahg*, the outer blades unfurling with a click, Vikagh said, "Do not toy with me, Tovoj. I was captaining Defense Force vessels when you were still sucking on your mother's teat."

From the door, a voice said, "Put that away, Vikagh." Klag looked over to see General Goluk, accompanied by Captain Kvaad of the *Kesh*. "The High Council has summoned us, and it is our duty to obey. You have no grounds for challenging Councillor Tovoj."

Closing the blades, Vikagh said, "The night is young."

"The reason for our being summoned is obvious," Klag said. He had assumed it had something to do with the Kavrot exploration, or perhaps the state of the *Gorkon*, but he now saw the true purpose. "All of us present are the surviving commanders in charge of the war against the Elabrej Hegemony. It is obviously of great importance to have removed the general and the captain from their posts."

"They are no longer our posts," Goluk said. He showed no emotion and did not elaborate.

Martok entered then, and everyone rose out of respect. Waving them off, Martok took his seat at the head of the table, between the statues of Kaarg and Azetbur. Behind him were four people: three men, one woman. Two of the men were from the *Yan-Isleth*, the warriors charged with protecting the chancellor, who took up position near the councillors' guards. The other man and the woman both wore the standard all-black of Imperial Intelligence. They stood on either side of the chancellor, the man in front of Azetbur, the woman in front of Kaarg. Everyone else took their seats.

Klag recognized the woman as B'Etloj, who had been assigned to the *Kravokh*. *This cannot bode well.*

Martok looked at each captain in turn with his one good eye as he spoke. "This meeting has been called by I.I. to determine if Defense Force resources were properly allocated during the campaign against the Elabrej."

Slamming his fist on the table, Puklik got to his feet. "What madness is this?"

"Be seated!" the man on Martok's left said.

"Or what?" Puklik asked snidely. "I.I. is exempt from challenges, but that means they cannot challenge, either."

Now it was Goluk who said, "Be seated, Captain. I do not believe you need to query *me* as to the consequences of disobedience."

Snarling, Puklik sat back down.

"The campaign has ended," Klag found himself saying. "Of what need is there to 'discuss' anything? Yes, by all means, let the record of battle be made available so warriors may study our tactics and learn from them, but this is not a class in the training academy, this is the Great Hall. Surely, I.I. and the High Council have more important issues to address."

The I.I. man said, "As a captain of a Chancellor-class ship, Klag, you should be aware of the importance of that class to our fleet. This campaign—against an unworthy, unimpressive, distant foe—cost us three of the twelve ships. These are our finest warships, the first line of defense against those who would destroy our empire, and now twenty-five percent of them have been lost to a pointless war."

"Pointless?" Now it was Klag's turn to rise. "The *Kravokh* was defeated, its crew taken prisoner and not allowed to die, but instead were *experimented* on like animals. Were we to let that insult go unanswered?"

"Of course not," B'Etloj said. "In fact, I contacted my fellow agents in the hopes of precisely such a rescue as your ship effected, Captain Klag. But there was no need to divert the fleet."

"If we did nothing," Goluk said, "the Elabrej would have kept coming. Instead of meeting them in their space, they would have come to find us in ours."

Vikagh said, "And what of other races? When Klingons are challenged, we must crush the challenger, or forever be thought of as weak."

"Was it truly necessary to commit so many of our most important vessels to the task?" the I.I. man asked.

Klag stared at the two councillors, who only made notes on a padd. He wondered what their purpose here was. Perhaps they were simply the councillors who dealt directly with I.I. Martok, too, was conspicuously silent.

"The fact that we lost so many of those ships," Kvaad said, "indicates that we did need to, yes. You described the Elabrej as inferior, but their weaponry was devastatingly powerful. It was only because their defenses did not match their offensive capability that we were so resoundingly victorious."

"Oh, yes," the I.I. man said, "quite the resounding victory it was." He pulled out a padd. "Let me read from your own report, Kvaad: 'The Elabrej economy was already in a shambles before they ever encountered the *Kravokh*. The Hegemony's entire wealth was concentrated into the oligarchs, who spent only on the military. The war against us destroyed their ability to produce anything of worth, and the entire solar system is resource-poor, at least for Klingon needs.'" Setting the padd down on the table in front of Martok with a clack, he went on. "The purpose of the Kavrot exploration was to add worlds to the empire so we may improve our economy, but this world would only drain resources."

Sounding impatient, Goluk said, "That is why we abandoned the worlds to their own fate. They would have been a drain on the empire."

"Nonetheless," B'Etloj said, "there were flaws in the campaign, flaws that could have been avoided—"

Deciding it was worth the risk, Klag said, "If I had ceded command to Trant? Is that not truly what this is about, B'Etloj? I.I.'s purpose in this was to provide intelligence, and they provided it well, but when Trant came to me and revealed his status as one of your agents, and then revealed that the *Kravokh* crew were being held prisoner, he attempted to take command of my vessel. That petition was denied." Now he looked at Martok. "With the full support of the High Council."

Martok stared right back at Klag. "A decision I stand by," he rumbled.

Klag let out a breath. Martok could easily have taken his tone for an insult. "Yes, we used our most powerful ships to defeat the Elabrej, but what does it matter that ships were lost? We may build new ones, after all. But to deliver any but the most crushing of defeats to the Elabrej would have cost us far more, and it would have been an irreplaceable commodity. We are *warriors*. If we do not give our all to the battle, then the battle is meaningless. If we hold back, if we reallocate out of convenience, then we are no longer warriors of a great empire but simple soldiers doing the bidding of self-serving politicians. We become the Jem'Hadar. I *fought* the Jem'Hadar, and I sit here today wondering why I bothered."

Silence descended upon the room. Klag could feel a palpable fury emanating from both I.I. representatives, in direct contrast to the calm radiating from Martok between them. Klag suspected that he had played right into Martok's hands.

In fact, the chancellor stood up. "This meeting has ended."

The I.I. officials' fury only increased at that, but it was Tovoj who spoke. "Chancellor, I believe there is more to be—"

"Silence!"

Tovoj recoiled as if Martok had struck him—and based on the look on the chancellor's face, that was probably his next step.

Martok continued. "I allowed this farce of a meeting due to the insistence of Councillors Tovoj and Merik. They *claimed* that I.I. had legitimate grievances against the manner in which the Elabrej campaign was waged. It has been proved to my satisfaction that these grievances are groundless." Turning to face both I.I. agents, Martok said, "At the next open council session, I will officially declare the Elabrej campaign a success."

Klag smiled. Such an official declaration in open council meant that I.I. could dispute it only by formally challenging the declaration—which would mean a *meqba'* and full disclosure of evidence, all in open council for the entire empire to see. I.I. functioned best in the shadows—which was why their attempt to discredit the war was being done in the back chambers of the Great Hall rather than in public.

It was, in Klag's opinion, to Martok's credit that he did not stand for this for very long.

Both I.I. operatives left the room quickly, and the councillors—who seemed very much to Klag like men who feared for their lives—ran after them, their bodyguards trailing them.

"You are all dismissed," Martok said to the others. "Except for you, son of M'Raq. I have an unrelated task to perform that requires your expert assistance. As for the rest of you: *Qapla'!*"

All at once, Klag, Goluk, Vikagh, Puklik, and Kvaad cried, "*Qapla'!*"

Klag remained in his seat while the others departed one by one under the gaze of Martok's predecessors. Martok himself took his seat and regarded Klag with his one-eyed gaze.

"You did well, my friend," Martok said after a moment. "It is my belief that I.I. contrived this entire exercise in order to achieve this very result. Their task is to keep the empire strong, and by being sure that all those in this room were united, they helped to ensure that."

Feeling he could speak freely, with only the two of them and the *Yan-Isleth* in the room, Klag said, "Their deception offends me."

"I doubt they will care overmuch," Martok said with a deep-throated chuckle. "In truth, I do not, either. This may have seemed a waste of time, but if it reassures me that the warriors commanding my finest vessels are honorable men such as yourself and Captains Vikagh and Puklik and Kvaad, then it was time well spent."

Bowing his head out of respect and gratitude, Klag asked, "What is the other task that requires my assistance, Chancellor?"

Martok smiled. "One of your officers is reporting to me at my request, and I thought you would find her report of interest. How are the repairs to your ship progressing?"

Grateful that his inspection of the *Gorkon* prior to reporting here was not in vain, Klag provided an overview of the report Kurak had given him. He left out her excoriations of the Praxis Station engineering staff, which alone cut the time to give the report in half.

Just as Klag finished summing up the report, another of the *Yan-Isleth* came in under the statues, trailing the familiar auburn-haired form of B'Oraq.

Standing, Klag said, "Doctor!"

"Captain!" B'Oraq smiled, tugging on her braid. "I was not told I would be reporting to you as well."

Martok said, "Klag and I had other business, and I asked him to remain to hear your report on the medical conference."

Klag winced. He'd already heard plenty from B'Oraq on that very subject. Martok had been the main advocate on the High Council for this conference, and he was unlikely to be pleased with her impressions of it.

"I am afraid, Chancellor, that the report will not be to your liking."

"My liking does not matter, Doctor. Our people's

medicine must improve, and that process will begin with the KPE. What I want is the truth."

"The truth is that the entire conference was a sham. Little to no useful information was exchanged, no minds were changed—nothing was accomplished. Sir, if the goal of this conference was to improve the empire's medical standards, it did precisely nothing to do so." B'Oraq tugged on her braid, then added, "Actually, that is not entirely the case. I did learn of two more physicians who feel as I do. One is a Defense Force doctor named Valatra, the other a civilian named Kandless. They assisted me in the rescue operation after Captain Stren flew into that building."

"Yes." Martok consulted a padd in front of him. "I see that your name is on the witness list of the *meqba'* for Councillor Kryan. Doctor Kowag has already made his report, which will be read into evidence. What will you add to that?"

Now Klag smiled. He'd already had *this* conversation with B'Oraq as well.

"Captain Stren is not to blame for what happened, Chancellor. His death occurred while flying the shuttle, and that death was the cause of the crash."

Martok stared at her. "You realize that you are challenging Kowag's judgment?"

"I've been doing that for years, sir."

That got a laugh out of the chancellor. "Very well. You will present your evidence. And I will consider your report and what it means for the KPE's continued existence." Martok then looked at Klag. "Your chief engineer has also placed herself on the agenda, Captain, to petition the council."

"I would not presume to speak Commander Kurak's mind, Chancellor," Klag said truthfully. "It is a disturbing place that I prefer to avoid."

Martok chuckled as he got to his feet and gave them each a salute. "Very well. *Qapla'*, Captain, Doctor."

Klag returned both salute and salutation, as did B'Oraq. Then Martok left the room, the three *Yan-Isleth* following.

She smiled and walked toward him. "Considerate of the chancellor to leave us alone."

"Indeed. I am sorely tempted to take you right here, under the eyes of the last six chancellors."

"I think not," she said with a chuckle. "Or at least, not Gowron's eyes. They're so wide and penetrating, I do not believe I would be able to perform to the captain's satisfaction."

Klag threw his head back and laughed heartily. "I intend to return home. My mother has finally come back, and we will dine together. You may join us."

"Would that I could, but I must return to the *Gorkon* to care for my patients."

Frowning, Klag said, "You could remand them to another facility."

"I'd prefer they get *good* medical care," B'Oraq said sourly. "Why do you think I transported them to the *Gorkon* in the first place? And unfortunately, Kandless has his own practice on Ya'Koraq to return to, and Valatra had to return to her posting, *and* Command hasn't seen fit to send me a new nurse yet, so I must care for them myself."

She playfully scratched his cheek. Klag shuddered with pleasure from the edges of her nails biting into his flesh and pulling on his beard.

"Very well." He smiled. "If you wish to continue this talk, we should leave, for I will not be able to restrain myself much longer, and then you will be forced to perform under Gowron's penetrating eyes."

"Well, I did say I had to return to the *Gorkon*," she said. "I did *not* say I had to return to the medical bay immediately."

Again, Klag threw his head back and laughed, and they left the chancellor's study for the Great Hall's transporter room.

TWENTY-TWO

Tabona's farm
Pheben III

The agonized wail awakened Wol from a sound sleep. Used to the call of the warrior, she went from dead asleep to awake and ready for action at a moment's notice. Tabona's restriction against wearing her armor meant she slept naked, and in that state, she leaped to her feet, reaching for a nonexistent *d'k tahg* at her side.

Still the pained cry continued. She'd heard such only from warriors whose injuries were so grave as to overcome their natural stoicism. Reaching to the floor for her armor, still where she'd left it after B'Ellor gave her a dress, she grabbed her weapon for real this time and ran out of the room, unheedful of her nudity. On Elabrej, after killing the scientist who experimented on her, she'd run naked through the entire government sphere, killing dozens of Elabrej and helping Commander Toq free the other Klingons held prisoner by those honorless *petaQpu'*. The lack of armor mattered less to her than the sound of a person in pain. That usually meant battle, and Wol would not pass up the chance to join in.

The last time she ran in her bare feet, it was on hard metal Elabrej floors. Now she ran on yielding dirt and grass and moved more quickly and efficiently toward the sound of the screams. She scented nothing different in the air—at this point, she had grown accustomed to the smells of the farm—and only a Klingon ahead.

Pushing her way through some brush, the branches slapping and scraping against her bare skin, she found Fuhrman lying on his side, his left arm caught between two curved metal bars.

"What happened?"

Fuhrman ceased his agonized cries, though he was shivering despite the warmth of the night air. He was fully clothed as well, yet Wol felt fine. "T-trap," he muttered.

Tabona and Kagak, both wearing nightdresses of different sorts, came running up, soon followed by B'Ellor, with Goran's lumbering strides right behind her.

Before Wol could say anything, Tabona said, "You stupid *yIntagh*, you set off the damn *korvit* trap, didn't you?"

"N-no, a *chuSwI'* did. I was t-trying to reset it, and it snapped."

"*QI'yah*," Tabona said with a snarl. "That damn Ferengi sold us bad goods *again*. I *told* you to buy from Grovalik, but do you listen?"

Wol knelt down and tried to pry the bars off his arm.

She could feel that the bone was shattered underneath the thin fabric of his shirt. "He needs to go to a doctor."

"Not a chance," Tabona said. "That butcher'll just cut the arm off, and what good would that do? I'll set it myself as soon we get that *khest'n* thing off him."

Gripping the cold metal, Wol pulled, the bars cutting into her fingers, but they did not budge.

"Kahless's hand, woman," Tabona said, having apparently just gotten a look at Wol for the first time, "put some damn clothes on, would you?"

"I heard the sounds of battle," she said, getting to her feet. "There was no time to dally." She turned to the big man. "*Bekk* Goran?"

"Yes, Leader?"

"Remove the trap from *Bekk* Kagak's brother's arm."

"Yes, Leader." Goran strode forward, put his huge hands on the bars, and yanked them apart. The trap shattered into several pieces with an ear-splitting snap.

Then, with a gentleness that seemed to shock Tabona, Goran guided Furhrman to his feet.

"Bring him inside," Tabona said. "I'll care for him in a moment."

"Yes, Grandmother," Goran said.

That prompted a snort from Tabona, but Wol could see how Goran, after only two days, considered Tabona to be a surrogate grandmother. Even those who didn't call her that spoke her name as if to say "Grandmother."

Goran moved toward the house, B'Ellor walking

alongside him. Though her brother was injured, B'Ellor was mostly looking up at the big man.

Wol said, "The bone was broken in several places, Tabona. It will take weeks to heal even with decent medical care." Months of serving with B'Oraq had made Wol forget what most Klingon doctors were like, though the disgust with which Tabona described that option served as a fine reminder.

"Yeah, I'll have to change his workload, keep him off anything involving lifting. That's not the real problem, though—I can account for work alterations due to injury, happens all the time. But the fights are in two days, and we don't have a fighter."

Kagak stepped forward, puffing up his chest, a gesture that would have been more impressive while wearing something other than a nightshirt. "Yes we do, Grandmother."

"Don't be an idiot, boy, you haven't got Fuhrman's skills—and he wasn't gonna beat Lak in any case."

"I am Fuhrman's brother, Grandmother. It is my *duty* to take his place. And besides which, I am a soldier of the empire. I have battled against many foes—Lak is simply the latest one."

Wol wasn't so sure. For all that Defense Force soldiers were supposed to be trained in hand-to-hand combat, most of the time warriors fought with *some* manner of weapon. "Kagak, are you sure?"

"The family honor is at stake," Kagak said, his chin thrust forward.

Tabona rolled her eyes. "Oh, spare me that nonsense, boy, this is serious."

"Who else will face Lak?" Kagak asked.

"Worse comes to worse, no one will." Tabona started walking toward the house. "Fuhrman's the only one who stands a chance, anyhow."

Kagak followed his grandmother. "The family cannot go unrepresented! We will lose our honor!"

"We'll lose a lot more if you put your fool head in the ring and get it handed to you." Tabona shook her head. "But you're right, I'll never hear the end of it if we don't send someone. And maybe the Defense Force taught you *something* useful after all these years."

Wol chuckled at that as she went with Tabona and Kagak into the house. She assumed Fuhrman was in good hands, and she needed her rest. She suspected she would be spending a great deal of time the following day going over the particulars of fistfighting with Kagak.

Hours later, she was awakened *again*, but this time by the bellowing of two Klingons. At first she thought it was a call to battle. Then she placed the second word as being "*jIH*," and she realized that she was hearing two people taking the Oath of Marriage.

Realizing that this was even less of a call to battle, Wol went back to sleep.

TWENTY-THREE

Kilgore Landing Bay
First City, Qo'noS

Toq and Ba'el disembarked from the *D'jaq*, met by a stooped, elderly Klingon wearing tarnished Defense Force armor. "You must be Commander Toq," the old man said.

"Yes."

"Lorgh sent me. He told me to tell you to go ahead to the Kilgore transporter station. Your friend'll be taken to the embassy, and you'll be taken to meet with him."

"What of—"

"I'm here to take care of the Rom body." He shook his head, his wispy white hair flying in all directions. "Damn pointy-eared *petaQpu'*, lettin' their damned corpses take up space that could be used for practical purposes."

As the old man entered the *D'jaq*, Toq started walking toward the transporter station. Ba'el struggled to keep up. "Toq!"

"What?"

"You hardly said a word the entire trip back."

Weakly, Toq said, "I thought you wanted to be alone with your grief."

"You could have asked me—but that would've meant talking to me. What did I *do*, Toq?"

Toq stopped walking and regarded this woman who had been his childhood friend. *But I stopped being a child a long time ago.* "It is nothing you did, Ba'el," Toq said truthfully. "There was more to this journey than avenging the loss of our families." He put a hand on her shoulder. "I am sorry that L'Kor and Tokath died. At least we know that they died well." He looked away. "Better than everyone else on Carraya."

He proceeded to the transporter station, Ba'el trailing behind him.

The transporter operator nodded to Toq, who stepped on the platform.

Ba'el stood next to the console and said, "Toq?"

"Yes."

"I . . . I don't know what to do now."

"Talk to Worf. He will help you as he helped me." To the operator: "Energize."

A red haze surrounded Toq's vision, and Ba'el and the transporter station grew indistinct. After a brief instant of all red, the haze coalesced into a similar transporter station, albeit in a darker room and with Lorgh standing at the console.

Toq had no idea where he was. The Kilgore Landing

Bay was designated for I.I.'s exclusive use, but everyone knew that. Lorgh's own offices would be in a secret location that Toq doubted remained in the transporter logs more than a second after his materialization.

Stepping off the platform, Toq pulled a padd out of his pocket. It was the one he had been studying after his argument with Tokath on the *D'jaq.* "Greetings, Father."

Lorgh regarded Toq with squinted eyes. "What concerns you, my son?"

"Gorrik is dead. So are L'Kor and Tokath. Only Ba'el survives of those who have lived on Carraya these past eight years."

"Where is she now?"

"She expressed a desire to see Worf, so I sent her to the Federation embassy."

Nodding, Lorgh said, "Good. I have already spoken with Worf, and we both agreed that it would be best for her to travel to the Federation. Her half-breed status would leave her unwelcome in Klingon or Romulan space." He indicated the door. "Come, let us retire to the mess hall."

Toq followed Lorgh out of the station's door, down a drab, dark corridor, and into a dark room that was filled with empty tables surrounded by long benches. It was about half the size of the *Gorkon* mess hall. Toq had seen no one else since beaming over—he wondered if anyone else was assigned here, and if not, why the mess hall was so large.

Walking to a replicator, Lorgh said, "Computer, two *warnogs.*"

With a mild hum and a brief glow, two mugs appeared. Lorgh grabbed them and handed one to Toq. "*Qapla'*," he said, holding one of them up.

Toq took the mug and returned the salutation, but did not drink.

After they sat at one of the long, empty tables, Toq spoke, his voice echoing off the walls of the huge space. "Father, I read the dossier on the House of Gannik that you provided for me."

"I expected you to."

"In it are transcripts of a communication between L'Kor and Gannik that indicate that he was scheduled to come to Khitomer. I also found a description of Gannik's holdings that included a weapons research company that was providing matériel to Khitomer— but none of it was on the official manifests signed by Commander Moraq. And then there was your own report regarding the secret development of metagenic weapons on Khitomer by Chancellor Kravokh without the knowledge of the High Council. I wondered why that report was in there, so I looked again at what Gannik was providing to Khitomer—and much of it could be used in the development of metagenic weaponry." He looked angrily at Lorgh. "Is *this* why all my friends died, Father? Is this why my *parents* died? Because Gorrik wanted to know if L'Kor knew his father's role in Kravokh's conspiracy?"

Lorgh chuckled. "Is that what you believe? I gave you all the pieces to the puzzle, Toq. I wondered if you would be able to deduce it from the evidence I provided, but you came to the wrong conclusion."

Toq slammed the padd down in frustration. "You speak in riddles!"

"That is what I do for a living, you young fool," Lorgh said angrily. "But for your benefit, I will speak plainly. Somehow, the Romulans learned about the weapons being developed. It might have been the spy that I sent Worf's father to Khitomer to find—"

"Ja'rod," Toq said, "of the House of Duras."

"Yes," Lorgh said testily.

Toq knew that from Worf's own public record, which Toq had studied at great length after his arrival on Qo'noS. He had wanted to know everything there was to know about his benefactor. The truth of Ja'rod's dishonor had been revealed to the public shortly after Gowron ascended to the chancellorship, which he had done with the aid of the House of Mogh.

"Or it might have been someone else. Ultimately, it does not matter—the Romulans learned of it and attacked the outpost, taking care to divert all Defense Force vessels away first. The Romulans did their work well—all the evidence of Kravokh's weapons development was vaporized in the attack."

Toq shook his head. "I do not understand. Why did Gorrik attack Carraya and take L'Kor?"

"Gorrik wished to know what truly happened at Khitomer—so he could profit by it. The House of Gannik had fallen on hard times, as Turok was the first of a series of bad investments over the past three decades. He used the last of his resources to set up that base you found him at and learned of Carraya from one of Martok's enemies on the High Council—Kopek perhaps, or

Krozek. He knew L'Kor and his father were close and thought L'Kor might know the truth."

Rising to his feet, Toq cried, "I still do not understand! Why did you send the three of us?"

"I told you: Carraya must be kept secret. And so must the truth about Khitomer. Kravokh's reign is known as a golden age among our people, and it must remain so. It was Kravokh who brought us out of the dark times following Praxis, Kravokh who made us a power in the quadrant again. *That* must remain his legacy, not as one who circumvented the High Council for his corrupt ends." Lorgh gulped down his *warnog* in one shot, some of it dripping into his gray beard.

Finally, Toq began to understand. "You told me before that not all your fellow I.I. agents were aware of this. That is true of Khitomer as well, is it not?"

"Yes." Lorgh smiled, apparently pleased that Toq had finally worked something out. "In truth, I fear for I.I.'s future. There are many newer, younger agents who attempt to manipulate the High Council for their own ends. They claim it is for the good of the empire, but I am not convinced of that. If this information fell into their hands—"

"So you used me."

"Of course I did, my son." Lorgh leaned forward. Toq could smell the *warnog* on his breath. "You wish to play at being I.I.? *This* is what it means. Oh, and don't give me that look, boy—the only way to get at the file on Khitomer in the padd I gave you was to use a code that I never provided for you. For that matter, there was the code word you used with B'Etloj on Elabrej."

Toq's eyes grew wide. "You know about that?"

"B'Etloj told me. She was angry, not because you used the code word but because I never told her that I had any other protégés besides her." He chuckled. "In fact, I have several, though they are ignorant of each other, and you are not any of them. You are very clever, Toq—it is why you are now first officer of the *Gorkon*—but there is a line between being clever and being dangerous, and you are dancing on it like a *trigak* in heat."

Lorgh got to his feet and went back to the replicator, ordering another *warnog*. After it materialized, he turned to face Toq, who was still sitting and nursing his own as yet untouched mug. "A toast, my son—to Tokath and L'Kor and the rest of the prisoners on Carraya."

For that, Toq was willing to drink. "To Pitzh and Q'Idar—and all the others of Carraya IV. May they sail with the Black Fleet in *Sto-Vo-Kor*." Even if Toq believed in the afterlife, he knew that all of Carraya's inhabitants would be on the Barge of the Dead, if anywhere, but what did it matter? It was all fiction—half-truths told to convince Klingons that there was more to the universe.

As opposed to Lorgh's stock-in-trade, which were half-truths told to convince Klingons that the universe made sense.

After gulping down his *warnog*, Toq got up, turned his back on his surrogate father, and walked out, heading back to the transporter room. He had a ship to report back to.

* * *

The sensation of being transported filled Ba'el with a thrill of wonder.

She'd been transported only a few times before the attack on Carraya, and that was when she was a girl, and her parents had grown tired of her endless questions about the supply ship that made regular trips to the planet. So she'd beamed up that she might see what a spaceship looked like. That desire had been satisfied, and she also got to see what home looked like from orbit—which was an amazing sight—but the thing she took with her for all her days after that was the wonderful tingly feeling of being transported.

For years after that, she always asked to be transported every time the supply ship came, and sometimes her parents and the supply ship captain indulged her. But as she grew older, she found new things to interest her, and she stopped asking, which she knew came as something of a relief to Tokath and Gi'ral.

After Worf, of course, she never asked either of them for anything again.

Klingon transporters were even more wonderful than Romulan ones. Less tingly but more comforting—where the technology of her father's people was like a mild shock, that of her mother's people was more akin to being wrapped in a blanket.

She materialized on the platform of a brightly lit room. On one wall was a blue emblem with three stars on it. Ba'el assumed this to represent that Federation Toq had spoken of to her.

Three people in strange black-and-gray-and-gold uniforms were in the room, one behind the console and two standing by the door. The latter two were armed with weapons that bore a vague resemblance to the disruptors the Romulans on Carraya carried but in silver rather than green. Ba'el had never seen a species like this before, but they seemed unfinished, somehow. Smooth, flat foreheads, stunted ears, very little hair—they had almost no distinguishing characteristics whatsoever.

A fourth was present as well, though he wore a brightly colored outfit. "You must be Ba'el," he said. "My name is Giancarlo Wu—Ambassador Worf's aide. If you'll come with me, please?"

Nodding, Ba'el stepped down off the platform and followed Wu out a door that slid apart at her approach. The technology had impressed her when she first saw it on Lorgh's ship—all the doors on Carraya were operated by hand.

Wu led Ba'el down a carpeted corridor. Her feet sank slightly into the dull orange rug. The bright walls were covered with tapestries and paintings that Ba'el found soothing, which she assumed to be the point. She passed doors that appeared to be made of wood with intricate designs on them.

After turning a corner to another similar corridor, Wu turned again, and a set of doors slid apart with a quiet hiss. Ba'el followed him through the doors, which led to a small enclosed chamber. Wu said, "Second floor."

The doors shut with the same hiss and then the chamber moved. Belatedly, Ba'el realized this was a turbolift. She'd used them on the supply ship but only there—everything on Carraya was at ground level.

Where the lifts on the Romulan ships had always made her nauseous, this one was quite smooth and pleasant. She wondered if that was due to Klingon or Federation engineering.

With a barely perceptible lurch, the lift slowed and stopped, and the doors parted again. Another unformed being—human?—sat at a wooden desk in the corridor that this lift emptied into.

"Hi, Giancarlo," the person at the desk said. "And you must be Ba'el. The ambassador's ready for you."

"Thank you, Carl," Wu said. He led Ba'el to a set of doors that parted at his approach.

Ba'el found her breath catching in her throat at what she saw.

The back wall of the huge room which she entered was made up of three windows that looked out over a magnificent cityscape. After growing up amid the modest structures of Carraya, to see such magnificent structures that climbed high into the cloud-filled sky took Ba'el's breath away. A dark river flowed tempestuously through the center of the metropolis, and she could see one particularly imposing structure atop the highest ground near the river—she assumed this to be the Great Hall, the center of Klingon government.

Inside the office, she saw a large wooden desk. The desk contained a workstation and several padds. The screen of the workstation was lit up with the image of an old Klingon being attacked by another Klingon whose face was masked.

Sitting at that desk was the man she loved.

Until this very moment, Ba'el hadn't been sure how

she felt. True, she'd fallen madly in love with Worf practically from the moment she first saw him on Carraya. Yes, she was younger then, and Worf was an impressive figure, appearing mysteriously, telling strange stories of worlds far beyond their experiences—plus he *smelled* wonderful. He opened her eyes to so many things.

As the years passed, though, Ba'el wondered how much of that was youthful enthusiasm mixed with nostalgia. Did she love Worf or just the memory of Worf? And was she fixated on him now because she had nothing left?

Seeing him switch off the screen and rise from his chair, dressed in the long cassock of office over a rust-colored suit, still with the powerful crest, probing eyes, and strong shoulders she remembered—though the smell she loved was muted—she realized whatever factor was played by nostalgia and despair was irrelevant. She still loved this man.

But does he feel the same?

Worf smiled, an expression she'd never seen in all the time he spent on Carraya. "Ba'el. It is good to see you."

She ran to him, wrapping her arms around his waist, pressing her cheek against his chest. "Worf. I've missed you so much." Tears welled up in her eyes, and she held Worf more tightly. So much had been taken from her these past few days—even Toq, truth be told, for he was no longer the boy she grew up with—and seeing Worf made her realize how much she needed *something* to cling to.

From behind her, Wu said, "Sir, as I was going to

fetch Ba'el, I was informed that the *Ky'rok* has achieved orbit around Qo'noS."

"Thank you," Worf said, his deep voice rumbling into Ba'el's very bones.

"Very good, sir."

Ba'el heard the doors open and shut. She presumed that they were now alone. Breaking the embrace, she looked up at his glorious face, and she cupped his chin in one hand.

Worf gently took her wrist in one hand, then stepped back. He indicated one of the chairs in the room and sat back down.

Unhappy—she wanted to stay in his embrace—she fell more than sat in the chair. "Aren't you happy to see me?"

"I am grateful that you survived the cowardly attack upon your world, Ba'el." He got a faraway look. "I have lost many who are close to me, and it would have pained me for you to be added to that list."

"Your wife? Toq told me that you'd married."

"Yes." His eyes went to the wall opposite the windows.

Ba'el followed his gaze and saw that the wall was filled with a number of items: a metal sash of some sort, an ornate medallion, several ribbons and chunks of metal, and three images. One was of Worf in a uniform that was vaguely similar to the ones worn by the humans in the transporter station, along with a Klingon woman with a weak crest and a boy. One was of Worf and another woman—possibly human, though she had odd spots ringing her face—dressed in what Ba'el assumed to be some kind of formal wear. The last was of Worf and a group of people of various species Ba'el did not know, all wearing the same uniform as well as strange headgear.

"K'Ehleyr was my first mate," Worf said. "She died in a cowardly attack by a worthless *petaQ*. It was with her that I sired Alexander." Ba'el realized that that must have been the Klingon woman. "Jadzia was my second—we were not able to produce children before she too was killed."

Ba'el smiled. "Also by a worthless *petaQ*?"

Worf nodded, still somber. "Both those deaths were avenged eventually."

"Toq mentioned that, too. He seemed to think that that made it all better."

Now Worf shook his head. "It does not. But it provides some measure of comfort."

They sat in silence for several seconds, which were agonizing to Ba'el. She'd waited eight years to see Worf again, and now she had no idea what to say to him, especially now that she saw that he had loved other women. *I've loved only him, and don't I feel like a fool for it?*

He didn't seem to know what to say, either.

Finally, unable to bear it, she asked, "What is the third image?"

That actually prompted—well, not a smile, but a softening of his features. "I was posted to a space station in the Bajoran system for several years. While there, several of the staff competed in a sport against the personnel from a Starfleet vessel."

"Were you victorious?"

"After a fashion." Worf leaned forward. "Ba'el—"

Holding up a hand, Ba'el said, "No, Worf, don't say anything. I don't expect us to just pick up where we left off. You obviously moved on with your life." *And I didn't.* She couldn't bear to add that out loud. "I didn't come here trying to renew our relationship." Thinking a minute, she then added: "I would not have objected if we did, though."

Worf closed his eyes. "Ba'el, right now—I cannot. Jadzia's death was but two years ago, and—"

"It's all right," Ba'el said, putting a hand on Worf's thigh, a gesture she feared might get her in trouble, but she didn't care. She knew how she felt. "All I wish from you is your help."

That seemed to put him in a more comfortable place. He straightened and said, "Whatever I can do to aid you, I shall."

"I have nowhere to go. Carraya was my only home. Toq told me about this Federation you work for. He said they took you in after your parents were killed—after my father killed them."

Worf's mouth twisted into something that might have been a snarl. "I do not know that your father was responsible for my parents' death—only that he was part of the larger Romulan force that destroyed the Khitomer outpost."

"It doesn't matter. Father is dead, and I have nothing—except you."

After staring at her with those damned dark eyes of his, Worf turned away and touched a control on his desk. "Mister Wu, report to the ambassador's office immediately."

Ba'el frowned, unsure what Wu could do for her.

The doors parted to reveal the human's pleasant, if odd, face. "Yes, sir?"

"Have Mister Mazzerone's requests for an assistant abated?"

Did Wu shudder? "I would say they have done the exact opposite, sir. Your predecessor did not entertain quite as many Klingon nationals as you, and the preparatory and—you'll forgive me, sir—cleaning-up requirements for Klingon guests are considerably greater than they are for most species."

At Ba'el's confused look, Worf said, "Eduardo Mazzerone is the person in charge of coordinating events that are held at the embassy. He requires someone who will assist him in these duties."

Putting her hand to her chest, Ba'el said, "Me?"

Wu said, "Your job will be, in essence, to do whatever Mister Mazzerone tells you to do, ma'am. I believe his primary desire is to have an extra set of hands to whom he can delegate certain pedestrian tasks so that he may focus on larger issues."

"You will be provided with a quarters here at the embassy," Worf said. "You will have—a place."

Breaking into a grin, Ba'el said, "*Thank* you, Worf! That's so much better than I expected! And I'll get to stay on Qo'noS, so I can see my mother's home, finally!"

"Yes."

"If that will be all, sir," Wu said, "I will inform Mister Mazzerone that his prayers have been answered."

"Of course," Worf said with a nod to his aide.

"Very good, sir." Wu departed.

Once the doors slid shut behind Wu, Ba'el got up and wrapped her arms around Worf's shoulders. "Thank you so much, Worf. I can't begin to tell you what this means to me."

Worf stiffened at first, then relaxed, though Ba'el noticed that he did not return the embrace.

Once she broke it, he gave a small smile. "Perhaps we cannot pick up where we left off, Ba'el—but this avails us of the opportunity to bring ourselves *back* to where we were eight years ago. I will not always be present here in the embassy, however—my duties will take me all across the empire, as well as sometimes returning to the Federation. Your duties will require that you remain here at all times." In a surprisingly soft voice, he added, "There is a galaxy of possibilities, Ba'el. It is past time you learned what they were."

"You have to make me one promise, though," she said with a mischievous smile.

Now Worf looked apprehensive. "What?"

"You have to tell me more stories about Kahless. L'Kor tried to tell them after you left, and so did some of the others, but nobody told them as well as you did."

Before Worf could reply, the doors slid open to reveal Wu once again.

"My apologies for the interruption, sir, but Mister Gorjanc has just informed me of some goings-on at the *qaDrav* that you need to be aware of. It involves the passengers on the *Ky'rok*."

Frowning, Ba'el asked, "What's a *qaDrav?*"

"I will explain later," Worf said, getting to his feet and approaching Wu. "Tell me."

Ba'el did not like the sound of this. As soon as Wu mentioned the *Ky'rok*, Worf stiffened, his fists clenched, his eyes hardened.

I wonder what that's about . . .

TWENTY-FOUR

**The House M'Raq estates
Outside the First City, Qo'noS**

Klag felt refreshed as he materialized on the porch of his family estate. B'Oraq was quite the enthusiastic lover, and the more time they spent together the more he realized he'd been a fool not to take her to his bed sooner.

He also thought that a mating might well be good for both of them. With Dorrek discommendated it was left only to Klag to keep the family line alive, or risk the House of M'Raq falling into the hands of one of his idiot cousins.

As he walked through the front door, he thought, *I shall have to arrange a meeting with her uncle, see if he can be convinced that linking his House to that of the Hero of Marcan and Elabrej is worth overcoming his disdain for the Defense Force.*

Thoughts of his future receded upon crossing the threshold, however, as he smelled Mother's distinctive *grapok* sauce. He had yet to determine what spices she used—she'd sworn she'd take the secret of her *grapok* sauce to the afterlife—but he knew the sauce's olfactory signature a *qell'qam* away.

It also meant that Tarilla had finally returned. "Mother!" he cried.

She came out from the kitchen, wearing a cooking drape. "It's about time you got home," she said with a smile. "I was not going to hold dinner for much longer."

"I have been home for many days now, Mother," Klag said. "I had a meeting with Chancellor Martok at the Great Hall." He did not bother to include his subsequent liaison with his physician.

"Meetings with the chancellor, eh?" Mother said with a smile. "You *are* doing well for yourself." Then the smile fell. "A pity the same cannot be said for all my sons."

Klag scowled. "You have only one son, Mother."

"Oh, spare me," she said with a snarl. "I carried Dorrek in my belly same as I did you. That makes him my son, even if he isn't part of this House anymore. And now he doesn't even have a ship."

Klag walked across the living room, past the Danqo tapestry that adorned the center wall and past the two metal chairs and the intricately carved wooden sideboard. "That was not my doing, Mother. General Kriz took away his command, and believe me, his discommendation had nothing to do with it."

"You expect me to believe that?"

Now Klag stood face to face with his mother. "Yes, I do. He engaged in an action that was condemned by Martok himself."

"'Martok,' is it? You're familiar with the chancellor now? And my other son is left to—" Tarilla cut herself off and looked away. "Never mind. We will not speak of this. My son is home, and I will feed him and we will talk of other things. Come, the meal is almost prepared." She turned and led him into the kitchen.

The house had a full dining room, of course, but for a two-person meal such as this, the small metal table in the kitchen served the purpose. Mother had arranged some *taknar* gizzards on a plate around a bowl of the *grapok* sauce, and she'd also made *rokeg* blood pie.

She brought both plates over to the center of the table, then went to the cabinet and retrieved two plates. Klag waited until she had done so before grabbing several gizzards and dunking them in the sauce. His exertions with B'Oraq had given him an appetite, and he devoured half the gizzards in two bites.

Nibbling on a bit of the pie, Tarilla said, "It is good to have you home again, my son. It has been too long."

"You know my reasons for staying away, Mother. As long as Father—"

Tarilla held up a hand. "I know. And in truth, I understood. If there had been some way—any way—I could have convinced your father to reclaim his honor, I would have done it, if for no other reason than to have our entire family together again." She let out a long breath. "But, for whatever reason, he could not rouse himself to do so. I do not know what he saw when he was a prisoner of the Romulans, but it obviously did something to him."

"That or his escape," Klag said quietly. "I too have often wondered what led him to his decision."

"Perhaps you should have asked him instead of shunning him," Tarilla said bitterly. "Perhaps he would have told his oldest son what he would not tell his mate."

Klag found he had nothing to say to that. He had given a great deal of thought to family these past few days, and to his relationship with both his brother and his father, but all that had done was confuse him further. So he grabbed more gizzards and dunked them in the sauce—which was particularly pungent today, just the way he liked it. In fact, it was even better than usual.

After he wolfed down more gizzards, he started to tell his mother how good the sauce was—but found that his mouth wouldn't work. Looking at his mother, he saw her split in twain, become two Tarillas instead of one. And she became fuzzy around the edges . . .

Mother? He thought the plaintive word but could not make his mouth actually form it. Stars danced in front of his eyes, and the kitchen started to melt and darken.

Blackness overwhelmed him as he realized that Tarilla hadn't touched the gizzards or the *grapok* sauce, and that the reason why—and the reason why the sauce was so much more pungent than usual—was that his own mother had poisoned him.

Images shimmered into being before him: M'Raq, as Klag remembered him when he and Dorrek were children, young and vital and strong; B'Oraq, naked and enticing; Me-Larr, the San-Tarah leader who defeated Klag in the circle; Drex, Tereth, Kornan, and Toq, the succession of first officers he'd had under him in less than a year commanding the *Gorkon*; Worf, trying to warn him about something; Martok standing before him, staring at him judgmentally with his one eye; Rodek striking him across the cheek . . .

Only after it happened a second time did Klag realize that Rodek was truly striking him, in the manner that preceded a challenge. Shaking his head, his vision clearing, Klag saw that he was no longer in his family's kitchen. He was outside, for one thing, wind howling in off a nearby river whose flow he could hear and the scents of dozens of Klingons mixed with the ozone tinge of a coming storm.

Clambering quickly to his feet, Klag realized that he stood inside the *qaDrav* in front of Command Headquarters, facing his second officer.

"Rodek? What is going on?" He looked around. "I was . . . I was home, and—"

"Face me, traitor!" Rodek screamed. The tone more than the request prompted Klag to face him. Since first reporting as the *Gorkon*'s gunner, Rodek had always come across as passionless, almost sedate. He was a good soldier, but he lacked the spirit one usually found in a Klingon warrior.

That tendency had improved of late, particularly since Klag elevated him to second officer after Toq took over as first, but this was something else entirely. Never had Klag heard such vitriol, such *hatred* in Rodek's tone.

"You took my life from me, son of M'Raq! You stole my identity, my very *soul*! Once I was Kurn—the son of a great House, a member of the High Council, a noble warrior! You left me with virtually nothing—and then you even took *that* away, having my foster father *murdered*."

Klag wondered if he was still hallucinating from Tarilla's *grapok* sauce. "Rodek, I do not know what you are speaking of. Who is Kurn?"

"I am Kurn!" Now Rodek—or Kurn, or whoever he was—turned to face the crowd that had gathered.

Following his gaze, Klag saw that Tarilla and Dorrek were at the front of the crowd, standing together as if united. *Of course they are together in this. I am doomed to be betrayed by my entire family.*

Looking back at his foe, he amended the thought. *And my crew as well.*

To the crowd, Rodek said, "I was born Kurn, son of Mogh! But *this* filthy *petaQ* conspired to have my memory erased, to make me over into a passionless bloodworm named Rodek, son of Noggra. Were that not enough, he had Noggra killed by an assassin!"

The crowd rumbled its disapproval, though whether it was with what Klag was accused of, or in disagreement with the charges, Klag could not tell. He knew Noggra only as Rodek's father, and had no idea he was even dead. As for Kurn, that name was familiar only insofar as he identified himself as being Ambassador Worf's brother.

All Klag could do now was speak the truth.

"Hear me! I know not of what this man says. Until now, I have always thought of Rodek as a trusted officer under my command. I have never heard of Kurn, son of Mogh, I know nothing of the death of Noggra, nor do I know anything of what he has said."

Rodek went on as if Klag had not spoken. "I challenge you, traitor! Face me and die!" To accentuate the point, Rodek unsheathed his *d'k tahg*, the outer blades unfurling with a click.

Having very little choice at this point, especially while standing in the *qaDrav*, Klag pulled out his own blade. He had no desire to kill a perfectly good second officer over what was obviously some kind of misunderstanding, but he would not back down from a challenge, either.

At least his head appeared to have cleared. Whatever his mother had done to him, she had not left him incapable of fighting. *She does not wish to dishonor me—only herself.*

That was for later, however. Now, he stood in a ready crouch, tossing the *d'k tahg* back and forth from one hand to the other. Although he'd been less assiduous about retraining with the *d'k tahg* than he had the *bat'leth* after his transplant, Klag had continued to practice so that he was facile with either hand while using the blade.

Rodek feinted, and Klag ducked. Then Klag did likewise, and Rodek dodged to the left.

They continued to circle each other, each waiting for the other to make a move. Members of the crowd shouted out cheers and jeers, some for Klag, some for Rodek, others nothing specific, probably interested only in seeing the fight and not caring who won.

Finally, Rodek lunged. Klag reached up with his father's hand, grabbed Rodek's wrist, and pulled it to the side. Rodek stumbled, and Klag swung his left arm up in an arc toward Rodek's now-outstretched arm.

With a clang of metal on metal, Klag's gauntlets struck those of Rodek. Klag had hoped to break his arm, but both of them were too well protected by their armor for that. However, the impact startled Rodek for a brief second, giving Klag time to whirl around and flip Rodek over his own shoulder, sending him crashing to the concrete floor of the *qaDrav*. Before Klag could deliver a kick to his face, Rodek brought up his knee into Klag's groin. Moving instinctively to protect himself, even though his armor was even stronger there than on his arm, Klag lost his chance to finish Rodek off.

Then Klag was sent reeling backward by Rodek's foot slamming into his stomach, smashing his own armor into his belly. There was no pain, but the force of the impact was enough to make Klag stumble backward to the iron railing.

Normally, Klag would be lost in the bloodlust by now. But this fight served no purpose. Klag found himself confused and angered by his mother's betrayal and by Rodek's absurd story, so much so that he could not focus on the fight itself.

"You will die for what you've done to me!" Rodek cried.

"I have done *nothing*!" Klag cried right back. "We fight for no reason, Rodek!"

"Do not call me that! Rodek is a fiction that *you* created!"

From behind him, a deep, powerful voice said, "That is *not* so!"

Whirling around, Klag saw Worf stepping through the crowd, forcing aside other Klingons in an attempt to reach the railing.

A guardsman Klag had not noticed before stepped forward with his painstik brandished. "There is a challenge in progress!"

Worf glowered at the guardsman. "I am Worf, Federation ambassador and member of the House of Martok. You *will* let me pass."

While the diplomatic post did not seem to impress the guardsman, Martok's name did. He stepped aside.

The crowd grew quiet.

Rodek was squinting at the ambassador. "Worf." The name was spoken as if it were a curse.

"Yes, I am the firstborn son of Mogh. And you are indeed Kurn, Mogh's second son and my brother." Worf now turned to address the crowd. "It is true that Kurn's memories were erased. It is true that 'Rodek, son of Noggra,' is a fiction. What is not true," and now Worf looked again at the man who was apparently his brother, "is that Captain Klag is in any way responsible."

"Why should I believe you?" Rodek asked.

"Because *I* am the one responsible."

Klag felt almost dizzy. "You did this to your own brother?"

"I had . . . what I thought were good reasons at the time, Captain."

"What of my father?" Rodek cried. "What of Noggra?"

Worf pulled a padd from an inner pocket of his floor-length cassock. "Noggra was killed by an assassin who interrogated him for several hours, forcing him to tell the truth of what happened to you." He held up the padd so that both Klag and Rodek could see the display.

The crowd grew restless. "I thought there was a challenge!" "Talk later, fight now!" "Kill him, Klag!" "Destroy the traitor, Rodek!"

But Rodek was focused entirely on the recording before him. "That is what Dorrek showed me—but only some of it."

Klag turned to see that his mother and brother were trying to lose themselves in the crowd. Immediately, Klag said, "Guardsman!"

The guardsman who had tried to stop Worf stood at attention. "Sir!"

Pointing at Tarilla and Dorrek, Klag said, "Detain those two!"

Two other guardsmen stepped forward, and the three of them quickly had both of Klag's family members surrounded.

Turning to Rodek, Klag said, "Dorrek wanted revenge upon me for discommendating him—not to mention his losing command of the *K'mpec*. He would have done anything to hurt me, including pitting me against my own officer."

Worf walked up to the opening in the railing of the *qaDrav*. "Klag is blameless in all this, brother. If anyone deserves to die for what has happened to you, it is me. If you wish to take my life, I shall not stop you."

Klag stepped back, giving Rodek room. He wasn't sure what the entire story was, but he did know that this was a feud between two brothers. In fact, it was two feuds between two sets of brothers, but he would deal with Dorrek shortly. Right now, he wanted to give the sons of Mogh the opportunity to finish this.

They stared at each other for several seconds. Shouts came from the crowd, who had been promised blood.

Rodek threw his head back and screamed to the heavens.

Then he threw his *d'k tahg* to the concrete floor and ran past Worf and into the crowd.

One of the guardsman, who was making sure Dorrek and Tarilla stayed put, asked Klag, "Should we go after him, sir?"

"No," Worf said. "Let him go."

Glowering at the ambassador, Klag said, "I am hardly inclined to do as *you* say right now, Ambassador."

Tarilla spoke up suddenly. "It does not matter, Klag. It would have been easier if you had died today, but I have already petitioned to speak before the High Council."

"Rest assured, Mother, you *will* speak before the council, but it will only be to explain your actions today." Turning to the guardsmen, he said, "These two are to be bound by law for attacking the head of the House of M'Raq in his own home."

The guardsmen all saluted.

Klag then turned to Worf. "As for you, Ambassador, you will explain yourself. And if I am not satisfied with the explanation, I will kill you myself."

TWENTY-FIVE

Baldi'maj District
Krennla, Qo'noS

By the time the dress rehearsal rolled around, G'joth had resigned himself to his impotence.

That resignation came when he remembered that he had left Krennla in the first place and never looked back. Years later, he remembered Klaad and Krom with fondness, but that was, he now realized, the haze of nostalgia. Distance from the actual event had made him recall only the parts he wanted to remember, completely forgetting that Krennla was a pit that he ran away from as soon as he could.

In turn, that revelation made it easier to deal with the opera. The Battle of San-Tarah was for Konn and Reshtarc what Krennla was for G'joth: a fond memory. The creators of the opera were interested in remembering only the parts that were important to them, just as

G'joth remembered only the parts of his childhood that were important to him.

Wol had been right to stay away from here. Were I sane, I would have done likewise. His memories were far more pleasant than the reality and also easier to maintain when he was in space far away from Qo'noS.

Still, he was here now, so he continued to "consult" for Konn. The one way he was actually useful was in showing some of the extras how to hold a *bat'leth*. They kept dropping them, mostly because they insisted upon holding them one-handed. In and of itself, that was fine, but you had to hold it a particular way for a one-handed grip to work, and they didn't know what it was. G'joth took it upon himself to show each of them either the proper two-handed grip or a one-handed grip that would allow them to hold onto it. It necessitated a reworking of some of the fights, which did not endear G'joth to Krelk, the choreographer, but G'joth was unconcerned. If Krelk wished to issue a challenge, G'joth suspected that Krelk would know only stage moves, and G'joth would kill him in an instant.

Speaking of challenges, the role of Captain Huss had to be recast when rehearsal was interrupted by the arrival of a woman who claimed to be the wife of the man with whom the actress playing Huss was sleeping. They fought a duel on the stage, the actress lost (for pretty much the same reason why G'joth expected to win a potential fight against Krelk), and one of the chorus was elevated to the role of Huss.

G'joth sat in the front row of the amphitheater as the dress rehearsal went on. This was the first opportunity he'd had to see the opera from start to finish, and he reluctantly had to admit to being impressed. Kenni deserved his reputation—he sang with passion and verve, enough to make G'joth's ribs vibrate on the lowest notes—and, while Klivv still looked nothing like Klag, he was able to convey the captain's heroism and spirit, if not his physical presence. (He also chuckled. G'joth did not think that the captain *ever* chuckled, and Klag's deep-throated laugh was legendary, but Klivv was unable to replicate it, and his one attempt to do so reinforced to G'joth that he should stick with the chuckle.)

As for his sister, it was impossible to make out her voice in the cacophony of the chorus, but the chorus as a whole did its job magnificently.

Of course, he would have preferred more use of the ground troops, but that, G'joth knew, was a forlorn hope in an opera. Klag's victories would be remembered forever. The fifteenth's victories would be forgotten outside the *Gorkon*'s decks.

After the rehearsal ended, G'joth accompanied Lakras downstairs to the dressing rooms. The aircar would take them back to Kenta District once they changed out of their costumes.

"I also need to see Kenni for a moment," Lakras said as she climbed into her own clothing. "Wasn't he *wonderful?*"

"He was . . . adequate," G'joth said with a smile, unwilling to give his sister the satisfaction of fawning over her love interest.

"Hmph. He was *brilliant*, and you know it."

"I will credit him with providing General Talak with

a nobility of purpose that the genuine article did not have. In the opera, Talak is misguided. On San-Tarah, the general was merely a dishonorable *petaQ*."

"Perhaps," Lakras said, exiting into the hallway and walking straight toward Kenni's private room, "but dishonorable *petaQpu'* make for boring opera."

"So I have been told repeatedly of late."

The opera house retained much of the same structure it had when it was first constructed centuries earlier, which meant that several of the doors were manual. Lakras pulled on the handle, saying, "You're just an old crank, G'joth. Admit it, you loved . . ."

G'joth was confused as to why Lakras trailed off. Then he looked past her to see Kenni scratching the chest of one of the other women from the chorus, who, in turn, was raking her nails across Kenni's back, drawing blood.

"Kenni? Ginva?"

Whirling toward the door, Kenni said, "Go *away*, girl, I'm busy!"

"But . . . but . . . I thought—"

"I said *go away*!"

Reaching past his sister, G'joth closed the door. He, at least, had no desire to watch. Voyeurism was never much of a thrill for him—he preferred to do rather than watch.

Lakras's eyes were wide, her skin and crest pale, her jaw hanging open. "I don't—I don't believe it. How—how—how could he—"

G'joth recalled one of the chorus members telling him that Kenni would discard Lakras soon enough.

Thinking about it, the person who'd told him that was the woman with whom Kenni was currently engaged.

Grabbing Lakras's arm, G'joth said, "Come, sister, let us go—"

"No!" She shook off his grip. "I am not moving from this spot until he comes out and explains himself!"

"Lakras—"

"I said *no!*"

"I am your older brother, Lakras, and I am telling you—"

"Telling me *what?*" She turned and screamed at him, her face now growing red with rage, spittle flying out of the corner of her mouth. "You went off to your stupid ship to fight stupid aliens all the time! You don't get to tell me *anything!*"

Then she turned her back on him and stood in front of the door to Kenni's changing room, arms folded defiantly over her chest.

Once again, G'joth resigned himself to impotence. *I have got to get out of this damned city.*

Eventually, the door opened. Both Ginva and Kenni were fully dressed. Ginva left the room, a triumphant expression on her visage as she passed both Lakras and G'joth.

Kenni remained in the room, staring at himself in a looking glass. G'joth felt nauseous.

"How *dare* you?" Lakras screamed. She grabbed a bowl filled with some items G'joth couldn't see off a sideboard and held it as if to throw it at Kenni. "We were—"

"Nothing," Kenni said dismissively. "An entertaining

diversion for a while, but I grew bored, so I moved on. Ginva gives me something you can't."

Now Lakras did throw the bowl, but Kenni ducked it with ease. The bowl crashed into the wall, the items clattering across the floor.

"I don't believe it!" Lakras cried. "What about all those things you said to me, those things you promised me?"

Laughing derisively, Kenni said, "Don't tell me you *believed* all that?"

"Why should I not have believed them?"

"This isn't a romance novel, Lakras, it's real life. Do you honestly think I would do anything but dally with the likes of *you*?"

Lakras grabbed a blade that was lying on the table. G'joth assumed it was Kenni's. "I should kill you!"

Another laugh. "Do not be a fool, Lakras. I am the finest opera performer of our time."

And the most modest, G'joth thought with a roll of his eyes.

He went on: "*You* are but a common woman."

"Do you truly think that will stop me from challenging you? I have every right—"

"Who cares about your rights, little girl? Do you even know how to use that thing in your hand?"

Lakras bared her teeth. "There is one way to find out."

"Even if I accepted your laughable challenge, what would come of it? If I win, you die, and no one cares—except perhaps your brother, there, but he'll be back on his ship in no time. If you win, you'll be known only as the girl who killed a great opera performer. What do you think that will do for your career?"

Tearing himself away from the looking glass, Kenni stepped past Lakras. "It was fun for a while, Lakras. And now you'll be able to tell your fellow commoners that you bedded the great Kenni. Take it for what it is and move on."

Kenni continued toward the exit. Lakras did not move—G'joth thought she looked stunned. She still held the blade in her hand.

Leaving his sister to her shock, G'joth followed Kenni to the entrance where a private aircar was no doubt waiting to take him back to his opulent home.

"Kenni!" G'joth called out just as the singer walked through the doorway.

"What is it?" he asked impatiently. "I have things to do."

"No doubt. I must give you credit. It is much easier to seduce common women secure in the knowledge that they cannot possibly challenge you without risk to their careers. But if you think I'm simply some soldier who will walk away, you are sadly mistaken."

Kenni, who was half a head taller than G'joth, stared down at him. "Are you threatening me, *Bekk* G'joth?" He practically sneered the rank.

"Merely stating a fact. You see, I have very little use for the opera or its practitioners, beyond what it means to my sister. All things being equal, I would have been quite content to go back to my ship and forget all about you, as you predicted. But that is not going to happen now—now you have my attention."

With that, G'joth turned his back on Kenni and walked back inside.

The sad thing was, it was an empty threat. If G'joth killed Kenni—and if he wanted to, he could have killed Kenni about twenty different ways without even trying hard—it would be a huge setback for the opera and would probably cause the same damage to Lakras's career that her challenging him would. With Father out of work, they needed Lakras to provide income to the household. Honor was all well and good when you had food in your belly, but it did G'joth's family no good to starve just so Lakras could save face.

Besides, she was a commoner. What face did she have *to* save?

A warrior did not make an empty threat, and the longer he stayed in this misbegotten city he once called home, the less G'joth felt like a warrior.

I have to get out of this place, he thought as he grabbed his sister, still in a state of shock, and took her home.

TWENTY-SIX

Market Circle
Pheben III

Wol's first thought upon seeing Lak was that he wasn't the biggest person she'd ever seen. But she'd also spent every day of her life since reporting to the *Gorkon* in the presence of Goran, who was bigger than any two Klingons—not to mention dealing with various alien species, some of whom were built quite large.

Besides, while Lak wasn't the largest Klingon she'd seen, excepting Goran, he was by far the largest Klingon on Pheben III. He was roughly the same height as the big man, with narrower shoulders, wider forearms, and a larger gut, no doubt from what his family farm produced. Given his streak of victories, Wol wouldn't have been surprised to learn that his family gave him the *trigak*'s share of the food produced by the family business to keep his strength up.

Wol had spent the previous day working with Kagak on his hand-to-hand skills. Tabona had said she was wasting her time, but Wol had insisted, and Kagak had agreed to take whatever assistance his commander would provide. For her part, Tabona kept a steady supply of the candied *racht* coming, since that provided a source of energy for both of them during the workouts.

At the end of the last session before the evening meal, Kagak had said, "Thank you, Leader."

"For what?" she had asked.

"Today is the first day that I truly feel like I am part of the fifteenth—that it is only now that you have accepted me."

Wol had bowed her head. "You brought me here, Kagak. That alone earns you the right to fight alongside us."

Today, they had come to the market. B'Ellor and Goran had said they would be right behind them. The pair of them had been spending a lot of time together, and Wol was concerned that it would come to a bad end. After all, they were reporting back to the *Gorkon* soon enough, which meant he would have to leave her behind.

Or he'll decide to stay here, and I'll lose the big man. Wol didn't like either notion. Goran was a very large part of the fifteenth's success, both literally and figuratively.

The market itself was a huge circular space, at least a *qell'qam* in diameter, with dozens of roads leading right to it. They had ridden in the thrice-damned Vikak, but this time Tabona drove, since Fuhrman's broken arm prevented him from doing so, and she drove more sanely than her grandson. *It could hardly be otherwise* . . .

Even over the noise of the Vikak engine, Wol could hear the sounds of shouting from half a *qell'qam* away. Haggling was performed at knifepoint, deals sealed by bloodletting and head butting. Wol had expected temporary structures as fitting itinerant merchants, but all the booths selling the various crops and merchandise were made of metal and strong wood rather than the canvas Wol expected.

Upon getting a closer look, she saw that stands were regularly kicked, punched, shot at, and had things thrown at them.

Wol had thought the farm to be a cornucopia of odors, but that was as nothing compared to that which assaulted her nostrils in the market circle: everything she got on the farm and more, plus engine fuel, a much more concentrated smell of pack animals, and an array of spices and fruits—Tabona's farm did not grow either, but others on Pheben III apparently did, based on the goods for sale. She also smelled assorted tree saps and sugars.

Turning a corner, she saw Lak for the first time. A small Pheben stood next to him, tentacles wiggling in a nauseating manner—it reminded Wol too much of the six-armed Elabrej—and trying to make herself heard over the din.

Once Wol got close enough—and had decided that Lak wasn't all that impressive—she could hear the Pheben's words: "Today at low sun, the seventy-fourth Pheben III tournament shall commence! The reigning champion is Lak, son of Til'k. He will fight until he is defeated—something that hasn't happened for seven seasons!"

Wol noted that very few people were paying attention to the Pheben's words. To Kagak, she asked, "Who is she talking to?"

"I have no idea. Honestly, you're probably the person here who knows least about the tournament. I think it's more of a ritual thing."

From behind her, Wol heard screaming. Whirling, she saw three young Klingons charging straight for Lak.

The Pheben skittered out of the way upon seeing them, but Lak did not move. He did, however, smile.

All three started pounding on Lak as soon as they reached him, fists striking his shoulders and chest, boots slamming into his legs.

Lak did not move.

"Cheater!" one of them cried. "My family starved because we lost money betting against you!"

That got Lak to smile wider. "Good. People who make stupid bets deserve to starve." Then Lak grabbed that one's head—he was the one doing the kicking—and threw him toward a stand. The youth crashed into it with a clatter, but the stand remained intact, though many of its wares were now scattered on the ground.

While the stand's owner slapped the youth on the back of his head and started yelling at him, the other two continued to pound at an unmoving Lak.

Finally, four bigger Klingons carrying painstiks came by. The ends of the painstiks glowing a bright amber, they touched all three with the bright ends, two on Lak, and one each on his remaining attackers.

Their screams filled the sky, though they did nothing to quiet the noise of the market. Few people even noticed what was going on, beyond the merchant whose stand had been disrupted and a small handful of spectators.

"Does nobody care about what's happening here?" Wol asked.

Tabona shrugged. "This isn't the real fight, this is just some people brawling."

"People brawling *is* a real fight," Wol said. "If something like this happened on the *Gorkon*, there'd be a crowd a *qell'qam* deep to watch—or participate."

"This isn't the *Gorkon*," Tabona said sourly. "These people have business to conduct that relates to their very survival. It's easy to waste your time on brawls when you know where your next meal's coming from, but these people," she waved out her arm, taking in the entire market circle, "are negotiating for how they're going to eat for the next season. When that's done, the tournament'll start—*then* they'll pay attention."

Tabona went off to do her own business, Kagak alongside her, fulfilling Fuhrman's role, leaving Wol to observe. What went on here today were the types of things she had always left to the House servants. If she needed, for example, sugar to make a particular confection, she told the House *ghIntaq* to get it, and he would send someone on the staff to do so. The actual process by which the staff did so never even occurred to her.

She walked around the market, watching the fights that broke out over prices, over the quality and/or provenance of the goods, and sometimes over the way someone looked at a family member or over some slight in the past. *In that, at least, it is very much like the* Gorkon, Wol thought with amusement.

As the sun got lower, the shouting dimmed, several of the stands started to close up, and people started drifting toward the center of the circle.

Lak, seemingly unfazed by being on the receiving end of two painstiks, stood next to the Pheben woman. He had stripped down to only a pair of brown pants—he had even removed his boots, leaving his ridged feet bare. Another Pheben, a male, was wheeling over a large slate on which was written several names. The only one Wol recognized was Tabona's.

"Leader!"

Turning around, Wol saw Kagak standing a few meters away, alongside Tabona and B'Ellor. Pushing her way through the growing crowd, she joined them.

Pointing at the slate, Wol asked, "Do those names represent the household?"

Tabona nodded. "The one on top's Til'k—that's Lak's father. Owns this tiny farm on the outskirts, can barely clear enough to live. Except, thanks to that *khest'n* son of his, he's the wealthiest man on the planet."

Wol looked at Kagak. "You shall have to change that. I see you are the fourth to fight." Tabona's name was listed fifth.

"Not exactly," Tabona said, before Kagak could reply.

Frowning, Wol asked, "What do you mean?"

Before anyone could answer, a burly Klingon came over to them. "Tabona, you madwoman, what're you up to?" Wol could smell the *warnog* on the man's breath.

"What makes you think I'm up to anything, Gralk?"

"I heard your grandson was scratched. So why are you betting your whole damn farm?"

Wol's eyes widened. "Tabona, Kagak is skilled, but—"

"You'll find out soon enough, Gralk." Tabona cut Wol off and glowered at her. "And if you're smart, you'll bet on my house instead of Til'k's."

"Bah!" Gralk stormed off.

"Tabona—" Wol started, but Tabona again cut her off.

"You don't know the whole story, Wol. While I'm grateful for your help in training Kagak, it wasn't necessary."

"Why not? Who will fight Lak from your household?"

Smiling, Tabona said, "Its newest member."

Before Wol could ask what Tabona meant by that, exactly, the Pheben female cried out, "Attention, citizens of Pheben III! The tournament will now begin!"

Cheers erupted from the crowd, and several people threw objects toward the center of the circle, which the Pheben ducked easily. Wol suspected she'd had a lot of practice.

"The reigning champion is Lak, from the household of Til'k. The first challenger is from the household of Vorbris."

A Klingon stepped forward, also stripped to the waist. He was about half Lak's size, and he looked like a newborn waddling up to an adult.

Wol noticed a few people—some Klingon, some

Pheben—bringing torches to the perimeter of the fighting area and lighting them. The sun was only just starting to set, and there was plenty of light, but, as Wol had learned, it got dark quickly on Pheben III.

The Pheben female said, "The fight will continue until one can no longer battle. Begin!"

Before the Pheben could even finish the instruction to start, the Klingon from Vorbris's household lunged forward with a left jab to Lak's chest.

"Keep it up," Wol muttered. At Kagak's look, she added, "The only way to beat someone that much larger than you is to get in close and keep pounding him as much as possible. If you stay inside his reach, he can't land a good punch."

"This is a grudge match," Tabona said. "Before Lak started fighting, Kriton was one of our best fighters. He usually lasted at least through four or five challengers before someone beat him. Now, though, he's just one more victim."

As Wol watched, she saw that Kriton was landing half a dozen punches, and Lak barely seemed to notice. Which was a pity, as Kriton's technique was excellent. He would jab several times with his left before coming in with a hard right. Against an opponent less—well, less huge, Kriton might have been well served. For his part, Lak lunged with several obvious punches, all of which Kriton dodged with ease. Were the fight based solely on punches landed, Kriton would be far ahead.

But a true battle required damage to one's enemy or it was no fight at all, and Kriton had done nothing to his. Not that Lak was all that impressive, either. Wol turned to Tabona. "How has Lak managed to win so many fights with such awful fighting ability?"

Even as she spoke, Kriton was a hair too slow in dodging one punch. It appeared only to glance off his head, but it sent him sprawling to the ground. Dirt kicked up and hovered in the air before settling again.

"That's how," Tabona said.

Lak threw his head back and laughed heartily, his guffaws echoing off the merchant stands. Kriton did not move from his prone position on the ground. Wol could hear grumbles as coins exchanged hands. "Someone thought he might still have the old fire," Kagak said.

Tabona said, "Possibly. Or, more likely, they're betting on how long Lak's opponent lasts. A few people still bet on his opponents winning, but that's mainly because the odds are so long that if it does happen, the victor will win very, very big."

"Like you apparently did on Kagak," Wol said. "Why?"

But Tabona only smiled.

Wol noticed that, for something that Tabona, Kagak, B'Ellor, and Fuhrman had all described as a major event on Pheben III, the crowd didn't seem all that excited. She would have expected cheers and head butts and other signs of enjoyment, but there was a tinge of impatience in the air.

The Pheben stepped forward even as another Pheben and a Klingon both hauled away the unconscious Kriton. "Lak, from the household of Til'k, is the victor. The second challenger is from the household of Rankak.

The fight will continue until one can no longer battle. Begin!"

A tall, wiry Klingon with scars all over his ridged chest stepped forward at the announcement. His hair was short, his beard weak, and Wol did not see what Rankak had to gain by sending one of its sons to be sacrificed so. He seemed to be very young, and Wol wondered if this was some child's foolish pride.

Where Kriton was a skilled fighter, the Rankak challenger was very much not. He never even landed a punch, and Lak literally hit him on top of his head, and he crumpled to the ground.

"Lak, from the household of Til'k, is the victor. The third challenger is from the household of B'Entrok. The fight will continue until one can no longer battle. Begin!"

This fight lasted somewhat longer, but only because the challenger from B'Entrok—a short, slim Klingon with a poor crest and a weak chest—was able to dodge every punch Lak threw. He accomplished this by staying far away. The crowd grew bored with this fairly quickly, and Wol could hear jeers and complaints from all around her. She was tempted to engage in one or two herself.

Instead, she stared at Tabona, who was also jeering: "This is a fight, not a dance!"

What is the old woman planning?

Eventually, as with Kriton, this foe fell when Lak finally got in a single punch, which brought him to the ground.

The Pheben almost sounded bored, now. "Lak, from

the household of Til'k, is the victor. The fourth challenger is from the household of Tabona."

Kagak did not move. He had not even taken off his shirt.

The crowd parted as leaves being blown by the wind to allow Goran to step forward. He had stripped to the waist, revealing several scars that Wol knew he had incurred during his time as a prison guard on Rura Penthe.

Wol's jaw fell open, even as several members of the crowd shouted in disbelief. "What is this?" "Who is this person?" "This is a fraud!"

The Pheben female didn't sound bored anymore. "Tabona, step forward and explain this!"

"There is nothing to explain," Tabona said with a smile. "This is Goran, the mate of my daughter B'Ellor."

Wol broke out in a huge grin, her tongue running across her teeth in an attempt not to laugh. *That's who I heard taking the oath. I should have realized.*

"This is not fair!" someone yelled. "We knew nothing of this! How do we know you do not lie to try to regain the shards of your lost honor?"

"Oh, do shut up, Til'k," Tabona said. "Everyone from three farms around heard them take the oath."

"It is true," someone from the crowd said. "Woke me up, they did!"

"I heard them, too," someone else said.

"No!" Til'k said. He had stepped in front of his son now, though the stooped, elderly Klingon was barely noticeable with Lak's girth behind him. "Tabona has broken the rules of—"

"I thought I told you to shut up, Til'k," Tabona said. "What are you concerned about, anyhow? Your son hasn't lost for many turns. The rules of the contest are that anyone who is from a farm family may participate. Goran here is one."

Wol stepped forward there, deciding that Tabona had earned her assistance. "Goran is also a soldier in the Defense Force, serving under Captain Klag of the *I.K.S. Gorkon*. I am the commander of his platoon, as well as that of *Bekk* Kagak. I can assure you that *Bekk* Goran is an honorable foe and would never dishonor himself or his platoonmate. If he tells you that he and B'Ellor are mated, then it is so, and any who would doubt it shall answer to me, to *Bekk* Kagak, and to the entire crew of the *Gorkon*."

A rumble went through the crowd. The name of the *Gorkon* carried weight, Wol knew. Operas had been composed about their exploits, and the information net was filled with their tales of glory in the Kavrot sector.

The Pheben female walked over to Til'k and waved her tentacles about, several of her eyestalks fixing him with a gaze. "Your protest has no merit, Til'k. Please remove yourself from the fighting range."

Til'k, though, was staring daggers at Tabona.

Wol stepped forward, interceding herself between Til'k and Goran's new grandmother. "You were given an instruction, old man. I suggest you follow it."

Lak put a meaty hand on his father's shoulder. "It does not matter, Father. I will beat this one as I beat everyone! I am too mighty to be defeated!"

That prompted a ragged cheer from several in the

crowd, though Wol couldn't help but notice that those cheers were even more muted than they'd been during the fights. Part of that was because plenty of people were too busy staring at Goran, who was far closer in build to Lak than anyone they'd ever seen.

Lak and Goran faced each other. Lak seemed nonplussed, and Wol wondered if he'd ever seen anyone eye to eye while standing up before.

Goran said, "You will lose."

"I've never lost."

"Today will be the first time. Because I am the biggest and the strongest."

"The fight," the Pheben said, "will continue until one can no longer battle. Begin!"

Immediately, Lak lunged toward Goran, throwing several punches right at the big man's head. Goran deflected one, ducked another, and then caught Lak's fist in his own hand. Lak's eyes grew wide; Wol suspected that that had never happened to him before.

Then Goran closed the fingers that were wrapped around Lak's fist. Wol heard the snap of bone echo off the stands, followed in short order by Lak screaming in what sounded like purest agony. Idly, Wol wondered if Lak had ever felt that kind of pain before. She remembered Goran saying in the mess hall once that he still recalled with perfect clarity the first time he felt any kind of agony, which was shortly after he'd enlisted in the Defense Force and his training *QaS DevwI'* used a painstik on him. Goran was sometimes hard-pressed to recall the specifics of last week, but he remembered that day quite well.

Goran flexed his wrist downward, and Lak's arm started to bend in a direction the Klingon arm wasn't intended to go in. He quickly fell to his knees rather than have his limb go the way of his hand.

Lak's face was now contorted into a grimace of agony. Silence fell over the crowd, as no one had ever seen Lak on his knees before.

Then Wol started shouting. "Goran! Goran! Goran!"

Kagak joined her, as did B'Ellor. Then Tabona. Then a few others nearby.

By the time the cheer spread to the entire crowd, Goran had let go of Lak's hand. He reared back and struck Lak with an uppercut to his jaw, which sent him sprawling backward, skidding across the circle, kicking up dirt and pebbles. Goran dove into the cloud and landed atop Lak. He used his knees to pin Lak's shoulders to the ground and then started punching the face that had been smiling and laughing only a few minutes before.

The cheers were all over the Market Circle now. "Goran! Goran! Goran! Goran!" People head-butted each other and raised their mugs and threw various items in the air.

As she led the cheer, Wol noticed that Til'k and those around him were noticeably silent, and their expressions could kindly be called sour.

Finally, Goran stopped punching Lak and got to his feet. "Rise up and face me!" Goran bellowed, loud enough to be heard over the crowd.

Lak did not move.

Now nothing even Goran's lungs could manage

would be heard over the din, as hundreds of Klingons and Phebens raised their voices to the heavens, cheering on Goran. About a dozen gathered around Goran and tried to hoist him into the air. Wol winced as they failed, and Goran fell to the ground, but he got up in short order.

B'Ellor pushed her way through the crowd and wrapped her arms around Goran's massive belly. He picked her up and bit her ear.

That just made the crowd louder.

Tabona was conspicuous by her absence. Looking around, Wol saw her eventually, collecting coins from a large number of Klingons. She would have expected the losers to be unhappy, but all who paid Tabona had smiles on their faces.

Wol walked over to Tabona and smiled. "Well played."

"You should get some of this, Leader," Tabona said. "Not that you'll get it or anything—I'm no fool—but in a fair and just universe, you'd get a share for your role in this."

"I did nothing, Grandmother," Wol said with a smile. "You orchestrated this."

"Yes, but you brought Goran here. And your stepping forward and throwing your rank around probably kept Til'k from declaring war on me right there." She smirked. "And you don't have to call me 'Grandmother.'"

"You are Goran's grandmother and Kagak's as well. They are my troops, and that binds us as closely as family—sometimes more so, though I would not presume it to be so with *this* family." She hesitated. Looking over, she saw that the Pheben female was trying to disperse the crowd around Goran and failing miserably. The tournament wasn't over, after all. Goran still had to fight the next six people on the slate.

Turning back to Tabona, Wol said, "I had a family once, a long time ago."

"I'm sure you did, Eral, daughter of B'Etakk. Oh, do not worry," Tabona added at Wol's wide-eyed stare, "no one else knows. Honestly, no one else is that clever."

Wol laughed.

Tabona shared the laugh and then went on: "It was obvious from the way you told that story that it happened to you. I thought it was dimly possible that you were B'Etakk, but Eral seemed more likely."

"I never knew my grandparents," Wol said. "They died in battle before I was born. My parents always spoke well of them, but they were only stories. You are the first person I have ever called 'Grandmother,' and I do not do it lightly. But you have earned it."

"So have you, Leader Wol." Tabona put a hand on Wol's shoulder. "You are always welcome in my house and at my table until you die with honor."

Wol smiled. "Assuming that is how I die."

"Pfah," Tabona said, waving her hand. "You couldn't die any other way if you wanted to. Now come—let's watch my new grandson-in-law win a few more fights."

The ride back to Yopak Port in the Vikak was even worse than the ride out.

B'Ellor piloted this time, and she did not know the roads as well as her brother. Either that, or there were just more divots in the road than there were a week ago.

Wol was still wearing civilian garb, having gone through several items in B'Ellor's wardrobe. She had considered changing into her armor, but neither Kagak nor Goran did, and Wol thought it might offend Tabona.

Besides, cloth was less abrasive when one was bouncing around the back of a Vikak than the metals and leathers of Defense Force armor. That quality was useful when one was on duty and wished to remain on guard, but just at the moment, Wol was seeing the value of comfort.

They had said their good-byes to Fuhrman and Tabona before boarding the Vikak. Kagak had arranged for transport on the *I.K.S. D'ghir*, which was on its way to Qo'noS for crew replacement. They had fought the Kinshaya and taken heavy losses, so there was plenty of room for three passengers, even one of Goran's girth. Their quartermaster was from a Pheben farming family and owed Tabona several favors, and so was able to find a place for the three of them on the ship.

During the ride itself, Wol mostly kept her eyes closed, as she could imagine then that she was in a ship under attack rather than being driven across uneven ground by her subordinate's mate.

When they finally arrived at Yopak Port, Wol couldn't get out of the Vikak fast enough. Kagak and Goran also clambered out, and Goran picked B'Ellor up out of the front stool and carried her to the ground outside with a huge grin on his face.

"I wish you did not have to leave," B'Ellor said, looking up at Goran's smiling visage.

"I will write you every day," Goran said. "I will tell you of our great exploits as we fight for the empire."

"And I will read them every day, twice a day, and read them at dinner to the family. They will love to hear about all of you." B'Ellor looked at Wol. "You're family now. No matter what happens, you can always come here."

"Thank you, B'Ellor," Wol said, meaning every word. "I must admit, I came here because I had nowhere else to go. I expected it to be tolerable at best. But you all proved me wrong, and you will always have my gratitude for that." She glanced over at the port doors. "If you wait here, I will change into my uniform so you can have this dress back."

B'Ellor held up a hand. "No, don't. Keep it."

"I could not possibly—"

"You can and you will," B'Ellor said in what she probably thought was a stern voice, though she was, in truth, far too timid to be convincing. "It is my gift to you."

"I have no right accepting more gifts from you or your family, B'Ellor."

"Nonetheless, you will accept it."

Kagak put a hand on Wol's shoulder. "Do not argue with my sister, Leader. She is more stubborn than a *khrun* and as difficult to move."

Wol had actually moved a *khrun* once, in Krennla, but that was a story she would not tell now. *I must save something for my next trip, after all.* Aloud, she simply said, "Very well. Good-bye, B'Ellor." She stood straight and put her fist to her chest. "*Qapla'.*"

B'Ellor's cheeks flushed brown. "I do not deserve such an honor."

"You and your family deserve that and more." Bowing her head, she then led Kagak toward the port door, leaving Goran and B'Ellor to say their farewells in private.

"Thank you, Leader," Kagak said as the port door rumbled aside to allow them ingress. The air was cooler inside, and while Wol missed the breezes of the outdoors, she did not miss the heat of Pheben baking down on them.

To Kagak, she said, "You are the one to whom I owe gratitude, *Bekk*. I had not wished to come, and G'joth was the one who convinced me to do so."

"Then I'll thank him when we get back." He grinned. "Perhaps next time, I will convince him to join us!"

The door rumbled aside again, and Goran stepped through, looking happier than Wol had ever seen him—and Goran was generally ecstatic after a battle, so this was no small accomplishment.

"Leader, something has happened that I did not expect." His face grew serious. "I hope you will not kill me when I tell it to you."

Wol frowned. She suspected Goran was overreacting— it wouldn't be the first time—so she simply said, "Tell me, *Bekk*."

"I had always thought the fifteenth would be the only family I needed. I served on many ships, but it was not until I joined the fifteenth that I felt I *belonged* somewhere. Now, however . . . now I feel like I belong somewhere else."

After exchanging an amused glance with Kagak, Wol

burst out laughing. A look of relief washed over Goran's face. "You will not kill me?" he asked.

"Why would I do that, big man? I feel exactly as you do. After I was exiled from House Varnak, I thought the only home I would ever know would be the Defense Force. Now I know better." She slapped Goran on his massive arm. "As do you."

"The only problem is that I cannot guarantee that I will be back next season. I might not be able to be there to fight Lak and everyone else again."

They walked toward the transporter station. "That may be for the best," Kagak said. "If you came back, you'd just do what Lak did. But now, Lak has been defeated, and badly. That will give his opponents new life and work against Lak."

"Good," Goran said. "I did not like Lak."

"I doubt anyone besides Til'k did," Wol said. "But enough of that. We have had our leave. It is time for the fifteenth to return to the *Gorkon*—and to glory!"

"Oh!" Kagak's eyes grew wide, and he dug into his satchel. He pulled out a clear bag that was filled with the candied *racht* that Wol had loved. "Grandmother gave us some for our trip back."

Wol smiled. "Excellent, but save them. We will wait until we return to the *Gorkon*, so G'joth may share in *some* aspect of Tabona's *yobta' yupma'* celebration."

"An excellent notion, Leader," Kagak said as he stuffed the bag back into his satchel.

The operator at the transporter station said, "Names?"

"Leader Wol and *Bekks* Goran and Kagak. We are transporting to the *D'ghir*."

Checking his console, the operator said, "Yes, I have you here. The *D'ghir* achieved orbit an hour ago." He looked sourly at Wol. "The captain was going to depart without you if you did not arrive soon."

"No he wasn't," Kagak said confidently. He leaned over to Wol, and added, "Not if he wished to eat again. Their quartermaster owes Tabona *many* favors."

Wol chuckled as she stepped up to the platform. "Something I'm sure many can claim." Once all three were in place, she said, "Energize."

In a silent glow of red, Wol and her soldiers were whisked into orbit, ready to face their next challenge.

TWENTY-SEVEN

A field
Qo'noS

Worf was not surprised to find that Kurn had come here.

His younger brother was sitting on a rock that stood in the midst of grasslands and trees. A guardsman was standing about half a *qell'qam* away, looking displeased. Worf approached him shortly after beaming to this place, and the guardsman looked almost relieved at the sight of the ambassador.

"I am Ambassador Worf, son of Mogh."

"It is good that you have come, Ambassador. The owners of this property are offworld at the moment, but their House *ghIntaq* wishes to know why he's there and when I can remove him. But he's a lieutenant in the Defense Force, I cannot just—"

Worf held up a hand. "I will deal with this, Guardsman. Return to your post."

"I will remain here," the guardsman said. "I promised the *ghIntaq* that I would prevent any harm to come to the lands."

"Very well," Worf said, not wanting to argue the point.

He proceeded to where Kurn sat. He had done no damage to the trees or the land yet, but he was armed, and Worf had no idea what his brother's mental state might be. Kurn was a great warrior, and even Rodek had developed into a fine one in his own right. If his brother now retained the memories of both personas, he might be a formidable foe. Worf bowed to no one in his warrior's skills, but he did not know if he could defeat his own brother—or even if he could bring himself to fight Kurn, after all Kurn had sacrificed.

"Greetings, Ambassador," Kurn said as Worf got close enough. Worf was approaching him from behind, and Kurn had not turned around. "I expected that you would be the one to come. I assume you know this place?"

Worf looked around the field. "I know what this used to be."

"Yes. Once a great estate stood here. The house stood empty for all the time you were in the Federation and I was raised by Lorgh."

"Lorgh once told me that he paid to have the house maintained."

"Yes. When the High Council seized the house as part of the condemnation of our father in the attack on Khitomer, that was when Lorgh orchestrated to have me placed aboard the *Enterprise* so you could challenge the High Council's ruling. When Gowron restored our family name, it became my home."

Finally, Kurn rose to his feet and turned to look at Worf.

The last time Worf saw Kurn as Kurn was in the quarters his brother had been assigned on Deep Space 9. He was drunk and despondent, ready to die, but unable to do so. His eyes were those of a man defeated.

Before that, Worf had served with Kurn on the *Hegh'ta*, fought with him, both in council chambers against Chancellor K'mpec's ruling against their father, and on the battlefield against the sisters of Duras who tried to seize power. Then, he had seen fire in his brother's eyes, fire that he had once thought nothing could dim.

On several occasions since, Worf had encountered Rodek, the man he had turned Kurn into, and he never saw either the defeat or the fire.

Until now. Now, he saw both.

"Ours was a glorious house, Ambassador."

Worf winced. Kurn refused to call him by name and would not call him "brother" but simply used his title, which he sneered as he said it.

Kurn continued. "Each room contained a grand double-door entrance, carved from the mightiest trees. Weaponry from the Third Dynasty decorated the walls, and the tapestry!" He smiled. "Our parents owned a Danqo, did you know that?"

"I did not," Worf said truthfully. He remembered almost nothing of his first six years of life on Qo'noS, only impressions here and there. He had suffered brain damage during the attack on Khitomer, enough that he did not even recall *having* a younger brother until Kurn showed up on the *Enterprise*.

"It took up the entire south wall, rendering Kahless and Lukara at Qam-Chee. The only thing missing was the family *bat'leth*." He blinked. "You had that."

Worf nodded. "I still do. It is the only remembrance I had of our parents for a long time."

Kurn turned away, staring off into the horizon. "When you protested Gowron's invasion of Cardassia, the House was dissolved, our lands seized. The items were all sold to line the High Council's treasury. The land itself was purchased by the House of Hurgas."

"I know of them," Worf said. "And according to that guardsman, their *ghIntaq* is concerned as to what you might do on their land."

Kurn whirled around. "Do they think me some kind of Ferengi, who despoils private property for personal gain? I am a soldier in the Defense Force!"

"That is why the guardsman has maintained his distance," Worf said dryly.

That elicited a grunt from Kurn. "Of course." Then he looked away again.

Kurn did not seem to be staring at anything save the horizon and a few trees, but Worf followed his brother's gaze anyhow. He had come here only after explaining himself to Klag. The captain did not seem pleased at what Worf did, saying it was not very Klingon. Worf took a small risk by pointing out how many people said the same about Klag's right arm, and that actually prompted one of Klag's bone-jarring laughs. "Besides," Klag had said, "this has taught me that my brother is not the only *wam* serpent in my home. Had it not been your brother, he would have found another with whom to manufacture a conflict. I will settle my family's affairs— I suggest you go and settle yours."

Worf had been grateful for Klag's acceptance—or, at least, his lack of outright condemnation. The son of M'Raq was a valuable friend and ally to Worf.

After a silence that went on for several seconds, Worf finally asked the question that had preyed on his mind since he first left the *qaDrav* with Klag: "Why did you not kill me?"

Kurn turned around, smiling, and for the first time, even with the new crest, Worf saw his brother. "It was very tempting. At the time, standing there in the *qaDrav*, I wanted very much to sink my *d'k tahg* into your chest and end you once and for all." The smile vanished and his gaze fell on the field. "But something stopped me. I was not sure what until I came here. Now, standing in the place where we were both born, in the ruins of the House of Mogh, I have finally figured it out." He stared back at Worf with an intensity that was also very much like Worf's brother. "I am *happier* as Rodek than I ever was as Kurn."

Worf blinked. This was not the reason he had been expecting.

Kurn sat back down on the rock. "Lorgh was a difficult father to grow up with. I did not understand why for a long time, until I reached the Age of Ascension. Not only was that when he told me of my true bloodlines but also when he revealed that he was an operative for Imperial Intelligence. For a time, I was content. I was a decorated warrior in the Defense Force—but then I revealed myself to you." He glowered at Worf. "From then, my life was a broken road to *Gre'thor*, only the road never actually reached the Barge of the Dead. First you forbade me from opposing Gowron."

"And I was right to do so," Worf said. "You only had the support of some of the Defense Force. Your opposition to Gowron would have made it a three-front war, and the empire would have—"

"Enough!" Kurn held up a hand, spit flying into his mustache. "You speak as a diplomat would. But I speak now of my *heart*. I did my duty as younger brother and I obeyed your instruction. I was rewarded with a seat on the High Council. At the time, I thought it to be a great honor. You may thrive in the world of politics, Ambassador, but I found it nauseating. As a soldier, I did battle for the empire. In council chambers, the battles were all useless words in the air. I yearned to return to the Defense Force. Instead, I was removed from the empire entirely due to the foolish actions of the head of my House. How easy it was for you to condemn Gowron's invasion of Cardassia, safe in your Federation."

Unable to resist, Worf said, "An invasion undertaken due to the actions of one of the Founders of the Dominion who was disguised as Martok."

"Which you did not know at the time." Before Worf could say anything else, Kurn held up a hand. "It does not matter. We could argue over this until the next *yobta' yupma'* and still not change each other's mind.

But what *does* matter is that as Kurn, son of Mogh, I was miserable. As Rodek, son of Noggra, I have served on the *Lallek* and the *Gorkon*. I am the second officer to one of the heroes of the empire. In Krennla right now, they are about to debut an opera about our campaign at San-Tarah. So I have decided." Kurn got back to his feet, his hands folded defiantly across his massive chest. "I will not restore my crest to that of Kurn. As far as the universe is concerned, Kurn, son of Mogh, is four years' dead. When the ship's repairs are finished, I will report back to the *Gorkon* as Lieutenant Rodek, son of Noggra, and resume my duties as second officer of that ship. And if ever our paths cross again, Ambassador, do not greet me as 'brother.' We are strangers now, because of a choice *you* made. I have refrained from killing you today; I will show no such restraint in the future if I am given cause."

Although Kurn's desire to remain as Rodek surprised Worf, his brother's animosity was no surprise at all. "If I give you cause, Lieutenant, I will not stop you."

Kurn—or, rather, Rodek blinked once then turned his back on Worf and walked away from him.

The final insult, Worf thought with a sigh. *And yet, a deserved one.*

Worf turned and headed toward the guardsman to reassure him that he would not feel the wrath of the House Hurgas *ghIntaq*. Then Worf returned to the embassy to make sure that Ba'el was settling in.

Tomorrow, the High Council would be in session. Worf planned to be in attendance.

TWENTY-EIGHT

Martok, son of Urthog, hated sitting in the chancellor's chair.

It had now been a full turn since Worf challenged Gowron and defeated him on Deep Space 9. Rather than accept the honor of leading the empire himself—an honor Worf had long since earned, in Martok's opinion—Worf designated Martok himself as chancellor.

Someday, Martok would consider forgiving Worf for that.

Morjod's coup had done a great deal to convince Martok that he belonged in this chair. Kahless once said that not having something was the best way to find out you wanted it, and while *want* might have been too strong a verb, Martok had at least come to accept that he was the right person for the job at this point in the empire's history.

But he still hated sitting in the chair. It always dug into his backside, and no amount of shifting in place made it better. The only upside was that the pain gave him even less patience with the inanities of council sessions, so he was able to take a hard line with those councillors and petitioners who wasted time.

The council had a full agenda for the day. As he walked from his office to the chambers, four members of the *Yan-Isleth* trailing behind him (none walked before the chancellor), Martok read over his padd to see that the crew of the *I.K.S. Gorkon* were involved in three of the proceedings. The council had summoned Klag and several members of his House to discuss what happened in the *qaDrav* yesterday, and Klag's mother was also one of three women who were petitioning the High Council for special dispensation to be made House head—one of the other two was Klag's chief engineer.

Then there was the first order of business: the *meqba'* looking into Captain Stren's crash into Novat. Klag's doctor had requested to present evidence.

Martok rarely looked forward to open council sessions, as the petitioners tended to be long-winded and tiresome. The only thing that cheered him was being able to occasionally condemn them to death, but that didn't happen nearly often enough to suit him.

When he arrived, he went straight for his seat in the raised chair at the back of the council chambers. A dark room with directed lighting casting long shadows, only the chancellor's chair and the trefoil emblem of the empire over it were fully lit. A second light was also used to illuminate those who spoke before the council.

A rumble of noise hovered over the room upon Martok's entrance, but it quieted to nothing as he approached the chair, the chamber steward announcing his entrance over the din.

The councillors took their place in a half circle radiating out from Martok's chair. One spot was empty, that belonging to Kryan. The results of the *meqba'* would determine whether or not he retained his seat on the council—and if he did not, a new councillor would be chosen before any other business was conducted.

In the front of the chambers, several Klingons stood, awaiting their turn to speak or simply observing the proceedings. Martok noticed Worf among the latter, and the chancellor was glad that he had come, as he had words to say to Worf regarding the previous day's events at the *qaDrav*.

Also in the observation area were Klag and B'Oraq, standing together, the latter tugging on the braid that rested on her right shoulder. Of Kurak, he saw no sign, but there were many dark corners and large pillars in the chambers she could have been hiding in. Tarilla and Dorrek were not present, either, but that was because they were in custody and remained under guard in a nearby antechamber until they were summoned.

Sitting on the edge of the chair rather than let it chew his spine, Martok said, "Kryan, son of Panich, step forward!" He deliberately did not use Kryan's title.

Kryan angrily stepped into the center of the chambers, followed by another Klingon, this one in Defense

Force armor. The light shone on Kryan, making the scowl on his round, pudgy face clear for all to see.

Martok went on: "You stand before us to answer for the dishonorable actions of your brother, Stren, son of Panich. It is the council's belief that Stren deliberately took his own life and that of several citizens of the city of Novat in a cowardly gesture. Who stands for you?"

The Defense Force soldier stepped forward. "I am Yakril, son of Wolkor. I will serve as the councillor's *cha'DIch*."

The steward stepped forward and handed Yakril the ceremonial *d'k tahg* that was given to all who served as *cha'DIch*. Kryan would be denied combat until the *meqba'* ended, so Yakril would stand for him. Peering closely, Martok saw that Yakril held the rank of ensign and also wore the emblem of the House of Mortran on his biceps. Councillor Mortran was a friend of Kryan, and while he could not publicly support Kryan while he was under suspicion, he could at least provide a *cha'DIch*.

"We will begin the *meqba'*," Martok said as soon as Yakril accepted the *d'k tahg*. "Kowag, son of Varkal, and physician for the Great Hall has prepared a report."

Councillor Krozek moved forward out of the darkness. His large, heavily ridged nose cast a long shadow on the left side of his face. Holding up a padd, he said, "I have Doctor Kowag's report."

Martok frowned. "Where is Doctor Kowag?"

"He is on a *targ* hunt with several colleagues, Chancellor. He felt that, since his report was complete, his presence was not required."

"That is a matter that I will discuss with Kowag upon his return," Martok said quietly, with a growl rumbling in the back of his throat. "What does the report say?"

Looking at the padd, Krozek said, "Doctor Kowag says that the cause of Captain Stren's death was a high-velocity impact-loading trauma—acceleration of the head following sudden deceleration of impact resulting in multiple comminuted cranial fractures as well as subluxation injury to the vertebrae of the neck when Captain Stren's head impacted against the shuttle bulkhead."

Martok doubted that Krozek understood what he was saying any more than Martok did. He thought he got the gist, however. "He died in the crash, then?"

"Yes, Chancellor."

Now B'Oraq moved into the center of the chamber. "I challenge the findings of Doctor Kowag."

Though Martok knew the answer to the question he was about to ask, it needed to be in the official record. "On what grounds do you challenge the official physician of the Great Hall?"

"On the grounds that Doctor Kowag is an incompetent fool."

That sent a rumble through the chambers. Kowag had many friends on the council, and B'Oraq was taking a huge risk by insulting him publicly like this. *But then, that one is used to huge risks.*

"Were he present," B'Oraq continued, "I would challenge him directly. Killing him would rid the empire of one of its greatest blights. I was on the scene when Captain Stren's craft crashed into Novat, and several

Klingons survived who might not have otherwise thanks to the presence of myself, as well as Doctor Valatra of the *I.K.S. Plorgh* and Doctor Kandless of the village of Ya'Koraq. We beamed many of the victims to the *I.K.S. Gorkon*, including Captain Stren. Before sending his body to Doctor Kowag, I performed an autopsy."

Krozek bristled. "What right did you have to do that, woman?"

B'Oraq turned on the councillor. "As I told you a week ago, Councillor, Stren was a patient in *my* medical bay. That gives me the right, and *you* approved my doing so."

"I did no such thing!"

"Yes, Councillor, you did." She held up a data spike and placed it in a padd. "This recording is taken directly from the *Gorkon*'s communications records."

First Martok heard B'Oraq's voice: "*Stren is a patient in my medical bay, Councillor. Standard procedure dictates that I do a full examination and write a report before I release him.*"

Then Krozek's voice. "*You are welcome to do so, but do it quickly and send the body to Kowag. That is all.*"

The councillor's face compressed into a scowl, but he said nothing. Indeed, there was nothing to say. He had authorized B'Oraq's examination and report, which justified the doctor presenting it to the High Council now.

Looking at each member of the council in turn except for Krozek, B'Oraq said, "Doctor Kowag's report is true on the face of it. Captain Stren did indeed suffer a high-velocity impact-loading trauma. But I suspect that anyone in this room who took even a cursory glance at the captain's corpse would be able to tell that from the rather large dent in the man's skull."

Martok was unable to suppress a chuckle at that. Neither were about a quarter of the people in the chamber, including both Kryan and Yakril.

"However, that was not the cause of death. The first indicator that it might not be was that the head wound did not bleed as profusely as most such injuries do. That implies that blood stopped flowing *before* the wound. So I examined *under* the wound—a methodology that seems to be beyond Doctor Kowag—and discovered multiple berry aneurysms that had burst. Those aneurysms indicated that Captain Stren suffered from T'Viad's syndrome—something that a competent doctor would be able to diagnose in an instant. Thus the captain's brain was an explosive waiting to detonate. Captain Stren died while flying the shuttle. The cause of death was herniation of the brain stem secondary to subarachnoid hemorrhage caused by the aneurysms. Extensive subarachnoid hemmorhaging consistent with rupture of the anterior communicating artery rendered him unconscious, with a subsequent increase in intracranial pressure causing the brain stem's herniation."

B'Oraq held up a padd and handed it toward Krozek. "This is my full report, witnessed by both Valatra and Kandless, and which includes the autopsy recorded by the *Gorkon* computer. Did Kowag provide such documentation or witnesses?"

Krozek's face, if anything, grew more sour. "No."

Now Martok spoke up. "Did Kowag actually *examine*

Captain Stren, or did he simply view the footage on the information net?"

"I am sure, Chancellor, that Doctor Kowag's examination was quite thorough."

"Would that I could be as sure, Councillor," Martok said. He stood up. Pronouncements, he found, came across better from that position. "In light of Doctor B'Oraq's evidence, it is the ruling of this council that there be no action taken against Councillor Kryan or any of his House. Councillor, you will return to your place." He put his arm to his chest. "*Qapla'*."

Returning the salute, Kryan said, "*Qapla'*, Chancellor." Then he took his place between Councillors Tovoj and Mortran.

Both B'Oraq and Yakril started toward the front, but Martok said, "Doctor B'Oraq, remain before us. Council has another pronouncement. It has become obvious that the Klingon Physicians Enclave has outlived its usefulness." He had already discussed what would happen next with the rest of the council, and while they were not unanimous, enough supported the notion that, unless there was some surprise revelation from Kowag during the *meqba'* (which there wasn't), Martok's next words came easily. Kryan's restoration made it easier, for he had supported the notion wholeheartedly.

The chancellor saw B'Oraq's eyes grow wide, and her hand moved to the pin that held on her braid.

Martok continued. "Council encouraged the KPE to hold a conference to demonstrate their usefulness to the empire's medical community, and from all accounts they demonstrated only that they are obsolete. Therefore, the High Council hereby disbands the KPE. It will be replaced with the Klingon Medical Authority, which the council hereby grants the authority to act on behalf of the empire's medical community. After this session concludes, Doctor," he said, staring at B'Oraq with his one eye, "you will meet with me to discuss the KMA's mandate."

"I will be honored, Chancellor." B'Oraq's smile practically illuminated the chambers all by itself.

Ignoring the rumbling from several councillors—all the ones loyal to Kowag, Martok knew—he moved on to the next order of business, to wit, the petitions for special dispensation. Women from the Houses of Lokak, Palkar, and M'Raq had all applied to be made head of their respective Houses. Preferring to save M'Raq for last, given its attendant complications, Martok saw B'Yor from the House of Lokak first.

He listened to her petition with only half an ear, for he saw no reason even to go through with the charade. Recalling his late wife Sirella, he knew full well that many women of the empire were perfectly capable of leading a noble House. Martok had already begun investigating ways to eliminate the need for this ridiculous process and simply allow women to lead. He had not done so only because so many of the most powerful Houses were dead set against it, and Martok could not afford to alienate them. At least not yet.

After granting B'Yor the right to lead her own House, Kurak came into the center of the chamber.

"I am Kurak, daughter of Haleka of the House of Palkar. I am also a commander in the Defense Force, chief engineer of the *I.K.S. Gorkon*, and builder of the former flagship, the *Negh'Var*. I am also the only able-bodied adult left in our House. The House was in the care of our *ghIntaq*, Moloj, but he has died, and no one is empowered to replace him."

Councillor Qolka spoke up. "There are *no* able-bodied males in your House?"

Kurak continued looking straight at Martok, not doing Qolka the honor of acknowledging him with her eyes. "The Dominion War claimed much of our family. My nephew, Gevnar, will not reach the Age of Ascension for another year."

Qolka started to speak again, but Martok held up his hand. "Enough! The House of Palkar has served the empire with distinction since the days of Emperor Sompek. To deny Commander Kurak's petition would be to destroy that House, and that I will *not* do. Dispensation is granted, Commander, and you are now head of the House of Palkar."

She smiled. "Thank you, Chancellor. I hereby name Karreka, daughter of Lyyroq, to be my *ghIntaq*. She will be the spear that defends Palkar."

A rumble spread through the chamber. While there was no proscription against women serving as *ghIntaq*, it rarely happened, and when it did, it was generally in smaller, less consequential Houses. To the best of Martok's knowledge, no House of the stature of Palkar had ever appointed a woman to that position.

From the front, a woman wearing a white dress stepped forward, followed by a white-haired man in Defense Force armor. The woman said, "I accept the honor,

Kurak of the House of Palkar. I will be your *ghIntaq* and serve your House until my dying day." Then she turned to the white-haired man, backhanded him across the face, and said, "Our marriage is *done!*" Then she spit on him.

Recovering quickly from the blow and wiping the spittle from his pointed beard, the white-haired man, a lieutenant from a House that Martok did not recognize, turned to Kurak and said, "I am Klingon!" Martok also noted that he wore a necklace of Cardassian neckbones. That necklace rattled as he grabbed Kurak's hand in his and enclosed his fist around hers. Even as blood seeped out of her palm, the lieutenant said, "My blood."

Kurak smiled and said, "Our blood."

A part of Martok was curious as to why she did not simply mate the lieutenant so *he* could become head of the House and save herself the trouble, but in truth, he did not care all that much and saw no reason to waste the council's time with a lengthy explanation. "Go begin your new lives, my friends," he said, "and let us continue our business."

The lieutenant bowed low, the necklace swinging outward. "The chancellor honors our union with his witnessing of it." With that, he turned and left, along with Kurak and Karreka.

To the steward, Martok said, "Bring Tarilla and Dorrek into chambers."

Saluting, the steward exited right behind the other three.

"Captain Klag, step forward."

Klag had been speaking with B'Oraq, but now he

came into the center of the chamber, the light shining on his proud face. Martok noted that Klag looked determined, which was well, as the next few minutes would likely be difficult for him.

Dorrek and Tarilla were brought in by two guardsmen. As members of noble Houses, they were not shackled, though Martok had been tempted.

Martok had put Councillor Grevaq in charge of the investigation into what, exactly, happened at the *qaDrav* yesterday. Normally, such matters between a captain and his second officer would be handled internally, and had Lieutenant Rodek challenged Captain Klag on the *Gorkon*, it would have been. But since it happened in the *qaDrav*, it became a matter for the council.

So when Dorrek and Tarilla took their place next to Klag—neither of them looking at him, Martok noticed—Grevaq then stepped forward, reading off a padd.

"At council's direction from the reports made by Captain Klag and Ambassador Worf, the Imperial Guard investigated the home of Noggra, son of Doqi, as well as Noggra's body. DNA traces were found in the home and on his person, which belonged to Captain Dorrek, son of M'Raq. Noggra's home security recorded someone wearing a holomask attacking Noggra in his home and interrogating him about his son, Rodek. That interrogation revealed that Rodek was a fiction, and that Rodek was born Kurn, son of Mogh."

Martok looked at Dorrek, who stared straight ahead, as did Klag. Tarilla, however, was staring at her younger son with an expression of fury.

The chancellor said, "Captain Dorrek, do you deny the findings of the Imperial Guard?"

"No." A rumble of shock went through the chambers. For a decorated Klingon warrior to admit to such subterfuge was almost unthinkable, even though the evidence was overwhelming. "While my brother may paint me as dishonorable, I am a true Klingon, and I will not lie before the High Council. My brother has brought dishonor to our once-noble House. He rejected our father, M'Raq, a mighty warrior who served the empire well! He disobeyed the orders of General Talak at San-Tarah and pitted Klingon against Klingon for the sake of mere *jeghpu'wI'*! And he desecrated our father's memory by placing his dead arm on his person! He is an abomination! But I had no avenue by which I could remove him, for he had manipulated events so that he was a hero of the empire. So I investigated his crew and discovered some anomalies in the history of his second officer, Rodek. I admit that I then committed the acts Councillor Grevaq described. I did so knowing it might mean my own death—as long as it also meant Klag's."

Martok growled. "You will get half your wish at least, Captain. You have killed without showing your face. You have no honor." Martok stood and unsheathed his *d'k tahg*. "You will not be allowed to leave this chamber alive." He moved forward. Around him, all the councillors did the same, unsheathing their own blades, the click of their outer blades unfurling echoing with a snap off the walls of the council chamber.

Klag and Tarilla stepped aside, the latter a bit more slowly, but Dorrek stood his ground.

Raising his blade, Martok plunged his *d'k tahg* directly into Dorrek's neck. Blood spurted out, but Martok found the smell of it to be far less intoxicating than it might, coming as it did from such a dishonorable worm as this.

Each councillor in succession plunged his own blade into Dorrek's body. To the captain's credit, he did not fall until the tenth wound—few, in Martok's experience, lasted past the seventh, particularly when the first was to the neck. Martok wiped his own *d'k tahg* on his sleeve. Perhaps it was his imagination, but Dorrek's blood even smelled foul.

To the steward, Martok said, "Remove that from our presence."

No one performed the death scream. Those who died by the council's hand in this manner did so because they had dishonored themselves. There was no point in shouting a warning to the Black Fleet that Dorrek was on his way, because Dorrek's destination was the Barge of the Dead. *Fek'lhr* could take care of his own warnings.

Once the body was removed, the council had retaken their places, and Martok sat back down in the uncomfortable chair, Tarilla stepped toward the chancellor, her arms flailing. "I knew *nothing* of this! Dorrek told me only that I had to make sure Klag was at the *qaDrav* at the appointed time. He did not tell me what else he planned. For all the reasons Dorrek gave, however, I must petition the High Council to make me head of our House. Klag has—"

"Your petition is denied," Martok said before she could go on.

357

Klag smiled.

"You must hear me out!" Tarilla cried, her fists clenched so hard blood seeped from her palms. "I cannot allow this creature I birthed to have control over my life!"

"Then you should have used a stronger poison," Martok said. "Klag will remain the head of the House of M'Raq. If you wish to remove yourself from that House, then I suggest you acquire some *adanji* and find someone to give you *Mauk-to'Vor*."

"No! You must listen to me, Chancellor!"

Martok smirked. "Many have told me what I 'must' do. Most of them are dead now. Would you join them?"

Snarling, Tarilla turned and stormed out of the chamber.

Leaning back in his chair, Martok tried not to squirm as the muscles of his backside started to contract.

The rest of the session went by surprisingly quickly. Somehow, Martok had forgotten that the last item on the agenda was regarding Krios—both the appointment of a new governor to replace Gortak, who died in battle against Kreel raiders, and the commissioning of a sculptor to create a statue of Gortak to place in Krios's capitol to honor his service. Once Berolik was made governor and J'lang commissioned to create the sculpture, the session was over.

Thrilled at the realization, Martok practically leaped to his feet, the pain in his backside having grown roots. He put his fist to his chest and said, "The session has ended. *Qapla'*."

Walking gingerly toward the exit, he told the *Yan-Isleth* to allow Worf and B'Oraq to see him, but no one else. They also kept councillors and others from getting near him while he beat a hasty retreat to his office, pausing only to hand off his *d'k tahg* for a proper cleaning. He didn't want any trace of Dorrek's foul blood on it any longer than he had to.

The door to the office rumbled shut behind him and he sat in the chair behind the office's small desk, which was only slightly more comfortable than the chancellor's chair. *Listen to me, complaining of my aching back. I'm growing soft in my old age.*

B'Oraq was the first to enter. "Chancellor, thank you," she said without preamble. "I cannot begin to tell you what this means."

"It means nothing yet, Doctor," Martok said with a smirk. "The KMA will only be as good as those who run it—and that will not be you."

That brought B'Oraq up short. "Why not? I have done more to expose the KPE's uselessness and bring about the need for the KMA than anyone!"

"Yes, and the landscape is well populated with the enemies you've made while traveling that road. There is a reason why warriors leave corpses in their wake, daughter of Grala—it means they cannot rise up and stab you in the back."

"Kowag." B'Oraq practically spit the name.

"Among others, but yes, primarily him. He has many high-powered friends, including the person you just made a fool of in open council. If you wish the KMA to be effective, you must not be involved in its hierarchy."

Shaking her head, B'Oraq said, "I wish Kowag *had* been present today. I *would* have killed him and taken great joy in the act."

"Kowag is a coward and a fool. His incompetence almost led to the disgrace of a respected councillor. That will not go unnoticed. Nor will your actions." Martok smiled. "You have friends as well, after all."

"I hope I may number you among them, Chancellor."

"For the moment—but a chancellor must choose his friends carefully and abandon them when expedient."

"Of course." She smiled back. "Including you, the list of my friends is now four—you, Klag, Worf, and Kryan. In truth, it is four more than I ever expected to have."

Martok chuckled. "You mentioned two other physicians who aided you in Novat."

"Valatra and Kandless, yes." B'Oraq squinted. "Are you suggesting—?"

"I believe they would serve the KMA with honor."

B'Oraq smiled. "I agree. Thank you, Chancellor."

The door rumbled aside to let one of the *Yan-Isleth* in along with Worf.

"Ambassador," B'Oraq said. "It is good to see you again."

Worf inclined his head toward the doctor, then turned to Martok. "You wished to see me."

"Yes, my friend, on a matter of great importance. That will be all, B'Oraq. I will inform Valatra and Kandless of their new appointment myself."

Her hands clutched together at her chest, B'Oraq said, "Again, Chancellor, thank you." Turning to Worf, she added, "Ambassador," then departed.

As soon as the door shut, Martok rose. "Explain to me, Worf, why is it that I had to learn from Councillor Grevaq that your brother Kurn now lives as Rodek, son of Noggra."

Worf's mouth twisted the way it did whenever he was about to say something Martok didn't like. "It was . . . necessary to keep it a secret. At the time, I could find no alternative to—"

Martok waved off Worf's words as he walked around to the other side of the desk so he could look the ambassador in the eye. "I do not care *why* you did what you did, Worf. It is done. What I wish to know is why you did not tell *me*! I made you part of my House, at a time when you were an enemy of the chancellor. I did so because of what I saw in the Jem'Hadar prison—I saw a noble warrior whose House had been taken from him and whom I would be proud to call brother." He turned away from Worf, looking up at the *targ* head mounted on the wall. That had been a trophy from the very first *targ* hunt he and Worf had gone on months ago. "Now I learn that you kept this from me." Turning back, he asked in a low rumble, "Why?"

"It was never my intention to deceive you, Chancellor."

"Bah!" Martok waved his arm back and forth. "Do not fill the air with meaningless titles. We are not chancellor and ambassador now, Worf. I am speaking to you as the head of our House!"

Worf looked down at the floor, as if it would provide comfort, then he looked back at Martok with a pained expression. "I could not speak of what happened with

Kurn to you—or to anyone beyond those who were present at the time. It was a . . . a family matter."

"*I* am your family, Worf!"

Speaking as softly as Martok had ever heard him, Worf said, "I meant it was a matter for the House of Mogh."

Though Martok hardly thought Worf needed to be reminded of this, he felt the urge to do so anyhow: "Worf, that House no longer *exists*."

Pointing to his chest, Worf said, "It exists *here*."

Martok found he could not argue with that. His anger burned to ashes, he went back to his desk and sat at it, becoming chancellor once again. "What will become of your brother?"

"He has chosen to remain as Rodek." Worf hesitated, then: "And he has promised to kill me if I give him cause."

Martok smiled. "Then I suggest, my friend, that you not give him cause."

Worf nodded. "If I may pursue other business, Chancellor."

It was not a question. "Of course."

"Klag informed me that an opera called *The Battle at San-Tarah* is debuting tomorrow night at the opera house in Krennla. I will be attending. Will you join me?"

His nose scrunching up, Martok said, "Krennla? Ah, Worf, I knew that foul place in my youth. And it has grown worse. Still, I suppose the opera house is tolerable. Besides, it at last gives me an opportunity to see Klag in action."

TWENTY-NINE

Kenta District
Krennla, Qo'noS

Krom's dwelling had the exact same design as Klaad's, only it was in a larger building that was in worse shape. There were no automatic doors, and G'joth had to shove his shoulder into the building's main door in order to get it open. The hairs in his nose practically retreated into his sinus cavity, the smell was so foul. Breathing through his mouth as much as possible, he went up the stairs to Krom's place.

G'joth had spent most of his time at the opera house, grinding his teeth while watching *The Battle at San-Tarah* come together. At home, he stayed in his room, rewatching the *Battlecruiser Vengeance* recordings he'd inherited from *Bekk* Tarmeth. Tarmeth had been involved with a mutiny on the *Gorkon*. The ship's security chief had put him to death after he confessed, and G'joth had claimed

Tarmeth's recordings of the century-old entertainment. The simplistic narrative and over-the-top melodrama of Captain Koth of the *Vengeance* were an especially nice palliative after suffering through the pomposity of the opera.

Lakras had been inconsolable, and her performance was affected to the point where Konn had almost put her to death. Only G'joth's own intercession had prevented that, but almost losing her life had served as a reminder to her, and she had performed well after that.

Watching the *Vengeance* recordings had also given G'joth an idea. On opening night of the opera, he told Lakras to go ahead without him, as he had an errand to run. Klaad hadn't been home, so he went to Krom's.

His other friend wasn't quite as broken-down as Klaad, but Krom still did not look especially well. All his teeth were gone, and one eye was milky and white, but he seemed more robust otherwise. His mane of hair was still dark, with only streaks of white. "Thought you might come by. What do you want?"

"I have something for your son, and for Klaad's, and for their other friend. It is something for them to share."

Unlike Klaad, Krom showed no sign of letting G'joth into his home. "What is it?"

He held up a satchel. "In here are data spikes containing every episode of *Battlecruiser Vengeance*."

Krom's good eye went wide. His bad eye didn't, a sight G'joth found somewhat nauseating. "They still make those?"

"No, these are the originals. I received them from

a crewmate. I remember how much we enjoyed these when we were young. Remember, we would roam the streets, each taking turns being Koth?"

Shaking his head, Krom said, "We were foolish youths."

"Perhaps. But sometimes it is good to be foolish." He looked around, even though all there was to see was a dilapidated hallway that smelled of rot and decay and a battered door. "There is little cause for enjoyment in this place. But while the adults may have no hope, the children should have some. They should dream of better things, the way we did. That is why I want all three of them to have these recordings."

"Perhaps they'll find them inspirational." Krom held out a hand, and G'joth placed the satchel in them.

It wasn't exactly a sacrifice—these were copies, after all. The hard part had been finding a merchant who had enough blank spikes on which to copy them.

"I will tell Gurlk what you have done and why you have done it for them. I cannot say if he will be grateful—but I can say that his father is." Krom stood up straight. "Thank you, G'joth. It *has* been good to have you back."

G'joth sighed. "Would that I could say the same."

He turned and exited down the staircase. *Thus far, I have learned that my father is a liar, my sister is an idiot, and my oldest friends are miserable. I should have gone with Wol and the others to Pheben III.*

Checking his wrist comm, he saw that he had just enough time to take a leisurely walk to Baldi'maj. He'd probably arrive right on time for the opening, which was good, as it meant he wouldn't be obligated to go to the preshow celebration. Konn had invited him, which Lakras said would involve a great deal of shouting, last-minute rehearsing, and drinking. G'joth had no interest in participating, especially since he might be tempted to slit Kenni's throat.

When he finally arrived at the opera house, there were Defense Force guards at every entrance. G'joth went to the cast entrance, where there were two guards, a tall one and a short one, who scowled at him, until they saw his uniform. "I'm *Bekk* G'joth."

The tall one said, "They said you'd be coming sooner. Go ahead."

"Why the extra security?" G'joth asked.

"Ain't you heard? Chancellor Martok's attending, and he's bringin' half the damn First City with him. Ambassador Worf, Captain Klag, Councillor Grevaq, Danqo, even Jo'Krat."

G'joth had no idea who Jo'Krat was, but from the way the guard nodded, he was a man of great fame.

The short one said, "Jo'Krat *never* comes to Krennla. This is *huge*."

Willing to take their word for it, G'joth moved past the two guards and went down the long, dank corridor to the dressing area. G'joth wondered what his captain would think of the opera. A part of him thought he might wish to warn Klag—but no, the captain was a warrior being honored by having his exploits made into an opera. Regardless of the accuracy of the opera in question, it remained a great honor. That, G'joth knew, would be all that mattered to Klag. *And in truth, should be all that matters to me.*

The smell of cheap bloodwine was almost palpable as he entered the dressing area.

The throat-coating bloodwine was drunk to excess right before the show. G'joth remained skeptical of the medical legitimacy of this practice—he would have to ask B'Oraq when he reported back to the *Gorkon*—but the singers all swore by it, and they were quite drunk.

Were he among fellow warriors, G'joth would have gladly joined them, but something about drinking with these performers left a worse taste in his mouth than the bad bloodwine was likely to. It didn't help that the bloodwine on the *Gorkon* was particularly good . . .

As soon as he got close enough, he saw Kenni standing at the center of attention, Lakras draped on his arm.

"I do not believe this," G'joth said. "Lakras, what are you—?"

He was interrupted by Klivv, who stumbled into him. "G'joth! Come, my friend, drink with us, for tonight we open!"

Pushing Klivv roughly aside—the singer barely seemed to notice—G'joth walked straight toward Kenni and Lakras. "What is going on?"

Kenni was surrounded by half a dozen other Klingons, only some of whom G'joth recognized. "Ah, this is my good friend G'joth. He has been an invaluable aid in maintaining the verisimilitude of the original battle. Without him, this show would be a mere shadow."

Several of the Klingons pounded G'joth on the back and congratulated him. Someone handed him a mug filled with bloodwine.

Snarling at Kenni, G'joth threw the mug to the floor, its clatter barely audible over the din of celebrating.

"G'joth," Lakras said, "what are you *doing*? Kenni is honoring you!"

"Hardly."

He turned his back on Kenni and walked back to the corridor.

"You dare to turn your back on me!" Kenni shouted.

Suddenly, the room got very quiet.

"You are nothing, G'joth. I spoke well of you for the sake of your sister, but now I see that you are a liar and a coward!"

G'joth smiled. He turned around. "Normally, I would consider such words an insult, Kenni—but only if they came from a *Klingon*. When they come from spineless bloodworms—well, I consider the source." G'joth walked back toward Kenni. "Listen to me very carefully. I have fought against Cardassians and Jem'Hadar, against Romulans and humans, against Kreel and Kinshaya, against Children of San-Tarah and creatures of Elabrej. I have not only survived, I have *thrived*. Do you truly imagine that after all I have done, anything you say could possibly matter to me?" Looking around at all the actors, singers, and sycophants (or whoever the unfamiliar faces were), G'joth said, "I have fought battles for the empire! I have bled and watched good warriors die! I have done this so we will have celebrations like this. I have done this so that our deeds may be enshrined in song, as they will be tonight!" Looking back at Kenni, he added, "And I am sure you will play the role of Talak well, for he too was a dishonorable traitor to the empire, and I cannot think of a better performer for his role than your pathetic self." He grabbed Kenni by his cassock; the singer flinched, which alone should have condemned him. "Tonight, you will perform brilliantly, and you will bring honor to the ship on which I serve. And that is why I am letting you live. If you ever dishonor me publicly again—or if you do *anything* that brings harm to my sister or any member of my family—I will not restrain myself." He smiled. "Oh, and the same holds true if you perform badly. My captain is in the audience, as is the Federation ambassador, and Chancellor Martok himself. I expect that the stage will be coated with drinks by the end of the show from the accolades. If I learn that the audience stayed quiet, if I learn that nothing was thrown on the stage in celebration, then I will return, and you will die—slowly."

With that, G'joth let go of Kenni and walked down the corridor to the exit.

The two guards were surprised to see him exit. "Where are you going, *Bekk?*"

"I have better things to do," G'joth said. Activating his wrist comm, he said, "G'joth to Praxis Station. One to beam to the *Gorkon.*"

With Klag at the opening, G'joth knew that word of how the performance went would shoot through the *Gorkon's* corridors at warp speed. That meant he was relieved of the obligation of actually watching it. He'd already seen the opera dozens of times—another would truly drive him mad.

Before the transporter took him, he looked around at the Krennla skyline, buildings climbing their desultory way toward the dark skies. His father had dishonored him, his sister had returned to being the lapdog of a fool, and his friends were not truly his friends anymore. *I have nothing here.*

As the red glow engulfed him, he swore that the only way he would set foot in Krennla would be to fulfill his promise to Kenni. That alone was reason to hope for a successful opening night . . .

THIRTY

I.K.S. Gorkon
Praxis Station, in orbit of Qo'noS

The man who still thought of himself as Lieutenant Rodek entered the bridge of the *Gorkon* with a song in his heart.

Toq was sitting in the first officer's chair and rose at Rodek's entrance. "The captain wants to see you, Lieutenant." The rest of the bridge crew went about their business. They were on duty, so Rodek thought nothing of their ignoring him as he entered. It was a surprise that Leskit, at least, did not say something—but then Rodek saw that Ensign Koxx was at the helm.

"Of course." Rodek moved toward the front of the bridge. "It is good to see you again, my friend."

Toq regarded him. "You seem unusually happy. In fact, I do not believe that you ever have been *this* happy."

"It is as if the galaxy has removed itself from the task

of crushing my skull, Toq. But I will tell you all about it in the mess hall later."

"Perhaps." Toq spoke hesitantly.

Frowning, Rodek asked, "What is it, Toq?"

Again, Toq said, "The captain wants to see you, Lieutenant."

With a shrug, Rodek moved toward the captain's office. He supposed that Klag might be a bit angry about the *qaDrav*, but he also knew that Worf and the captain had become comrades. Rodek had very little use for Worf, but he knew that the ambassador was, at heart, an honorable man. He would smooth the ground for Rodek with his captain.

The door rumbled aside at Rodek's approach, meaning that the captain knew he was coming. He was seated behind his desk, examining a padd.

"Lieutenant Rodek reporting for duty, sir."

"I think not," Klag said without looking up from his padd. He dropped it to the desk with a clatter and picked up another.

"What?" Rodek asked, confused.

Rising from his chair and now glowering at Rodek with his pitiless brown eyes, Klag said, "We served together, Rodek. I made you my second officer. And what is the result? Betrayal!"

"Sir, I'm sure Ambassador Worf explained—"

"Worf told me precisely what happened, and the *meqba'* in council chambers told me what he did not know. I am *fully* aware of the chain of events that led to you trying to kill me in the *qaDrav*. And that is why you will be gone from my ship and *never* set foot on it again!"

Rodek took a step back, half expecting the captain to challenge him. But no, that was unnecessary. He was Rodek's superior—Klag had only to order him away, and Rodek could not question him.

But question him he did. He had found contentment on this ship, found a place in the universe that he had not had as Kurn for many turns. Why would the captain take this from him? Aloud he simply asked, "Why?"

Klag stepped closer, fury in his eyes, spit flying from his mouth. "You *dare* to ask that? Ten months, Rodek! For *ten months*, we served together. We even fought against Dorrek! I believe that I asked you to fire on Dorrek more than once. My call to battle at San-Tarah included taking up arms against my dishonorable brother, whom I then discommendated from our House. You *knew* all this! And yet, a mere fifteen-minute conversation with that same *petaQ*, and you betrayed me. Ten months of service done away because you believed a creature so base, he killed your father without showing his face and died in ignominy on the floor of the council chambers. Either you were too addled to make a sensible decision, or you are as foul a creature as my brother. Whichever it was, I cannot afford to have you under my command where you might betray me again." He stepped in close enough for Rodek to smell the *raktajino* on his breath. "So you will not remain. You have been rotated off my ship, permanently, with the reason on your record. Now get off my ship!"

With that, Klag turned his back on his erstwhile second officer.

Rodek stared blankly. At first, he thought, *How dare*

this toDSaH *speak to me this way! I am a member of the High Council!*

But, of course, he wasn't. He had chosen the life of Rodek over that of Kurn, thinking it to be a better one.

Saying nothing—he had tempted Klag's wrath enough with his questioning why—Rodek turned and left the office.

As soon as the door to the office closed behind him, all members of the bridge crew got to their feet, crossed their fists in front of their faces, and turned their backs on him.

The only one who did not was Toq, who walked up to him. "You have betrayed your captain. You have betrayed *our* captain. I wish it were not so, Rodek, but it is. There can be no forgiveness for what you have done."

Then Toq, too, crossed his wrists and turned his back on Rodek.

A memory came to him all of a sudden, one of Kurn's: in the Great Hall, after Worf had accepted discommendation from the empire, when the entire High Council did to Worf what the crew of the *Gorkon* now did to Rodek. The last person to do so was Worf's brother, Kurn. Kurn had not wanted to accept the dishonor—he was willing to die to preserve the family name. But Worf's actions, damn him, were the right ones and led to the House of Mogh's honor being restored.

Reluctantly, Kurn had turned his back on Worf. Rodek sensed that reluctance in Toq now.

For all the good that it does me.

As he moved to the rear door that would take him

to the turbolift, and thence to the transporter room to leave forever this ship that he had called home, Rodek's chest grew heavy with the realization of the magnitude of what had happened today.

Klag was right—Rodek had betrayed him. He had been so lost in his confusion of who he was that he readily accepted Dorrek's lies. So eager was he for answers that he accepted the first set of them that were put before him, and he disregarded what he knew about Dorrek.

Dorrek was in *Gre'thor*. Rodek wondered if he might be better off following him. Not only had he betrayed a captain he respected as much as or more than any other in the fleet, but he had also guaranteed that no captain who considered Klag a friend or comrade would have him, either. His only recourse was to find a ship with an enemy of Klag's in command—or, at best, someone who was indifferent to the captain.

Dejected, Rodek instructed the lift to take him to the transporter room.

The lift doors opened at the tenth deck to reveal Leskit and Kurak, whose hands were entwined around each other.

Kurak scowled. "Hasn't Klag kicked you off the ship yet?"

"He just did," Rodek said quietly.

Leskit put a hand on Rodek's shoulder. "I will miss you, my friend, truly. But what choice did Klag have?"

"Should've done it months ago," Kurak said. "I *never* liked you, Rodek."

Rodek ignored the engineer—they'd served together

on the *Lallek* prior to this posting, and one of the first things Rodek had learned about Kurak was that she didn't like *anyone*—and said to Leskit, "I will miss you as well, Leskit. I doubt the mess hall on my next assignment will provide the joy that this one has." He looked around at the bulkheads. "Nor the battles that this ship has won."

"Perhaps not." Leskit put his fist to his chest. "*Qapla'*, my good friend. May you recover your honor and die well."

"*Qapla'*, Leskit." Turning to Kurak, he added, "And to you as well, Kurak."

Kurak just spit at his feet.

With a sigh, Rodek pushed past the couple and headed to the transporter room. *I will not forget that kindness, Leskit.* It wasn't at all the proper thing for Leskit to do—that would've been to do what Toq did—but the next time Leskit did the proper thing would probably be the first.

Good-bye, my friends, Rodek thought, as he left the *Gorkon*.

"No, *Bekk*," B'Oraq said with a laugh, "bloodwine does *nothing* to help the singing voice. But try convincing an opera singer of *that*. No, they must have their rituals."

The *bekk* from the fifteenth—B'Oraq honestly could not remember his name—nodded sagely. He had come into the medical bay with the question. B'Oraq was stunned, since most of the warriors on the *Gorkon* would rather face a Kreel unarmed than enter the medical bay for any reason other than injury. "I suspected as much.

When I saw the performers carousing, my first thought was that this was what they should be doing *after* the opera. My second was that it would ruin their voices."

"Which performers would that be?"

"*The Battle of San-Tarah*. It was playing at—"

"Baldi'maj, I know, I was there. It was quite the performance. Nothing like the real thing, of course, and I could've lived without Tereth as Klag's love interest, but it was a very well-performed opera. The chorus was especially magnificent. I've rarely seen a chorus that could make itself heard over the audience's cheers as well as this one."

The *bekk* smiled. "I'll be sure to pass that on, Doctor." By way of explanation, he added, "My sister Lakras is in the chorus of that company."

"Ah. Well, the next time you talk to her, give her my compliments." With a chuckle, she added, "And tell her that if she abstains from bloodwine before a performance, her career will last an extra ten years. I know of only one opera singer whose career lasted into old age, and that was Kabrerr. Know what he drank before each show? Water. Nothing else."

Bowing his head, the *bekk* said, "I will do that, Doctor." With that, he left the medical bay.

B'Oraq tugged on her braid. Her new nurse—a recommendation from Valatra—was due to report today, along with several other crew replacements. The *Gorkon* would be setting out into space once again. The KPE had been disbanded, and B'Oraq had more hope for the future of Klingon medicine than she'd ever had since she began her crusade a decade ago.

The doors to the medical bay opened to reveal Klag. "Captain!" she said.

"Doctor." As soon as the door closed, he grabbed her and bit her cheek.

The feel of his teeth on her flesh intoxicated her, but she forced herself under control. "We are on duty, Klag. Should we not practice discretion?"

"Discretion is for humans," he whispered into her ear. "Besides, I escorted you to the opera yesterday, to a performance attended by the chancellor. I doubt our being *par'Mach'kai* is any kind of secret."

"True." She smiled. "In fact, I have a message from my uncle excoriating me for being seen in public with you."

Klag broke the embrace and smiled down at her. "What did you tell him?"

"That my captain ordered me to come to the opera with him, and I could hardly refuse a direct order from my captain." She smiled back. "He agreed that that was the case, never mind that you never gave such an order."

His smile modulating into a thoughtful expression, Klag said, "Perhaps it might be wise to try to convince your uncle of my merits." At B'Oraq's questioning look—all things being equal, she would have no problem mating with Klag, though she did not wish to alienate her uncle, either—Klag said, "My mother's intransigence may prove to be problematic. The House of M'Raq might need a new Lady of the House."

B'Oraq considered. She would make no kind of House lady, but Klag knew that—this was for appearances' sake more than anything, and to make it clear that Tarilla, the shrew, was no longer running the household. "I am surprised you did not have her put to death."

"No," Klag said softly, and now his face was sad, a show of emotion he rarely allowed anyone on board to see. "She only wished to have her son restored to her. I can blame no mother for that, least of all my own."

She rested her hands on Klag's massive chest. "I will speak with my uncle again soon and see how he reacts to the notion."

"Thank you." Klag grinned. "Though I do not wish to be seen as simply imitating Kurak and Leskit."

Laughing, B'Oraq said, "Indeed. They do make an excellent couple, I think."

"Yes, and Leskit will make a fine second officer."

B'Oraq tilted her head. "*He* will be third in command?"

"Why not? He has proved himself time and again, and he has more experience than anyone else left on the ship. My lone concern regarding Toq was his youth—Leskit will counter that."

"I think it is an excellent choice."

Klag grinned. "Your approval is noted, Doctor. Now then, I have some free time. I was considering a *bat'leth* drill with Kohn. Or, perhaps, some *other* exercise . . ."

G'joth headed down to the centermost deck, where the *Gorkon's* troops had their bunks. The last time he had been there was when he'd convinced Wol to join Kagak and Goran. The leader had promised to slit G'joth's throat if she had not enjoyed herself. *After what I went through in Krennla, I may ask her to do it regardless.*

379

But when he approached the fifteenth's bunks, he heard gales of raucous laughter from three voices. *It seems I get to live another day.*

"May one assume," he said as he approached the threesome, who were all standing in front of the bunks, each holding something, "that the trip to Pheben III was a success? And what is that you're eating?" It looked like dead *racht.*

All three turned. Goran bellowed, "G'joth! You have returned!"

"Of course I have. It's not like this squad can get by without me." G'joth plastered a smile on his face. Goran and Kagak both laughed, but Wol was staring at him.

G'joth stared back with a look that he hoped conveyed his thoughts: *We will speak more later.*

Wol nodded, comprehending. She'd lived in Krennla, she would understand.

Then the leader handed him one of the dead *racht.* "We have been waiting for you in order to share this."

"What is it?" It felt oddly sticky for *racht.*

"A specialty of my grandmother," Kagak said. "Eat it!"

Reluctantly, G'joth put it in his mouth and slowly, gingerly chewed.

After the second bite, he chewed much faster. "This is *amazing.*"

"So's our grandmother," Goran said.

G'joth looked up sharply at that. " 'Our'?"

"I have mated!" Goran said proudly.

"To my sister," Kagak added. "B'Ellor and Goran are now mates."

Turning to Wol, G'joth said, "Obviously, I missed a great deal."

"Yes, you did," Wol said with a warm smile. "Would that you had heeded your own advice to me."

"Indeed." G'joth had never seen Wol this content before. And the big man was positively giddy.

After taking some more of the *racht*, G'joth looked at Kagak. "It seems you're one of us at last."

A voice said from behind G'joth, "As am I, now."

Whirling around, G'joth saw *Bekk* Moq. "You're our fifth, Moq?"

Moq nodded. "*QaS DevwI'* Grotek informed me when I reported that I'd been promoted to the fifteenth." To Wol, he said, "Leader, I can think of no greater honor than to be posted to your squad. I hope I can live up to your standards."

G'joth frowned. "Weren't you in the one-seventy-fifth?"

"One-seventy-seventh, actually," Moq said.

"However," Wol said, "Moq was instrumental in identifying the mutineers at Elabrej. The entire ship—or at least, those who remain loyal to Klag—owe him a debt. I believe the promotion was well earned."

Wol's word was good enough for G'joth. He held out his hand. "Have some candied *racht*, Moq. And welcome to the fifteenth."

Grinning, Moq grabbed the confection and stuffed it in his mouth. "This is fantastic!" he said with a full mouth.

The others all laughed and ate heartily.

It is good to be back home, G'joth thought.

FIRST EPILOGUE

Federation Embassy
First City, Qo'noS

"**R**emember, Vulcans do not eat meat, so make sure there are plenty of vegetables for them."

Eduardo Mazzerone was a short, round human with a head that was too big for the rest of his body—no mean feat, given how stocky he was—and a high, raspy voice. Of all the humans that Ba'el had met in her short time at the Federation embassy, she found Mazzerone to be the most difficult to deal with.

Unfortunately, she now worked for him, so she had to make the best of it.

The oddest thing about humans to Ba'el was that they didn't smell like much of anything. And they were all so *small*. Ba'el had a hard time taking them seriously as a species.

Still, Mazzerone was her supervisor, which was the

only reason why she didn't remind him that he'd told her about Vulcans' vegetarianism six times already.

"Also, the Trill like that yellow-leaf salad, so stock extra of that—and *do* try to limit the amount of *gagh*. I know the ambassador loves the stuff, but I swear we get at least six people throwing up when they see the worms move, and at least one idiot who insists on 'going native' by eating one and forgetting to chew it thoroughly first, and we have to send them to medical."

Ba'el had been taking notes on the padd Giancarlo Wu had given her, but now that Mazzerone was repeating himself, she just nodded a lot. The reception was not to be held for another twenty-four hours, and Ba'el was fairly certain that she would be able to make sure that Mazzerone's instructions were followed.

"Now remember, I'm going to be *far* too busy making sure that the performers are lined up. Last time, we had Sinnravians, and I *still* get migraines just thinking about it, so I have to ride herd on *that* before it gets out of control. So I'm trusting you with the food, all right?"

"Of course, Mister Mazzerone," Ba'el said. "I promise to make sure that all your orders are followed."

"Good." Mazzerone stared at her with his beady little eyes. "Well, why are you just *standing* there? Go! Do your job!" With that, Mazzerone wandered off, muttering to himself.

"Ba'el."

Turning, Ba'el saw Worf standing in the entryway to the dining hall where the reception was going to be held. "Worf!" she said with relief. She practically ran toward the entrance so she could stand in front of him, take in his glorious scent. After spending the day around humans, she reveled in his musk.

"How are the plans proceeding?"

"They would proceed faster if Mister Mazzerone were not so fond of repeating himself."

"No doubt." Worf spoke with the air of someone who had long suffered this particular problem.

Not wishing to talk about Mazzerone, Ba'el instead said, "Thank you for taking me to that opera last night."

"If you wish to learn about Klingon culture, then the opera is a good place to start."

Ba'el hesitated. "Does the audience always . . . *throw* things like that?"

Worf let out a small smile. "Only when it is a *good* opera."

"I *did* like the love story between Klag and Tereth. I just wish it had a happier ending."

"It does—after a fashion," Worf said.

"What do you mean? Tereth died."

"It is—" Worf hesitated. "It is a long story, and it is not my story to tell."

Then Ba'el put it together. "That woman the real Captain Klag was with! Was that the real Tereth?"

"No, Tereth is truly dead, though she died at Narendra III, not San-Tarah. But B'Oraq is Klag's true *par'Mach'kai.*"

"Good," Ba'el said. She preferred happy endings since real life rarely saw fit to provide them. "Might you take me to another opera?"

"I am afraid that I have many meetings between now

and tomorrow night's reception—and as soon as that is over, I must travel to No'Mat. I will be gone for several days." He bowed his head. "We will revisit the possibility upon my return."

With that, Worf took his leave. Ba'el, for her part, went to the kitchen to see what was already in stock and what needed to be procured.

She allowed herself a glimmer of hope. The opera had indeed been wonderful—and she was grateful that Worf's position allowed them to sit in the front row near the stage, as she doubted she'd have been able to enjoy the performance if she was behind so many crazed Klingons showing their appreciation by shouting, singing along, and throwing their drinks onto the stage—and she wanted to go to another.

Her life had been taken away from her. She would never stop grieving for the family she had lost on Carraya. But where most Klingons, even Toq, seemed to think that the best response to death was to avenge it, Ba'el thought it better to honor the memory of those who fell by living a good life.

She hoped to do so with Worf's help. Perhaps that help would only be as her employer. Perhaps she would be able to convince him to let her be his—what was the word he'd used? Yes: *par'Mach'kai*.

Either way, she would *live*.

SECOND EPILOGUE

Imperial Intelligence Headquarters
Qo'noS

"**W**hat was the point of that exercise?" Lorgh asked B'Etloj as his *mek'leth* sliced through his opponent's belly.

B'Etloj stood against the wall of one of I.I.'s workout rooms. Lorgh had chosen this place for two reasons: he wanted a workout, and he wanted to question B'Etloj while she was forced to watch Lorgh kill things.

The things in this case were holographic opponents, all female Klingons who looked similar to B'Etloj.

He swung his *mek'leth* around so it struck the neck of another woman, holographic blood spurting out against the wall and floor.

B'Etloj said, "The fleet response to the Elabrej threat was—"

"Entirely proper. The Elabrej needed to be made an example of. Klag was correct—ships can be rebuilt. Honor cannot be. All you did was give I.I.'s detractors another blade to put in their belts when they attack us. We work best in the shadows, B'Etloj." Lorgh was not even out of breath as he took down two more of his opponents while dodging their *bat'leth* swings. He had programmed the holograms to be poor fighters. The idea was for him to win, after all, and he was getting too old to rely on his fighting skills all by himself, especially when there was a larger point to be made to his subordinate. "The only time the High Council should even be aware of us is when we give them information. Now when Martok thinks of us, he will not be reminded of the intelligence we provided that allowed us to win at Elabrej. Instead, he will think of Trant trying to take Klag's command from him, and of you and D'khon and Councillors Tovoj and Merik wasting his time and that of his generals and captains." With a final swing of his *mek'leth*, Lorgh sliced through the thigh of his last opponent, who stumbled to the floor. He then kicked her in the face, knocking her onto her back, and then plunged the *mek'leth* into her chest.

That done, he looked back at B'Etloj. "Am I understood?"

B'Etloj's face was almost vibrating, as she attempted to hide her emotions. That alone disappointed Lorgh. She should have been a good enough operative to have better control of herself. It was difficult, he knew, for Klingon society encouraged outward showing of passion, but if B'Etloj was to succeed in I.I., she needed better discipline than that.

Not to mention learning not to waste the time of the chancellor.

Finally, B'Etloj said, "Councillors Merik and Tovoj—"

For the first time, Lorgh raised his voice. "I asked you a *question!*"

Recoiling as if he'd struck her, B'Etloj said, "Yes, sir, you are understood!"

"Good. Tomorrow, you will receive your new assignment."

Again B'Etloj did not keep her emotions in check, this time by letting the relief she felt show on her face. She probably thought that Lorgh was going to end this discussion by doing to her what he did to the holograms.

As she walked toward the door, Lorgh decided to answer her unasked question. "If I wanted to put you to death, I would have done so at the outset. There is no point in teaching a lesson to someone who will not live to learn from it."

"Thank you, sir," B'Etloj said and departed.

Lorgh walked over to the control panel on the workout room wall and removed the holographic corpses from the floor. That same action removed the holographic blood from his *mek'leth*.

Nevertheless, he walked over to another wall, on which hung rags, and he began the ritual cleaning of the blade. His mentor, the great I.I. agent Kveld, had taught him always to clean his blade after using it, whether it was *d'k tahg*, *mek'leth*, *bat'leth*, *tik'leth*, or *qutluch*, though he used the latter rarely.

As he ran the cloth over the metal, he thought about how things had gone.

Toq had learned his lesson. The boy probably didn't even realize it, but he would soon enough. He understood that the universe was an infinitely more complicated place than he'd imagined, and he knew just how difficult it was to keep a secret—and how important it was, as well. Toq probably knew that intellectually, but seeing the disastrous consequences of the secret of Carraya getting out probably drove the point home effectively.

Kurn had his memories back. Lorgh had always been grateful that Worf had not given Kurn the *Mauk-to'Vor* he'd asked for. Indeed, his solution was very much an I.I. one. Years ago, when he was a very young I.I. agent, Lorgh had been sent undercover as part of General Worf's staff. The old diplomat had become a good friend to Lorgh, and in return, Lorgh had become a good friend to Worf's son, Mogh. When Mogh went to Khitomer at Lorgh's request, Lorgh had agreed to care for Kurn until they returned.

Of course, they never did, and Lorgh had raised Kurn as his own. He had plans for both of Mogh's sons, and they would have come to naught had Worf killed Kurn on that Bajoran space station.

But he did not, and now Kurn was restored to life, for all that he still insisted on calling himself Rodek. True, his transfer off the *Gorkon* was disappointing, as having Toq and Kurn on the same ship simplified things, but Lorgh could play *klin zha* with whatever game pieces he had available.

Still, the plan remained in place.

Lorgh just hoped he wouldn't have to implement it.

With one final swipe, he finished cleaning the blade, replaced the rag, sheathed the *mek'leth*, and left the workout room. There was work to do.

GLOSSARY OF KLINGON TERMS

Most of the language actually being spoken in this novel is the Klingon tongue and has been translated into English for the reader's ease. Some terms that don't have direct translations into English or are proper nouns of some kind have been left in the Klingon language. Since that language does not use the same alphabet as English, the transliterations of the Klingon terms vary depending on preference. In many cases, a more Anglicized transliteration is used instead of the *tlhIngan Hol* transliterations preferred by linguists (e.g., the more Anglicized *bat'leth* is preferred over the *tlhIngan Hol* spelling *betleH*).

Below is a glossary of the Klingon terms used. Anglicized spellings are in **boldface**; *tlhIngan Hol* transliterations are in ***bold italics***. Please note that this glossary does not include the names of locations, people, or ships. Where applicable, episode, movie, or novel citations are given where the term first appeared. Episode citations are followed by an abbreviation indicating show: TNG = *Star Trek: The Next Generation*, DS9 = *Star Trek: Deep Space Nine*. Note that a word in the text with the suffix *pu'* is the pluralized form. It is listed in the glossary in its singular form, without the suffix.

adanji. Incense used in the *Mauk-to'Vor* ceremony. [First seen in "Sons of Mogh" (DS9).]

bat'leth (*betleH*). Curved, four-bladed, two-handed weapon. This is the most popular handheld, edged weapon used by Klingon warriors due to its being favored by Kahless, who forged the first one. The legendary Sword of Kahless now held by Chancellor Martok is a *bat'leth*, and most Defense Force warriors are proficient in it. [First seen in "Reunion" (TNG).]

bekk (*beq*). A rank given to enlisted personnel in the Defense Force. [First referenced in "Sons and Daughters" (DS9).]

bok-rat liver (*boqrat chej*). Food made from the liver of a *bok-rat*, apparently cooked to some degree, making it unusual among Klingon foods. [First seen in "Soldiers of the Empire" (DS9).]

bolmaq. An animal native to the planet Boreth that makes a bleating sound and tends to run around in circles a lot. [First referenced in *Honor Bound*.]

bregit lung (*bIreQtagh*). Food made from the lung of an animal, presumably a *bregit*. [First seen in "A Matter of Honor" (TNG).]

cha'DIch. Literally, "second." During a legal proceeding, the accused is denied combat and so must have a second, called a *cha'DIch*, to defend him or her. [First referenced in "Sins of the Father" (TNG).]

chech'tluth (*chechtlhutlh*). An alcoholic beverage best served heated and steaming. The word seems to derive from the verbs meaning "to drink" and "to get drunk." [First seen in "Up the Long Ladder" (TNG).]

chuSwI'. A rodent that mostly lives underground and makes an annoying noise. [First referenced in *Enemy Territory*.]

chu'wI'. Literally means "trigger" but has also come to be slang for "rookie" or "beginner" (or "newbie").

d'k tahg (*Daqtagh*). Personal dagger. Most Defense Force warriors carry their own *d'k tahg*; higher-born Klingons often have them personalized with their name and House. [First seen in *Star Trek III: The Search for Spock*.]

gagh (*qagh*). Food made from live serpent worms (not to be confused with *racht*). [First seen in "A Matter of Honor" (TNG).]

ghIntaq. A type of spear with a wooden haft and a curved, two-bladed metal point. Also the name given to a person who serves as a close and trusted adviser to a House. It is possible that the latter usage evolved from the first, with the adviser being analogized to a House head's trusted weapon. Sometimes Anglicized as *gin'tak*. [Spear first seen in "Birthright Part 2" (TNG); adviser first referenced in "Firstborn" (TNG).]

ghojmoq. Nursemaid. [First used in "Sins of the Father" (TNG).]

gonklik (*ghonglIq*). A vegetable, usually served sliced.

grapok sauce (*gha'poq*). Condiment, often used to bring out the flavor in meat dishes. [First seen in "Sons and Daughters" (DS9).]

Gre'thor (*ghe'tor*). The afterlife for the dishonored dead—the closest Klingon equivalent to hell. Those who are unworthy spend eternity riding the Barge of the Dead to *Gre'thor*, led by *Fek'lhr*. [First mentioned in "Devil's Due" (TNG).]

grinnak (*ghInaq*). A game that involves tokens and wagers. [First referenced in *Honor Bound*.]

hurkik (*HurqIq*). A fruit grown on Klingon farms.

jeghpu'wI'. Conquered people—more than slaves, less than citizens, this status is given to the natives of worlds conquered by the Klingon Empire. [First used in *Diplomatic Implausibility*.]

jIH. "I am."

jInjoq. A type of bread. [First referenced in *A Time for War, a Time for Peace*.]

khest'n (*Hestlh'ng*). Adjective with no direct translation, generally a curse word. [First used in *The Final Reflection*.]

khrun (*Hun*). A riding beast.

klin zha (*tlhInja*). A popular board game. [First seen in *The Final Reflection*.]

klongat (*tlhonghaD*). A beast native to Qo'noS that is much larger than a *targ* and more difficult to subdue. Sometimes used as a riding beast. [First referenced in *Honor Bound*.]

korvit (*qorvIt*). A rodent that eats through plants, commonly found on Klingon farms, where farmers have to set traps for them.

krada legs (Qa'Da'). Food made from the extremities of a *krada*. [First mentioned in "The Sound of Her Voice" (DS9).]

loSpev. A particular type of wheat grown on Klingon worlds.

lotlhmoq. Predatory bird native to Qo'noS that swoops into the water to catch food. [First referenced in *Enemy Territory*.]

Mauk-to'Vor (ma'Do'vor). Ceremony whereby one is killed by a family member or other comrade in order to die with honor without the stigma of suicide. [First seen in "Sons of Mogh" (DS9).]

may'ron. A musical instrument, similar to an Earth accordion. [First seen in "Melora" (DS9).]

mek'leth (meqleH). A swordlike one-handed weapon about half the size of a *bat'leth*. [First seen in "Sons of Mogh" (DS9).]

meqba'. When evidence is presented to a court or some other judicial body, such as the High Council. [First seen in "Sins of the Father" (TNG).]

Mok'bara (moqbara). Martial art that focuses both the body and the spirit. [First seen in "Man of the People" (TNG).]

par'Mach'kai (parmaHay). A term for "lover," though the Klingon word is far more intense than the human one. [First used in "Change of Heart" (DS9).]

petaQ. Insult with no direct translation. Sometimes anglicized as *pahtk*. [First used in "The Defector" (TNG).]

qaDrav. Literally "challenge floor," it is a raised, fenced platform in the plaza outside Klingon Defense

Force Headquarters where challenges between warriors were once regularly held.

Qapla'. Ritual greeting that literally means "success." [First used in *Star Trek III: The Search for Spock*.]

QaS DevwI'. Troop commander on a Defense Force vessel, generally in charge of several dozen soldiers. Roughly analogous to a sergeant in the modern-day army. [First used in *The Brave & the Bold* Book 2.]

qelI'qam. Unit of measurement roughly akin to two kilometers. Sometimes anglicized as *kellicam*. [First used in *Star Trek III: The Search for Spock*.]

QI'yaH. Interjection with no direct translation. [First used in "Sins of the Father" (TNG).]

QongDaq. A Klingon bed. [First seen in *The Brave and the Bold* Book 2.]

qutluch. A weapon favored by assassins, which leaves a particularly vicious wound. [First seen in "Sins of the Father" (TNG).]

Qu'vatlh. Interjection with no direct translation. [First used in *A Good Day to Die*.]

racht (raHta'). Food made from live serpent worms (not to be confused with *gagh*). [First seen in "Melora" (DS9).]

raktajino (ra'taj). Coffee, Klingon style. [First seen in "The Passenger" (DS9).]

rokeg blood pie (ro'qegh'Iwchab). Food apparently made from or with the blood of an animal, possibly a *rokeg*. [First seen in "A Matter of Honor" (TNG).]

Sto-Vo-Kor (Suto'vo'qor). The afterlife for the honored dead, where all true warriors go, crossing the River of Blood after they die to fight an eternal battle. The closest Klingon equivalent to heaven. [First mentioned by name in "Rightful Heir" (TNG).]

taknar (*taqnar*). An animal, the gizzards of which are sometimes served as food, and the droppings of which are particularly foul smelling. [First referenced in *A Good Day to Die*.]

targ (*targh*). Animal that is popular as a pet, but the heart of which is also considered a delicacy. [First seen as a pet in "Where No One Has Gone Before" (TNG) and as a food in "A Matter of Honor" (TNG).]

tik'leth (*tIqleH*). An edged weapon, similar to an Earth long sword. [First seen in "Reunion" (TNG).]

tIngDagh. A stringed musical instrument, traditionally played during operas.

toDSaH. Insult with no direct translation. Sometimes anglicized as *tohzah*. [First used in "The Defector" (TNG).]

torgot (*torghotlh*). A large animal native to Rura Penthe that is difficult to subdue.

trigak (*tlhIghaq*). A predatory animal with sharp teeth that it bares before attacking. [First referenced in *Honor Bound*.]

wam. A type of serpent. [First referenced in *Honor Bound*.]

warnog (*warnagh*). An alcoholic beverage. [First seen in "Rightful Heir" (TNG).]

Yan-Isleth (*yanISletlh*). The chancellor's personal bodyguard, sometimes referred to as the Brotherhood of the Sword. [First seen in "Apocalypse Rising" (DS9).]

yIntagh. Epithet with no direct translation. [First used in *A Good Day to Die*.]

yobta' yupma'. A Klingon harvest festival. Literally translates as "the we-have-completed-harvesting festival."

zilm'kach (tlhImqaH). Food made from something orange. [First seen in "Melora" (DS9).]

ACKNOWLEDGMENTS

Primary thanks go, as ever, to Marco Palmieri, my editor. It's under his guidance that this new direction was conceived, and his insights made this story as good as I hope it is. I've done some of my finest work for Marco, and I hope that trend has continued with this volume.

Secondary thanks go to Paula Block of CBS, who approved the story and manuscript with her usual deft touch; to Lucienne Diver, my wonderful agent; to John J. Ordover, with whom I initially developed the *Gorkon* crew for the novel *Diplomatic Implausibility* and who edited several of Klag and the gang's subsequent adventures before moving on and Marco taking over; and to Pocket's other noble editors, Margaret Clark, Edward Schlesinger, Jennifer Heddle, and Jaime Cerota.

Thanks also to the actors who gave voice and face to several of the characters seen in these pages: Nicole deBoer (Dax), Robert DoQui (Noggra), Michael Dorn (Worf), Aron Eisenberg (Nog), Jennifer Gatti (Ba'el),

Acknowledgments

David Graf (Leskit), Richard Herd (L'Kor), J.G. Hertzler (Martok), Sterling Macer Jr. (Toq), Tricia O'Neill (Kurak), Alan Scarfe (Tokath), Alexander Siddig (Bashir), Ron Taylor (Kaga), Brian Thompson (Klag), and Tony Todd (Rodek/Kurn).

I cannot begin to express my gratitude to Marc Okrand, who created the Klingon language, and Dr. Lawrence Schoen, head of the Klingon Language Institute (www.kli.org), who were of invaluable aid with many Klingon words and phrases.

There have been many Klingon episodes of all five *Star Trek* TV shows over the years, and I wish to thank the writers of all those episodes, but in particular Gene L. Coon (who created the Klingons in the original series episode "Errand of Mercy"), Ronald D. Moore (who wrote *a lot* of Klingon episodes, among them "Sins of the Father," "Redemption," "The House of Quark," and "Sons of Mogh," stories that had a particular influence on this novel), and René Echevarria (who wrote "Birthright Part 2," one of the finest and most underappreciated episodes of *The Next Generation*), for laying some of the groundwork for *A Burning House*. Thanks also to my fellow *Star Trek* novelists David Mack (*A Time to Kill*), Jeffrey Lang and the aforementioned J.G. Hertzler (*The Left Hand of Destiny*), Kevin Ryan (the *Errand of Vengeance* and *Errand of Fury* trilogies), Dayton Ward (*In the Name of Honor*), Michael A. Martin & Andy Mangels (*Forged in Fire*), and especially the late John M. Ford (*The Final Reflection*) for excellent and inspirational work with Klingons in their books.

At almost every convention I've been to, there have

been Klingons, and they've all been incredibly supportive of my work, as have dozens and dozens of others who've e-mailed me over the years. They are far too numerous to name here, so I hereby thank every single one of them all at once. Having said that, I will single out two groups in particular: Joe Manning and the rest of the gang at the Camp Dover Peace Conference in Ohio and the wonderful folks who organize the Klingon end of things at DucKon in Illinois, who had me as their guest in 2005 and 2006. You guys are the best.

Dr. Ilsa J. Bick, fellow *Trek* novelist and MD, was of tremendous assistance with various medical details, and she deserves much thanks and praise.

The usual gangs of idiots: the folks at the café who plied me with coffee during my marathon writing sessions; CGAG, the bestest writers' group ever; the Forebearance, in particular GraceAnne Andreassi DeCandido, for editorial and emotional guidance; and *Kyoshi* Paul and my fellow students at his dojo, for keeping my spirit high.

Finally, thanks to them that live with me, both human and feline, for regular encouragement, love, and understanding.

ABOUT THE AUTHOR

Keith R.A. DeCandido has written a wide variety of *Star Trek* material in an equally wide variety of media: novels, short fiction, magazines, comic books, and eBooks. It began in 1999 with the *Next Generation* comic book miniseries *Perchance to Dream* and most recently includes three items in celebration of *TNG*'s twentieth anniversary: the novel *Q&A*, the short story "Four Lights" in *The Sky's the Limit*, and the concluding eBook in the six-part miniseries *Slings and Arrows*. His other contributions include two novels and a novella in the acclaimed series of post-finale *Deep Space Nine* fiction, three pieces of *Voyager* fiction that don't take place in the Delta Quadrant, eleven eBooks in the *Corps of Engineers* series, the duology *The Brave and the Bold* (the first single story to encompass all five TV series), the political novel *Articles of the Federation* (singled out by *TV Zone* as the standout *Trek* novel of 2005), *A Time for War, a Time for Peace* (the *USA Today* best-selling lead-in to the movie *Star Trek Nemesis*), and more.

About the Author

However, Keith is perhaps best known for his work with the Klingons, from the 2001 novel *Diplomatic Implausibility* (which introduced the *I.K.S. Gorkon*), to the three books under the *I.K.S. Gorkon* banner (*A Good Day to Die* and *Honor Bound* in 2003 and *Enemy Territory* in 2005), to the historical epic *The Art of the Impossible* (part of the best-selling *Lost Era* miniseries in 2003), to the Klingon issue in the *Alien Spotlight II* comic book miniseries, to short stories in the *Tales from the Captain's Table*, *Mirror Universe: Shards and Shadows*, and *Seven Deadly Sins* anthologies.

Beyond *Star Trek*, Keith has written in a wide variety of media universes, including TV shows (*Buffy the Vampire Slayer*, *Supernatural*, *CSI: NY*, *Farscape*, *Gene Roddenberry's Andromeda*), video games (*World of Warcraft*, *Starcraft*, *Command and \Conquer*, *Resident Evil*), and comic books (Spider-Man, X-Men, Hulk, Silver Surfer). He's also written the original high-fantasy police procedural *Dragon Precinct*, along with several related stories. Keith—whose work has been praised by *Entertainment Weekly*, TrekNation.com, *TV Zone*, Cinescape.com, *Dreamwatch*, and *Publishers Weekly*, among others—is also a musician, a practitioner of *kenshikai* karate, and an avid New York Yankees fan. He lives in the Bronx with his fiancée and the world's two goofiest cats. Learn too much about Keith at his official Web site at DeCandido.net, or just send him silly e-mails at keith@decandido.net.